SHADOW'S EDGE

KYN KRONICLES BOOK 1

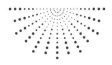

JAMI GRAY

CELTIC
MOON
PRESS

Copyright © 2011 by Jami Gray
All rights reserved.
Shadow's Edge - Kyn Kronicles - Book 1
Revised Publication: November 2018
Celtic Moon Press
ISBN: 978-1-948884-16-7 (ebook)
ISBN-13: 978-1-948884-17-4 (paperback)

Cover Art: Robin Ludwig Design, Inc.

First Publication: October 2011
Black Opal Books
ISBN: 978-1-626940-54-3 (ebook)
ISBN-13: 978-1-937329-15-0 (paperback)

Copyright © 2016 by Jami Gray
All rights reserved.
Submerged in Shadows - Tangled in Shadows - Kyn Kronicles Short Story Collection
JG Pub
ISBN: 978-1-626944-25-1

ALSO BY JAMI GRAY

Caught in the Aftermath

Fear the Reaper

DEDICATION

*For my mom and dad, who spent years not minding the typewriter
on the table at dinnertime and never said I couldn't do it.*

*For the 7 Evil Dwarves, without who this story would've never seen
the light of day.*

*To Ben and my boys—I thank God every day you chose me. There
is no way I could do this without you—and Pizza Hut.*

ACKNOWLEDGMENTS

As with every book I write, there are a great many people who take the time to respond to my strange questions without calling the authorities. So all my military, firearm experts, and first responders who took the time to help me out, I give you a big thank you, and proclaim any errors solely mine.

CONTENTS

CHAPTER ONE

With a quick twist of her wrist, Raine slipped the blade between Quinn's ribs. His heart gave one last desperate beat, then fell silent. He slid slowly down her body to his knees, ending up in a strange, lover-like tableau.

Wrenching her blade out with a soft grunt, she held him in a gentle grasp, carefully lowering his lifeless body to the cracked concrete floor of the deserted warehouse. She closed his now dull brown eyes, knowing they would join the handful of others haunting her dreams.

As she knelt to wipe her blade clean on his shirt, her hands shook slightly. Shaking hands were good. It was a sign she hadn't yet slipped off the crumbling edge into the same deep hole holding the monsters she hunted. A small comfort, but a comfort all the same.

She was careful to keep her knees away from the creeping trickle of blood inching outward. Standing, she caught her breath in a near-silent hiss of pain. A reminder of a stupid mistake on her part. She knew better. Every time she thought she'd seen it all, something came along and bit her in the ass. Or, in this case, distracted her enough to get past her guard.

The four-inch gash along her ribs was a small price to pay for her inattention. The illusion Quinn had used was good, damn good. Almost good enough to save his life.

She slipped her knife back in its wrist sheath, careful not to touch the iron blade. Not wanting to leave a blood trail, she stripped off her coat and long sleeve shirt, leaving her pale skin covered in a simple black tee. She tore the sleeves from the shirt creating a primitive binding for her ribs. Resetting her trench coat, she moved out into the night-shrouded streets of downtown Portland.

Although her mixed heritage helped her heal faster than a normal human, she needed to get home and clean out the wound. Thanks to the spell Quinn had so thoughtfully wrought on his own weapon, it would probably need mending. Damn, how she detested needles and the skin-crawling sensation when they pierced skin. It always brought back the sick helplessness of being a living pincushion for a demented scientist and his distorted visions of grandeur.

Destructive memories rose causing her steps to falter. Wresting her personal demons back into their cell, she blew out her breath in a deep sigh, her long strides making quick work of the winding streets in the deserted neighborhood. In seconds, she disappeared into the shadows, leaving behind the hazy-yellow streetlights shining feebly through the misty fog.

A few blocks later, just as a soft rain began to fall, she opened the door to her dark-green SUV and climbed in. The Northwest was a great place to live, so long as you didn't mind being wet and growing mold.

She did a fast scan of the deserted parking lot before turning the key in the ignition. It would just complete her night to finish this assignment by getting car jacked by some tanked-up group of mortal teenagers or a pack of hormonal shifters. One look at her five-foot-five frame—okay five-foot-seven with her thick-soled boots—and they'd think easy mark. A mistake people rarely made twice. Even Quinn knew better.

A glance at the dashboard clock showed it was past three in the morning. She grabbed the cell phone from the glove compartment and hit a programmed number. It rang once before being picked up.

She didn't wait for a greeting. "This is McCord, the job's done."

Silence answered. Not surprised, she hit disconnect and tossed the phone into the center console. Flicking the stereo on, she let the throbbing bass and heavy guitars pound through the speakers as she turned out of the lot and headed home.

Spending the money on the protection spell for her leather trench coat was definitely a good investment considering she wasn't bleeding out next to Quinn right now. In her line of work, protection spells were as important as a finely sharpened blade, both of which were oft used line items in her well-funded bank account.

That same account bore testimony to the generosity of her employer, Taliesin Security. However, even the top security company in the U.S. didn't tolerate mistakes, as evidenced by the fact they were now down one employee. *Poor, psycho Quinn wouldn't be collecting any more checks.*

Truth was, she liked Quinn. Liked him enough, she had tried to bring him in alive. Unfortunately, he hadn't felt as accommodating.

Maybe it was the thought of facing Raine's boss, Ryan Mulcahy, which made Quinn attack tonight. Something Raine understood all too well considering her personal experiences with the infuriating man left her craving violence. A master artesian when it came to manipulation and control, he made her wonder if those two characteristics had been listed as requirements on his job application. *"Wanted: one powerful, arrogant, type-A, control freak to head up the Fey population in the Northwest."*

She snorted. It wouldn't surprise her.

The SUV hit a pothole, causing her to wince at the aching reminder of Quinn's final exit interview. His name had been linked to the disappearance and bloody murders of two college students, a situation that normally would ping on Taliesin's radar despite the resulting ripple left in the human world. But, if one of the few government agencies who knew about the Kyn linked Quinn's name to the crime before Taliesin—well, that ripple could turn into a tsunami, creating a potentially cataclysmic threat to the magical community. *That* was why Mulcahy assigned Raine, one of his specially trained Security Officers, to deal with Quinn.

Why he killed those girls was a mystery, but Raine had a few hunches. One of Quinn's weaknesses was an addiction to power. Wanting what he couldn't have, hating those who had it, and doing whatever necessary to obtain it. Whichever one was at play had caused him to break the unbreakable rule— never take out the innocents, especially if they're human—it was bad for business. Should you break that rule, Taliesin had a very literal termination policy, one that included a permanent demotion to a lovely, airless box six feet under.

Hell, no matter how you looked at it, Quinn's decision had been just plain stupid.

Sirens jerked her attention back to the wet road rushing under her tires. She glanced in her rearview mirrors and caught the flashing red and blue lights streaking toward her. Her fingers whitened on the steering wheel. She couldn't afford to be pulled over right now. There were too many hidden weapons on her person and in her vehicle to get out of this with a simple ticket.

She checked her speed. *Nope, not speeding.* The blare of the siren rose above the pulsating music, and the spasmodic lights filled up the side mirror.

Muttering a string of epitaphs under her breath, she lifted her foot from the gas and began pulling her SUV over to the shoulder. Mentally she scrambled to piece together a believable story. Before she could come to a complete stop, the siren and lights blasted by her, spraying a fine mist of grit and water across her windshield.

Sweeping relief left her slumped in the driver's seat as she watched the red brake lights fade into the night. A shaky laugh escaped as her adrenaline level dropped. *How ironic would it be to get stopped for speeding, only to be arrested for the small arsenal she was transporting?*

Not to mention the additional headache of answering the question of whose blood stained the metal of the knife strapped to her body. It wouldn't take much to match the unusual blood on her blades to the soon-to-be discovered corpse back at the warehouse. Even humans could connect the dots if given enough clues.

The Kyn had managed to keep their existence quiet for hundreds of years. Unfortunately, the advent of modern technology made blending into the shadows difficult.

Decades ago, some of the human governments, various high level military personnel, and a select handful of others became privy to the Kyn's existence. A decision was made to keep their presence a closely guarded secret. The humans in power didn't want to scare the masses by admitting that the nightmares of campfire stories were alive and kicking. The Kyn, secretive by nature, didn't argue.

Raine pulled back out onto the freeway, and finished her drive, minus any other heart attack inducing events. She slowed as she approached the turnoff, and released a quiet sigh as she exited the highway. Tires crunched onto a gravel road heading into the mountains. Home wasn't far now, and she looked forward to a warm shower and a cup of hot tea.

The SUV bumped over the bridge spanning the dried-up riverbed. When the tires touched the other side, the steady vibrations of her primary wards, which served as a basic magical warning system surrounding her land, seeped into her bones. Their strength was a surprise, since warding magic wasn't her greatest skill, but she knew enough to avoid spending money on a professional Warder. Since the wards appeared undisturbed, her remaining tension the night's activities slipped away. She loved living out in the middle of nowhere. It was her haven, her refuge.

She parked the SUV in the detached garage and opened her door. As soon as her foot touched the ground, the disquieting jangle of her inner wards that protected the house's interior scrapped over her nerves.

Something, or someone had breached them.

A powerful someone or something, since they managed to bypass the outer wards without tripping them. Muttering a brief oath, she caught the edge of the car door before it slammed shut. Granted, her element of surprise was already shot to hell since her approaching headlights had been far from subtle.

Still, she eased the door almost closed, until the interior light clicked off. Then she stood by the SUV, an unmoving shadow. In complete silence, she slipped into the surrounding shadows as the soft rhythm of falling rain and the slight rustling of the breeze through the dense tree leaves covered her movements.

Under the concealment of the garage's heavy darkness, she scanned her front and side yards. There were no visible signs of life from inside, the small bushes strategically position under the windows remained undisturbed, and no strange cars were parked nearby. Whoever it was either flew in, or parked somewhere out in the surrounding woods.

She sent out a flicker of energy to read the house wards. They didn't offer much help. All she could sense was one intruder.

One trespasser versus her and her knives? Easy odds.

Sinking into a crouch, she crept toward the wrap-around porch. She slipped over the porch railing, and dropped softly to the deck. She avoided the windows and kept her back to the wall as she moved toward the door from the left. She came in low, in case whoever, or whatever, waited inside, decided to take a shot. No sense in creating an easy target.

With a flick of her wrist, her blade dropped out of its sheath into her right palm. Her left hand twisted the door-knob and began inching the door open.

"Raine, it's Gavin." A deep voice emerged from the darkened interior, freezing her in place. "I have a message for you."

Far from being reassured, she shoved the door wide, but kept low. Her night vision kicked in as she did a visual sweep of the entrance hall. Sure enough, a large man, his dark form outlined in a reddish-orange glow, was sprawled in her favorite cushy chair.

He reached for the switch on the wall and as the soft light flicked on, she blinked, her vision rapidly adjusting to normal. She straightened and shifted her knife down at her side. Out, but not readily visible.

"Deliver it and leave, Gavin." Her voice was quiet as she stepped fully inside and closed the door. Her gaze never left the man in front of her.

Gavin Durand made her uneasy, itchy. She wasn't the only one to experience an undeniable reaction when confronted with his presence. More than a few female conversations at the office focused on his exotic looks.

Something about his golden skin, lean muscles, and long legs sent all the women drooling.

If she was honest, she'd have to admit to drooling—once or twice—herself. That well-hidden flaw created a crack in her hard-won control, making her resent every inch of his enticing six-feet-four body. She and Gavin had worked together before on a few, rare assignments for Taliesin, and her cautious reactions around him seemed to provide him endless amusement.

"Could I get a cup of tea, at least?" His green eyes regarded her steadily as he leaned a shoulder against the entryway between the front room and the hall. With his arms crossed over his broad chest and his hands empty he sent a clear message he wasn't armed.

She took that message at face value, deciding he was probably here to irritate. Ignoring the weight of his gaze, she slid the knife into its sheath as she moved toward the hall closet. "If you want tea, there's the kitchen."

She was proud of how level her voice was because Gavin always set her nerves on edge. Especially here in her own home where he watched her, his thoughts hidden by a mask of mild amusement. She hated that particular expression of his as much as she disliked the tumultuous feelings he always managed to invoke. He not only rubbed her metaphoric fur the wrong way, but was an attractive pain in the ass.

A fact that pissed her off, even as she reminded herself that nerves were a sign of weakness, not desire. "Go put the water on."

She reached the hall closet, yanked the door open, and grabbed a hanger. Her movements were less than graceful and jarred the injuries Quinn inflicted. She winced and turned, only to find Gavin standing uncomfortably close.

The damn man moved quieter than a cat. "Dammit, Gavin, step back." Her frustrated snarl ended in a slight hiss of pain as she yanked her coat off, the rough movement pulling at the wound marring her side.

"Hurt?" His dark voice tumbled down her spine, spreading unexpected chills.

"It's just a scratch." Her jaw tightened with frustration and the unwanted awareness she couldn't hide as she met his brilliant green eyes. "I need to clean it up."

Unwilling to stand there like some girly-girl, and let him crowd her, she put her palm on his broad chest and pushed him away. She moved warily around him, surreptitiously wiping her tingling palm on her jeans, trying not to breathe in his woodsy scent, as she continued to the kitchen. Unused to having people in her house, she was hyper aware of the man pacing behind her and watching every move she made.

Screw it, it was her house, and Gavin wasn't here on her invite.

Unsettled and off-balance, her anger flickered and her pulse accelerated. Gavin being here meant something was up, something serious. Not only was he a fellow Security Officer for Taliesin but, like her, he was also part of the Wraiths.

The twelve member, highly skilled, specialized group of Kyn warriors who operated in similar fashion to a human military black-ops group were the Kyn's last line of defense for the supernatural community and were not publicly acknowledged. Not even within the Kyn community.

They existed in whispers and stories meant to keep the monsters in line, and were granted the authority to use whatever powers and skills necessary to get the job done while maintaining the the fragile peace between Kyn and humans.

One thing was for certain, Wraiths did not visit other Wraiths in the dead of the morning for tea.

Once in the kitchen, she beelined to the sink. She grabbed the bottom of her black T-shirt and pulled it off, throwing it in the trash. Tattered and bloody, the T-shirt was a loss, so was the ripped black tank underneath. She didn't bother with the rough binding yet. Instead, she removed both wrist sheaths, revealing an abstract pattern of old scars on her arms. Her wrists held a matching set of marks, circling them like bracelets. A lasting set of impressions left from an old nightmare.

She laid the wrist blades on the counter to clean later. If Gavin chose to start something, he would at least play fair and give her a chance to grab them. Besides, she still had the two in her boots. She started to unravel the makeshift bandage from her ribs.

The hair along her neck rose as Gave closed in behind her. She stiffened as he reached around her with the empty teakettle, flicked on the faucet, and filled the container.

Intent on ignoring him, she pulled up her tank top, knowing she would be flashing a colorful glimpse of the delicate Celtic artwork of intertwining lines and lithe cats cradling her lower back, but it was necessary.

She studied the wound, and then opened the drawer next to the sink, grabbed the first aid kit, slamming it into the counter. As pain danced across her ribs, she gritted her teeth, then set about cleaning the cut.

Suddenly, Gavin was there, taking over the task. "Here, let me do it."

He didn't wait for permission, but grasped her left shoulder with one hand and the first-aid kit with the other. The contrast of his darker skin against her own pale flesh shot a spark of heat through her bloodstream. He tugged her away from the sink and guided her to the kitchen table.

"Sit." He pressed firmly down on her right shoulder. When she balked, he kept his hand in place and pushed until she reluctantly sat in one of the straight-backed chairs.

His long fingers lingered over the second tattooed band

of ancient knots and ravens covering the upper part of her right arm. "Nice ink."

She couldn't stop herself from going stiff, but muttered, "Thanks."

He dropped his hand, set the kit on the table, and pulled out a second chair, positioning it so he was facing her. When he sat, he angled his head to study the wound. "It needs stitches."

"Yeah, I figured." She jerked her chin toward the first aid kit. "There's surgical thread and needle in there."

Shadows played over the intriguing angles in his face as he scrounged through the well-stocked kit. When he found what he needed, he neatly laid his supplies out for easy access.

Watching him prepare the needle, she couldn't hide her slight grimace.

His small smile proved he caught it. "Ready?"

Giving a short nod, she took a deep breath. Years ago she had been used as a lab rat, making her fairly immune to pain. Yet, for all the horror she endured, needles tended to make her inwardly cringe.

Bending over her side, he worked the needle in and out of her flesh, the tug and pull of it moving through her skin causing a dull, discordant pain. What was worse were the flashbacks it triggered.

The bone searing ache of cold iron as it burned its lasting impression into her wrists, ankles, and neck. Her body seizing as rivers of fire and ice ran through her blood. Inhuman noises ripping from her raw throat as she fought not to lose her mind to the agony consuming her. Men in white lab coats watching it all with emotionless eyes.

The shrill whistle of the teakettle snapped her back to her kitchen.

Gavin finished the last stitch, and looked up. His gaze sharpened.

"Go, make the tea." Her voice came out hoarse, and she could feel the thin film of cold sweat coating her face. She needed a moment to pull herself together, before he saw more than she was comfortable with. "I'll put the bandage on and clean up this mess."

He watched her for another moment, but she knew what he saw because it was all she would allow him to see. He finally got up and moved toward the kettle.

Her black hair was unraveling from its tight braid and straggling around her face, the complete opposite of his neatly pulled back, sherry colored hair. Thanks to her partial Fey heritage from her mother, she looked like she was in her late teens, early twenties. Most people mistook her for a kid, until they got a good look in her eyes. Silvery gray, they mirrored the coldness and knowledge of someone who had gone through hell—with a couple of repeat tours. She'd overheard the word "eerie" used a few times. That look, along with the faint scars on her wrists and the one resembling a collar around her throat, generally made people walk cautiously around her.

It was either her looks or her take-no-shit personality. Privately, she preferred to attribute it to her personality.

She took her timing getting to her feet, and kept a hand on the table waiting for the light-headedness to pass. When she was sure she wouldn't end up on her face, she grabbed the gauze and tape, then covered the neat row of stitches.

The delicate chimes of her teapot on her mother's china sounded behind her. When she was finished cleaning up, she turned to find Gavin at the counter near the stove, arranging two cups of tea. Leaving him to it, she went to the sink, feeling the weight of his gaze as she tossed the soiled bandages in the trash before rinsing the used needle.

Finished, she faced the silent, disturbing man invading her kitchen. Wiping her hands on a towel, she decided to get to tackle the elephant in the room. "Okay, you have your tea. Now what's so important you had to break through my wards at—" She glanced at the clock behind him. "Three-forty-five in the morning?"

"Your wards were good, just not complicated enough." His critique rasped over her temper.

Something in her face gave her away because his mouth twitched.

He took the two cups to the table, his voice suspiciously innocent, "Would you like me to re-do them?"

It was a hell of an offer considering his proficiency with warding magic was legendary, a gift from his very powerful witch mother.

"No." She kept a close eye on him as she followed and sat in her chair, wondering what the truth was behind his visit. "Answer my question."

Wraiths rarely made house calls, or to be more accurate, they were rarely *caught* making house calls. His unexpected appearance triggered a tendril of unease as thoughts of past sins haunted her. She shoved them down ruthlessly. Her secrets were still safe. Hopefully.

Gavin settled in across from her with his usual sardonic expression, which gave nothing away. "Mulcahy wants you to report in later this morning." Leaning back in the chair, he crossed his long, jean-clad legs at the ankles and sipped his tea. "There's a new, high level job waiting for us."

This was unexpected. "High level" was another way of saying the job was Wraith material. Despite Gavin's casual appearance, she knew he was judging her reaction. Previous experience taught her his nonchalant attitude was a front hiding his lethal mind and lightning-fast body.

Forewarned, she gave him nothing. "Us?"

Loners by nature, Wraiths didn't work well in pairs. The highly secretive nature of their work wasn't conducive to lasting partnership—professional or personal. Only in extreme circumstances did they team up.

So what did the boss consider so dangerous it required the top two Wraiths?

Granted, Gavin's main strength lay in his use of magic, but his weapons skills followed as a close second. Raine, on the other hand, was a living weapon, nearly unstoppable when armed with anything holding a sharp edge. Magic had its uses, but she didn't have the patience needed to master such a fickle force.

The one thing she and Gavin both shared was their belief that rules were merely suggestions. Mulcahy, their boss, was very aware of this fact since he commented on it many times, usually accompanied by gritted teeth and growls.

"Yeah, us," Gavin drawled. "And no, I don't have a clue what it is."

She took a sip of her tea, her mind churning. Ryan Mulcahy held dual roles. In the human world, he was the CEO of Taliesin Security. In the Kyn world, he was the head of the Fey contingent and, more importantly, the captain of the Wraiths.

Taliesin housed the four heads of the Northwest Kyn community, which consisted of the Fey, Shifters, Magi, and Amanusa. The worldwide magical community was divided into global regions, and each region's power structure was determined by its ruling majority or, as in Taliesin Security's case, ruling majorities.

The Northwest held one of the highest concentrations of Kyn, thanks to the vast amounts of untouched nature running from northern California up to the western edge of Canada. It provided a huge power source for those whose magic came from the natural world: the Fey, the Shifters, and the Magi.

Those in the fourth group, the Amanusa, were less able to tap into that source. Since their magic came from a darker power the other Kyn didn't want to play with, they were on their own. Their population might be small in comparison to the other Kyn species, but the reputation of the half-demon crowd was more than enough to make the supernatural community step lightly around them.

For Mulcahy to call on Gavin and Raine, something big was behind the request. She hadn't heard any unsettling rumors recently, so it left her curious. Obviously Gavin shared that curiosity, since he managed to hunt her down. He probably thought she knew what was going on. He was out of luck. The realization almost made her smile.

"Fine, what time am I to report in?" Her voice was far from friendly.

"*We*," he stressed, "have to be there at seven."

"Let me guess?" Sarcasm coated each word. "You lost your cell phone and couldn't just call me?"

Answering humor lit his emerald eyes, causing her breath to hitch audibly. Proving he didn't miss much, his lips twitched. "Maybe I just wanted to see if I could get past your protections." When she refused to acknowledge his double meaning, he raised his teacup in an informal salute. "Besides I heard your tea was good."

She snorted. "Couldn't have been from anyone breathing." Restless she rose, taking her empty cup to the sink. Rinsing it out, she decided to be blunt. "More like you wanted to know if I knew anything. I don't, so you're out a few hours of sleep for tea."

She heard the chair shift as he stood up. Turning her head, she dried her hands with a towel. "Good night, Gavin."

She gave him empty, yet pleasant eyes. "I'll see you out. Unlike others, I like my sleep."

Moving with a rolling gait no female could fail to appreciate, he brought his cup over, crowding her as she turned fully to face him. Trapped between his big, hard body and the counter's edge, pressing into her spine, she was stuck there. Unless she planned to maim him.

Tempting thought.

Invading the hell out of her personal space, he rinsed the cup and preceded to dry his hands on the towel she still held, his knuckles brushing her tense abs. As he placed the cup gently on the counter behind her, he leaned in, bending close. "Good night, Raine." His voice, low and quiet, stroked down her spine like the rub of soft fur.

Chills danced up her arms.

He bent his head a fraction closer, his mouth hovering over her ear, making her visibly shiver as his warm breath caressed her. "Just to clarify, it wasn't the tea I wanted to check out."

She fought to hide her body's reaction and didn't look away.

His smile was slight, his amusement evident. "I'll see myself out, thanks."

She didn't move, couldn't move, as his tall figure walked down the hall and out her door.

CHAPTER TWO

W eak sunlight filtered through the huge windows, outlining the figure seated behind the deep mahogany desk. Physically, the man wasn't imposing, but the mantle of authority he wore made you sit up and take notice.

Ryan Mulcahy looked to be in his mid-forties, but as with most Kyn, he was much older. How much, no one knew for sure, nor did they dare to ask. There was no white in the thick sable hair brushing his narrow shoulders. His coffee-brown eyes were far from warm and friendly—more like dark and deadly—as they focused on her and Gavin.

Gavin's battered boot rested on his jean-covered knee as he sat in the deep leather armchair to the left. A striking floor to ceiling oak bookcase stood to his right. Raine took a position next to it, her shoulders braced against the wall, arms folded.

"I need both of you to do some investigating." Mulcahy's voice was deeper than one would expect. Built along the lines of a long-distance runner, his voice would be more at home on a wrestler. "One of you will cover a series of deaths we've been asked to look into. They've been labeled as accidents, but the client feels there may be more to it than that."

He shifted his gaze to the open folder in front of him. "Food poisoning, accidental fall while mountain climbing, drowning in a pool after one glass too many, a fatal mugging, one suicide, and a two-for-one in a car accident." He glanced up. "Seems to me this group has had some seriously bad luck over the last few years, or else someone is trying to take them out."

Mulcahy's recitation sent Raine's internal alarms clamoring. Fighting for calm she raised an eyebrow, and shifted her suddenly damp palms behind her back. "And the other assignment?"

Gavin shot her a look. "Not bloody enough for you?"

Bearing her teeth, she answered sweetly, "Actually, no." She tilted her head slightly, mocking him. "Besides, I've noticed you don't mind invading the privacy of others."

A wolfish grin flashed his white teeth. "It's the challenge, babe. It's always about the challenge."

She curled her lip. "Isn't that always the story?"

Clearing his throat, Mulcahy demanded their attention. "The second assignment is investigating a minor security breach. A couple of employees have been fielding an unusual number of questions about Taliesin."

Gavin stiffened slightly in his chair, and Raine's body tensed in sudden interest. Breaching Taliesin's intimidating security was no accident.

"What kind of questions?" She forced the question from her tight throat.

"Interesting ones, including inquiries into internal processes. How we're organized, what services are needed the most, what skills are required, questions on past assignments, and who sits on the board." Mulcahy leaned back in his chair, his gaze steady. "I don't like nosy questions. We need to know who's asking, why they're asking, and more importantly, who's holding their leashes."

Across the globe, the Kyn used companies like Taliesin Security as public fronts. The companies provided a protective environment where the Kyn and their specialized skills could be put to use, quietly but effectively. In the modern world, the need for corporate and personal security provided the perfect outlet for many warriors of the Kyn. Protecting the weak, righting wrongs, the whole superhero thing, worked for most Kyn.

Raine wasn't most Kyn.

Neither was Mulcahy. His face hardened and his smile was more a sneer of cynicism than true mirth. "I'm a bit concerned at the timing of these two cases. It's a little too coincidental for my tastes."

"What's the connection?" A deadly seriousness underlay Gavin's question.

"The client?" Raine guessed, not believing in coincidence any more than her boss did. She searched Mulcahy's unreadable face. "Who is it, Mulcahy?"

An indecipherable something flashed through his eyes, and she knew she was not going to like his answer.

Mulcahy kept his cold gaze locked with hers. "Jonah Talbot."

Yep, that would be the name.

"Talbot?" She couldn't completely hide her quiver of shock and shifted her stance, hoping to mask her involuntary jerk, but knew Mulcahy caught it. "The Talbot Foundation, Talbot?" She was proud of how steady her voice sounded. Too bad the rest of her teetered on shattering.

Mulcahy nodded. "It seems Talbot is a bit concerned how some of his associates have been dropping like flies. He's afraid he might be next."

If only they could be so lucky.

Her mind raced, wondering how much her boss suspected. "If that's the case, why not hire a personal security detail from Taliesin? Why simply investigate the deaths?"

"An answer I'm sure Gavin will learn." Mulcahy leaned forward. "I want to know if these deaths are connected, or if it's a ploy set in place by Talbot. There are seven deaths in total and they stretch back almost seven years. If they're real, I want to know who's behind them."

Gavin nodded once. "Do you want to be able to talk to them, or would you prefer a report?" The question was asked in a deceptively bland voice.

Mulcahy's lips twitched at the other man's unsuccessful attempt at subtlety. "I want to talk to them, especially if it's one of ours."

Before Raine could open her mouth, Gavin cut in, "Ours?"

"Quite possible."

Quickly squelching a skin-numbing combination of fury and panic, Raine fisted her hands at her side. She didn't want to dwell on the reasons behind her panic, but the ones behind her anger were easy to identify.

No way in hell did she want to deal with Jonah Talbot. She would rather be skinned alive. Problem was, she might not have a choice, especially when the two cases connected. A connection that held a high probably of being made considering Mulcahy's instincts tended to be dead on.

Locking her internal chaos down, she returned to the conversation at hand. "What makes you think it's one of ours?" Her unasked question being what connection did Mulcahy see that others missed? It wasn't something she could blurt out since asking questions of her boss was akin to finding a solid patch of ground in the middle of a marsh.

"Call it a hunch." Mulcahy studied her, his expression blank, eyes steady. "Looking at the deaths separately, there are no obvious ties. As a group, it becomes a bit murky. The lack of a pattern and the length of time it took to knock off Talbot's associates speaks of patience, planning, and cold ruthlessness, at least in part." His shoulders rose in a negligent shrug. "Perhaps it might be best to offer such an individual a job with us, unless they're already ours."

For Mulcahy to believe the killer may have a link to Taliesin, meant he suspected a Kyn. Based on the skills needed to pull such a series of killings off, if they were Kyn, then chances were even higher that they would be a Wraith.

It was an uncomfortable assumption, but each of the twelve Wraiths could claim those identifying traits. After all, every one was an expert assassin, and patience and planning were necessary elements of well-planned assassinations.

The tricky part was the Wraiths' identities were not common knowledge. In fact, only Mulcahy and the other three Kyn leaders knew all twelve individuals. Raine knew only a few.

Mulcahy's voice broke into her dark thoughts. "Regardless of how it plays out, I want to make sure we covered all our bases. Either Talbot is playing some sort of game with us, or someone wants him dead."

"And if it's both?" Gavin pressed with quiet intensity.

"Let's hope they get Talbot first," she muttered as she uncurled her fists, flexing her numb fingers.

"Is there a problem, Raine?" The rumble of danger in Mulcahy's voice speared shards of dread into her bones.

Yanking her head up, she caught Gavin's sharp look. She had to get a grip. "There are rumors surrounding the Talbot family." Her tone was cautious. "I'm not so sure it's such a good idea for Taliesin to be involved with him."

"Do you know Jonah Talbot?" Her boss's casual position didn't alter, but she wasn't fooled.

She had to tread carefully. "Not really, but from what I've

heard, it might be a better option to help out whoever is knocking these guys off." She shrugged stiffly, trying to release the fine line of tension in her shoulders. It didn't work.

"Are you saying that you, a top level employee, would be unable to do your contracted job?" Ice coated Mulcahy's words and a razor-sharp threat lay underneath them.

After years of enduring unspoken criticism from this man, she should have expected the cut, but it never made it easier to bear. Temper and panic simmered under her skin, triggering an immature need to push the lethal man behind the desk.

Taking a deep breath, she met his eyes and managed not to flinch. Barely. "No, I can and will do it. Besides, there's no guarantee these two assignments will overlap." Okay, so she might nudge him a little. She was never good at backing down.

Mulcahy's eyes didn't warm. "And if they do?"

Then she was screwed. Instead of sharing, she played his detested game. "Why are you so certain they will?"

"You're not the only one who finds it curious that Talbot wants us to investigate this series of accidents, but won't hire Taliesin Security for protection." He paused, straightened a perfectly aligned pad of paper, then continued, "The current increase of interest in our company from various points outside, plus Talbot's sudden request to look into a series of accidents, some of which are years old, doesn't sit right."

"Especially since he's had plenty of time to question these so called accidents." Gavin leaned forward, bracing his arms on his knees.

Their boss nodded. "Exactly. The last few deaths have been relatively close together, which may explain why questions are being asked now."

"But…" she prompted. Really, she didn't want Mulcahy to focus on her, but she was curious to what was whirling in that Machiavellian mind.

"The Talbot Foundation has fingers in everything from genetics and nanotechnology to religious artifacts. More disturbing to me, are Jonah Talbot's ties to those agencies, both political and military, who know what Taliesin truly houses. A careless word in the wrong ear might expose the Kyn." He grimaced. "Although according to his company's press releases, all their research and discoveries are for the benefit of mankind."

"You don't believe it." Gavin's voice was sure.

Mulcahy templed his fingers and flicked an unreadable glance at Raine. "No. I've found the more powerful you think you are, the more you think you can get away with." He shook his head. "Talbot has a healthy ego, one which would normally question why a great many of his long time business associates are suddenly dying. His timing is suspicious. If, in fact, he knows Taliesin Security is the largest local employer of the Kyn and houses some of the world's top warriors, wouldn't an intelligent man start by finding out if we were the ones doing the killing?"

He pushed back from his desk and rose from his chair. "It doesn't add up." Walking to the front of his desk, he leaned back, and folded his arms across his chest. "Whatever either of you find, you share with the other. I want regular reports."

He twisted, and picked up two slim folders from his desk. "What information we have is in here." He handed each of them a file. "Raine, trace these questions back to the source, quietly. If I'm right and it's Talbot, it's a well-known name. Taliesin does not want, or need, the bad publicity. Gavin, you start looking into these deaths." He studied them both. "Questions?"

They shook their heads.

"Good."

Both she and Gavin turned to leave. As her hand touched the doorknob, Mulcahy's voiced floated over, "Watch each other's backs."

CHAPTER THREE

R aine was going to be late for her appointment. She was currently trapped in crawling traffic on a two-lane highway heading west toward the coast. It was the middle of October, and normally traffic wasn't this insane. To make things even worse, the gray skies threatened rain. If Mother Nature made good on her promise, she would go from a frustrating crawl to a dead stop.

Gavin, on the other hand, was meeting a demon and enjoying an excellent meal at one of Raine's favorite restaurants, the Portland Chart House. Not only did diners enjoy a stunning view of the Willamette River, but the food was excellent.

She didn't envy Gavin and his date. Okay, maybe a little. Especially as she was currently stuck behind Ma and Pa Winter driving their dreaded fifth wheel from Kansas as they stay a good ten miles below the posted speed limit on a road never meant to handle the heavy traffic.

To be fair, Gavin was pursuing his leads with Natasha Bertoi, a blonde, petite Fey and half-demon combination, who proved beauty truly was a treacherous bitch.

Natasha's mind was as sharp as Raine's blades, and just as able to draw blood. She was one of the Kyn leaders in possession of the names of the Wraiths. More importantly, she was the ruling head of the Amanusa house, which the half-demon contingency called home.

Yet Raine had every confidence Gavin would walk away unscathed from his luncheon. Females, even demonic ones, were endlessly fascinated by him. She'd bet good money Natasha wouldn't prove to be any different.

The flash of brake lights in front of her, made Raine quietly curse as she slowed even more. If she ever made it to the coast, a witch waited for her. Not just any witch, but the head of the Northwest Magi house, one whose word was rarely questioned. Not that anyone dared, since the power he wielded was intimidating enough.

She checked the clock on the dash and winced. Nothing good ever came from keeping powerful people waiting, especially someone like Cheveyo. No one was quite sure what blood ran through his veins, but his black hair, dark eyes, and bronzed skin hinted at Native American. Like most Kyn, he appeared younger than he was, and since he looked to be in his mid-thirties, his age was anyone's guess.

Today he would be her intermediary with Paul Dixon, the young male witch who had some disturbing stories to share. Paul, a compu-geek who worked IT security for Taliesin, discovered an electronic breach in one of the company's public-facing firewalls. Since she shied away from computers, as they tended to do everything, including explode, whenever she tried to use them, having Cheveyo there to translate should be helpful.

From what she had read in the file, a specialized Trojan virus was discovered in the company's email system. Designed to gather information about Taliesin's network, it located vulnerable ports within the firewall. Once in, it recorded security clearances and employee information, before sending a copy back to the hacker.

Luckily, Taliesin's own anti-virus program caught it before more than basic information was compromised, and shut the virus down. It managed to trace the originating hack, only to discover it was now defunct.

Paul was one of Cheveyo's pet students. After reporting the virus to Mulcahy, Paul requested his mentor's presence for any future questions.

Raine snorted softly.

The rumors of the company's internal investigations seemed to grow more menacing each year. It made her wonder how the general Kyn population would react if it ever came to light that the Wraiths weren't just some scary story. Her lips twitched with dark humor. However, the expanding stories explained why so many employees felt the need for representation before things became too involved.

In her experience, witches were more liable to think everyone was against them than most. A holdover from The Burning Times, when they were put to the stake by anyone who could light a match. Back then, the ability to sense upcoming events was extremely handy. Unfortunately, that little talent only helped the real witches, not the poor, unfortunate humans who didn't fit society's idea of "normal", and in the end, more humans died than actual witches, but still the wariness remained.

Today she planned on using that same paranoia to see if she could get information that hadn't been in the report. Perhaps through their contacts in the Kyn community, Cheveyo and Paul could link any potentially strange happenings to the current situation—okay, strange by Kyn standards, at least.

She finally made it to the edge of town. Traffic was still a bitch, but she could see light at the end of the road. Some of the larger vehicles were pulling into the gas stations and hotels lining the main street.

She checked the clock again, grateful to see she might actually make it in time. Turning into the maze of local streets, she searched for the elusive public parking lot that wasn't already full.

She hadn't bothered to call ahead, since the note in the file Mulcahy gave her stated she was expected by the two men at an address near Cannon Beach. Weaving her way through the small town, her search ended at a small, half-empty parking lot.

Shutting off the SUV, she opened her door and stepped out. The cold wind fluttered the edges of her trench coat, creating the faint sound of kites snapping.

The wind crept through the thin silk of her shirt and tickled icy fingers over her torso, making her wish she had thought to grab a heavy sweater before leaving Taliesin's offices. Weapons would have been nice, too, but this was supposed to be a friendly get together. So the eight-inch blades hidden in her boots would stay put, and her other, longer blades stayed tucked away in the SUV.

Pushing her hands into her pockets, she pulled her coat closer, hoping its illusion of warmth would become a reality, and headed down the boardwalk to the beach. The address, one of the many seaside homes peppering the coastline, lay in the direction of Haystack Rock.

Dodging the small meandering crowds milling in and out of the shops dotting the boardwalk, she moved into a narrow walkway between a gray, weathered two-story and a pale rose, one-story cottage.

October might not be prime tourist season, but the wildness of the Northwest Coast and fabulous saltwater taffy kept people coming year round. Turning slightly, she barely missed being plowed into by two small boys arguing over a bag of the gooey treats.

It didn't take long to reach her intended target, the more contemporary, light-blue cottage facing the roiling waves of the Pacific.

Pausing at the small gate surrounding the carefully tended front yard, she let the salty scent of the ocean fill her lungs. It rode the wind as it mixed with the furious energy of the storm clouds rumbling distantly over the turbulent sea. The people walking around her faded as the call of natural magic thrummed through the air and vibrated faintly under her feet with each breaking wave.

Instinctively, her powers stretched to gather what the world offered. It pulled on the swirling magic, surfing the waves, gently urging it toward her. The nearby humans remained oblivious to the innate magic swirling around them. Their ignorance left her amazed. For the Kyn, the physical world was akin to a deep ocean of magic.

The slight click of a door opening to her left had her turning to see a slender man with shaggy, dirt blond hair watching her warily. "Ms. McCord?"

She nodded once. "You must be Paul Dixon." Releasing her hold on the magic, it slipped like an undertow back into its endless sea. She stepped through the gate, hearing it latch behind her.

Paul returned her nod. "Please come in." He stepped aside, motioning her through.

She stopped a couple of steps below the porch. Entering a room with someone she didn't know at her back wasn't happening. "After you."

He took a cautious step back. "Of course, if you'd follow me then?" He moved through the door into the warm interior beyond.

She followed and pushed the door shut without turning.

Pale wood floors graced the open spaces where functional, yet tasteful, furniture rested. Large windows framed the constantly changing view of the ocean. Yet it was the pictures on the walls, which caught her attention. Some captured the sense of wildness found in nature, both of prey and predator. Others framed the surreal beauty found in the rugged forms of wind twisted trees and lightning-kissed skies crowning dark mountains.

Paul headed further back to the kitchen where Cheveyo stood at the gleaming stove dressed in crisp khakis and a forest green shirt. His black hair barely brushed the collar as he turned to her.

She couldn't keep her lips from twitching at the somewhat feminine-looking apron tied at his waist, sporting the saying 'It's a witch thing. You wouldn't understand.'

"Like it?" His voice rumbled as he gestured one handed to his attire.

"It suits you," she managed with a straight face. If a six-foot-six witch could pull off wearing such a girly apron, he would be the one.

He snorted and turned back to the pot on the stove. "I'm making chowder. Have you eaten yet?"

"No, actually, I haven't had the chance."

"Well, consider yourself invited. Paul, grab some bowls for us, would you?"

Paul walked to a cupboard and took down three soup bowls. He set them on the stone counter, then moved around the kitchen, pulling out utensils and cups.

"So, take off the coat and have a seat, Raine." Cheveyo motioned to the table standing to her left. "I give my word you have nothing to fight in my house today."

Some of her tension eased. Witches didn't give oaths lightly, as they had a nasty way of coming back to them threefold if broken.

Laying her coat over the back of a chair, she settled in, watching Cheveyo open the oven door. The smell of warm bread filled the kitchen as he pulled out a pan. He sat it on the counter to cool as Paul filled a copper teakettle with water. After placing it on the stove, Paul dished up the soup while Cheveyo cut thick slices of steaming bread.

Once lunch was on the table, only the occasional clinking of spoons against bowls broke the comfortable silence. She didn't feel the need to rush into things, and the two men seemed to agree.

Finishing her meal, she met Cheveyo's steady gaze. "You're an extremely good cook. Thank you for lunch." It may not have been the Chart House, but it was close.

He inclined his head slightly. Paul cleared the bowls from the table and set out tea. "So Mulcahy asked you to find out who breached Taliesin's security, and who's asking questions?" Cheveyo asked bluntly.

"Yes." She sipped the light herbal tea. "I saw the submitted report. Mr. Dixon was able to trace the virus back to a defunct address. Do either of you have any idea of the hacker's identity?"

The younger witch finished rinsing the dishes and turned to look at her. His washed-out, blue eyes moved nervously from her to Cheveyo as he walked back to the table.

"It was a dead end." His voice was steady, despite the trembling hand he ran through his disheveled hair. From the looks of it, he'd been running his hands through those strands a lot today. "It led back to a dummy account under Belinda Curtis, who doesn't exist as far as I can tell. I checked all the available databases, both public and ours. Neither one hit on anything."

She traced the handle of her cup as she studied the younger man. "So, some hacker just got lucky and managed to find a chink in our firewall?"

He shook his head. "No. Taliesin's firewalls are challenging, so it had to be a really good hacker. They didn't get very far before the updated virus scan caught it."

She'd have to take his word on that. "The list of names that got copied, do you know any of them?"

Paul shot a quick look to Cheveyo before he nodded. "Yes, one or two."

"And?" she prompted.

"One of them was a low level witch, Diane Layton. She schedules the security systems' assignments. The other was a wizard, Justin Black, who does secured runs."

Runs were assignments involving transporting objects from one place to another in secure settings. Depending upon the client—Kyn or human—these objects could be either magical or religious in nature.

When Paul paused, she nudged. "Are they friends of yours?"

"Diane is." Cheveyo's deep voice was laced in steel. His black gaze was intimidating, a clear indication she needed to watch her tone. He expected respect, and since she wasn't planning on starting anything, she needed to remember whose house she was in.

"She's a fountain of gossip," he continued. "She told Paul of a situation which he feels might be connected."

Witch paranoia at its finest.

She was quick to squelch the thought since the very lethal man in front of her might take exception to it. Instead, she made sure to show only polite interest as the two men continued their retelling.

According to Cheveyo, Diane's gossip had Justin picking up a woman at a local dance club and bringing her home to show her his collection of old manuscripts.

As a pick up line it seemed just as lame as others Raine had heard.

After a rousing night of metaphorically reading dusty tombs and drinking large amounts of alcohol, Justin woke in the morning with a hell of a hangover. The mystery woman was gone and his house a little less clean than before. Nothing was taken, and luckily nothing would've been found, as he was a low level employee.

His security clearance as a runner prevented access to any vital information. Unfortunately, the only name the wizard had managed to get, before his late-night reading session, was Linda. Paul thought it close enough to the non-existent Belinda Curtis on the hacker account to tell Cheveyo.

Mulcahy's file recorded the same information, but she wanted to see if any new facts would emerge.

"None of this is news to you," Cheveyo stated evenly, dark gaze studying her intently.

He was right. Mulcahy's file recorded the same information, but she wanted to see if any new facts would emerge.

"However, I have something else that could be connected." Cheveyo's lips shifted briefly as his large frame relaxed into the chair. "Which is why you are here." A tone of arrogance squeezed through his words.

It looked like her rusty diplomatic skills were about to be put to the test. "You know the rules, Cheveyo, I only answer to Mulcahy." She shifted back from the table, crossing one leg over the other. She wanted to make sure she could get to one of her blades fairly quick in case things got dicey.

No pun intended.

It never failed to amaze her how little it took to make a person feel in control of a situation. Within the Kyn, information played a vital role in the power struggles pushing back and forth among the magical throng. The downside? That information always came with a price tag.

Cheveyo's asking price to Mulcahy was her fighting hellish traffic to the coast to accommodate Paul's request for the older witch's presence. Otherwise Paul could have been picked up and brought into a conference room at Taliesin. Taliesin didn't sweat the ACLU.

But bargaining with another Kyn leader was tricky. Especially for Wraiths, since they answered first to Mulcahy, then to their own respective leaders. Only Mulcahy could demand their services anywhere, at any time, and have them go without question.

Cheveyo's dark eyes gleamed as his gaze roamed over her figure. "I know the rules, Raine. This is a personal request." He turned to Paul. "Privacy please."

Without a word, the younger man got up and left the room. His footsteps echoed on the hardwood floors, and then the came the sound of the front door opening then closing.

The thick silence left in the wake of his departure made her uneasy. The chowder she'd eaten began to curdle.

Just how personal of a request was Cheveyo going to make? Please don't let it be something she'd have to try to kill him for.

Going up against the Magi head was as productive as gouging out her own eyes. Except self-mutilation would be preferable to whatever he could devise—the repercussions could be more than even she could handle.

His enigmatic gaze studied her intently. Suddenly, he smiled, a real smile. "Oh relax, Raine, I'm not asking for sex. I like emerging from my bed alive."

Color stole up her face. Being so easily read left her feeling foolish. It didn't help that her first thought was, *why the hell wouldn't he want her*? Irritated at him for being so damn contrary, and defensive from embarrassment, she snapped out, "So what do you want?"

"I want you to do something for me." His smile left his face, but not his eyes, as if he could read her mind and was privately amused. "When this assignment is over, I want you to study under me for a couple of months."

Surprise widened her eyes and had her tensing in the chair. "Excuse me?"

"I've heard stories," he continued. "Stories indicating you have some skills which are uniquely yours. However, you've chosen not to explore them."

"You know better than to believe in rumors," she scoffed. "They're rarely based in fact." She reached for her teacup, dropping her eyes to hide her building anger. Noticing a faint tremor in her hand, she steadied it.

She didn't know what he'd heard, but there were parts of her hidden deep. Powers she buried because of the havoc they created and the price they exacted were too steep. Already a misfit in the Kyn world based on her unknown bloodlines, she didn't need anything else to set her apart.

"They aren't just rumors." Cheveyo didn't back down. "You can't ignore what you are forever, or what was done to you."

Shock shattered her composure. Not bothering to hide her chaotic emotions, she met his steady regard. "Even if the stories are based in fact, you have no right to ask this of me. I'm quite aware of exactly what I am, Cheveyo."

"I have the right, because I was asked to approach you years ago. I saw no need for it." His voice stayed level, his dark eyes steady. "Until now."

She dropped her leg and leaned forward, setting her cup down. Her grip on the edge of the table whitened her fingers as she took a deep breath trying to control the fury burning through her. No one used her, not ever. "Who talked to you? Who would ask you to take in a mongrel?"

He just looked at her, remaining silent, but she caught the flicker of pity.

Her face paled as it hit her. Only one person could have

told him, the only person who knew what had happened fifteen years ago. The sense of betrayal sliced deep, but she couldn't change what had been done.

Closing her eyes, she fought back the anger and pain. *Deal with it later.* Right now she needed to stay focused and calm. Had to think. Find the traps in his proposal.

Cheveyo wouldn't take her on just because of some sense of responsibility or curiosity. He had to get something out of this. Otherwise, he would have come to her years before when he was initially asked.

She knew she was different from most Kyn. Each of the Kyn chose a house based on their bloodlines. Not only was her heritage a mystery, as she had no idea what her father was, but only her mother's Fey blood allowed her to stay in the Fey house.

The real problem lay in the same past Cheveyo was determined to drag into the light. Being changed at a molecular level in a lab when she was fifteen hadn't helped. Neither she, nor those who treated her after her escape, could figure out exactly what had been done during those dark months. Even now, she knew there were parts of her still untapped.

It took a shit-ton of work and time, but she finally managed to find some sort of peace about the skills she was comfortable wielding, and tucking away those she wasn't. Now, Cheveyo was asking for her, to not only acknowledge these powers, but to embrace them. But doing so would make her stand so far outside the Kyn community, she wasn't sure she'd ever find her place. This bargain would shake the foundation of the world she had made for herself.

Still…it was worth considering. Especially since lately, small insidious threads of curiosity started to intertwine with that fear, making her wonder what she was truly capable of being. A whisper of rationality pointed out this might be the safest way to get answers to her personal questions.

Therein lay the temptation.

Determined not to reveal her inner turmoil, she kept her voice indifferent. "What do you get out of this, Cheveyo? Altruism is not your strongest trait."

"No it's not," he acknowledged. "You intrigue me, Raine. Chalk it up to curiosity."

She shot him a fierce smile. "Let's hope your curiosity doesn't get you killed." On the other hand it would serve him right if she did this and it came back to kick him in the ass. Realizing what she was considering, her smile faded. "There are conditions to my acceptance."

His presence suddenly darkened as his innate magic snapped to attention. Setting restrictions on the head of the Magi house was not smart.

Right now, a little voice in her head was asking how lucky she felt. The answer was, not very.

Finally, his instinctive flare of power died down, and he nodded.

Taking a steadying breath, she continued, "First, whatever we discover from this, you won't tell a soul. I want your oath on this. Second, my job trumps your teaching. Third, whatever powers develop, they are mine to use or share. I owe you nothing for this. When we're done, we're done."

He did not look happy at her list. It made her wonder what he had planned for her, and how much of her own grave she might be digging.

"I have an apprentice." His voice was cool. "I don't expect you to become my witch-warrior from this agreement. Whether you want to believe this or not, I like you, most of the time. I figured this would give you a chance to safely see how far you can go."

She wasn't going to let him know she agreed with that bit

of logic, and her lack of expression didn't alter as she waited for his oath.

He was quiet a moment, studying her. Finally, he snorted in disgust. "Agreed. You have my oath on it."

Hearing the words, her muscles uncoiled enough to ease the strain along her spine. She rolled her shoulders.

Cheveyo shook his head. "You need to learn to trust, girl. It will save you some grief in the long run."

"It hasn't so far," she responded coolly. "What did I just pay for?"

He brushed imaginary crumbs from his hands. "I ran across a couple of Kyn who don't work for Taliesin, but who were aggressively pursued to take part in a drug trial by a research company."

This made no sense. "Drug trials? From a human drug company?" At his nod, she grew more confused. "Did the company know they were Kyn?" If so, it meant the company had ties to some very scary government agencies. Not a good thing.

He shrugged. "I agree."

She traced the wood grain on the table with a finger. "Why would they want Kyn for the testing? We don't carry their diseases, nor has anyone come close to figuring out why."

The most widely shared theory was something in the cellular make-up of the Kyn prevented mortal diseases from infecting their supernatural hosts.

"I don't know, nor do the two people I talked to," he said. "Neither one accepted the offers, as they had the same thought you just did. The monetary compensation increased with each refusal. However, the company finally backed off when they realized neither one was going to play lab rat."

Such pushy tactics triggered warning bells. "What's the name of the research company?"

"Polleo Research." His face hardened. "I haven't been able to unravel the maze of corporations who fund it to find the head."

"How does this tie in to the questions being asked about Taliesin and the virus that was turned loose?"

"I think the better question is, what kind of drug could possibly be tested on Kyn? Humanity's leaders have tried for centuries to figure out what sets us apart from them." He shook his head, obviously caught in his own unpleasant memories. "Their constant greed for power and quest for immortality are generally the fuel behind such situations."

"That may be," she responded. "But you have no proof there's any diabolical tie-in with this drug testing thing."

He met her gaze, something she didn't understand moving behind his dark eyes. "Actually, I do. Dmitri Rimmick, the wizard who was approached, has disappeared and the witch has gone into hiding."

"They hit a wizard and a witch for testing?" Okay, maybe there was a reason to worry.

Those humans, who knew the truth, only knew it as far as the Kyn let them. Even now the Kyn were still keeping secrets. Deeper truths and realities—such as the fact some of the Kyn held powers, which could send good little humans running for the mountains and screaming for their guns—were not allowed out. It was one thing to come out of the magical closet to a privileged few, another to come out blasting to the masses.

Humans thought witches and wizards were inter-change-able. But that wasn't true. The difference between the two lay in how each drew on magic and used it.

Witches used primarily earth magic, and wizards relied heavily on spells and potions. Neither side got along very well since their basic tenets stood on opposite sides. For example, witches held sacred their threefold law—whatever you do, comes back to you threefold. Wizards, on the other hand, always looked out for themselves.

For a research company to pick one of each showed a more complete knowledge of the Kyn world than was comfortable, and could be an indicator of something much more ominous.

She worried her lower lip. "Are you sure the wizard didn't just piss someone off?"

Cheveyo snorted. "Not this particular one. Dmitri is not that good. He hung on the fringes, dabbled in the darker spells, but could never seem to get them right. I'd be more inclined to think he played with something he couldn't handle, but those few that know him said he wasn't working on anything at the time."

"And the witch?"

"She won't talk to you." His slight grin was more a bearing of teeth. "She only came to me when she found out Dmitri was missing. I don't even know where to look for her."

As the head of the Magi House, Cheveyo was the acknowledged leader for the witches, shamans, and a handful of wizards living in the Northwest. He knew enough of the various cultural quirks of each to make a sound decision, which was what Raine counted on now. "So, you think he's missing, not just vacationing, and that the witch could be in trouble because of this research company?"

"Oh, most definitely." His confidence was evident in his voice. A sense of foreboding crept over Raine as he continued, "And I think this is just the beginning."

CHAPTER FOUR

Raine headed back to Portland, the deafening sounds of heavy bass chords filling the interior of the SUV. The leaden clouds followed through on their threat and rain pelted the windshield in time to the driving beats as her wipers whipped back and forth. Letting the music move through her in rhythm with her chaotic emotions, she turned Cheveyo's proposal over in her mind.

The devastating sense of betrayal lingered, leaving her floundering. Fifteen years ago, she trusted her rescuer to keep his mouth shut. Until now, she had no reason to think he hadn't kept his word. She thought she was safe, that no one would ever find out what she endured all those years ago.

She never shared her past with anyone, not wanting or needing anyone's pity. Life could sucker punch you without batting an eyelash. You made a choice—either lie down and let it screw you over, or fight back and make sure it thought twice before hitting you again.

Well, she made a life out of hitting back, harder and

faster. With very few friends and no close family, she was content in her solitude.

Right?

She ignored the insidious memories of Gavin's touch and the ache it brought. Over the years, that ache had deepened. Although their interactions were few, they were intense. He tempted her on a level no one had ever before reached. He was hard to resist, but the past had shown her the devastating price of caring for someone.

Was she really considering taking such a risk?

There was no quick answer, which added another confusing layer to her unstable emotions, and unable to deal with that haunting question, she shifted mental gears.

Why had Cheveyo been told? The past was starting to ooze under the door she placed between it and her current life. If the door ever cracked opened, she would quickly become the hunted instead of the hunter.

She couldn't afford to lose the respect of the other Wraiths, and her leaders—respect she worked tirelessly for—not to mention the hard-won self-respect she managed to carve out despite her past.

Maybe her rescuer playing some kind of game? If so, she'd better learn the rules quick or better yet, rewrite them. The last thing she needed was to start questioning her life. She didn't have time for an existential crisis, or for the fallout the unknown answers would bring. Gods knew, it would screw things six ways to Sunday, and she needed things to stay the way they were, stable and under her control.

That last thought made her snort in derision.

As if any of this was under any sort of control? Here she was, battling back a hailstorm of emotions, heading to confront a man who probably wouldn't blink an eye if she no longer existed.

Taking the exit off the freeway, she drove toward Taliesin

intending to get some answers. *Why had he told Cheveyo? Had he told anyone else?*

Damn him, he knew how she felt about her past, her privacy. What did he get out of this, anyway? There had to be a reason.

Shivers crawled down her spine. She feared very little in this life, but this man, he could make her blood run cold. As she turned into the parking lot, she sent up a fruitless prayer there would be a valid explanation, something she could live with. Putting the SUV in park, she took a deep breath, and did her best to rebuild her inner walls into something resembling her normal, stoic demeanor.

She blinked, and realized she spent the last few minutes staring out the windshield as she worked to pull herself together. Shutting off the engine, she yanked open the door, got out, and then strode through the rain toward the warm light coming from the seven-story structure housing Taliesin Security.

No one would ever guess who and what was behind the brick and mortar. It was no different from any other corporate building park. Clean lines, manicured landscaping, even a security guard at the front door. Stalking by the guard she headed straight to the elevators, ignoring the trail of water she left on the marbled entry floor in her wake.

When she stepped into the elevator she barely noticed the wide berth given to her by those in the standard office uniform of suits and skirts. The other occupants hugged the wall, eyeing her warily as they metal cage rose.

She exited the elevator and headed for the reception desk that sat atop a pale lush carpet that stretched across the opening and guarded the main offices. The receptionist—a sleek professional woman named Rachel, all expensive silk and tasteful gold—looked up.

Her angular face paled slightly as she saw Raine bearing

down. Rachel quickly ended her phone conversation and nervously pushed a strand of professionally dyed red hair back behind her ear. She stood and moved to intercept Raine. "He's in a meeting." She tried for a conciliatory tone, but a slight panicky note still made it through.

"Not for long." Raine's gaze flickered up and held the woman's hazel eyes, then she reached for Mulcahy's door. Pushing it open, she barely refrained from slamming it shut. Nevertheless, Rachel stepped back quickly as Raine closed the door in her face.

Mulcahy didn't startle at her interruption, but annoyance shimmered around him as he watched her move across the carpeted floor to his desk. Aware of a blond-haired, blue-eyed man sitting in front of the desk, watching her approach, she didn't take her focus off her target.

Mulcahy's baritone cut through the sudden silence, his dark eyes never leaving Raine. "Mr. Talbot, it seems we'll have to finish this conversation at a later date."

At the name, she turned toward the man in the chair. "Talbot? Jonah Talbot?"

The man smiled, humor lighting his blue eyes. "Yes, and you are?"

Thrown off stride, she quickly recovered. "Raine McCord. My apology on interrupting your meeting with Mr. Mulcahy, but something's come up that needs his immediate attention."

The smile widened into a grin. She subtly searched his face. There was nothing out of the ordinary. No burning light of fanaticism in the light eyes, like the ones that burned through her nightmares. His voice was pleasant, charming. "I understand. When one runs a successful business, unexpected situations seem to occur more often than one would think."

Talbot got to his feet, and she realized he was nearly as

tall as Gavin, nicely muscled, more lean than big. He held his manicured hand out to Mulcahy, who had also risen. "I hope to see you there then, Mr. Mulcahy." Talbot's voice stayed amused, showing no irritation at the interruption. "I will look forward to your reports." He turned, nodded to her, then headed out of the office.

She was still trying to process her first meeting with Talbot when the door shut softly behind him. Putting it aside for now, she turned to Mulcahy. His anger was well hidden, but meeting his cold gaze, she felt her own rage resurface.

"What's the problem now, McCord?" His voice went low with fury at her unannounced presence.

"Why the hell did you tell Cheveyo?" The question tore through gritted teeth. All her earlier resolve about dealing with this rationally blown apart by the raging emotional storm she couldn't calm. "You swore no one would ever know! You lied to me!" Hearing her voice rise, she stopped, taking a deep breath despite the smothering pain in her chest.

His annoyance and anger faded as he registered what triggered her outburst. "I was concerned."

"About what?" She tried to fight back the fury and hurt so she could think. "What in the hell could so concern you, that you went behind my back? You broke your oath, dammit!"

"You. I was concerned about you." He sighed wearily as he studied her. "Sit down."

She dropped onto the edge of the chair behind her. Her hands twisted tightly together—much like her chaotic emotions—her legs shook. "I don't understand."

"I know, and I'm not sure I can explain it." He got up and moved to the front of his desk, taking the chair at her side so he could face her. "You were young, Raine. You'd focused so utterly on your training, you seemed to have nothing else in your life. The anger that makes you good at what you do, it twisted you. You took unnecessary risks. You wouldn't willingly work with anyone on exploring or controlling your abilities. You were reckless, almost unstable." His professional mask dropped for a moment, exposing lines of concern and tiredness she refused to acknowledge. "You studied the basics, just what you needed to do the job."

She sat there, staring at him, a brief flicker of disbelief running through her. That he had seen her so clearly, knocked her off balance. Did he know the things she had done? Things, even now, she never really thought about. "I needed the fighting skills. They were more important," she countered, hoping her fear of being found out wasn't reflected in her face.

He shook his head sharply. Raising his hand, he almost touched her, before clenching it into a fist and resting it on his knee. "No, Raine, they weren't." His voice gentled, "You're my niece, my responsibility. I owe my sister, your mother, that much. I may not have saved her from those labs, but I can damn well try and save her daughter." He watched her, his emotionless mask firmly back in place. "Cheveyo doesn't know everything, only that your magic was tampered with when you were taken."

But it was more than anyone else knew. Didn't Mulcahy understand? Couldn't he sense her humiliation at having Cheveyo know even that much of the story? She searched his face, still not finding the comfort or understanding she spent most of her life looking for.

He may have pulled her shattered body out of the human labs when she was fifteen, but she hadn't been his first priority. She knew that. He'd gone in to save his half-sister and the male who had been their bodyguard. Unfortunately for her uncle, Raine was the only one left alive when he arrived.

Sitting next to this powerful being who was her only blood family, she felt an old, familiar ache. Her uncle would never be able to accept her as she was. He may have loved his sister, but her child was another story. For years she knew this intellectually, but by telling Cheveyo, Mulcahy made it brutally clear she was another pawn in his power games.

Her last faint delusion of familial comfort shattered into dust. Her laugh was bitter as the awareness of how little she meant to this man sank in. "I'll just have to trust you on that, Uncle. Forgive me if I don't put much stock in it right now."

His eyes hardened and his jaw clenched. He pushed himself up and loomed over her. "You're a stubborn child sometimes. I want you to master your own magic. You've been so busy running away from it, you haven't stopped to think what it could change for you."

She leaned back in her chair, arms negligently draped along the sides. "Change?" Mockery heavy in her voice. "For me or for you?"

She could tell he was holding his temper by a thread. Was the urge to shake her riding him hard? Did she really give a damn? She kept her tone scathing. "I don't want to change anything, I was…am doing just fine. Do you have any idea what will happen when I start poking around inside my own head?"

He straightened and unclenched his jaw and fists. He took a deep breath and leaned against the edge of his desk. "No, and neither do you." His gaze was steady and his voice cold. "That's the problem." Something in her expression triggered a flashing of his teeth. "So far you've been lucky, but it won't last."

"Yeah? Well, let's just hope it doesn't kill me and Cheveyo." She heard the hostility in her voice. She must have a death wish to keeping pushing her uncle like this. You don't back a hungry tiger into a corner and keep poking it with a stick. Eventually, the tiger will get bored and rip your throat out.

"You accepted his offer?" Both his face and tone were carefully blank, all traces of his anger and frustration tucked behind his normal professional mask.

"What was I going to do? Turn it down?" She rubbed one hand absently over the back of her neck. "I needed the information he had." A sudden suspicion hit her and she narrowed her eyes into a glare. "You knew when you sent me that this would happen."

He didn't answer. He didn't have to. It was reflected in the brief glimpse of satisfaction she caught in his eyes.

She shook her head, suddenly tired. She didn't want to continue this conversation anymore. There was no way it would end how she needed it to. Nor would she ever be able to figure out her uncle and his convoluted machinations.

Mulcahy read her capitulation, because his own tense posture relaxed fractionally. "After his first refusal, I didn't push too hard as you seemed to find some sense of balance in your life." His tone was a couple steps up from his earlier frostbite. "You slowly came out of your shell. You were isolated, but seemed to be functioning better." He shrugged, circled his desk, and then sat in his chair, his gaze holding her in place. "I thought I'd wait and see if you would make the decision to explore your talents. I didn't think it would take this long."

She leaned her head back against the chair and closed her eyes. "You should have," she said, her voice empty.

"I know," he agreed. "When I called Cheveyo about the security breach, he mentioned he was thinking of approaching you. I didn't disagree with the timing."

"Of course not." Her eyes opened, the ceiling taking up her field of vision, but she didn't lift her head. "You think I'm a ticking time bomb."

He ignored her sarcasm. "Yes, I do. You're no good to me

as a Wraith if you self-destruct because you're too scared to push your own limits."

Familiar with her uncle's ability to divorce emotionally from any family ties when it came to Taliesin, didn't make it hurt any less. It was the primary reason they agreed to keep their family bond quiet.

No use in anyone thinking she got where she did because of blood ties, as laughable as that was. It would've been yet another reason to keep her on the outside. She never regretted the decision, yet right now, she envied Mulcahy's control.

Pushing her body out of her chair she stood. "Don't worry, I'll do my job. I always do. Just like you taught me." Her lips twisted into a bitter smile. "Who knows, Uncle, maybe when Cheveyo's done, I'll be the warrior you want me to be. I wonder if it'll be enough." She turned on her heel and left the office, not bothering to wait for his answer.

CHAPTER FIVE

B arefoot, hair drawn back in a serviceable braid, Raine systematically pounded the punching bag with sharp, blurring vicious movements. Using short quick strikes, she let her anger reign. Just because she imagined Mulcahy's face on the bag meant nothing. It was no more than a focal point.

The conversation in his office ran through her head in an endless loop, pushing her hands faster. After years of intense training, her body moved in an instinctive rhythm. Sweat trickled down her face, but was ignored.

Her muscles stretched and flowed. Her mind emptied and settled, as her body shifted and contorted into various offensive and defensive positions. Caught up in her workout, it took a second for a slight rustle of cloth to filter through and catch her attention.

Recognizing Gavin's long-limbed figure, she came to a gradual stop. Putting her hands out to hold the heavy bag steady, she watched as he moved through the dim light of the second floor gym open to all Taliesin employees.

She'd never admit it aloud, but she got a secret thrill out of watching him move. All that leashed violence wrapped in such a tempting package. No, it wasn't just her exercise making her pant. She closed her eyes and used her arm to wipe the sweat off her forehead. What the hell was wrong with her lately? Males never hit her radar like this. They were too much work. Yet, this man drove her crazy. Only Gavin seemed to send her from furious to horny in under a minute.

He stopped just in front of her. "What did it do to piss you off?"

Her damp, gray tank stuck to her back as she wiped her hands down the side of her black sweats. "I didn't like its tone."

She realized she'd lost track of time. She was supposed to meet him and go over what they discovered in their separate meetings. Thanks to the discussion with her uncle and its emotional upheaval, she'd missed the appointment.

Damn. She winced and shrugged. "Sorry, I got sidetracked."

Sharp green eyes studied her. "I was able to track you down, so no harm done." He walked to the other side of the hanging bag and gently pushed it toward her. "Need a live opponent?"

Sending the bag back, she answered, "If you're up for it." She welcomed the challenge of facing someone who would actually hit back.

The gym's lighting illuminated the small signs of tension around his mouth, leaving her curious. Perhaps she wasn't the only one who needed to blow off a little steam. It took a great deal to push Gavin's buttons—she should know, she tried often enough and learned his need for control rivaled hers.

She tracked his lithe progress into the locker room as he went to change. What would it be like if two tightly controlled people trusted each other enough to let loose?

She snorted softly and went to pick up her bottle of water from the floor, ignoring a brief flare of regret that she'd never risk finding out. Trust wasn't something she could easily give, and her secrets meant his trust could never be earned.

A few minutes later he returned, wearing a faded pair of sweats. His chest was temptingly bare, except for the tattoos covering his right shoulder and upper arm. The inked images mirrored a separate band on his left arm, and a strangely haunting pattern traced down his left side. She recognized the spelled protections in the markings on his shoulder, but not the ones on the left. In addition, like any warrior, he bore his own share of scars.

He stopped a few feet away and bowed. She returned it. Moving into a defensive stance, she turned her body to the side, presenting the smallest target, while keeping her legs balanced and her breathing and gaze focused.

His opening form was one from Kyoskushin-Kai, a powerful Japanese style of Karate. The style leaned on quick multiple attacks, breaking, breathing, and killing techniques. Her own preference was a combination of Aikido and Krav Maga, which utilized efficient, but lethal movements. It eliminated wasted motions, giving her split-second advantages over other styles. It was, in her opinion, the most realistic form for street fighting.

He came at her in a blur. Barely blocking his first hit, she responded with a snapping series of punches and kicks, before dodging back out of reach. He advanced, his hands striking out, only to be followed by a quick foot-sweep.

She landed on her back, twisted to the side, crouched, and got her feet set, before kicking out. A solid hit to his thigh knocked him off balance, enough for her to pull back and set up for her next move.

Back and forth they danced, focused and deadly, the

silence broken by occasional grunts and the thick sound of flesh hitting flesh. Fifteen minutes later, they stepped back and bowed to each other.

Raine, chest heaving, was grateful to see him breathing equally hard. There would be bruises and aches tomorrow, but the physical outlet banked her rage, leaving a steady calm in its wake.

Meeting his hooded gaze, she found an echo of the primitive joy she always experienced after a fight. Watching him in predator mode touched her primal feminine core. Without thinking she gave him a fierce grin, receiving a similar baring of teeth in return.

"So, now that the preliminaries are out of the way," she said. "What next?"

He chuckled and shook his head. "You're one of the few females I know that gets off on fighting."

"Hey, a girl has to have a hobby." Her voice was muffled as she wiped the sweat off her face with a towel. "You have to admit it was fun."

"It's definitely one way to blow off a little steam." Grabbing his own towel, he began to wipe his chest.

The motion caught her gaze and her breath hitched briefly before steadying out. His chest was truly fascinating, but looking was a dangerous indulgence. However, her silent warning did not stop her damn hormones from clamoring for attention.

"I can think of other things that work just as well, if not better," he offered, his voice dark, seductive as he caught her staring. The flare of arousal stained his cheeks, while something much lower made an unmistakable appearance. "Like what you see?"

More than he'd ever know. "It's distracting, but I'll live." Her quip came out husky. This attraction was just a mess waiting to happen. Time to ratchet things down a bit. "How went the meeting with Natasha?"

His lingering grin faded. "Challenging as ever. I was able to gather some more information, though." He tossed the now damp towel toward the bin outside the locker room. When it landed on top of the others, he shot her a look. "We should probably head somewhere to trade stories. I want to hear what you found out from Cheveyo that sent you storming into Mulcahy's office."

She shook her head, giving a small huff. "The gossip mill here is worse than a bunch of old crones."

"And you're surprised because?"

"I'm not." She shifted, throwing her towel toward the bin. "Regardless, my meeting with Mulcahy had nothing to do with what we're following."

He raised an eyebrow. "Really? Now I'm definitely curious as to what could have possibly triggered your ever infamous temper."

She grimaced. "It was simply a difference of opinions." Time to change the topic. "Speaking of infamous tempers, what did the demon queen have to add?"

He took her not-so-subtle hint. "You've got a one track mind. Let me clean up first, and I'll meet you back here. Then we can figure out where to go to chat."

She shrugged. "Sure, just give me a few."

Turning, she headed back to change, and was back in the gym twenty minutes later. Her damp hair was braided, her tank and sweat pants exchanged in favor of well-worn jeans and a white button down fleeced shirt she kept in her locker. At least now, her trench coat would be warm. She really needed a better coat. Although leather looked cool as shit, it was not great for maintaining warmth.

Gavin was leaning up against one of the gym walls, talking

to a heavily muscled man. She recognized Chet Hilliard's brown hair, streaked with blond. His face was an interesting blend of scruff and lines. His blue eyes held spots of gold, like tiny starbursts, and a scar twisted from his left temple down to his chin.

As she drew closer, the slight vibration in the air surrounding him nipped at her. Chet was a shifter and another Wraith, one of the few she knew and actually liked. Right now his constantly smiling mask was missing, leaving behind the grave and dangerous hunter he truly was.

Both men turned to watch her walk toward them. As an oddity in the male dominated world of warriors, she was use to the scrutiny. She didn't stop until she stood beside both of them.

"Hey." She nodded to Chet. "Something up?"

"Not sure," he answered. "I was supposed to get a report from a bodyguard covering one of my assignments last night. He never showed."

"Did you ask Mulcahy where he was?"

"Chet was just telling me," Gavin answered blandly, watching her, "that the boss man indicated Quinn had left the company."

Training kept her expression from altering. Although it was known that Wraiths would, at Mulcahy's orders, take care of removing any employee who violated the laws, when a situation arose, names of those doing the removing were not shared. From Gavin's look, he had put one and one together and figured out where she was the night before.

Chet grimaced. "Mulcahy indicated his leaving was permanent, which puts me back to square one as I tried to figure out what leads have already been traced. "

Hearing that, she relaxed a bit. Chet understood Quinn wasn't going to be reporting in anytime soon, unless he found a necromancer willing to act as a go-between.

Gavin kept his sharp gaze on her as he asked Chet, "What will you do next?"

Chet sighed, and ran a large hand, etched with scars, through his hair. "Retrace his steps. See if I can figure out what he found. Then I get to fill his shoes as a bodyguard until I can come up with someone else to cover it." He shot an appraising look at the two of them. "I'm guessing you two can be crossed off that list?"

She gave him a small smile, and tried to ignore Gavin's unsettling stare. "Yeah, Mulcahy has us working two different cases that may, or may not, be connected."

"Figures." Chet grinned back. "I had hoped to convince one of you to take the assignment on." As they both shot him a look, he shrugged his powerful shoulders. "Oh well, on to the next unlucky name on my list." His curious gaze moved between them, noting the fact they were both dressed to leave. "So, Gavin, who'd you curse to end up working with Raine?" Speculation kindled in his eyes, and smug humor colored his tone. The comment earned him a quick jab in the arm from Raine.

Gavin quirked an eyebrow at Chet. "Wouldn't you like to know?"

Chet just laughed and rubbed his arm. "Well, luck to you both, then. Let me know if there's something I can help with. I'm off to teach a few new recruits some old tricks."

The clamor of an arriving training group drew closer as Raine and Gavin said good night to Chet. The three of them received some speculative looks, but before any of the wide-eyed trainees could get up the courage to approach, she and Gavin headed out.

CHAPTER SIX

The light rains from earlier left the night air clean and cool, while bright moonlight weaved between the scattered clouds. Walking through the Taliesin employee parking lot, the hem of her trench coat nipping at her calves, Raine led the way to her SUV. Beside her, Gavin matched his long stride to her shorter ones, his own dark coat zipped.

"Any preference where we go?" Her question broke the quiet of the night.

He looked down at her. "Got some place in mind?"

She gave him a tiny smile. "Actually, yeah. I have a friend who runs a small pub down in the Pearl District."

An up-and-coming spot, The Pearl District was home to art galleries, riverside condos, warehouse lofts, restaurants, and brewpubs. Currently, it was under siege by hard hats and cranes as every street corner seemed in the midst of a facelift.

Reaching the SUV, she unlocked the doors so he could climb in. She turned the key and muted the abrupt explosion of music with a turn of her wrist. He raised an eyebrow but said nothing.

Once on the road, she shot him a swift glance. "So, what's the story from Natasha?"

She could hear him shifting his body—probably so he could watch her. It was a habit she was beginning to dread.

His voice cut through her thoughts. "It seems a couple of her people in lower level jobs at some of Talbot's research companies heard some interesting stories floating around the water cooler."

"How interesting?" She kept her eyes on the rain-slicked road.

"Puzzling might be a better word." He paused for a second. "What do you know about Talbot's father, Aaron?"

Her fingers tightened on the steering wheel as she chanced a quick look at him. "Just old rumors and stories. Why?"

The weak light from passing street lamps cast shifting shadows across his face, making it hard to read his expression. His voice remained neutral with no hint of where he was going with his questions. "It seems of the seven deaths that have occurred, the first four were close business associates of the father's. Not the son's. While the last three deaths were men the son, Jonah, had handpicked to help run his various ventures."

"I know old man Talbot was the one who moved the fading family business into scientific research." She kept her voice level, burying her own opinions of the topic down deep. "I vaguely remember reading about it when he died in that car accident some years back."

Gavin was quiet for so long that she dared another glance, only to catch him watching her. She wished she could see him better. There was something going on behind his shadowed face, and it caused a small shiver to work its way down her back.

When she turned back to the road, she felt, more than

saw, his small head shake before he looked away. Finally, his low voice continued, "From what I was able to gather from Natasha, the rumor mill is leaning toward a personal grudge on the last three."

"These low level employees know Natasha how?" Was Gavin seriously basing theories on rumor, or was there something I was missing here?

"Well, they didn't exactly check the 'Other' box on their applications," his tone was wry. "But it seems they're both half-demons who fall on the weaker side of the power lines."

She nodded. "Which means they're better able to play with the humans."

Some of the less powerful half-demons could and would pass themselves off as humans. A common decision for those who didn't want to get pulled into the dominance games riddling Natasha's domain.

"Right," he said. "So the information is about as reliable as we're going to get, unless we actually sit down with Mr. Jonah Talbot."

"Probably more reliable." Raine didn't bother to hide the scorn in her voice. "Men like Talbot tend to get off on keeping as much information as they can to themselves."

"You said you didn't know Talbot." There was a sharp edge to Gavin's comment. "Somehow, I'm getting the impression you do."

Damn, the man was just too perceptive by half.

"Look, I know of men like Talbot. Whether they're Kyn or human, give a man money, power, and influence, then sit and watch as they elevate themselves to godhood."

"Jealous?" he mocked.

Her lips curled in disgust. "No, but it gets old after a while." She glanced at him. "You can't tell me you haven't noticed the same pattern?"

He shrugged. "True, but there can be exceptions."

"I don't think Talbot is going to be an exception," she replied tightly.

He didn't respond to her comment, just changed the subject. "Speaking of power and influence, how did your conversation with Cheveyo go?"

Remembering her own discoveries, her shoulders tensed. "It went." Her short tone earned another sharp look from Gavin.

"It went where?" he prodded.

Avoiding the personal aspect of the afternoon's conversation, she kept the retelling short and to the point, sharing the tale of the missing Dmitri, and Cheveyo and Paul's assumptions as she turned into one of the public parking lots scattered throughout the Pearl district.

Gavin didn't say anything as they got out and walked through the lot to the sidewalk. They both ignored the wary looks they gathered when they passed an art gallery, a restaurant, and an antique shop.

Raine paused next to a large smoked glass window beside a heavy wooden door. Before Gavin could grab the twisted black metal door handle, she put her hand on his arm, ignoring the flare of heat the touch of his skin caused.

"By the way, this place is warded," she warned.

He raised an eyebrow, lips tilted slightly in the age-old male answer to a perceived challenge. "How strongly?"

"Very." She dropped her hand. "It's a refuge for both Kyn and mortals, hence the name." She indicated the letters etched in the window.

"Zarana's? What's that?" He pulled the door open and gestured for her to precede him.

Giving him a slight smirk, she stepped back and waved him first. He shrugged, then crossed the threshold, only to stiffen momentarily when he hit the edge of the ward. His head turned slowly back to her, his gaze a bit shocked.

"I did warn you." She gave him a half-smile. "The name's Sanskrit. It roughly translates to a place of shelter or refuge."

Bracing for the ward's impact, she followed, refusing to visibly react to the shocking sensation of having her magic cut off.

Considering Gavin's reaction, he must have more Fey blood in him than she'd guessed. Those who could lay claim to Fey blood could feel—like a constant white noise—the natural magic, which still existed in the world. The amount running through your veins determined the volume of that noise. That ability also meant some wards could be used as a barrier between you and your magic.

A pure blooded Fey was a rarity. Actually, finding a pure blooded Kyn of any line was an oddity nowadays. With so much intermingling among the supernatural races, those who could claim pure blood status were either very old, or Shifters.

A long life and low birth rates were Mother Nature's solution for keeping the Kyn and human populations balanced. Humans outnumbered the Kyn, but what the Kyn lacked in numbers, they made up for in power.

As the door swung shut behind them, the noise level dropped then quickly resumed. Looking around the warmly lit pub, she spotted a group clearing out of a booth in the back. Taking the lead, she headed over.

As they threaded through the crowded tables, she heard her name called. Turning to the long bar on the side, she smiled at the diminutive figure currently pulling a couple of drafts.

"Go ahead and grab it before someone else does." Raine gave Gavin a slight push toward the now open booth. "What do you want to drink?"

"A black and tan," he answered, still moving toward the empty table. He reached it just before a group of four could stake their own claim. Shooting him wary looks, they moved along.

She turned back toward the bar and took off her coat as she made her way over. A nervous looking man took his drink from the bartender, then turned and headed toward a nearby table filled with, what appeared to be, a bunch of female executives. The man looked as if he was gearing up to ask one of them out.

When Raine passed the table, a slight vibration danced lightly over her skin. The small blonde closest to her was probably a shifter. Grabbing Nervous Guy's recently vacated spot at the bar, Raine waited for the bartender to return.

It didn't take long.

"Hey McCord, tell me it's your night off, uh?" Dark eyes sparkled with humor out of a face that could be called cute, even with the four long, thin scars running from temple to chin. However, telling the small female drink-slinger she was cute could get you cut off at the knees.

Raine grinned with true warmth at the woman on the other side of the counter. "No worries, Alexi. I'm just here with a business associate."

Alexi looked at Gavin sitting in the booth, and her smile widened, as her gaze sharpened with speculation. "So, you're finally getting a social life?" She set a glass in front of a bleary-eyed executive a couple of seats down. Wiping her hands on the white towel at her waist, she moved back in front of Raine. "Good lord, girl, let's break out the good stuff."

Raine was constantly amazed to find herself friends with Alexi. The woman loved to flirt and considered sex to be part of a balanced diet. "Not quite. It really is business. Let's just stick with my usual, and he'll take a black-and-tan."

"You've got to be kidding me!" Alexi's gaze was reproachful, her tone admonishing. Her short cap of dark curls danced in time with her quick movements as she pulled Gavin's drink and then poured Raine's cup of tea. "You're a foolish woman to be passing up something like that. I can't think of a better way to mix business with pleasure."

Unfortunately, even though she knew better, a small part of Raine agreed whole-heartedly with her friend, but getting involved with Gavin was not smart. Not now, and the outlook for the future wasn't too shiny either. Grabbing the drinks as Alexi was called away by another customer, she wove her way back to Gavin.

Handing him his drink, she sat down across from him.

He looked at her cup. "Tea?" She could see the silent laughter in his eyes. "It's a bar, Raine. Don't you drink?"

She warmed her hands around the mug and shot a deliberate look at her tea. "It's liquid. That equals a drink in my world." She didn't like the taste of alcohol, or the resulting loss of control.

He turned back to the bar, watching the diminutive bartender. "A friend?"

She nodded. "Alexi Savriti, she owns Zarana's." When she stopped, he turned toward her obviously waiting for the rest of the story. She sighed. "We met a few years back when someone I was tracking ran in here looking for a place to hide."

She took a sip of her tea, not wanting to go into the details involved in following a psychotic necromancer into the bar. He made the mistake of thinking since it was a refuge, he would be given sanctuary. Alexi was all about providing neutral ground, but when the crazy man told the bartender she was the main course for his zombie, she helped Raine open his line of communication with the dead a lot wider than he expected. Then, together, the two women terminated his communication. Permanently.

"Going to share?" Gavin was still looking for an explanation.

She turned her cup around in idle circles. "Since this place is kind of a neutral zone, she picks up all sorts of interesting tidbits. We help each other out occasionally." She figured Alexi kept her around to keep the more exotic customers in line.

Her friend provided a safe place for Kyn and human alike, and that alone demanded respect. This was the one place the two worlds could coexist in relative harmony. No one questioned how weird your behavior was. Instead everyone enjoyed the food, drink, and entertainment, leaving the outside world on the other side of the door.

But more than that, Raine cherished the fact at Zarana's she could just be another anonymous face, not the dreaded Wraith or the weird misfit.

Gavin interrupted her internal musing. "She's a witch then?" Raine's puzzlement must have been obvious because he explained, "The warding, it's damn strong."

Immediately she understood why he'd make that assumption, especially considering he most likely inherited his warding skills through his witch mother. Witches were notoriously good at setting wards. Just not in this case. "No, she's actually a human/half-demon mix."

His eyes widened in disbelief. "That's not possible. Half-demon blood drives the human half insane by the time they hit puberty. They fall apart and generally end up dead—by their own hand or someone else's."

"True," a throaty voice broke in. The woman in question sat next to Raine, who scooted over to give her some room. "Except I'm thinking my gypsy blood helped to counter that particularly nasty side effect. Though some would argue differently, especially when I'm a tad upset." She flashed a quick, flirtatious smile at him. "I'm Alexi, and you are?"

"Gavin Durand," he answered with his own devastating grin, proving even he wasn't immune to a little flirting.

Raine could never figure out what it was about her friend, but the woman drew men like a magnet. If Raine could ever figure it out, she'd make a fortune, or at least end her own dry spell.

Alexi turned to Raine, curiosity plain on her face. "What are you looking into now?"

Raine shifted a glance at Gavin, before meeting Alexi's gaze. "Actually, we're both looking into separate situations. The boss thinks they're connected." Her friend may not know she was a Wraith, but she did know Raine was a Security Officer, whose job description sometimes included hunting down outlaw Kyn on behalf of Taliesin.

Alexi was Raine's ace in the hole when it came to obscure information on various members of the Kyn world, because the barkeep's information was always gold.

Alexi listened while Raine repeated what they knew. She was quiet, her gaze unfocused as she thought it through. "So, not counting the stud boy—"

"Justin Black," Raine cut in.

Alexi waved her hand dismissively. "Fine, Justin, who was scoped out, you have a missing wizard and a witch in hiding, both approached for testing, and someone going around knocking off humans involved with the Talbot Foundation." She searched Raine's face. "You think the research company is one of Talbot's don't you?"

Raine did actually. Those supposed stories about old man Talbot were true. He'd been snatching up Kyn and screwing with their DNA in an attempt to create beings that were never meant to be. He even picked up the occasional human just to test his obscene theories.

Unfortunately, due to the lack of living, breathing witnesses, it was not common knowledge. Those precious surviving few were so broken they would probably prefer death, and were in no shape to share their horror stories.

She wouldn't be surprised if Talbot's son was following in his father's footsteps. Few knew the old man had actually succeeded with some of his experiments, but Raine couldn't focus on that. Faded screams and blurred faces flashed in her mind's eye before she pushed them back.

Returning Alexi's look, and hoping her nightmares weren't showing, Raine aimed for a casual tone. "Don't know for sure yet, but I should by tomorrow morning. I have someone at the office connecting the dots."

The barkeep turned serious, obviously following the directions of Raine's thoughts. "You know those old rumors about his father have never been proven. You can't go after a human based on past gossip. Pissing off someone like Talbot could get you hurt. That man's got some serious influence in this town."

Raine couldn't keep her hands from tightening on her cup any more than she could eliminate the frustration from her voice. "So I'm supposed to ignore the possibility of someone with enough power to hide horrific experiments on Kyn for profit? Ignore the fact that a human research company is doing its best to lure Kyn into an unsanctioned trial of some unknown drug right before that same wizard disappears into thin air? And when it comes up that this Polleo is connected to Talbot? What then? Should I just believe it's a big coincidence?"

"Just be careful," Alexi's tone softened in an obvious effort to calm Raine. "You're not indestructible."

Raine tried to ignore the worry on her friend's face.

"You're leaving out the murders," Gavin cut in, reminding her he was silently following their conversation. She heaved a mental curse, and wondered what he would pick up from her little rant.

He took a sip of his beer before continuing, "If you believe the logic of what you're thinking, Raine, and Talbot is picking up where his father left off, it could explain why some of his top people are being picked off. It wouldn't explain all of them, but it's a place to start."

And that was the last thing she wanted to give him, despite her unthinking rant. *Hell, this was why she preferred working alone.*

Gavin was the type who wouldn't stop until he had every scrap of information on these deaths, every last one of them, and as much as she admired his tenacity, right now it was a pain in her ass.

"Look," Alexi said before Raine could say anything to throw Gavin off. "I don't have much to add, except if I hear anything you can use, I'll let you know. Especially about Dmitri, okay?"

Raine nodded, grateful that Alexi was backing down. She gave the smaller woman a brief hug before Alexi headed back to the bar.

Silence filled the booth as Gavin eyed the milling crowd. Lost in her own thoughts, Raine sipped her now lukewarm tea. She needed to wait until tomorrow to find out if she was right about Polleo. If she was, she'd have to let Mulcahy know his hunch might once again be spot on.

Then she needed to decide how much information she would share with the increasingly disturbing, but attractive man sitting across from her. Because she was fairly certain the term "full disclosure" played into Gavin's definition of a partner, just like it did for her.

She leaned her head against the back of the booth and brooded. Unfortunately, in this case, full disclosure could mean the end of their tentative partnership. No way did she want to instigate that volatile discussion. Inwardly, she winced, because should that discussion take place, she had no doubts he would be ticked—actually more like wickedly pissed.

She was so screwed.

"What's next?" His voice cut through her dismal thoughts.

Turning her head, she brought his face into focus, even as fatigue crept in. Add in the few hours of sleep she managed last night, plus all of the emotionally packed revelations from today, and she wanted to close her eyes and drift for a while.

"Now, we get some sleep." She sighed and straightened. "There's nothing to do until we find out whether or not Polleo is linked to Talbot."

Finishing her tea, she rose from the booth and stretched her arms above her head, her spine popping and her shoulders loosening. Dropping her arms, she made a grab for her coat and caught him watching her. She could have sworn she saw fleeting hunger, but he downed the last of his drink and the impression was gone. She cursed her overactive imagination for tripping her up around him and blamed it on lack of sleep. However, she knew better. He was getting to her.

She waved to her friend as they headed back out into the chilly night. It was still clear and neither said a word as they walked back to the SUV, dodging puddles from the earlier rain. As they moved closer to the parking lot, and away from the more populated areas, the shadows increased. Soon their footsteps were the only sound on the cracked sidewalk.

They passed two darkened buildings when the hushed sound of metal against cloth whispered through the air. It was followed by the soft sound of water squelching under foot.

She didn't falter, and neither did Gavin. A couple of steps more and she had both wrist blades in her hands. The black coated blades blended into her own dark garments, their silver runes turned in toward her body so no light would reflect off them.

She shot a look at Gavin and saw his hand down by his thigh, a long darkened blade tucked close to his leg.

She'd have to remember to ask where he kept that thing.

Neither of them had guns, since firearms tended to stop working without warning for those with magical means. It didn't mean their follower couldn't have one. She still had her trench coat with its protection spell, but she wasn't sure how strong Gavin's spells were. Though, short of a head shot with cold iron, they should survive.

His free hand made a series of short motions and she gave a tiny nod to let him know she understood.

At the next narrow alley, they darted around the corner. Banking on the fact most people couldn't see in the inky darkness, Raine utilized that weakness and faded into the shadows to wait, while Gavin continued forward, luring their stalker in.

Unfortunately, within a couple of steps they realized they weren't alone in the alleyway. It seemed the bad guys were a bit more prepared than usual.

Inside the darkened depths of the alley, three new figures spread out, trapping Raine and Gavin between them and their pursuer. Raine spun around, putting her back to Gavin's. She was slightly miffed when she saw that instead of one person, two individuals blocked the opening closest to the street.

Damn, how had she missed the second one?

From their muscular outlines, they were male, dressed in all black, their faces hidden. With no vibrations in the air, it meant they weren't shifters, nor did they seem to be using magic. Which left human assailants.

Weak moonlight reflected off the guns in their hands—yep, definitely human. Either they didn't know Gavin and Raine were Kyn, or they carried the typical mortal arrogance that bullets could solve any problem.

Here's hoping their aim was off.

Clearing her mind, she pictured a thickening in the air surrounding her, as she set up a protection circle to slow down the bullets once they started flying. Behind her, she could feel the line of tension radiating from Gavin, and then the slight thrum indicating he invoked his own protection circle.

The two spelled circles merged into a warm line of energy, and on some deeper level, something clicked—a key to an unknown lock. The strange sensation was pushed aside as she focused on their attackers, waiting for the bad guys to move first. It always helped if you could honestly say the dead men struck first. Self-defense at its finest.

At some unseen signal, the five shadows struck as one.

A bullet hit her circle and slowed down before grazing her left shoulder. A second one nicked high up on her right thigh. It was enough to throw her balance off, dropping her to her to her right knee. Letting one of her blades fly, it found a lethal home in the throat of the taller of her assailants.

His body folded, sinking to his knees, his fingers frantically trying to remove the knife. His eyes slowly blanked, his hands stilled, then dropped from his wound, and blood trickled from his open mouth as he fell over, dead.

His partner, realizing their bullets weren't slowing her down, pulled out his own wicked-looking knife. He bent his knees, arms loose, knife ready, and moved in.

Unbalanced and in a half-kneeling position, Raine blocked his first series of punches and kicks. His next kick got lucky, knocking her blade into the darkness. She caught his knife with a rising block of her forearm and the edge of his blade left a stinging line of fire.

Getting back on her feet, she brought her left leg around in a solid roundhouse kick. The knife clattered to the ground while the sound of bones snapping like twigs indicated she broke his wrist. The howl of pain following shortly there-after was icing on the cake.

Back in a steady defensive stance, she landed a few well-placed strikes, dropping her second attacker to the ground with a solid thump. With her two down, she turned to help Gavin.

Except he seemed to have it under complete control. Two of his three attackers were already motionless lumps on the concrete. The third was on his knees, doubled over Gavin's foot.

Her quick once over noted a bloody stain marring Gavin's gray T-shirt. Another rip, high on the shoulder of his jacket indicated someone else managed to get close before they met the pavement. A flashing movement caught her attention as his foot solidly connected with the side of the kneeling man's head, sending him down with the other two lumps on the ground.

Gavin stood still, catching his breath. The dim play of moonlight and shadows across his face mesmerized her. This was the real Gavin. The green eyes glowing in anticipation, full lips pulled back from sharp white teeth in a predatory snarl, his warrior's body primed for action. This was a male capable of protecting what was his. His gaze caught hers, and the heat of battle was quickly replaced by a more dangerous heat.

A corresponding fire filled her veins.

He took a deliberate step toward her, his larger frame looming over hers. Caught in the feral intensity of his gaze with the heat shimmering through her, she was hypnotized. The urge to protect herself from this man was drowned out by her need to touch, to luxuriate in his strength. Momen-tarily lost, she pressed her hands to his chest, his T-shirt a useless barrier against the heat radiating into her palms.

He lowered his head, his mouth coming closer, tempting her. Helplessly, she rose on her toes to close the distance, but the faint sound of drunken laughter broke the spell.

In unison, they turned toward the mouth of the alley, watching as a group of oblivious partygoers stumbled by. Reality slammed home, dousing the heat with ice.

Stepping back, she dropped her gaze and caught a small flash of her blade against the wall next to her. She covered her obvious retreat by kneeling and retrieving her blade. Behind her, she heard his deep inhale.

Without a word, they both started going through the pockets of the downed men. Not surprisingly, they didn't find anything to indicate who they were, or what they had wanted. Now that she was once again thinking straight, she realized none of the men in black had said a word. That small fact left her uneasy. It just didn't seem normal.

"Did you leave any alive?" Gavin's low whisper echoed slightly in the alleyway.

She glanced up and saw him kneeling next to the last man he downed. Desire shimmered under her skin, urging her to reach out. She shook her head clear.

Job first, personal shit later.

She felt the neck of the man she kicked and couldn't find a pulse. She met Gavin's eyes, knowing her own were just as calm and cold. "No."

Getting to her feet, she retrieved the knife she had thrown. After locking her emotions down, she drew the blade out, ignoring the slight sucking sound, and then wiped the blood from her blade on the dead man's sweater. Only then did she put it back in its sheath.

She studied the bodies. Based on their attack she felt safe making one guess. "How much you want to bet that they're ex-military?"

"It's a sucker's bet. The question is, who are they working for?"

She was pretty sure they belonged to Talbot. She'd wager her next year's salary a Taliesin investigator had finally connected Polleo to Talbot, which meant Talbot knew he was being looked at. *How had he found them so fast?* Hell, it was something to puzzle out later. Right now, there were other things to worry about.

"First thing's first, we need to make this look good for the authorities. Someone had to have heard those gunshots and made a call." Her adrenaline started to level and exhaustion slowly crept back in. *How do you make five dead bodies look natural?* "We can't just drag them to the river and toss them in. It would take too long."

She and Gavin had a short discussion of their options, before finally settling on a few minor changes so it looked as if two men had gone against three. They stripped some of the bodies so they weren't all in black, which would be too weird for any explanation.

Raine positioned the knife she managed to kick away, into the throat of her first attacker. Good thing most of the men had white T-shirts on underneath considering how hard it would be to explain bare-chested men in the middle of October in Portland. Bad enough some of them wouldn't have jackets.

Heeding Gavin's suggestion, they returned to where they initially stood their ground, and picked up the spent bullets and the matching casings. Since none of the men had bullet wounds it was better to get rid of any evidence of the spent ammunition. Hopefully, the police would assume any gunshots heard had gone wild. It would also make identifications that much harder.

They'd let the authorities try to tie it all together. Questions would be raised, but the possible conclusions would either run along the lines of smugglers using abandoned warehouses as an illicit meeting place, or to a drug deal gone sour.

Whatever came about would be better than the truth. Humans rarely looked beyond the obvious. She and Gavin were counting on that trait to hide their involvement.

Scene set, they walked quickly back to the parking lot and left. They made a couple of detours on their way out of the district to dump the bullets and casings in separate spots. Then with the night clouds playing hide and seek with the moon, they headed out of the city.

CHAPTER SEVEN

R aine took Gavin home with her, rationalizing it was quicker to go there than back to the office—although even her inner voice wasn't buying that one—an unprecedented move she hoped no one at Taliesin would ever hear about. If they did, the rumors would grow to grossly elaborate proportions, filled with all sorts of innuendos and sly asides. As far as she was concerned, office gossip comprised an outer level of hell just by its nature of twisted truths and sheer vindictiveness.

The drive passed in silence, and she pulled into her detached garage, shut off the engine, and listened to the ticks of the cooling engine resonate in the resulting quiet. She leaned her head back against the headrest and dropped her hands to her lap.

"We stepped on someone's toes," Gavin's voice was low and soft.

With lifting her head from the headrest, she turned to study him, only then noticing the small lines of pain bracketing his mouth. The tiny indicators tugged on her conscience, urging her to get them both inside, but she couldn't find the energy to move. She blinked, long and slow, not bothering to respond.

In the darkness, his eyes were pale jade, and his light earthy scent reminded her of a deep forest glen after a rain, comforting and disconcerting all at the same time. She had the strongest urge to trace those pain lines away.

That last, unexpected observation was disturbing enough to reignite her earlier tension and to get her moving. She opened her door. "Come on, let's get cleaned up and get some sleep. I'm barely functioning right now."

His door opened, and his feet hit the ground, then followed her to the house. Once inside, he followed her into the kitchen and muttered, "Déjà-vu."

After once again dragging out her first aid kit, she threw him a look over her shoulder. "Except we've switched places."

His low chuckle answered.

Gathering what she needed, she turned and made her way to where he sat in a chair, shirtless. There was no way she could avoid gawking.

His gray T-shirt was on the floor and the exposed expanse of golden flesh had her thoughts scattering for balance. Realizing she was just standing there, staring, she mentally shook herself like a wet dog, and yanked her rioting thoughts back into line.

She grabbed another chair, dragged it next to his, took a seat, and faced him. She was so close her left thigh brushed his outstretched right leg with every move. She bent over to inspect his wound. "We need to clean you up, though I don't think you'll need stitches."

He said nothing.

She slanted a glance up to find him watching her—like some big cat just waiting to pounce. She forced her attention back to the work at hand, and despite the slight tremble in her fingers, she made quick work of cleaning the blood off the now half-closed wound.

Warmth radiated from him, sending chills racing down her arms. Her awareness of him as a male raised her tension level—which, in turn, pissed her off. Her eyes whipped to his. "Whatever you're doing, knock it off. I don't like games."

At her outburst, satisfaction darkened his face. "I'm not doing anything." His other arm darted around her neck, his fingers wrapped around her braid, and he drew her head down to meet his lips. "But I can change that."

She tried to tell herself it was shock holding her immobile in his firm grip, not curiosity, but then his warm, full lips whispered across her mouth. She pressed closer, her hand flattening on the burning skin covering his chest, as her own lips softened under his.

Before the kiss could even start, he raised his head, lightly tracing her lips with his tongue and then sat back, his half-lidded gaze drifting over her face. There was no time to hide her internal confusion, and his flash of male triumph meant he caught it.

Straightening slowly, she moved back so his hand no longer held her neck. "Don't," her voice was almost a whisper. "I'm not up to this right now."

"For now," he agreed, his voice equally quiet.

She dropped her eyes, veiling the swirling emotions, and began putting things back into the first aid kit in her lap.

He reached out and absently stroked his fingers over the old scars on her wrist.

Her hands stilled.

When she went to stand up, his hand shackled her wrist.

"Some of that blood isn't mine." He nodded to the rust colored stains standing out starkly on her white, fleeced shirt. "How bad is it?"

She twisted her wrist slightly, and escaped his restraining

fingers. "They're just nicks. It's not all mine." She moved to the counter, and put the kit back in its drawer. "Let me show you where you can sleep."

Wisely, he kept his mouth shut.

He followed her down the left hand hall to the second bedroom, and despite being keenly aware of his presence, she held it together as she opened the door.

The king bed, covered in a patchwork quilt of faded red and blues, dominated the far wall. A nightstand holding a lamp sat tucked on one side. Against the near wall a set of drawers sat under a mirror.

After showing where the extra towels were, she bid him a good night, and headed into her room at the other end of the hall.

Shutting her door softly, she leaned her head against the smooth wood. She fought back the small voice urging her to open the door and follow through on his earlier unspoken invitation. Refusing to acknowledge the regret swirling inside her, she reached down and turned the lock, ensuring she would be tempted to give in.

She let her breath out slowly. Turning, she pressed her shoulders against the door while she slid to the floor. *What had she been thinking letting him kiss her?*

She ran a hand over her face. Good grief, she wasn't some silly twit whose higher brain functions crashed when confronted with a half-naked male. Nor was she a simpering virgin. Her few sexual experiences fulfilled a basic need, supplying a simple release, nothing more. Sex itself could be good, but she had a sinking suspicion if she and Gavin ever ended up in bed, good wouldn't be enough to cover what would happen.

Exhaustion. It was the only sane explanation for her aberrant behavior. It wasn't normal for her to be sitting on the floor, thinking about Gavin and sex in the same sentence. Maybe her hormones were making her delusional.

She pushed to her feet, pulled her stained shirt off, and tossed it toward the basket next to her bathroom. Restless and edgy, she crossed the shadowed hardwood floors in the moonlit darkness, not bothering to turn on the lights.

On the way she removed her wrist blades and stashed them in the drawer next to her high-set poster bed. She'd clean them in the morning. A quick check under her pillow ensured the seven-inch dirk she inherited from her mother was still tucked away.

Talk about a security blanket.

Turning away from the temptation of her bed, she entered her bathroom and flicked on the switch. A warm glow spilled over the oversized tub to her left, and illuminated the stone-tiled shower that was large enough to easily hold three people. There was even a shelf that ran along one side that could double as a bench. She twisted the handle, and water fell from the hidden spouts in the ceiling.

She stepped back, and leaned against the granite counter, waiting for the water to heat. Steam rose and quickly filled the confines. She stripped, got in, and let the warm water cascade over her aching muscles. With her eyes closed, she fell into a half-asleep haze. The half-healed nicks gained in the recent fight slowly went numb under the spray. Ignoring the small stings, her mind slowed its chaotic whirl and finally calmed.

Time passed, and as tempting as it was to leave Gavin with nothing but cold water, she finally turned off the shower. Grabbing a towel, she wrapped it around her body. Too tired to dry her long hair, she left it damp, even though she'd pay for it tomorrow morning with nasty tangles.

Back in her room, she grabbed a long sleeved T-shirt and an old pair of sweat pants from the shelf in her walk-in closet. With Gavin in the house, she didn't want to be caught in her normal T-shirt/underwear combination. No sense in playing with fire.

Climbing into bed, she pulled her down comforter close, and snuggled into the warmth. The faint sounds of Gavin moving around in the hall bathroom drifted to her, and left her wondering what she was thinking, bringing him here.

With no ready answer, she sighed wearily, settled deeper into her bed, and let herself drift into sleep.

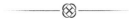

MUCH LATER, as the silence lay deep and shadows surrounded the darkened house, Raine moaned softly, her body twitching. She couldn't breathe. Her legs thrashed, but she couldn't break free of what held her. Something wrapped itself around her body and tangled her limbs.

On some level, she was absently aware that she was dreaming, but caught deep in the throes of her nightmare, she couldn't will herself to wake. Her eyes darted from side to side, searching for the approaching danger.

Lab technicians in white coats bustled around her, their voices blending together. *"Exhibiting unusual signs of energy... blood work showing interesting formations...need a few more samples to confirm...recent discoveries from the bone samples show...'"*

Pain was a crushing weight.

She struggled against the iron cuffs that dug deep into her flesh. Blood trickled over her wrists and ankles while cold, impersonal fingers roamed over her clammy flesh. Sharp pricks and stings assaulted her as samples were taken again and again.

A scream echoed from behind her, full of horror, agony, and rage.

That wasn't her, that couldn't be her.

Thuds of flesh hitting flesh interrupted her panic. She tried to wrench free to help the person being tortured behind her. Unable to move, her chaotic emotions crested to a boiling point.

Suddenly her arm was free, and her hand, now a grotesquely shaped claw, whipped out and tore open the throat of the nearest white coat. Blood fell like a warm rain across her face and an inhuman howl escaped her sore throat.

With violent twist of her body, her restraints disappeared, leaving her crouched on all fours on top of a cold metal examining table. When more men in white coats appeared, her lips drew back in a feral snarl.

Strangely, they turned their backs to her, their attention on a large cage. She pushed off the table, and broke through their circle, raking out indiscriminately to leave behind gaping wounds on two of the faceless men.

The image wavered and stretched, morphing into a long dark hallway, lined on both sides by heavy bars. Light gleamed dully off the metal. She charged down the hall, snatches of nightmarish forms, trapped behind bars, swam in her brain.

Panic strangled her.

In an effort to escape her pursuers, she grimly kept moving forward. Then, without warning, the floor disappeared, leaving her to tumble through the dark. Mocking laughter and evil taunts followed as she landed in a heap. She looked up and saw the bars of her own cage. Shoving to her feet, she struck out at the bars, barely noticing the burning pain of iron against her flesh.

Her sense of helplessness morphed to a burning rage that scoured her soul. Underneath, hopeless despair rose. She couldn't stop them. She was nothing but another lab rat, another monster brought to life by the demented vision of one man.

The sound of approaching footsteps had her turning to watch an older man, his gray hair immaculate, and his craggy face creased with a pleased smile. But it was his gaze that warned her. Those light eyes were cold and dead. The flames burning inside her, shoved outward, slowly swallowing her body. She couldn't control this, didn't want to control it. And, as the heat grew, the chasing tidal wave of emotions slammed her to her knees.

With a gasp, she woke among her tangled sheets. Her skin was clammy with sweat and her hair a tangled mess around her face. Haunted by the lingering terror, her gaze darted around the room, searching the shadows. Tremors racked her body, and she raised her trembling hands to rub her face.

It was a struggle to calm her breathing. She pushed up to a sitting position and, with a small whimper, drew her knees up to her chest, wrapping her arms around them. She lowered her head to her knees, and slowly brought her body and mind under control as time ticked by.

There was no going back to sleep, but with Gavin in the house she couldn't leave her room undetected. She prayed to whoever was listening for the strength to face her own demons and finish this assignment with her sanity intact. Then she stared out the dark window, her dry eyes burning, as she watched the sky begin to lighten.

CHAPTER EIGHT

While Taliesin's investigative department continued to travel through the money maze, Raine tried to track down friends of the missing wizard. Even with the list Cheveyo had given her, it was like chasing ghosts.

Dmitri Rimmick's associates seemed to have left town en masse, and no one was willing to talk. At least not to her. A lesser being might have taken it personally. She didn't. If it hadn't been for the fact that Cheveyo wouldn't deliberately mislead her, she'd have thought putting her on Rimmick's trail was a twisted joke. Even his neighbors, in the older section where the small rundown apartment was located, had rarely seen him.

A little breaking and entering—more entering than breaking, since the flimsy locks wouldn't keep out a fly—proved the wizard wasn't hiding out in his apartment. The place was grungy and dim. If not for being Kyn and immune to infectious diseases, she would have donned a Hazmat suit before entering.

His home was a clutter of crap, with no real purpose other than to collect dust. The cheaply made bookshelves in the front room were tightly packed with tattered books in various languages, a weird collection of stones, misshapen pottery, and bones. Then there was the small mountain of rumpled clothes spread across a faded puce-colored sofa, its middle sporting a dip the size of the Grand Canyon.

An old black and white TV sat on a couple of stacked milk crates. On top of the television, torn notes lay like snowflakes. She was amazed to see rabbit ears in the age of digital. She nudged one metal ear out of the way and grabbed the small pile of ragged papers before moving on.

The small kitchen was in dire need of sand blasting to remove the layers of grime and growing mold cultures that coated every available surface. Since the highest level of alien life forms she wanted to encounter was the stuff growing on the counters, she refused to open the refrigerator. That might turn out to be a lethal mistake.

She turned the one and only dank and smelly bedroom inside out, doing her best not to think about what could possibly leave such noxious stains. Then, she scoured the small closet, digging past worn out shoes, and old camping equipment.

In the very back, was a pile of boxes. It didn't take long to recognize the illusion spell and break it, revealing a small hidden space. Inside was a tattered notebook. After a quick scan of its contents, Raine decided deciphering the cramped handwriting could wait until later. Pocketing the torn paper scraps and worn notebook, she retraced her steps through the messy apartment and left, locking the door behind her.

Despite Rimmick's non-existent housekeeping skills, she was fairly certain no one else had searched the apartment before her. Whoever had taken him probably thought they snatched a wizard who wouldn't be missed. It was a noticeably human mistake.

Time and time again, she witnessed humans make

assumptions about the Kyn solely based on how their own reality worked. Granted the various Kyn communities were spread throughout the world, but unlike humans, the supernatural community kept watch over their members. They might not know your favorite food, but if your face suddenly disappeared, someone would eventually notice. Then, since information was a key commodity in a great many Kyn circles, it would be remembered and mentioned.

Back in her SUV, she attempted to read through the notebook. As far as she could tell, most of it was incomprehensible rambling. The entries on the last few pages indicated that recently Rimmick thought he was being followed. Not a surprise considering that knowing your target's routine played a vital role in a successful kidnapping.

In the small pile of torn messages she pocketed, she found the phone number to Zarana's, another number to one of the Kyn owned bookstores located downtown, and one to the electric company. Which could mean anything from Rimmick having a meet at Zarana's, to him trying to find some obscure text, or working a deal to keep his electricity on. Nothing she could trace to the research company. The rest of the torn notes were too vague to be of any use.

Frustrated and grimy, she headed back to Taliesin. Maybe she'd get lucky and there would be news about Polleo. If not, at least she could grab a shower.

CHAPTER NINE

With her hair lying wet against her faded concert T-shirt that topped equally faded jeans, Raine was once again comfortably clean as she walked out of Taliesin's gym and toward her office. Chasing Rimmick had eaten up most of her day, but she found time to ask Taliesin's investigative department to untangle Polleo's financial maze and find her a name. She was hoping that name would be on her voicemail.

She made her way through the sixth floor hallway which held the Security Offices. As it was close to six in the evening, the normal din of phones, computers, and muted conversations was missing. Most of the S.O.'s were either out on assignments or had left for home already. The few doors leaking light proved even Kyn had a hard time leaving work at the end of the day.

Opening the door to her dark office, she flipped on the light and looked toward the black phone on her desk. Sure enough, the little red light was blinking away, indicating a message.

She slipped into the leather chair behind the battered oak

surface, and reached around the thin monitor to grab a pen and a sticky note. Her elbow bumped the monitor, waking the slumbering electronic beast, which flickered to life with a vibrant desktop of some faraway landscape. Dialing into her voicemail, she held her breath.

It didn't help.

Within moments the monitor flickered, then with an audible pop, the screen went dark. In her ear, one of the investigative drones confirmed that after working through dummy corporations and complex tax shelters, they found the name—Jonah Talbot, head of Talbot Foundation.

The pen in her hand snapped in half.

A ball of icy tension and dread coalesced in her stomach, unable to freeze out the anger born of desperation and fear. Remnants of her nightmares whispered through her mind and she vowed not to let the past repeat itself.

Carefully, she hung up the phone, dropped the pen pieces onto her desk, and stared blindly out her office door. Her mind spun, considering and rejecting various scenarios involving her, Talbot, and a knife.

A sharp acrid scent of something burning interrupted her pleasant musings of violent revenge. Wrinkling her nose, she caught a wisp of smoke rising from behind her screen. With a snort of disgust at the idiosyncrasies of technology, she tucked away her bloodthirsty indulgences for later.

No matter how certain she was that the younger Talbot was taking after his dear old dad, Mulcahy and Gavin would demand actual proof. She picked up her phone and dialed Gavin's extension. The phone rang twice, then went to voicemail. She hung up, and dialed Rachel's extension.

"Good evening, Raine," Rachel's calm voice floated over the line.

"Hey, Rachel, do you know if Gavin was in today?" Raine asked.

"Yes, I saw him in his office about forty minutes ago. However, I believe he was getting ready to go home."

"Thanks, I'll try his cell then." Eyeing her now dead screen, she added, "Um, could you call tech support for me?"

"Not a problem." There was a pause. "What's the issue?"

Raine could hear the implied *this time*. Damn, she hated computers. "The monitor died."

A very delicate snort was quickly muffled. "I'll let them know. Hopefully, they can have it fixed by tomorrow."

"Thanks." Raine hung up before Rachel could start laughing.

Raine left the office and made her way to the elevators. She held her phone and took a couple of deep, calming breaths, before dialing Gavin's number. Three rings later, a gruff "Yeah" answered.

"Hey Gavin, it's Raine."

"What's up?" His voice smoothed out.

"Am I interrupting anything?" She stopped at the elevator doors, not wanting to lose her signal.

"No, I was just fixing dinner."

"I just got a message back on Polleo's finances. They got a name." Leaning against the wall, she shifted the phone to her shoulder and dug her keys out of her pocket.

Gavin paused, and the sound of rhythmic thumps filled the line. "And?"

"And, it came back as Jonah Talbot." She kept her voice as bland as possible. Not an easy feat.

There was a pause in the thumping, and then he surprised her. "Why don't you come over to my place for dinner?"

"Dinner?" She almost dropped her phone. "At your place?"

"Yeah, why do you sound so shocked?" She could hear the smile in his voice. "You do eat, right? 'Sides I have some more information from my end as well."

"Okay, fine." Her knees weaken, either from fear of what he found out, or nerves at the thought of being alone with him, she wasn't sure. "Can you give me directions?"

He rattled off a series of streets and turns. She repeated it back as the soft thumping sound resumed, pricking her curiosity. "What are you doing?"

"Cutting basil for the pasta, why?"

An absurdly sexy image of him in nothing but an apron almost made her break into hysterical laughter. She cleared her throat. "Just having a hard time imagining you in an apron."

His dark chuckle sent chills down her arms. "Well, then you should hurry and see for yourself." He hung up before she could answer.

TWENTY MINUTES later Raine parked her SUV in front of an old bungalow-style home overlooking the Willamette River. She walked up the steps and knocked. Gavin answered the door and invited her in. She followed, surreptitiously taking in his bare feet and long legs, her eyes landing on his great ass showcased in ratty jeans. In an effort not to get caught ogling, she quickly averted her gaze and took in his home.

In direct opposition to Dmitri, Gavin's housekeeping skills were excellent. Either he was a neat freak, or someone cleaned for him.

Most of the furniture was oversized but well made. The obligatory flat screen dominated the front room. Underneath the cut out dividing the kitchen and living room sat a couch with a couple of easy chairs flanking it. There were more rooms off to the left, but Gavin was heading into the kitchen, leaving her to do the puppy dog routine and follow.

He moved to the stove, still facing away from her. "Go

ahead and make yourself comfortable." He turned his head to watch her take off her jacket, as he stirred something in a pan. "We can eat at the table."

She laid her jacket over the back of chair and sat down. Being alone with him made her feel twitchy, nervous. *When was the last time she'd done dinner with a male?*

She came up blank. Choosing to ignore what that indicated, she angled toward the French doors framing the winding river below. The sun was sinking behind the green-carpeted hills and a few boats trolled through the waters. It was as quiet here as it was at her home. "Have you had this house long?"

He took a pot from the stove to the sink. "Awhile, yeah." He began to pour the pasta into the drainer in the sink.

"It's nice," she murmured, her gaze going back to the river outside.

"It may not have the land you have, but it brings me peace." The kitchen faucet turned on.

With out looking away from the view, she asked, "Why do you need peace?" The wistful words were out before she could stop them. *Oh Lord and Lady!* She shot him a quick look as hot color stained her cheeks. "Never mind, it's none of my business."

The water shut off, and then he finished preparing dinner. It wasn't long before he had two plates filled with pasta and vegetables and brought them over to the table. He set one in front of her, and then put his in the place opposite.

Using her fork, she pushed the pasta around and mentally cursed herself for overstepping her bounds. She had never been good at the whole male-female social thing. When it came to business, she had no problems saying what needed to be said, or doing what needed to be done. But in normal conversations, she was socially inept, which was why she preferred being alone.

She took a bite and lifted her gaze to find him watching her intently.

"I need the peace so I can go back out and face reality." Unvarnished truth added a dark depth to his rumbled voice.

Since she considered the woods surrounding her home a sanctuary, a bit of the wild she could lose herself in when life got too hard, she could relate. "I can understand that."

He raised an eyebrow. "I don't doubt it." Then he took a bite, breaking the strange tension.

They continued to eat in companionable silence, and bit by bit the edgy unease faded. When her plate was empty, she broke the quiet. "What did you find out?"

He leaned back in his chair and wiped his mouth with a napkin. "I found a link with one of Talbot's dead men."

At his statement, her breath hitched, but her question came out steady. "What link?"

"Between the man and Polleo." His answer restarted her lungs. "It seems Miles Prewitt, the supposed suicide, worked in an advisory position at Polleo."

She fiddled with her napkin. "Were you able to find out what he was advising on?"

He noted her nervous movement, but didn't comment. "Prewitt's team was working on the cultivation of a new anti-virus."

She shot him a questioning glance.

"No." He answered, indicating he understood her silent question. "No one has any idea what type of anti-virus it was, and there's no public information available either."

She grimaced. "Well, doesn't that just figure?"

Unable to sit still, she gathered their dishes and took them to the sink, dodging his considering look. Once at the sink, she began rinsing the dishes. "So Polleo, a company positively linked to Talbot, is looking for Kyn volunteers for research. Probably for this anti-virus drug of Prewitt's. But we can't ask him because he's conveniently dead." She held one of the rinsed plates up, and cocked her head.

"The dishwasher," he answered.

She quickly set the plates in the machine. Closing it, she looked up. "Now what?"

He smiled with no humor. "Tomorrow morning we go to Mulcahy and lay out what we have so far."

She narrowed her eyes until they were mere slits. "You have a plan." It wasn't a question.

"Yep, and it involves getting into Polleo and its files." He watched her dry her hands and replace the hand towel.

Before she could say anything more, his phone rang.

He got up and went to the counter where his cell merrily chimed its head off. A number splashed across the screen and his face closed down, but he still answered. "Yes?"

His frigid tone was downright scary and she prayed it would never be directed at her. Not wanting to intrude, no matter how curious she was, she stepped around him, intent on giving him privacy.

He shifted until he blocked her way.

She looked up and quirked an eyebrow.

One of his hands brushed her shoulder, setting her hormones clamoring. He moved the phone away from his mouth, and kept his voice soft, "Don't leave yet. I'll be done in a minute."

She nodded and headed to his back porch.

"What do you need now?" As he moved farther into the house, his voice remained somewhere in the Arctic region.

Once outside, Raine closed the French doors behind her and took a seat on wooden swing, relishing the serene view of the river.

This attraction she felt for him was getting to her. Although it was dangerous to let it develop, she discovered that maybe she didn't want to be so alone anymore.

Cautiously, she imagined what it would be like to have someone be there for her. Someone who could understand how her life was a contradictory mix of vicious realities, well-hidden pockets of peace, and brief flashes of happiness. *What would it be like to trust a person so completely you wouldn't have to worry they would turn from the real you?*

The faint bellow of a boat's bullhorn cut through her musings and brought her back to the here and now. Reality was, she couldn't let him get that close. Her secrets were deadly and twisted. If she couldn't understand some of her darker decisions, how could she expect him to?

A hollow ache set up shop and she rubbed the heel of her hand against her chest in a futile attempt to ease it. Lost in her thoughts, she was startled when the swing shifted as Gavin sat next to her. It wasn't that big, so she ended up pressed against his side. He laid his arm along the back of the swing and used a bare foot to keep the slow momentum going.

She stiffened, but as moments passed and his body heat seeped into her, she relaxed and finally settled against him. Shadows from the falling night painted mysterious patterns over his face as he gazed out over the river. She wasn't sure, but the coldness that appeared with the phone call seemed to be fading.

Without thinking she reached out and traced a finger softly along his jaw line. Her voice was unconsciously gentle. "You okay?"

Those too-knowing, green eyes dropped to hers, and she found she couldn't look away. Didn't want to look away. He captured her exploring finger in his grip and slowly tugged her hand to his mouth. If she hadn't watched his head dip down to press a soft kiss into her palm, she could have believed she imagined the feather light touch.

"I will be," he answered. He dropped their joined hands to

his thigh, his attention going back to the river. His finger absently traced the back of her hand. "What do you know about my mother?"

Taken by surprise by his out of nowhere question, she racked her brain for the bits and pieces she heard throughout the years. Uncertain where he was going with it, her tone was cautious. "Not much, just that she's a strong blooded Fey witch, who's extremely good at warding magic." She watched his finger move back and forth, thinking in just a minute she'd move her hand. Right now it felt...nice.

"She is that." He took a big breath and let it out slowly. "That was her on the phone."

Lifting her head and tilting it to see his face, she tried to catch his expression, but the shadows had deepened with night's entrance, rendering him almost faceless. "Sounds like you two aren't close."

"Not anymore, no." He stopped his absent minded caress and combed his fingers through his hair. "Let's just say, that awhile back, she and I agreed to disagree on some things." He recaptured her hand and met her puzzled gaze. "What about your family?"

She stiffened as his question triggered unpleasant memories that snaked through her fragile peace like tiny serpents. "My mother died when I was young," her voice was tight and empty. "I don't know what happened to my father."

"Sorry to hear that," he said, his voice soft.

Not comfortable with the personal questions, she tugged her hand free, and stood up. "I should go." She got to the French doors and stopped. "Why don't you call me tomorrow and let me know when we're suppose to meet with Mulcahy?"

She didn't need his reflection to know he was right behind her. She could feel him. She did her best to ignore him as she opened the doors and stepped inside. She made a beeline for her jacket. In the midst of putting it on, she half-turned, only to come up short.

He stood inches away. "You can run and hide, Raine." His eyes were dark. "But, I'm a damn good hunter."

His challenge sparked her pride, and she shocked them both when she reached up and threaded her fingers through his thick hair. She ran her nails against his scalp, secretly pleased when visible chills cascaded down his arms.

Using the velvet strands as a handle, she brought his head down for a kiss. Not some wimpy kiss either. If she was doing this, she was doing it right. It may be her only chance.

With the tip of her tongue, she traced his lips, startled at how soft they were. When they parted for her, she took advantage of his offering and slid her tongue inside.

Her eyes drifted close as hunger and need swept through her. She arched closer, in some mindless urge to absorb his heat. It was like moving into the warm sunshine after standing in the cool shadows.

Desire licked under her skin, warming places she hadn't known existed. His taste, like warm sherry and dark spices, made her breath catch. She lost herself in the moment, with this man.

And she wanted to stay lost.

The unfamiliar thought jerked her eyes open, only to find his green ones focused solely on her, dark with arousal. Seeing such a totally male expression on his face brought an unexpected flare of pride.

With her body fully pressed against his, there was no escaping how in the moment he was. Slowly, she ended the kiss. Her fingers relaxed, releasing his hair, letting the strands slide over her skin. She glided her hands to his shoulders. He truly was a beautiful man.

Then, because it was almost too serious, she leaned up

and dropped a light kiss on the tip of his nose. Catching his startled grin, she pulled out of his arms.

Her voice was unsteady, almost husky, "I wouldn't call it running, Gavin."

Turning on watery legs, she walked down the hall to the front door, while every hormone screamed for her to stay.

He followed, reaching above her to hold the door open as she stepped onto his front porch. "Then what would you call it?"

She turned and met his eyes, her gaze as serious as her voice. "Trying to decide if you're worth the risk."

His eyes flared briefly, but he said nothing.

She left him there and strode down the steps to her SUV. As she drove away, she couldn't help biting her trembling lips as the unique taste that was Gavin swarmed through her bloodstream.

She glanced in the rearview mirror and saw him framed in the open doorway, tall, proud, and oh so dangerous.

CHAPTER TEN

The next morning found Raine and Gavin once again in Mulcahy's office, this time to go over what information they collected so far. Mulcahy, in his customary place behind his imposing mahogany desk, faced the two leather chairs that held her and Gavin. They each took their turn running down their various interviews, reciting the attack outside Zarana's, Raine's search of Rimmick's apartment, and Gavin's latest find with Prewitt.

Mulcahy turned his chair to the side and gave them his profile as he listened to their reports without commenting. When they were done, he stared out his window. A few minutes passed before he spoke. "What's your next move then?"

Gavin answered first. "We need to get into Polleo's offices. See if we can find out what this anti-virus is that Prewitt was advising on."

Mulcahy continued to look out his window. "I'm assuming you have a plan?"

"We do. I had the blueprints pulled for the research

center." Gavin slid a glance at Raine. "Raine and I will go over them this afternoon to find a way in."

Mulcahy nodded and then turned until he was facing them. "You need to be careful. Security will be tight and you don't want anyone to know you've been there."

"If we find Rimmick," Raine spoke up, her voice all business, with no trace of their previous confrontation, "do you want him out?"

Mulcahy's dark brown eyes were equally impersonal when he answered, "If he's able to move, yes. If not, make sure there's nothing left to be used."

She nodded. For her, killing Rimmick wasn't an issue, especially if he was in bad shape. In her opinion, he'd be better off dead than left to be used for more testing. A quick end was preferable to being a living science experiment, something she knew all too well. The fact she didn't want to add another pain-filled voice to her overcrowded nightmares was beside the point.

Mulcahy's voice cut through her morbid thoughts. "If we can find out what's going on at Polleo and how it impacts the Kyn community, I'll set up a meet with Cheveyo, Bertoi, and Vidis. I'll need you both in attendance to help plan a strategy."

Vidis was Warrick Vidis, the alpha shifter at Taliesin. Raine knew him by reputation only. More than any other Kyn leader, he preferred staying in the background.

She and Gavin left Mulcahy's office a few moments later. When they reached Gavin's office, he ducked in and picked up the sealed tube sitting on his desk. They headed toward a conference room where they unfurled the blueprints to reveal a detailed schematic of Polleo's offices. He pointed out the research teams offices, located on the second floor of the three-story building.

Taliesin's own research teams uncovered the details to

Polleo's security system. Using the detailed information and consulting with one of Taliesin's security experts, Raine and Gavin were able to identify the weak points—the few that existed.

Outside measures consisted of the normal obstacles of armed guards, a handful of guard dogs, and video surveillance. However, Gavin and Raine had an advantage no human security system could counter.

Shadow Walking.

An ancient, volatile magic, generally attributed to the Fey house, where the user could literally use deep shadows to step out of nothingness, strike, and disappear, all within the space of a single breath. Very few of the Kyn could master the control needed to perform the trick safely, but some of the Wraiths with Fey blood had. Walking the shadowed paths was hard to explain. The best comparison Raine heard was walking down a dark corridor of fun house mirrors while arctic winds tried to rip you to pieces.

To traverse the shadowed paths, the walker needed visual anchors, something to hone in on. Inside the magical corridors, cold, vicious energy whipped around a walker like cutting blades, tearing them off course. They could see the outside world, but it was warped and twisted. The only way to stay on the right road was to use recognizable visual points.

Using the detailed blueprints as reference, Gavin and Raine planned their route from outside Polleo's security fences to the interior rooms. They factored in how to bypass the guards, their dogs, and the surveillance cameras. The downside was the amount of energy required to travel in such a manner. After weighing their options, they decided the energy drain was worth the risk. There were too many things that could go wrong if they didn't take advantage of Shadow Walking.

At one point in the discussion, Raine asked, "These cameras aren't using heat signatures, right?"

"Right," Gavin said. "They may pick up some shifting in the shadows, but nothing clear should be caught on film. Our bigger threat is the dogs."

"True," she agreed. "They're much more perceptive than humans."

"We'll have to time it between their patrols."

They discussed their options once inside the building. Security lights ran throughout the building, dispelling the necessary areas of darkness needed to Shadow Walk. To help combat the internal video surveillance in the hallways, one of Taliesin's security experts had given them an electric jammer designed from the details gathered on Polleo's security system. It worked from the inside only, shutting down the motion detectors and looping the video surveillance.

Scanning the electrical layout, they identified spots where the lighting wouldn't reach, which gave them the benefit of shadow pockets for possible entry points. There was only enough room for one person at a time, so Raine would go in first.

They only had forty-five seconds before the system reset for Raine to get the jammer in place, have Gavin come in, and then both would disappear into an office where no cameras existed. If motion was detected in the halls, or a door was open, the alarms would sound. So long as the jammer remained in position, the video loop would show an empty room.

Gavin was rolling up the blueprints, when Raine asked, "How did Talbot know we were at Zarana's that night?" The question had been circling in the back of her mind for the last couple of days.

He put the blueprints back in the canister, moved to one

of the chairs, and took a seat. "You're assuming they were Talbot's men."

She frowned. "Well, they weren't in the bar. So they weren't out for a friendly game of pool, were they?" She ignored his small smile. "A response that quick means there had to be a mole at Zarana's."

"True," he agreed. "The question now is, are they human or Kyn?"

Pulling out a chair, she sank down and took a moment to think about it. "I'm leaning toward Kyn."

"How do you figure?"

He stretched his long legs in front of him, crossing them at the ankles and drawing her attention. The fleeting image of running her hands up those jean-clad legs almost made her groan aloud. Almost. *Focus, dammit.*

She rubbed her tired eyes, shoved her rampaging desire away, and got back on point. "They knew who we were, or at least had an idea of what we were." She dropped her hands and frowned. "No one sends out five armed men to take out two ordinary people. It's overkill."

"But, they weren't prepared," he pointed out softly. "They had guns with normal bullets. If they knew who we were, their ammunition would have been lethal."

She raised her head. "They never spoke, Gavin. Not once. They didn't ask for anything, didn't demand anything. Doesn't that strike you as strange?"

Pushing up from her chair, she began to pace. "If you're sent out to warn someone off, you threaten. You tell them, 'Back off or else'. The only time you don't chat is when you know exactly who your target is and there is no room for negotiations." She stopped abruptly as a sudden insight struck her.

"They weren't planning on warning us." Her voice was soft as she worked it out, momentarily forgetting the man watching her. "No lethal ammo means they either didn't have time to get the right materials together before being sent out, or…" Dread crept in.

"They wanted us alive," he finished.

The implications froze her blood. She sank slowly onto the edge of a chair as her mind quickly ran through various conclusions. Was Talbot gunning just for her? Or had he been going after whichever Kyn came nosing around? If she was the target, she would have to tell Gavin everything. The thought left her stomach in knots.

It wouldn't be safe, not to mention fair, to keep him in the dark. She would tell him—just not yet. This thing between them it was new—precious—and for once she wanted a chance at something for herself. Besides, there was nothing to indicate Talbot knew who was poking around, or who she was.

She took a deep breath, and let it out, forcing her pounding pulse to slow down. Thankfully her voice sounded steadier than she felt when she answered, "Maybe, but the fact remains we have an internal snitch. If we can figure out who it is, we might find Talbot's ace in the hole."

"That bar was crowded. There's no way we're going to be able to pick out who made us." His fingers drummed absently against the container in his hands. "It's not like we blend in."

"Maybe you don't," she retorted. "But I never seem to have a problem with being part of the crowd."

"Right." He scoffed. "Just keep telling yourself that." He stood up abruptly. "Come on. Let's get things together before we head out."

CHAPTER ELEVEN

The night was cold, and the moonlight sporadic as thick clouds moved through the sky. Raine was grateful for the deep shadows the night provided as well as for the lack of rain. It would be tricky enough without the added risk of slick surfaces.

She and Gavin crouched outside of Polleo's fenced grounds. They decided to approach from the rear of the property, which backed up to the woods. The thick foliage supplied cover while they timed the guard's routine and waited for the next guard to approach.

As they prepared to start their Shadow Walk, she absently stroked her wrist blades before checking the telling movement and forcing her body to stillness. There was an additional blade down her spine, and two stuck in the tops of her boots. She finally figured out Gavin's possible hiding spots for his long blade. It was retractable, so it fit snuggly up a sleeve, down a boot, or along his spine.

The crunch of leaves and gravel underfoot heralded the second guard and his dog as they approached. She caught

Gavin's quick signal to be ready and froze in the deepest shadow until the sentry pair moved past.

When they were gone, she straightened, took a deep breath, and drew the memorized layout of the building to the forefront of her mind. Focusing on distinctive architectural points, she opened the metaphysical doorway to the shadowed paths and stepped into the cold space.

Frigid energy whipped sent shards of ice into her bones. Concentrating on her anchors, she ignored the distorted shapes writhing on the edges of her vision. The temptation to turn and stare in horrified fascination pulled at her, but she holding her final destination in mind, she fought it back.

Every step was a struggle, as if she was trudging through knee high drifts of snow. Time ran strangely on the shadowed paths and her mental countdown was the only thing keeping her moving. Between the icy, violent energy swirling around her and the shifting shadowy surroundings, her reality was slipping away. She refused to listen to the chittery voice in the corner of mind urging her to flee.

Relief swept through her when her last visual anchor came into view. A few more steps and she emerged from the magical maze into the real world. She shoved the metaphysical door closed and let out a shaky breath. As the warmth of the room replaced the chill of the shadows, sweat broke out over her skin. With no time to waste, she located the hall security camera.

Luck was with her. It faced the other way. Sticking to the shadows, she pointed the jammer at the camera. The door to the targeted office she and Gavin had identified sat at the end of the hall.

Then came the hardest part—not disrupting the electronics of the jammer. To do that, she had to contain her emotional reactions. Utilizing her formidable self-control, she locked away the chaotic mix of nerve, anger, and anxiety.

She was relieved when the small green light on the device remained steady. In a matter of seconds, it blinked twice, indicating it was now synced with the camera.

Gavin materialized out of the darkness behind her. She gave him a nod and he moved toward the door at the end of the hall, barely brushing against her. She followed him into the research team's office and, without a sound, eased the door closed. She turned off the jammer, and noted they had fifteen seconds to spare. She slipped the jammer in her pocket and surveyed the room.

Gavin headed straight to the first desk near a filing cabinet. There were two other cabinets, a second desk on the other side of the room, and a large circular table in the center. It was obvious the office was doubling as a conference room.

She moved to the two cabinets in the back and flicked her fingers on her right hand. A small ball of low light appeared. It was a necessary indulgence as she needed to take pictures of the files. With a twist of her wrist, she moved the small globe to her shoulder and started flipping through files.

She found nothing of interest in the first cabinet. The second held a couple of intriguing documents regarding test designs centered on magic-based skills. She used the small, finger-length camera supplied by Taliesin to record each page before replacing the files. When she was done, she moved back to Gavin where he sat at the desk.

Since his computer skills were far superior to hers—and less volatile—he was the one accessing the hard drive. In the time she spent scanning through the two filing cabinets, he managed to bypass the computer's security.

When the monitor flickered and Gavin shot her a dark look, she moved to the third and final filing cabinet. There was nothing in the files and it left her frustrated. She eyed the cabinet. and going on instinct, she did a more in-depth examination and found a discrepancy. Excitement sparked. One of the drawers wasn't as full as the others, and the back end sat about half an inch higher.

She pushed the files toward the front and out of the way, then ran her fingers over the bottom of the drawer. When she felt a raised edge, she grinned. *Jackpot.*

It took a second to pop the false bottom and reveal a slim opening holding thin folder. She tugged it out and rapidly scanned the contents. It looked like a family tree, but instead of names, there were coded labels, making it cryptic as hell. Instead of wasting time trying to decode it, she quickly snapped her way through the documents.

Once she had them back in their hiding spot, she turned to see Gavin removing the memory stick he used to store the copied hard drive. He shut the computer down and repositioned the chair. He glanced up, his expression grim, and lifted his chin in silent question. She nodded once, indicating she had what she needed, and then extinguished her little ball of light.

She hadn't found any mention of Rimmick, but going by Gavin's expression, he had. His hand was a warm weight on her shoulder as he leaned in close. His low voice was as unsettling as the look on his face. "We need to go down and check the lab in the basement."

She searched his gaze. "Security?"

"Don't know." His voice stayed quiet. "But we have to try."

She squelched the useless urge to argue. If Rimmick was here, they couldn't afford to leave him behind. Together, they moved toward the smaller door that led out into Polleo's inner hallway.

Based on the blueprints, the jammer wouldn't work in this area because they had multiple hallways to get through. Finding the darkest shadows in the far corner of the room, she watched Gavin's broad back wink out of sight as he stepped into that space between worlds.

The additional Shadow Walking would seriously deplete her energy. Still, she took a deep breath, slowly released it, centered her spirit, and mentally pushed the door open. Ignoring the disquieting sense of her body melting into the frigid shadows, she let her being become insubstantial, making it easier to blend in to the darkness.

They Shadow Walked down the twisting corridors until they reached the basement. Stepping back into the real world, Raine stumbled. Gavin shot her a questioning look as she steadied herself against his frame, but she shook her head and straightened.

She looked around and realized they were in a huge cavern of cement and shadows. The sterile, glass-walled room crouched in the middle of the dimly lit basement held a metal examination table that gleamed softly in the dim light. Just beyond the glass enclosure was a solid rock wall lined with cages. The jarring scene revived nightmarish memories. While not unexpected, panic still dug vicious claws into her chest.

Barely settled after traversing the shadows, her stomach dropped, leaving a sickeningly hollow feeling behind as her gaze remained riveted on the examining table. In the muted light, patches of shadows lay across the table and spilled into a macabre pattern on the floor. The illusion was so strong it tore a soft whimper from her closed throat.

A dark figure rose between her and the ominous table, breaking the spell. Strong hands grasped her upper arms, while a low voice called her name and cut through her rising nightmare. The harsh noise of air rushing in and out of her lungs replaced nightmarish cries. Blinking she found herself staring into Gavin's worried face.

"Raine?" His eyes were intent. "Can you hear me?"

Taking another noisy breath, she managed a shaky nod. His fingers loosened, then dropped away. She stepped back, closed her eyes, and took a moment to get a grip. Falling apart in the middle of a mission was not allowed.

"Keep it together," he warned in a soft hiss.

She fought to clear her mind, and concentrate on why she was here. When she opened her eyes, she hoped she looked steadier than she felt. "I will." She cleared her throat. "Sorry."

Taking her at her word, he continued toward the back of the lab.

She followed, refusing to look back to the glass examination room. The rear of the basement was shrouded in fragmented shadows, but it was soon evident Rimmick was not here.

Since they were pushing their time frame, they turned to head back to the double-door entry. At the sound of booted feet tromping steadily down the hall, they jerked to a stop. Security was making its rounds.

They moved to opposite sides of the door and stilled in the concealing shadows as the guard got closer. The unsuspecting man pushed open the door in front of Raine. She held her breath, pressed back against the wall as far as she could, and watched as the door stopped just before her toes. The guard stood with one hand on the open door, and peered around. Obviously satisfied everything was as it should be, he turned and headed back into the hallway.

As the door closed, she silently exhaled. She caught Gavin's considering gaze and gave him a weak smile. His answering one was quick, and then he was gone, back into the shadowed paths.

She followed and when they were back in the empty office, she pulled the jammer out of her pocket. When the light flickered to green, she nodded to a now pale Gavin. He looked as shaky as she felt, the energy drain from their multiple journeys into the shadows considerable.

With the small device in hand, she inched the office door open enough to monitor the security camera. When the camera rotated away, she slipped out, aimed, and triggered the jammer. When the green light blinked twice, she tapped the door, signalling Gavin.

He slid by her, and moved into the hall's deep shadows. Giving him a head start of a few seconds, she darted after him. A deep breath and she was once again surrounded by the icy darkness. Drawing on her waning reservers, she made it to their spot outside Polleo's fences and stumbled into the moonlit air, leaving the twisted paths behind.

Once she and Gavin hit the tree-line of the woods, they sprinted to where they left her SUV. Next stop—dropping off their findings at the office so the investigators at Taliesin could download their files.

If luck was on their side, those files would give them some idea of where to find Rimmick as soon as tomorrow. On the other hand, since luck was on vacation, sipping a Mai Tai and laughing her ass off, Raine was betting they were more likely to raise more questions.

CHAPTER TWELVE

"Damn it." Raine rubbed her tired eyes yet again. For the last five hours, she and Gavin had plowed through the seemingly endless piles of paper. She had a headache from trying to translate abbreviations, which used every letter of the alphabet. It was bad enough most of the readable text was so cryptic it could've been anything from a grocery list to supplies needed for world domination.

They were set up in the conference room at Taliesin, and white paper covered the long table like huge flakes of snow. Gavin sat at the opposite of her, meticulously working his way through the stacks. He looked up from the document he was scanning and leaned back, arms stretching over his head. Neither had spoken much except for the occasional question, or to add some point on the whiteboard sitting next to the table.

She reviewed what they had been able to piece together so far. It wasn't much. There was no doubt some sort of testing was happening at the lab. Neither she, nor Gavin, understood the chemical compounds used in the trial formulas, and they had passed those on to Taliesin's labs for translation. However, one thing was clear, based on the custom-made, ten-foot-square cages noted on one of the down-loaded invoices from Polleo's stolen files, the test subjects were much bigger than rats.

What was more worrisome was a series of notes she found. They recorded a lab assistant's disjointed observations on the effect of *"parapsychological input on S3M's reactions to injected stimuli"*. Whatever the injected stimuli was, S3M did not perform as expected. Words like: *"faulty conditioning"*, *"unusable strands"*, and *"unstable cellular walls"* left her futilely hoping S3M didn't meant what they were beginning to fear.

Sprinkled throughout the documents were a handful of other letter-number combinations. W8F, DL2M, WF5F, and so on. Going with Raine's belief the lab was using Kyn as test subjects, she and Gavin created a rough key, hoping Polleo's scientists didn't possess much of an imagination.

The first letter denoted the bloodline of the individual Kyn subjects—W for witches, D for Demon, L for Lycos or Shifter, WF for witch/Fey, leaving S for wizards. The S stumped them both until Gavin mentioned wizard and witch were both W's. Which led to the question of what else humans called wizards. Raine hunted down a Thesaurus and they came up with sorcerer.

The second designation appeared to be the number assigned to the subject. The fact the numbers were on the low end gave them hope that whatever was happening, hadn't been happening for long. The last letter was always M or F. Logic dictated that was gender—male or female.

There were other combinations as well, ones they couldn't fit in to their theory. Still, breaking even that much of the code didn't prove anything. Those letters and numbers could easily stand for some esoteric scientific terminology. Even what she first thought to be a genealogical chart ended up being indecipherable. There were no names, just symbols and equations.

Frustrated, she got up and paced. On her third pass, the telephone on the table rang. Gavin hit the speaker button and Rachel's smooth voice filled the room. "Mr. Durand, you have a call on line three."

"Thank you, Rachel." He hit line three and picked up the receiver. "This is Durand." His eyes narrowed and his spine stiffened as he listened to the voice on the other end. "Fine, but it better be good." His tone hardened, as if angry at the interruption, but Raine caught the flare of excitement in his eyes. "When and where?"

He grabbed a pen and scribbled something on a piece of paper, then flicked his gaze up to her. "I'm bringing someone with me."

She heard the sudden sharp exclamation on the other end. The caller obviously didn't want an audience. She rested her hip against the edge of the table to watch the call play out.

Undeterred, Gavin didn't bend. "It's that or you come in. Your choice." A moment later, a predatory smile creased his face.

Guess he won the argument.

He hung up the phone and leaned back, crossing his arms behind his head as he flashed a heart-stopping grin that hid nothing and contained pure satisfaction. "Want to take a ride with me?"

That look, one rarely seen, fascinated her and left her wanting more. It didn't help that his innocently phrased question caused her imagination to paint a bizarre scene of her straddling him like some sexually deranged cowgirl and kissing that grin off his face.

Damn, he was dangerous to her peace of mind—in more ways than one.

Rubbing a hand on the back of her neck, she slammed her unruly imagination into a dark corner. "Sure." She motioned to the covered table. "I don't think I'm going to get much more out of these."

He reached for his coat, and moved to hold the door open when she walked out ahead of him. Unaware of her prurient thoughts, he raised an eyebrow in silent surprise at her quiet thank you as she passed. Keeping him unbalanced made her feel better. She wasn't one to ignore when someone was unique enough, in this day and age, to demonstrate simple courtesy.

Gavin remained quiet as he led the way downstairs to his car. Expecting his preferred mode of transportation to be one of those lovely fast motorcycles you practically laid down on, she was surprised by the deep blue, sleek two-seater, hardtop convertible, he led her to. A soft beep and its lights winked as the security system disengaged.

It was her turn to raise an eyebrow. "Yours?"

"What were you expecting?" He popped the lock on her side, and held the door open as she slid into the supple leather.

"Not this." She ran her hand down the buttery surface. It fit his sexy predator image, and beat the heck out her SUV for comfort. However, taking this baby off-road would be a huge no-no. The slightly funny, yet absurd image of this low slung sports car barreling along a dirt track, with Gavin trying not to ding his pretty paint job, almost made her laugh.

He raised an eyebrow when she failed to stifle a small chuckle. He shut her door and walked around to the driver's side. He folded his long frame into the driver's seat and let a comfortable silence fill the interior as they headed out.

She relaxed into the plush seat, and cocooned behind the

darkly tinted windows, watched the scenery race past. "So, are we going very far?"

"A bit. We're heading north."

"Who's up north?"

"Hopefully, someone who can shed some light on those deaths at Talbot." His casual answer triggered an instinctual warning.

The momentary pleasure gained from his alluring presence and sweet ride disappeared into coiling tension. It could be a coincidence. North covered a lot of territory. A slow creep of dread left her voice tight. "What's the name?"

He steered his car through traffic, and missed the change in her tone. "Bane Mayson."

The name hit hard and she winced as coincidence slapped her upside the head. *Dammit!* "How did you find him?" Strangely enough, her voice came out calm, considering her internal battle against throwing up.

"I didn't. He found me." Gavin shot her a look. It didn't take long for him to catalog her tense shoulders and pale face. His grin faded, and was replaced by something harder and darker. "What aren't you telling me?"

Well, no one could claim he wasn't perceptive.

Her continued silence shot the tension between them into the danger zone, and his eyes narrowed as his jaw locked.

Guilt was a traitorous bitch and Raine fought the urge to go for her weapons in automatic defense. She was out of time.

His fingers clenched the steering wheel as his frustration clogged the air. Without warning, he zipped across three lanes of traffic, ignored the irritated blares of horns in his wake, and took the next exit. The abrupt move pulled her out of her spiraling thoughts as she braced against the door. Gavin drove the car a ways down a deserted road before pulling off to the side. Gravel pinged against the low-slung car as he slammed on the brakes. Raine's body jerked against the seatbelt.

He slammed the car into park and ordered in an harsh voice, "Out."

She sucked in a shaky breath, released the seatbelt, and opened her door. She followed his tall figure as he strode toward a small clearing, his fury evident in every step. When he stopped next to a large moss covered tree trunk, she went to stand opposite of him, staying out of arm's reach.

He glared at her, the sharp edge of suspicion darkening his gaze. "Enough of this shit, Raine," he spat. "Whatever you're hiding, spill it."

She struggled to keep her face blank, doing her best to hide the emotions tearing her apart. "It's a long story," ice coated her voice. "Do you really want to go into this now?"

He snarled something vile and pulled out his phone, dialing from memory. His voice was short, "I'm running late. Don't leave." Not giving Mayson a chance to argue, Gavin snapped his phone shut without another word. His gaze pinned her like shards of colored glass, and his face was hard, unreachable. He crossed his arms, leaned against the tree, and waited.

She circled the conversational pit and hedged, "I've used Mayson for information in the past."

"What kind of information?" His question hit the air like bullets.

She held up a hand in warning, knowing if she didn't start from the beginning, chances were high he'd kill her outright. "I'll explain, but you need to hear it from start to finish."

"The whole story?" His expression didn't change, nor did the chill in his eyes lessen. "Wouldn't that be refreshing? I so like being kept in the dark."

She winced as his tone sliced through her. In that moment, she lost the partner from the last few days and faced the dangerous warrior. Tension kept her stiff and unmoving, but she forced herself to meet his stony stare. "I spent my fifteenth birthday chained to a lab table."

A swift ripple of shock flared in his eyes before they went back to cool calculation.

She didn't stop. "I know you've heard stories at Taliesin. Even I've heard some of them."

"How much is true?" He had no idea how much his question hurt.

"They barely scratch the surface." She gave an awkward shrug. "I'm Fey, but no one's really sure what else is in here."

"So those rumors of you being the result of some forbidden affair or magic gone wrong?"

Gritting her teeth, she looked away. "Magic didn't do this to me. Humans did."

His poignant silence scraped at her nerves.

"They used me for their experiments. I lost track of how many. Each one did something to me, to my magic. But my mother…" Her throat closed around the choking pain and shame. With a ragged cough, she continued, "She died during one of those experiments."

Raising a shaky hand, she massaged her temple, hoping to stave off the impending headache. Unsettled, she began to pace. She couldn't stand still and look at him while she relived her past.

Reverting to the necessary distance to get through the retelling, her voice cooled. "It was late at night. My mother and I were at home when they came." Memories of cracking wood, harsh commands, grabbing hands, and her mother's screams swam across her mind. "When I woke up, I was chained down on a table. Wrists, ankles, neck and waist. They used iron restraints. The pain of it burned so bad, I couldn't think. I spent the first few hours screaming myself hoarse." Her hand absently rubbed over old scars at her wrists as the phantom ache woke.

"Men in white lab coats would come in, run their tests, and leave. I tried asking questions." Begged and pleaded, more like—two words she would never admit out loud. "But they ignored me, talking over me as if I was nothing." She was deaf to the bitterness echoing in her voice.

"They took samples of everything. Flesh, blood, bone, whatever they could use. They tried every stimulus they could come up with." Searing agony in dancing flames, breath-stealing cold, the unnerving feeling of something inside her she couldn't stop. "It didn't matter how much I fought, they kept going."

The nightmares seeped through her mental walls as she gave him the whole twisted story. Her vision darkened, like clouds before a storm. "Do you know how many different types of pain there are?" It was a rhetorical question. Giving a sharp shake of her head, she pulled herself back from the black pit of memories.

"It took me awhile to figure out, but their little 'tests' left me different." Her lips twisted in a tight smile, and her voice turned harsh. She flexed her hand, releasing the tight fist at her side. It looked so normal now, but before...before she could make it change into something deadly.

"Whatever they were looking for, I wasn't giving it to them. My body, my mind, my magic, wouldn't respond how they wanted. I knew it wouldn't be long before my time as a lab rat came to an abrupt end. I was a threat, too uncontrollable, too unpredictable. So, I learned to hide my growing skills because they managed to create something all right, just not what they expected."

She stopped moving, not really seeing him or their surroundings as she stared at the trees in front of her. "I started planning my escape. I stopped responding to their tests, burying my magic deep. I made them believe I was no longer able to function. Therefore, I wasn't a threat. One night before I left, I heard two technicians discussing the termination of a separate project." The last word emerged as a hiss. She hated that word—her tormentors had labeled her mother a project.

"Which project?" His voice cut through her memories.

She realized she had fallen silent as she got lost in her past. "My mother." Deliberately opening both her hands, she studied the bloodied half-moon marks on her palms, a curious detachment settling in. "She didn't survive their latest implant." Needing to move so she wouldn't fall apart, she paced away from him.

Memories of the two techs as they speculated to the reason the test subject failed rose. Their clinical observation of her mother's death attributed to "the host body rejecting the implant". It took a bit as the conversation continued before Raine understood what they had done to the most important person in her life. They impregnated her mother with some perverted genetic structure, all the while hoping for a live birth. Instead, her mother had hemorrhaged to death. Not that anyone tried to stop it. The implanted embryo caused too much internal damage to justify keeping her alive.

"You escaped by yourself?" Gavin's question dragged her back from the agonizing memories.

She shook her head. "No, a few days later, while I was getting out of my restraints a man came in." No point in detailing how she managed to slip out of those restraints, how long it took her to thin out her wrist, morph it down, to slip through the cuffs. Or the deadly claws that sprouted, giving her the only weapon she had at the time. No, better not to share all that. "It took a few minutes to realize he wasn't one of the scientists. He got me out of the lab."

Turning, she met Gavin's gaze without flinching. "We were outside, almost to the woods, when their security caught us. We were trapped, but I wasn't going back. I used the power they'd created, just like they'd hoped. I burnt each man to the ground." No preliminaries, just a statement of fact. She gave Gavin credit, his expression didn't change.

"I'd do it again if I had to." Cold, she turned back to the trees. "We weren't the only test subjects at that lab." She braced, knowing what she said next would change everything. "My rescuer was Mulcahy." Out of the corner of her eye she caught Gavin's jerk of surprise. *Yep, knew that would get a reaction.*

Almost done with the story, she hurried on, wanting it all out. "After killing those men, I blacked out. When I woke, Mulcahy was carrying me. We were about two hundred yards out when there was an explosion. The lab went up in flames. The explosives he used did their job. Nothing was left but a pile of rubble."

She rubbed her arms. "I spent a year recovering. I got my strength back, and pulled myself together. I joined Taliesin just before my seventeenth birthday." She wanted, no needed, him to understand, but from his unforgiving expression it was futile wish. "My job gave me focus, helped me to function as normally as possible."

No sense in sharing she trained from the beginning to be a Wraith. Needing to hone her skills, to become an unbreakable weapon so she would never again feel helpless or out of control again. From the moment she used her magic to kill those men, she hadn't felt one iota of remorse. Instinctively she understood the danger she faced. The scientists and their tests managed to create an unpredictable, dangerous animal. A very pissed off predator who only wanted to hurt.

It would be so easy to give in and become the monster they created. Something held her back, forcing her to choose, to continue to choose, not to let her magic corrupt her sense of self. It had taken years to master control, but she kept her vow to not become what the twisted humans created, to stay true to her sense of honor. Problem was, her sense of honor was a bit skewed.

"I was twenty-two," she continued. "When I finally figured out who the power men were behind that lab."

"The deaths at Talbot?" It hadn't taken him long to put the pieces together.

Clever man.

She sighed and rubbed a hand wearily over her face. "The first four were mine. I have no idea on the last three." Not missing his skepticism, she tried explaining. "The first four are tied to Aaron Talbot. Even you figured that much out. Aaron was the moneyman behind the lab. The other three, Austin Santos, Leon Bishop, and Danilo Rostislav were all heads of various departments at the lab. Matthew Peyton was the senior Talbot's right hand man."

"Did you kill Aaron Talbot?"

"No, his car accident was just that, an accident." She held his unemotional gaze without flinching, knowing what he saw. She spent years facing it in her mirror. "I didn't do it, but I didn't shed any tears about it either." There was no remorse, no satisfaction, just emptiness. "The other four— they had to answer for what they did."

"Who made you judge and jury, Mc Cord?"

Him using her last name was a bit disconcerting, but not unexpected. If she was honest, she would be thrilled to leave this little clearing alive. Everything else would be gravy. "I was the last one standing." Her answer wasn't a plea for understanding, but stated a brutal truth. "They killed my mother. They killed countless other Kyn and humans. They were so intent on playing some demonic god to find a way to outrun mortality. They had no right!"

Her breathing turned choppy, and she took a moment to recapture her shredded emotions. "They took what wasn't theirs, what they could never understand, and warped it into unrecognizable forms. They created nightmares you have no concept of." The depth of her emotions made her throat and eyes burn. "Gods willing, you'll never have to find out."

He remained unmoved. "That doesn't explain why you hid what you did. It doesn't explain why you supposedly stopped after those four." He began stalking her, each step echoed by an accusation. "It doesn't clear you for the last three. It doesn't even make sense that Mulcahy wouldn't come up with your name first, or why he wouldn't sanction the hits. It doesn't cover how you came to know Mayson." His voice grew harsher, colder as his anger pushed through his thin control. "It sure as shit doesn't explain why you didn't tell me this last night!"

Like a curtain being ripped away, his pain and anger at her perceived betrayal became brutally clear, leveling her in one vicious punch. It was too late to apologize—his temper well and truly snapped.

"Did you get a kick out of watching me chase my tail?" It came out on snarl. "Or wasting my time tracking leads to your kills? Did you think you were so damn good no one would figure it out? Were you ever going to tell me? How much of you is a lie, Raine?" The last question exploded in her face as he backed her into a thick tree trunk. He slammed his palms against the rough surface, caging her in without touching, while his words sliced her open. "Maybe I should be the one deciding if you're worth the risk."

There it was, what she dreaded from the beginning. Whatever relationship they may have started was gone before it even really began. No way would he believe her, no matter what she said or did. None of it would change the fact that she hadn't told him everything straight out. Now, when it was too late to fix it, she managed to destroy something fragile, something she wasn't sure she'd ever find again.

"I didn't tell you because I've never told anyone," her voice was soft, trying to talk to his rage. "You know as well as I do what happens to the Kyn who go after humans. Mulcahy wouldn't change the rules." She flinched in anticipation of his reaction as she finished, "Not even for his own blood."

He stumbled back a step. His piercing eyes searched her face. "What do you mean 'his own blood'?"

"Mulcahy is my uncle." Gavin wanted it all? Fine, she'd give it to him. "It's why he was at the lab that night. My mother was his half-sister. He received a tip one of his Wraiths and his sister were being held in a hidden lab. He went in to retrieve both of them." She fought to keep her voice from shaking. "He found his Wraith beyond saving and his sister dead. He overheard some of the personnel talking about a subject scheduled for termination the next day. Curious, he went looking. He found me."

"Don't try to play me." Gavin's face darkened. "If he was your uncle, he would have gotten you out regardless."

"Maybe." She fought back old doubts, but Gavin didn't need any more unpleasant truths. Those truths whispered her uncle may have cared for her mother, but her daughter was only useful in how she could help him. "Regardless, he got me out. Once he destroyed the lab, he didn't feel the need to dig any deeper. His intelligence indicated all those involved were at the site that night."

As she uttered the words, old resentments rushed her. She ached for the child who had been reborn into some unnatural creature who would never fully be a part of the Kyn. When she looked in the mirror, the beast peeking out served to remind her why being a Wraith was her only option. Without the safety valve of her job, her bloodier tendencies, which made her such a good Wraith, were the same ones that would lead to her becoming the hunted.

Doubt and disbelief were clear on Gavin's face as he studied her. "You're saying they weren't all killed?"

"Aaron and his little gang were at a different location." She carefully stepped away from the tree. "It took me years to track those four men down. Years to figure out how to make it look like accidents. Mulcahy never thought to look beyond the information he was given. To this day, he thinks it was a small renegade group of scientists. For him, the problem was solved. He was wrong."

"Why not go to him? He would have helped."

Why try explaining the non-existent relationship with her uncle? Hell, she could barely comprehend it herself. She shook her head, not taking her gaze off of him. "I didn't track those men through documented lines. I tracked them down through other survivors. Most of whom were considered crazy or delusional. I knew the faces in the lab. I knew their names. I listened when those scientists talked, as they pulled samples off my body, while they ran their tests, while they discussed how I wasn't giving the expected reactions."

Fighting down her rising resentment at still having to defend her actions, she kept her voice level, "Mulcahy would not take the word of an angry, somewhat crazed child and a handful of tortured, mind-broken Kyn who barely managed to escape. It wouldn't be worth the risk, not to him or to Taliesin."

Frustrated by Gavin's continued disbelief, she dared to share more, laying a part of her bare. "The year it took for me to heal? I spent half the time seeing things that weren't there, reacting to strangers like a rabid animal, and hours not moving or speaking, just watching, waiting."

Only for him would she attempt to explain the hell of that first year of recovery. A maelstrom of emotions wrapped tight fingers over her throat, but she got the words out. "Those experiments opened a door to abilities I didn't understand, couldn't control. It was like being drowned in noise and brutal urges. I couldn't turn it off, I couldn't turn it down. It was all I could do not to strike out at those around me." She shuddered as the memories clawed closer.

"When I was finally able to surface, it still took time for me to understand those people were trying help." Her voice dropped as the emotional upheaval hit its peak and blessed numbness began to seep in. "When Mulcahy finally let me join Taliesin, I was grateful. The training was so intense it took over everything. I used my training to grow strong enough to eventually close the door and lock it."

Gavin didn't waste time putting the rest of the story together. "Mayson was one of those Kyn wasn't he?"

She nodded, saying nothing. What she shared with Gavin, she had never shared with another. Nor could she see ever doing so again. It brought back too much pain, too much anger, too much helplessness.

"Why did you stop after the first four?" He watched her face carefully, as if her answer would reveal something vital.

After all the half-truths and lies, he wouldn't believe her. Hell, if their positions had be reversed, she'd be hard pressed to believe anything he said. Yet, she had to try. "It became too easy to hunt and kill. There was a part of me that liked it."

Contempt flickered through his face. Catching the expected reaction, what was left of her heart shattered, and finally the numbness settled in for good.

His voice betrayed nothing. "So because you liked spilling their blood, you stopped?"

She nodded, once.

His bark of harsh laughter made her jump. "Bullshit! You're a Wraith for fuck's sake. We kill people. It's what we do. If killing bothered you that much, you wouldn't be standing here." He leaned in, filling her vision, but kept a careful, revealing distance between them. "Lie to yourself, if you want, just stop lying to me."

His derision cut deep, deeper than expected. Burying her pain with the hundreds of other bitter and painful emotions, she wondered a bit distantly if the little room holding all that mess would ever fill up. When it did, what happened next?

She lifted her chin, refusing to be cowed. "Believe what you want. I've answered your questions. Your turn to answer one of mine."

He took his time stepping back. "Ask."

"Are you telling Mulcahy?" She needed to know in order to determine her next move.

He stared at her, his thoughts hidden. "I don't know yet."

She buried the burst of relief as his answer. It meant she had some time to figure shit out.

He looked at his watch. "We have to leave. We're late."

Without waiting for her response, he turned and stalked back to the car, anger still shimmering around him.

Raine took a deep, shuddering breath. One small positive —she was still breathing. She'd count that as a positive, even as she ignored the small, hidden part of her crying silently as a hollow ache settled in her chest. Gavin would never trust her again, which meant she could never turn her back on him.

Following his lean form, she reminded herself it was better this way. If she could stop worrying about his unsettling presence in her life, she could stay in control. Besides, if he kept his distance from her, there was a good chance Talbot would only target her when it all hit the fan.

CHAPTER THIRTEEN

S uffocating silence filled the car for the remainder of the drive. Still reeling from the last go around, Raine let Gavin stew. She had nothing left to say anyway. Just outside the small town of Sheldon, Washington, he pulled into a small parking lot half filled with worn out pickup trucks and a few older model sedans. As she got out of the car, Raine was greeted by the squeak of the chains anchoring a weathered sign that advertised a lunch special for five dollars and ninety-nine cents. Below that stunning deal it proclaimed Saturday's were Honky Tonk nights at Mackey's.

As Gavin stormed across the pavement and up the steps to the planked porch running the length of the bar, his anger rode the air. Raine followed a few cautious steps behind to give him space. He pulled open the heavy door, and a cowbell clanked in welcome as they walked into the dim interior.

Faces, mainly male, turned to watch as they headed to the back where two pool tables stood. An empty booth sat on the left wall. Gavin slid in on one side and she took the other. A blonde waitress in painted on jeans and a green T-shirt—a couple sizes too small for the overflowing manmade chest—strolled over.

"What're you having?" Her light blue eyes devoured Gavin.

Raine was unsurprised by her reaction as he was clearly a step up from the nearby options.

"Nothing, thanks." Gavin's smile was a sexy invite and carried no trace of his earlier fury. "We're waiting for a friend."

The blonde preened a bit, leaned one ample hip against the edge of the table, and gave Raine her back. Not the smartest move. Then the waitress took it one step further, and played her chipped red nails over Gavin's hand. "Anyone I know?"

Irritated, Raine resisted the urge to snap a quick kick to the back of Blondie's knee. Yeah, it was immature, but it would make Raine feel better. Maybe. She must have made some noise because Gavin shot her a knowing smirk.

He turned back to the waiting woman. "Bane Mayson. Know him?"

She pulled her hand back as if burned, her heavily painted lips twisted into a grimace of distaste, and a small flash of fear flared in her eyes. "Oh sugar, you don't want to be mixing with the likes of him."

"And why is that?" Raine's voice was sharper than intended, but it had the side benefit of forcing Blondie to acknowledge her.

Blue eyes narrowed in annoyance at being addressed by someone else with breasts. "He's strange."

"Really?" Gavin's tone was all conspiratorial, inviting her to share more details.

She huffed at Raine, turned back to Gavin and took him up on his offer. "Lots think he's into that voodoo stuff, y'know?" Blondie's voice stayed low as if she didn't want to be overheard.

Gavin matched it. "Why?"

The bouncing ponytail perched high on her crown moved as she tilted her head. "Not real social. Keeps to himself. Always wearing those black long-sleeved hooded things, hiding his face. He'll come in every now and then, have a couple of drinks, and leave. Always sitting in the back, in the dark." A summons from the bartender snapped her back to her duties. "I'll be back for your orders." She turned and worked her way through the room, gathering orders.

Gavin's flirty smile faded, only to be replaced by hard angles and empty eyes. Raine waited until he meet her gaze, proud when her voice came out even. "So do we wait for him here, or go looking?"

Instead of answering, he pulled out his phone, dialed, and held it up to his ear. After a few moments, he hung up, a wrinkle of concern narrowing his eyes. She waited, unwilling to play this game. If he didn't want to talk to her, fine, but she wasn't going to beg for his attention.

He tapped the table's surface as he studied her. She remained unmoved under the weight of judgment. She was who she was, and if he couldn't accept that, it wasn't her problem.

After coming to some internal decision, he broke his silence and started to get out of the booth. "Let's go find out why he's not answering."

She sighed quietly as she followed in his wake. It was going to be a long day.

The chilly silence continued as they got back in his car and headed out. As he drove to a destination only he knew, he made two more calls, both remained unanswered. Fifteen minutes later, he pulled in to a graveled drive that led to a small, gray, manufactured house nestled in the trees. Sunlight glinted off the nearby waters of Lake Cushman.

Privacy was clearly a priority for Mayson because his neighbors were few and far apart. Right now that privacy was shot to hell. Two police cruisers, an ambulance, and two unmarked cars were scattered through the front yard. The EMT's stood near the empty ambulance, and two officers were in a heated discussion near the police cruiser.

Rocks settled in Raine's gut as she took in the scene from where she sat in the car. Raine was almost certain they wouldn't be talking to Bane any time soon. Next to her, Gavin muttered a quiet curse. When he turned to shoot her a dark look, she couldn't miss miss his brief flash of speculation. Her temper slipped.

"Screw you, Durand. I had nothing to do with this." Yanking the door open, she climbed out, and slammed it shut hoping the window would shatter. No such luck. She stalked to the uniform walking their way, and heard Gavin's door click shut behind her.

"Excuse me, ma'am, but this is a crime scene. You need to stay outside the barrier." The cop's uniform was neat as a pin, leg creases so sharp you could cut yourself on them. His eyes were equally sharp as he stopped in front of her and brought her to a halt. "Can I help you?" His voice, a pleasant baritone, matched his slightly husky form topped by straight brown hair buzzed down into a military style.

"We were supposed to meet a Bane Mayson, but he didn't show." Gavin came up behind her, but she ignored him. "We thought we'd come out to see if he was still here."

The officer studied them, his expression unmoved. "Your names?"

"Raine McCord and Gavin Durand." She looked at the officer's badge. "What's going on, Officer Kirkwell?"

"I'm afraid I can't tell you, Miss McCord," his voice remained polite. "However could you answer a few questions for us?"

When she nodded, Kirkwell led them to the cruiser. A second uniform stood nearby, this one a bit more rumpled than his immaculately pressed counterpart. The second officer was pale and shaky as he leaned against the car, but as they got closer, he carefully straightened to attention.

"Officer Lake here, will take your statement, Miss McCord." Kirkwell turned to Gavin. "If you'll come with me, Mr. Durand?"

"Of course." Gavin followed him out of hearing range.

Lake stared at Raine, his throat working convulsively. He took a crumpled notebook and pen from his pocket. "Miss McCord, if you could please tell me how you know Bane Mayson?" His voice was high. Whatever scared Lake wasn't stopping him from doing his job.

Knowing Mulcahy wouldn't approve of having too many details of the case under human scrutiny, she kept her answers as vague as possible. Not as easy as it sounded. "Gavin, Mr. Durand, received a phone call from Mayson earlier, requesting a meeting today."

"About what?" Lake's voice began to level.

"I didn't take the call, I'm just along for the ride."

His hazel eyes narrowed at her somewhat evasive answer. "Have you met Mr. Mayson before?"

"Yes, a few years back. He was able to provide some information for me on a situation I was handling."

"Situation? What is it you do?"

"I'm a Corporate Security Officer for Taliesin Security in Portland."

Recognition sharpened his gaze. "Security? What kind of security?"

"Corporate and personal." Movement near the home caught her attention as a tall man in a navy blue suit that screamed 'federal agent' emerged from inside. He clocked Gavin and Raine's presence, ducked under the yellow police tape, and strode toward them.

The young cop let out what sounded suspiciously like a snort of disbelief. "Uh-huh. Well, what would a Portland based security business have in common with a recluse like Mr. Mayson?"

Before she could answer, the tall man closed in, and Lake's back went poker straight. Raine wasn't surprised. Local and federal agencies never seemed to get along, not with both sides determined to act like a dog protecting its best bone.

As the agent got closer, he flicked a glance over her, but switched directions to Gavin. She and Lake watched him address Kirkwell, before leading Gavin in their direction. Kirkwell glared at his back, looking decidedly unhappy. Raine would bet Lake was going to be feeling the same way very soon.

Gavin and his federal escort stopped in front of them. "Thank you, Officer Lake, but I'll take it from here."

Lake's jerky nod didn't hide his flare of resentment, but he closed his notebook with a sharp snap and stormed toward his partner.

Now that the agent stood in front of her, Raine noted the touches of white in the deep brown strands combed back from a high forehead. Based on the bags under the equally brown eyes, sleep wasn't his friend.

"Agent Victor Osborn, FBI." His voice was gravelly, as if he smoked one too many cigarettes. "Out of the Seattle Field Office." He held out his blunt fingered hand.

She took it, and calluses rasped against her hold. *Hmm,*

seemed Osborn hadn't always worn a suit. She gave him a polite smile. "Raine McCord."

Osborn dropped her hand and turned to Gavin, who was currently imitating a stone. "Mayson's dead, Durand. I want to know why you're here." His clear frustration and irritation proved the two men had met before.

Gavin shrugged. "Look Osborn, I got a call from Mayson asking to meet. He didn't show, so we headed over and found you." His stance was relaxed as he met the agent's questioning gaze. "I'm not sure what I can tell you that will help here."

"Fine," Osborn bit out, but Raine didn't think he was buying Gavin's nonchalance. "What information did Mayson have that has you driving all the way up here?"

"I don't know. That's why we were meeting."

The agent's gaze went razor sharp with speculation. "What are you investigating?"

"Corporate espionage."

"For which companies?"

Gavin shook his head, and a small smile played around his mouth. "You know I can't tell you. Our clients expect a certain amount of confidentiality when they hire us."

Frustration radiated from the older man. "Look, you and I have danced to this tune before, but I'm not up to it today. I need something, because what's left in there isn't giving me anything." Osborn ran a hand through his dark hair. "I got called in on my way up from Portland. The locals are spooked, and my superiors want this swept up quick."

Gavin stiffened slightly, but his focus stayed on the agent. "Do you want me to look at the scene?"

Osborn considered him a second without answering. Instead, he turned to Raine. "Do you work with Durand?" At her nod, he continued, "And your position at Taliesin?"

"Corporate Security Officer."

With a small, aggrieved sigh, Osborn looked back to the house, then back to Gavin, before coming to a decision. "Fine. Follow me, both of you. Don't touch anything. Just tell me what the hell I'm looking for."

With that cheery endorsement, he started toward the house leaving Gavin and Raine to follow.

CHAPTER FOURTEEN

Raine walked into the dim house and braced for the usual smell accompanying a violent death. It was one she knew well. A distinctive scent that reminded a person of raw meat and coppery blood. A scent that warned whatever you found, it would no longer be recognizable.

As she made her way down the short entryway a few steps behind the two men, she realized there was no odor. No blood, no raw meat. She let out the breath she was holding, and her other senses stretched out in curiosity. A trace of spine tingling magic raised bumps along her skin as she drew closer to the front room.

Two agents passed her, heading out of the house, each carrying small evidence bags in their gloved hands. Osborn stopped just to the left of the front room's entryway, while Gavin halted in the middle of the opening, blocking her view. She stepped around to his right and came to an abrupt stop, puzzled.

Bane Mayson was sprawled on the faded green couch under the picture window. At first glance, the scene made no sense. There were no visible wounds, no horrific mutilations, nothing to show how he died. Just the skitter of magic down her spine that made the deceptively calm view in front of her that much more ominous.

"Can you give a positive ID?" Osborn's rough voice regained her attention. He was looking at Gavin, who wasn't answering.

To find out why, she looked and realized Gavin was staring at her. "What?"

"I've never met him," he said blandly. "Just spoke to him on the phone."

"Oh." A little disconcerted, she addressed the waiting agent. "Yes, that's Bane Mayson."

Osborn gave her the universal version of cop eyes— steady and cool. "You've met him?"

She shrugged, and resumed studying the weirdly peaceful scene. "We met briefly about six or seven years ago."

"Is that so?"

She caught the note of skepticism in his question, so she turned and met his gaze. "He had a lead for me on one of my cases."

"Was your case official or unofficial?"

She quirked an eyebrow. "Excuse me?"

Osborn closed the distance between them and then lowered his voice. "I'm highly aware of what Taliesin is, and my team was specifically called in as we're the ones who handle strange cases. Based on my past experience, strange generally involves Taliesin." He pointed to the body on the couch. "This definitely qualifies as strange."

Yes, it certainly did. She was unsurprised the humans had a special unit to deal with the Kyn, but confidentiality had its place. "Mayson provided information, and only information, to Taliesin, Agent Osborn. He was a computer genius. If you're familiar with our company, then you know that's all I can disclose."

Osborn's jaw flexed as he clenched his teeth. "Mr. Mayson seems to be a regular font of knowledge for you two." His voice was close to a growl. "So here's a question. How does a reputed recluse get access to such important information if he never gets out?"

Cops were a damn suspicious lot by nature, but she couldn't blame Osborn for not swallowing the whole corporate espionage story. Since Gavin shared history with the agent, she'd let him field the question. For now, she'd keep her mouth shut unless she had something worthwhile to add.

Granted, Osborn could pull them both in for obstruction and make Taliesin's top-notch lawyers earn their fee, but, there was no way she or Gavin could make any allegations involving Talbot. Not unless Mulcahy cleared it.

Gavin picked up Osborn's gauntlet. "As Raine said, Mayson was pretty good with computers. In this age of technology, you don't have to leave your home to do much." He gestured around the dusty, shabbily furnished room. A top of the line computer sat on a wooden table against one wall. "Taliesin didn't worry about how he got his facts, as long as his information was reliable. I'm fairly certain he wasn't comfortable out in public."

That last observation was an obvious understatement. From where she stood in the entry, Raine studied the slumped form on the couch and thought Mayson's physical appearance would be difficult enough to explain to the locals, never mind explaining how he ended up dead. Thankfully, both tasks belonged to Osborn and not her.

Mayson's long, sprawled legs were ensconced in faded blue jeans, and his feet were bare. He wore a dingy white, short-sleeved T-shirt, but his arms were twisted ropes of scar tissue. When she first met him and saw those horrific marks, she asked him point blank what made them.

His answer was, "A test gone wrong."

Now, Mayson's hands were clenched into loose fists that showed a fine webbing of more scars. If his hands had been unfurled and nothing had changed in the last six or seven years, his nails would bear an uncanny resemblance to a wolf's claws — sharp, long, and slightly curved. *Which had to have made typing on the computer a bitch.*

Osborn's voice cut across her mental observations. "Fine, Durand. Let's see if you can tell me what killed him." The agent entered the front room, and motioned for the two of them to follow. "What happened?"

Mayson's chin rested on his chest, and his long, stringy brown hair provided a partial curtain that hid most of his face.

"Magic." Gavin drop to a squat, putting him at eye level with the body. "Do you have gloves we can wear?" He aimed his question at Osborn. "I don't want to contaminate your crime scene."

Osborn pulled out two sets of latex gloves from a box sitting on the side table and handed them to Raine and Gavin. It took her a few seconds to get them on, and then she flexed her fingers, getting used to the powdery feeling of latex against her skin. Once her hands were covered, she knelt at Gavin's right, and faced Mayson.

Gavin's glove-covered fingers gently tilted Mayson's head up and strands of hair fell back, revealing his face. Osborn sucked in a sharp breath, but Raine didn't flinch. Mayson's face was heavily scarred and bloodless lips barely covered his elongated canines. But his most disconcerting feature, the amber eyes of a wolf, were closed. It was as if two unfinished sculptures of a human male and wolf were merged into one warped image. It was a shifter's worst nightmare brought to life—an incomplete transformation.

Except Mayson had never been a shifter.

Something about his face was bothering Raine, and it

took a second before she figured it out. She flicked a glance at Gavin to see if he noticed.

He had, and his lips were pressed into a thin line. "The eyes are missing."

She nodded. The eyelids were down, as if Mayson was asleep, but instead of the normal slight roundness that lifted the lids out that tiny bit, they were sunken. She cupped her hand around the lower part of his chin, and held Mayson's face still while Gavin gently pried open the right eye.

She could stop her shocked inhale. The eye wasn't gone, but it appeared as if the liquid filling it had evaporated. The amber iris ringed in red was still visible, the black pupil remained dilated, and the white sclera was clear of any trauma, but the orb itself was flat, like a deflated balloon. Gavin let the lid drop, and wiped his fingers absently along his jeans.

She let go of Mayson's chin carefully and touched the arm nearest her. The cool skin felt like tissue paper, fragile and thin. She pushed a bit deeper, hoping to find bone, and instead hit something spongy. Where both the ulna and radius were supposed to be was now a soft substance.

She lifted a puzzled gaze to Gavin, and disbelief kept her voice soft. "What the hell happened?"

Gavin's expression was just as confused. This close to Mayson's body, the traces of magic were stronger, and gave her an idea. She dropped her mental walls and skimmed her hands mere inches above his body, hoping to get a sense of what magic was at play.

Instead she got nothing. With a small, frustrated sound, she pulled the gloves off, and did it again, this time going up the arm to the shoulder, across the chest, and stopping about mid-chest. She closed her eyes, and sent a flicker of her own magic out, hoping it would find an anchor.

She wasn't ready for what she got back. Her magic hit

something and sparked like an electrical current. The silent explosion sent her flying back into the wall behind her. Her head hit with a resounding *thunk* and she collapsed into a heap. Whatever it was, wasn't done. It sucked her magic down into the body on the couch.

Frantic, she tried to pull back, only to encounter agony. Fire and pain whipped through her as if she was being simultaneously burned from the inside out and crushed to death. Struggling to draw a breath and yank her magic back, she couldn't find her voice to call out for help.

For a few disconcerting moments, panic reigned, then she realized that the more she tried to escape, the stronger the drain on her magic. Making a split-second decision, she opened the lock on her magic and powered it down the tethering lined in a desperate bid to overpower whatever was dragging her under. Her magic rushed forward and the two opposing forces collided. The impact body-slammed her to the ground and sent pain radiating through every limb.

Strong hands tightened on her shoulders, and the unexpected touch snapped the magical connection. She opened her eyes, and Gavin's face swam in her vision.

"Raine, can you hear me?"

"Yeah." Her voice came out rough, her throat raw. She blinked until Gavin's face stopped moving, and raised a hand to rub the back of her head. She was going to have a doozy of a headache.

Osborn knelt on her other side. "What the hell just happened?"

"She tried to read the traces of residual magic." Exasperation came through loud and clear in Gavin's tone. "Not the smartest move in the world."

"Well, next time you do it," she muttered. With Gavin's help she pushed up and sat with her back to the wall. He settled in next to her. It left her facing Mayson's body with Gavin on one side and Osborn on the other.

Osborn rested his arms on his upraised knees. "Did it tell you anything useful?"

"Yeah, it was a spell, and it didn't like being poked at," she said.

"Can you tell who, or what, cast it?"

She shook her head and the ache in her head increased. "Not definitively, but I can give you a couple of choices by the taste of it."

"Taste of it?" Osborn eyed her closely.

"I don't know how else to explain it. Magic leaves images behind, like afterimages when you've stared too long into a bright light. Sometimes another magic user can figure out who did the spell by how it feels, how it tastes mentally." She disliked explaining magic to anyone, especially humans. For her, it was instinctive, but finding the right words to explain any of it was awkward.

Osborn appeared to grasp the idea she was trying to get across. "So what did it taste like?"

She held Gavin's gaze when she answered, "It's either a demon or a wizard. I'm not sure which one." She rolled her head back to Osborn. "Whatever spell they used, it drains the victim."

"Explain that please."

"It pulls magic out of the victim, and I would bet once it drains the magic, it moves on to the next step." She considered Mayson, and recalled the painful sensations before she overpowered the lingering pieces of the spell. "I think it also burns and crushes its victims from the inside out."

Osborn's voice was hard. "Which would explain the lack of fluids and softened bone mass."

She nodded, but there was something else that bothered

her. "It doesn't explain why his skin is so cool. Shouldn't his body temperature be warm?"

Osborn's attention snapped to her. "Why do you ask?"

"I spoke to him on the phone roughly four hours ago." Gavin absently rubbed his hand along her arm, his earlier anger seemingly set aside, as he focused on Osborn. "That doesn't seem to be enough time for a body to cool, especially if they've been cooked from the inside out."

Osborn didn't comment, but ran a hand over his face. "I don't suppose you know any demons or wizards who might be in this area?"

Gavin bared his teeth. "If I did, I'd hand them right over."

The agent pushed his body upright with a huge sigh. "I don't believe you."

Gavin shrugged, not bothering to argue.

"How did you find him so fast?" The question was out before Raine could stop it. Osborn stared at her. "Look," she continued. "You said it yourself, Mayson was a recluse. I know you were coming up from Portland, but I didn't notice any close neighbors when we drove up, so how did you find him?"

A cynical light sparked the dark eyes. "Would you believe an anonymous tip?"

The flippant answer triggered her temper. "Fine, but we leveled with you. It would be nice if you could stop with the inscrutable federal agent shtick and give us a straight answer."

His only reply was a raised eyebrow.

Uncomfortable sitting on the floor, she started to stand up. Her body wasn't quite as excited with the prospect, and she gratefully accepted the arm Gavin offered. Once on her feet, she let Gavin go, and started to carefully walk away, doing her best not to aggravate the ache in her head. She wanted out of this house. She was tired of the questions, and even more tired of looking at the dead body on the couch.

Osborn's trailed behind her, his voice grim. "Let's finish your statements and get your contact information so you two can go back to Portland."

It was a clear dismissal if she ever heard one. Damn Federal agents, they never shared anything important, which made working with them the equivalent of working by yourself, blindfolded. Or like working with the Kyn.

"Yeah let's," she growled, as she stepped out of the house with Gavin at her side.

CHAPTER FIFTEEN

R aine tried not to think about Mayson, but it was a futile exercise. The image took its place among others in her nightmarish collection. It wouldn't be the last one, either, before this job was finished.

Her headache was almost gone now. She carefully rolled her head to the left, and watched the early evening sun play over Gavin's face as they headed back to Portland.

"How did you meet Osborn?" Her soft question fell into the quiet interior of the car.

He flicked a glance her way. "We met on one of my cases a few years back." His smile was wry as he turned back to the road. "We've met up a few times since."

"Is he a good agent?"

He nodded. "He tries to keep an open mind and use whatever tools he can. He's gotten pretty good within the Division."

The Division was actually the Preternatural Crimes Division, a deeply cloaked, specialized unit within the FBI, created ten years ago. It had taken a while for those humans in the know to admit a more than normal investigative unit was needed to handle supernatural crimes. Rogue Kyn of any bloodline could create quite a stir in the mortal world. To help hide the Kyn's existence, the alphabet soup of agencies handpicked humans with varying psychic skills and created the Division. After all, who better to help solve the unexplainable than those who were unexplainable themselves?

"I guess that's something then." She sighed. "I'm not sure what he's going to be able to accomplish against whoever set that spell. It was nasty."

Gavin's attention didn't leave the road. "I'm betting we'll run across whoever it is before he does."

She grimaced. "You're probably right. I'm going to talk to Cheveyo about what we can use against it."

Gavin rolled his shoulders. "Why not ask Natasha?"

"No thanks." No way in hell was she doing that. "I'm really not into pain. She doesn't trust me, and I don't trust her. Makes for a tricky working relationship." Realizing her last statement could now include him, she fell silent.

He slashed her an indecipherable look, his voice thick with sarcasm. "Now why wouldn't she trust you?"

She stiffened as renewed tension thrummed in the air. The pounding in her head made a comeback and left her in no mood to be tactful. It was time to handle this, just as she handled everything—straight up, no apologies. If she didn't believe in her own actions, then she had no business being a Wraith. "Look, I've apologized for not telling you sooner."

"There's a 'but' on the end of that."

She rubbed her forehead. "Yeah there is. Trusting people hasn't gotten me anything nice."

His eyes stayed on the road. "Sounds like a pretty isolated way to live."

She gave a harsh laugh. "Oh yeah, like you're a big old teddy bear yourself."

"You disappoint me, Raine. I thought you were stronger than that."

"Than what?"

"It doesn't take strength to be alone, because there's no risk. Trusting a person, having friends, partners, that takes strength."

He didn't need weapons to wound her. He did just fine with words. She didn't bother to argue, and instead brooded over his statement.

Logically, she knew he had a point. She closed herself off from others, fearing one more rejection, one more loss, would loosen her tenuous hold on sanity. But trusting, caring for someone weakened you, turned them into your Achilles' heel. She worked hard not to have a weakness. She needed to be unbreakable.

Deep down she knew she was damaged, but she held on to the small spark of hope she would find someone who could accept her, warts and all. But realistically, if she couldn't face what she was, how could she ask anyone else to?

She stared blindly out the passenger window while his apt criticism scored internal wounds that bled. "I may be lacking, but you're proof that I'm justified."

"How do you figure?"

"Oh, please!" She turned awkwardly—trapped by the seat-belt—and glared at him. Her fists were clenched in her lap. "Cut the crap. I saw your eyes when I told you what I'd done, what I am. You're like everyone else. You may be a Wraith, and maybe you tell yourself when you kill it's justified. You looked at me and decided because I took pleasure in killing those men, it makes me less than you."

Her voice was harsh as all the resentment she kept bottled up came spewing out. "You said I was lying to myself, but you're way off base. You have no clue what it's like to know you don't belong, or to not even know what you are! I'm an aberration, created by a bunch of demented scientists."

Raking her hands over her face, she turned away. "Did you see Mayson, Gavin? Did you get a good look at him? Do you know who put those scars on his body, gave him the claws and eyes of a wolf?"

Turning, she studied his profile through narrowed eyes. "The same four men I killed." Her breath heaved. "You asked me why I was judge and jury. Mayson is one reason, my mother is another. Let's not count the other Kyn and innocent humans they twisted and murdered. I still hear their screams. Someone has to stand for them. They sure as hell can't do it themselves."

"You escaped," his voice was even.

Her body trembled, and a scream of frustration beat at her, but she locked it behind her teeth. *How could she make him understand? Should she even bother?* "None of us really escaped. Death was the only true way out. Those who were rescued, or escaped, were like Mayson. Mentally, he was a mess. He stayed inside, and kept to himself because it was the only way he could control his environment. I was the only one left to strike back. It was my responsibility to make those men pay. I can't apologize for it. I won't."

Gavin's expression remained stony. "I don't think less of you." When she gave a snort of disbelief, a thin layer of warmth rode his tone. "What I'm finding hard to understand is why you continued to be a Wraith if the fact you like the hunt, the kill, disturbs you so much? Why not do the last three men? Why not kill Jonah?"

Disappointment spiraled through her and left her numb. It was useless, and she was tired of trying to explain, tired of justifying her actions. He could never truly understand. Defeat haunted her voice, but she blamed the burning in her eyes on the steady pounding of her head. "Being a Wraith is all I know. I never wanted to be a victim again, so I became a weapon. A damn good one. Those four kills were personal. My job is not. It's business."

Hearing the words out loud, it hit her just how close she once skirted the edge of right and wrong. "Matthew Peyton, the food poisoning, was when it hit home. I was becoming exactly what they tried to create. I didn't want to be that."

Gavin didn't say anything, and silence flowed back into the car.

She closed her eyes and shut him out. Her thoughts going back to the night she followed Peyton to a Japanese sushi restaurant in London.

After months studying his habits, she had his routine down. He liked to take chances—such as escorting his attractive young companion around while his wife was out of town. He was with his young thing, and enjoying his favorite dish— fugu, also known as blowfish, dipped in bitter orange sauce. His taste for the exotic made initiating his death a simple thing. A couple of milligrams of tetrodoxin—blowfish poison—when Raine stumbled into his server and his already dangerous menu choice became a fatal one.

She sat at a corner table and watched the older man and his decidedly younger female partner laugh while they chatted throughout dinner. Peyton's tongue occasionally flicked out to wet his lips. Raine's research indicated those lips had to be going slightly numb. He drank his saki while his gaze wandered around the dimly lit restaurant. He stopped briefly on her table, and never realized who she was.

She played the role of student, with books spread out around her, as she enjoyed her bowl of rice and Tempura. Heavy rimmed glasses hid her gray eyes, and her long dark hair was drawn back into a braid. A small bit of glamour covered her tattoos and scars while she kept an eye on the dining couple.

Peyton paid the check and wiped his mouth once on his sleeve. Raine gauged the time from ingestion, certain the numbness had time to spread to Peyton's entire mouth at that point. When the couple left and headed down the street, she followed. Their laughter drifted back as the young woman related a story of a drunken student who mistook a sink for a toilet.

Peyton's left arm dropped from the girl's shoulder, and he stopped to shake it as if it had fallen asleep. Raine stepped into the shadows and continued to watch, anticipation snaking through her icy resolve. Her gaze never wavered as Peyton clutched at his companion's arm. He missed, and off-balanced, he fell to the sidewalk, clutching his throat. Unable to keep the smile off her face, a tide of dark joy rose as Raine watched Peyton struggle to breathe.

His date's shrill voice tore through the night, "Matthew? What's wrong?" Once she realized he couldn't breathe, she started screaming. She rolled him over, loosened his tie, and kept begging for someone to call an ambulance.

Peyton's panicked gaze swept over the slowly gathering crowd and found Raine. Their gazes locked, and she watched the horror and knowledge spill into his eyes.

She stood there, no longer hiding behind the illusion of glamour, a small smile curving her lips as he asphyxiated. She never took her gaze from his. Not even when Peyton's silent screams for help echoed in his eyes, and his life drained away. She was still smiling when he took his last labored breath, the light in his eyes finally disappearing.

It wasn't until she was getting ready to sleep on her flight out of London, that it hit how much she enjoyed watching Peyton suffer. *She could get addicted to that feeling.* The small realization rocked her. That night she made her decision. She wouldn't hunt down any more of Talbot's men. She wandered too close to being the monster they created, and that was unacceptable.

Yet, on some level, she worried it was already too late. Not going after Aaron Talbot had proven almost painful, but when he died a few years later in a car accident, she considered it her reward for not killing him, and took her peace where she could.

The discordant sound of the tires going over the bridge heading into Portland pulled her out of the past and back to the present. Gavin had stayed quiet, leaving her to wonder what was going through his head while she wandered through her twisted past.

Before they hit the office, she needed to know. Turning to him, she asked, one last time, "Are you telling Mulcahy?"

"For now, no," his tone was careful. "I can't see what it would accomplish."

Her shoulders slumped, and relief left her shaky.

He stopped at a red light and turned to face her, his face carved in stone. "Understand this, Raine," his voice was utterly cold. "If I find out you've lied to me about the last three murders, I will personally drag your corpse into Mulcahy's office."

She didn't need the pitiless emptiness in his voice and eyes to understand it was not an empty threat. She could even understand it. That core of him echoed the core in her that allowed her to do her job. She nodded.

His cell phone rang and shattered the strained silence. The traffic light flashed green and he turned back to the road even as he picked up the call. "Durand." He listened to the caller as he drove, and then his tone changed fractionally. "When?" Another pause made her turn to watch his face. "Did anyone see anything?"

An expression flashed across his face. It was so fast she might have imagined it. The only sign of his unease was the whitening of his fingers around the cell phone. Whoever was on the other end of the phone was not sharing good news.

"We're about twenty minutes out." His face returned to his normal inscrutable expression. "We'll be there." He hung up, tossed his phone in the center console, and put both hands on the steering wheel. She waited while his fingers flexed on the grip. He kept his eyes forward. "They found Dmitri Rimmick."

She blinked. "Alive?"

He shook his head. "No, his body was left out behind Zarana's."

"Witnesses?"

Again, Gavin shook his head.

She moved on to the next question. "How'd he die?"

He shrugged. "I don't know, but let's see if Mulcahy does. We're to report to his office when we get back."

She took a deep breath and forced her mind back on their case. "It has to be a message." From the edge of her vision, she caught his nod and her stomach knotted with dread. A grim certainty grew that whatever Dmitri was involved in would link to Talbot.

It bothered her that Dmitri's body was dumped in neutral territory, with no one being the wiser. Someone should have seen something, heard something. Her stomach clenched as a nagging worry raised its ugly head. "Who found him?"

Gavin's jaw clenched, his voice flat, "Alexi Savriti."

A spark of fear ignited. This was why she shouldn't let anyone close to her. If it was Talbot, had he figured out who was hunting him? Did he know how Alexi helped her? Had going to Zarana's endangered her friend? The questions chased one another until the spark of fear became a burning flame. As soon as she realized how scared she was, she got angry. Anger was good. It was a hell of a lot better than fear.

"If it's Talbot, we have to move fast." Gavin was obviously followed the same logic.

She let her anger and fear harden her resolve. "If it's Talbot, it won't be fast enough."

Gavin didn't argue and the resulting heavy silence lasted all the way to Taliesin.

CHAPTER SIXTEEN

I nky darkness pressed against the windows in Mulcahy's office. With the two chairs in front of Mulcahy's desk already filled, Raine, her arms folded, listened to Gavin recite what happened at Mayson's as she leaned against the wall by the bookcase. Cheveyo's long frame was folded into the chair nearest her.

In the other chair, closest to Gavin, sat a small, delicate looking blonde. Natasha Bertoi. Her nylon-clad legs were demurely crossed. Deep blue, three-inch heels encased her small feet. Her elegant hands lay calmly in the lap of the matching short skirt. A jacket of the same deep blue hue topped her icy-lavender scoop camisole. The dramatic color combination brought out the periwinkle blue eyes in her triangular face.

Mulcahy had called in both Cheveyo and Natasha in hope they would be able to shed some light on what magic had killed Mayson. Gavin concluded his summary with what happened when Raine tried to touch the remnants of magic, and Natasha turned her strange gaze to Raine.

Raine found the woman's face almost witchy, but men

seemed to be endlessly fascinated. Kind of like rabbits with a snake—except this snake would do more than just swallow a man whole. Natasha Bertoi did not become the ruling head of one of the most powerful demon houses by being the epitome of delicate femininity she resembled.

Something about the woman always set Raine's nerves on edge. It wasn't because the ultra-feminine, half-demon made her feel like the ugly duckling. No, it was the calculation that lurked behind those eyes. As if Natasha continually examined the angles before deciding who, or what, she could and couldn't use to her advantage. That level of ruthlessness meant Natasha could only be trusted to look after her own ass in any situation, because everyone else was on their own.

"What made you think it was a demon or wizard?" Natasha's husky voice flowed through the room, her gaze flat and dispassionate. "If the trace magic could affect you so strongly, your magic may not be up to judging who set the spell."

Raine stiffened at the implied insult. "I'm an expert in killing methods, Ms. Bertoi, and what was used was a death spell. It wasn't meant to simply harm, it was meant to kill, as slowly and painfully as possible. In my experience, the only Kyn able to put that much hate and malice into a spell are those who get a kick out of hurting others."

Natasha's gaze remained steady. "Pain and suffering could appeal to anyone. Why not a witch from the Magi house, or someone from the Fey house, Ms. McCord?"

The demon bitch would know all about pain and suffering, wouldn't she?

Raine refused to back down. "Witches hold their three-fold law inviolate. I've yet to find a witch willing to risk that much negativity coming back to them. Nor did the spell hold traces generally associated with Fey magic. Shifters are out because they would either eat him, or tear him up. That leaves the wizards and demons."

Mulcahy cut off the impending argument. "Wizards or demons, we need to know which Kyn is out hunting."

"And who they're hunting for," added Gavin.

Mulcahy aimed a sharp look at him. "Do you have any idea who this killer might be working for?"

Raine's pulse raced as she strove to keep her face blank and unreadable. She had no choice but to trust Gavin not to reveal her part in the case.

Gavin flicked a look her way. "We think Mayson's tied to Talbot."

"How?" Mulcahy's question was sharp.

Cheveyo and Natasha stayed silent and waited for Gavin's answer.

"The one name that keeps coming up on every thread we pull is Talbot, and Mayson can be tied to the senior Talbot, Aaron. It's possible Jonah Talbot is picking up where the rumors say his old man left off." Gavin didn't look at Raine, but gave Mulcahy steady eye contact. "It seems Aaron was involved in questionable experimentation with Kyn and humans. Mayson happened to be one of those experiments."

An explosive silenced filled the room before Cheveyo asked, "How do you know that?"

Gavin turned, giving Cheveyo an inscrutable look. "I have my own sources, and they don't need to be revealed."

Cheveyo's expression hardened. "They can be trusted?"

Deep inside Raine stilled as she waited for Gavin's answer.

"Yes, I trust them." Only then did he turn his attention to her, his expression unreadable.

She was the first to look away, only to realize her uncle was watching them both, his thoughts well hidden.

"Durand," Mulcahy addressed Gavin, even though his

gaze was narrowed on her. "Why did you go to Mayson's in the first place?"

"He contacted me," Gavin replied. "Said he had information on who was taking out Talbot's men."

Disbelief replaced Mulcahy's speculation as his attention finally shifted to Gavin. "If Talbot's father tortured him, why would Mayson want to help you find the killer?"

Gavin shrugged. "I didn't get a chance to ask."

Natasha took over the questions. "Can you prove Jonah Talbot is following in his father's footsteps?"

"Not yet," Gavin said. "I want permission to get more information on Talbot. Especially since Rimmick's name appeared on Polleo's hard drive. The wizard had to be held at their lab before we got in. We need to figure out who's keeping Talbot one step ahead of us."

Mulcahy's gaze narrowed. "You think there are two separate individuals involved, don't you?"

Gavin gave a short nod. "If I'm right, then Talbot has a Kyn tipping him off. It would also explain how they're luring in those like Rimmick. The murders Jonah asked us to look into were a ploy to get us involved. I'm betting he really didn't think they were connected."

"Are you saying they are?"

"Not sure." Gavin didn't flinch under Mulcahy's penetrating stare. "It's highly probable it's the work of one of his experiments looking for payback."

"Speaking of Rimmick," Raine cut in. "How did he die?"

Natasha made a small sound of disgust as impotent fury washed across her face. "Someone wanted it to look like a demon attack, but it was a poor imitation."

Raine blinked at the unexpected answer. "What do you mean?"

"He was eviscerated." Despite the small hand clenched into

a fist, Natasha's voice didn't betray any emotion. "Something tried to lay him open. His heart was missing, along with his eyes and tongue. He'd been pulled apart at the joints. There was a rite circle carved around him, and the etched runes belong to the Minuo branch. However, they were in the wrong order."

Not familiar with that particular Amanusa branch, Raine asked, "Minuo?"

Natasha threw her an unfriendly look. "Demons who can draw blood from any being without making a wound. There wasn't enough blood at the dumpsite, so whoever drew the runes and circle wanted whoever found him to believe it was the work of a Minuo. However, they don't know their demonology because a Minuo would never pull the body apart, nor would they remove parts."

Raine didn't dare ask why any demon, even a Minuo demon, would refrain from tearing a body apart. She could guess. Rogue demons enjoyed playing with a human body. Possessing a mortal form allowed a demon to create chaos between both Kyn and mortals.

Natasha made a good point. Whoever killed Rimmick really didn't know demons because destroying a perfectly good body made zero sense. Even for a rogue demon.

"Let me play devil's advocate here," said Mulcahy. "If someone is trying to imitate a demon, is it possible it wasn't demon magic that killed Mayson?"

Cheveyo shook his head. "Mimicking the actions of a rogue demon is one thing, but you can't copy someone's magic. If your Wraith feels it was a demon or wizard, I'd say chances are you're looking for a demon or wizard."

"Would a wizard imitate a demon?" Gavin asked.

Cheveyo was silent as he thought it over. Finally, he shook his head. "No, I don't think so. Most wizards know enough about runes to not put them in the wrong order."

Mulcahy studied the witch. "You're leaning toward demon then?"

Cheveyo nodded.

"It's not one of mine." Natasha's voice was certain.

Mulcahy studied her. "How do you know?"

"None would dare bring such attention to my house." Raine caught a brief hint of the beast hidden inside the diminutive form as a feral little smile played over her face. "They all know how displeased I would be. There is no one who would risk it."

Mulcahy took Natasha at her word. He pushed up from his desk, and walked over to the night-blind windows, his hands crossed behind his back. Then, without turning, he spoke. "Before anyone else goes missing, we need more information. What McCord and Durand retrieved from the lab at Polleo is a start, but even that is too vague for our people to translate. We need stronger lines to tie Talbot to Rimmick and Mayson's death."

Raine studied her uncle's back. "Just how are we going to do that? Talbot's too smart to leave incriminating evidence lying around. He wouldn't want to risk his precious foundation. In the time it would take to drag that dirty laundry out, he could take another Kyn."

The older man's shoulders tightened fractionally, the only sign of his growing frustration. "You and Durand will be attending his fundraising ball, as representatives of Taliesin. Ask him."

CHAPTER SEVENTEEN

Raine hated shopping and today's little expedition didn't alter her opinion one bit. Unfortunately, her limited wardrobe options forced her to endure the pushing, shoving, and innate rudeness of those armed with a shopping bag. Going to the ball with Prince Charming ranked just below getting poked with needles on her list of not-so-fun things to do.

Most of her morning and part of the afternoon was shot looking for the perfect dress. Trying to find something sophisticated, comfortable, and able to hide various weaponry was more difficult than she expected.

She walked across the mall parking lot as the plastic covered dress and accompanying shoes banged along her left side. Popping the back hatch of her SUV, she shove it up and looped the items over the garment hook.

Shutting the rear door, she checked her watch, and decided to swing by Zarana's to check in with Alexi. Not only did she want to make sure her friend was okay, but she had a few questions to ask. She climbed into her SUV, and headed to the Pearl District in downtown Portland.

It was mid-afternoon and it didn't take her long to find a parking spot. She got to the bar, and pulled open the heavy bar door. The wards hit as she stepped across the threshold and left a shiver over her skin. Despite the shadows that laced the edges of the room, the bar wasn't as dim as normal.

Although there was nothing to indicate Raine's arrival, a muffled voice came from the back room. "I'll be just a minute."

Raine sat on one of the padded barstools and waited.

The sounds of heavy boxes being shoved around was followed by the distinctive clink of bottles. Then light foot-steps preceded the appearance of the dark haired barkeep. Alexi's normally bright face appeared slightly drawn, which highlighted the dark circles under her eyes, and her smile was a pale imitation of its normal self. When she caught sight of Raine, a bit of life chased away the signs of strain. "Hey, McCord. What brings you here in the light of day?"

Raine cocked her head. "You doing okay?"

Alexi set down the bottles she carried, and then motioned for Raine to follow her over to one of the tables. Once seated, the smaller woman's fingers began a tap dance on the table-top. "Did you want your usual? I forgot to ask."

Raine shook her head. "Don't worry about it. Looks like you could use a stiff drink."

"Yeah, but I'm afraid one won't cut it. 'Sides, the owner of the bar can't come to work blitzed."

"Want to talk about it?"

Something Raine couldn't read flashed through Alexi's eyes, and her tapping fingers paused. "Not particularly," her tone was more scathing than Raine expected. "But I'm sure you'd like to hear about it."

Feeling the rebuke, but knowing it was necessary, Raine kept her gaze steady. "I wouldn't ask if I didn't have to, Alexi, believe me."

A slight blush worked its way up Alexi's face, and dulled the angry edges. "Sorry, I shouldn't take my frustrations out on you." Her fingers resumed their erratic dance, as her gaze restlessly roamed the room.

Alexi couldn't seem to settle, and watching her stretched Raine's nerves tight.

"It was horrible. I had nightmares all night," Alexi's soft voice trembled, her face bleak. "How do you get that image to go away?"

Raine didn't have an answer, and the frustration of not being able to comfort her best friend left her stomach tight. Alexi didn't deserve to be dragged into this, and the frightened look on her face was one more thing for Talbot to answer for. "I don't know, but I swear it fades eventually."

Alexi's curly mop bounced as she shook her head. "I find it hard to believe right now, but let's hope you're right." She took a deep breath and let it out, visibly steadying herself. She lifted her head and met Raine's gaze. "Okay, what do you need to know?"

"Just tell me what happened, what you saw."

Alexi shifted and stared out across the empty room. "It was a busy night, and one of my busboys had to take his boyfriend to the hospital. Appendicitis, I think. I let him leave and tried to help cover both his duties and my own. We had a live band, so the noise level was pretty high, but I felt a vibration from the wards as if something had slammed up against them."

She shook her head, her face puzzled. "I haven't felt anything like it before. Everyone knows Zarana's is neutral territory, so I've never had any serious interference with the wards. This was different. Like a really strong shove. I went out back to find out what was going on, opened the alley door, and there he was." She shivered and rubbed her arms as if cold.

Raine kept her voice gentle. "Did anyone pass you on the way out the back?"

Alexi blinked as if trying to dodge the horrible images in her mind. "No, the crowd was up front with the band. There wasn't anyone there."

"Did anyone in the crowd stand out?"

The barkeep shook her head. "We had a lot of new faces. We generally do when a band comes to play. No one sticks out though."

"When you first saw Rimmick, did you see anything?" Raine pushed. "Sense anything?"

"You mean besides the pieces?" Alexi's short laugh was bitter. "No, just him and the blood…oh gods, Raine he was like some horrible jigsaw puzzle. I didn't want to push past that circle. Those runes were demon magic and they made my skin crawl."

"Are you sure it was demon magic?" Raine hated what she was putting her friend through, but she needed whatever information she could get. It was a race to see if she and Gavin could figure this out before another Kyn showed up missing, or dead. "Have you ever felt it before?"

Alexi nodded, a little too rapidly, and again a flash of something unreadable swam through her eyes. "It was definitely some sort of demon magic. Did you see those runes? I may not have been trained, but I know enough to recognize the stench."

"What do you mean 'stench'?"

The barkeep spread her slightly shaking hands out across the table. "I don't know how else to explain it, but when a demon invokes magic it leaves a burning stench. It was faint but there. I didn't think demons tore their victims up."

"They don't usually," Raine answered.

"This doesn't make sense." Alexi raised wide eyes. "Why would they leave him outside my bar?"

It was Raine's turn to sigh and look away. "I don't know. None of this is making sense."

The scraping of chair legs against the hard floor pulled Raine's head up. The smaller woman walked to the bar, her movements jerky, as she rounded to the other side and grabbed a towel, before wiping down the counter. After a few minutes, she started on the line of bottles on the far wall, and kept her back to Raine.

"You never answered my first question, Raine," her voice cut through the deepening silence. Alexi made eye contact through the large mirror behind the bar. At Raine's blank look, she gave a small smile. "What brings you down here in the light of day?"

Raine's confusion cleared. She sighed and went to the bar. "I had to do some shopping."

Alexi turned, her face a study of surprise. "Shopping?" Her eyes narrowed. "Who are you and where's Raine?"

Raine smiled. "It's for work, so I didn't really have a choice."

"Does it involve the walking wet dream you brought in the other night?" Alexi ran the towel absently through her fingers.

Raine felt her face heat. "Unfortunately, yes."

Her friend raised her eyebrows, and then her gaze turned speculative. "What do you mean, unfortunately?"

Raine hunched her shoulders and looked away. "We've had a slight difference of opinions."

"What did you do?"

Her question triggered Raine's defenses. "Why does it have to be something I've done?"

Alexi rolled her eyes. "Because you don't let anyone get close to you. The minute they start trying, you pull back behind your fortress of solitude."

Raine felt her eyebrows rise. "Fortress of solitude?"

Alexi's expression turned serious. "Whatever you want to call it, it's what you hide behind so no one hurts you."

She wanted to argue, but since Alexi was right, it was pointless. "Well, this time it wasn't me. It was him."

"How so?"

Raine had never told her friend about her past. With Gavin's response still achingly fresh, she wasn't about to risk this relationship as well. "I let him in the fortress of solitude, but he didn't like the decor. So he left."

"He didn't strike me as the wimpy type." Alexi tilted her head, her gaze knowing. "What dragon do you have hiding in there?"

Raine shrugged. No way could she share how Gavin couldn't handle the fact she was a sociopath who enjoyed hunting people. If a man who killed for a living couldn't handle it, there was no way her gentle-hearted friend could. "I guess some knights just don't live up to their armor."

Sympathy played over Alexi's face. "I'm sorry, Raine." She laid a hand over Raine's. "Sorry he wasn't what you thought he was."

Her empathy was enough to make Raine's eyes burn. She blinked a few times to chase the sensation away. "No worries." She forced a grin. "I've got enough on my plate to worry about right now."

Alexi took the hint and changed the subject. They chatted for another hour and then it was time to open. Raine followed Alexi to the door, gave her a quick hug, then slipped outside with a wave as her friend switched the door sign to OPEN.

ON RAINE'S drive home the early evening air was crisp, carrying the scent of burning leaves as it drifted through the open window of her SUV, and triggered half-formed feelings of peace and comfort. She wasn't sure why, but she loved that particular smell. Maybe it had to do with the time of the year. Fall was coming to an end and winter was just around the corner. Patches of yellow gold, vibrant orange, burnt amber and deepening green flashed pass her windows, a tribute to the changing seasons.

She turned onto the road leading to her house, and passed through the leafy tunnel parading the autumn colors. All that contentment went up in a puff of smoke when a black Jeep Wrangler sitting outside her wards' perimeter came into view.

Unless Gavin had more than one car, it didn't belong to him. Besides, they were meeting at Taliesin before Talbot's party.

She slowed and palmed a wrist blade. As her SUV came to a stop, the Jeep's driver-side door opened and Cheveyo's tall form emerged. He walked around the front end of the Jeep and waited for her to approach.

She turned off the engine and got out. *Why he was here?* His unexpected arrival left her unsettled. She debated the wisdom of just ignoring him but knew it was pointless. Still, she didn't replace her blade. "Hello, Cheveyo. What brings you out to my neck of the woods?"

He leaned against the Jeep. "Well, I figured since I was in town I might as well visit."

"Uh-huh."

"Nice piece of land you have here." His gaze roamed and came back to her. "Isolated. It suits you."

"It hasn't seemed isolated enough lately," she muttered.

He laughed. "Poor Raine, too much company?"

She let out a sigh. "Not to be too blunt, but why are you here? I have a party to get ready for, remember?"

"I know. It's why I'm here."

"What? Are you my new date?" Her tone was dry, sarcastic, but deep inside there was a little twinge as she wondered if Gavin had backed out.

A purely male grin crossed Cheveyo's strong face, making her wonder, yet again, if this witch could read her mind. "Not this time. I actually have a gift for you."

"A gift?" There was no hiding her shock.

Something close to pity flashed across his face at the disbelief even she could hear in her voice. "What? A man can't give a beautiful woman a gift?"

She shrugged. "Yeah, he could. But it's me, so what's the deal?"

Cheveyo opened his mouth to say something and then apparently thought better of it. "Look, I thought about what you said happened at Mayson's. If whatever set that spell makes an appearance tonight, I wanted to give you some protection."

Where was this leading? "I appreciate the thought, but I don't have the time to learn a spell right now."

He shook his head. "It's not a spell, it's a charm. You're going to be spending energy on glamour tonight to hide your tattoos and scars. This," he held out his hand, "will help offset the drain and provide an added layer of protection."

In the center of his palm lay a beautiful silver lynx. It was wrapped around a deep blue tanzanite gem that was strung between beads of onyx and a delicately pink hued kunzite on the braided leather. He held the leather, letting the charm dangle. The light caught on the tanzanite and reflected purple flashes. "This particular animal is known as a guardian and keeper of secrets."

She reached out and let him drop it into her palm. Then she tentatively traced the handcrafted lynx. The silver was warm. Thankfully silver didn't seem to burn her as it did some of the other Kyn. Cold iron, on the other hand, tended to leave a nasty reminder behind. "It's beautiful Cheveyo, but you didn't have to do this."

"No, I didn't."

She searched his eyes, confused. They were a deep velvet black that made her think of a starless sky. She shook away the fanciful thought. "It'll match my outfit perfectly. Thank you."

She moved the blade, still hidden on her left side, into her jacket pocket, and then reached out and took the necklace. Closing it in her fist, she paused, "Wait a second." She narrowed her gaze on his face. "How did you know what I'm wearing?"

He touched the tip of her nose, startling her. "I'm a witch. I know a lot of things." He went back to his Jeep. Just before he opened the door he turned and shot her a cocky smile. "Enjoy your ball, princess." Then he got in and started the engine.

She watched him leave, then looked at the necklace lying in her palm, and shook her head. Men were the most confusing creatures on earth. She wasn't even going to try to understand what had just happened. She put the necklace in her other pocket, re-sheathed her wrist blade, and then headed home to get ready for the next unexplainable male encounter.

CHAPTER EIGHTEEN

Raine pulled into Taliesin's parking lot with only minutes to spare. The damn outfit took longer to put on than expected. The ankle length black leather skirt fell in a straight line, while the blue tinted silver material of the bodice gave the impression of a corset, complete with leather laces up the back. After fifteen minutes of contortions proved she wouldn't be able to lace it herself, she left it loose, hoping Rachel would still be at the front desk to help tighten it.

The outfit's major selling point was the skirt—long enough to wear heeled boots where she could hide two of her blades—the side slits starting just above her knees gave her quick weapon access. The hilts would rub against the outside of her knees—uncomfortable, but not as uncomfortable as being dead. Hiding other blades with this outfit was tricky, but she managed to tuck one more down the front of her top. It worked, unless she bent over too fast.

Cheveyo's braided charm-necklace lay against the base of her throat resting below an elegant silver lace choker. The choker's matching wristbands were half-hidden under the shimmery material of her sleeves. Not wanting to mess with conflicting jewelry, she wore diamond studs in her ears. Her glamour pulsed softly along her skin, hiding her scars and tattoos from sight and touch. It was one magic she perfected and was an instantaneous disguise at the flick of a wrist. Its only flaw was that you had to alter your clothing. Nevertheless, it had saved her skin more than once.

The whole make-up and hair situation frustrated her. If Mulcahy hadn't been so adamant about her and Gavin playing up the glamorous Taliesin image, she would've left her hair down. She didn't have the patience to come up with something elaborate, so she settled on a simple chignon and stuck with the basic cosmetics, something she rarely wore.

Even those slight changes made her squirm. In her rearview mirror, her pale gray eyes surrounded by heavy lashes, seemed opaque, and her crimson covered lips were a startling contrast to her pale skin. It gave her a delicate, but foreign, appearance and should fulfill Mulcahy's orders nicely.

Getting out of her SUV, the night's chill barely made a dint thanks to her one indulgence, an opera length black velvet coat. She headed into the quiet building and noticed Gavin's car parked near the doors. She stepped off the elevator at the office level and groaned at the empty front desk. As she headed towards Mulcahy's office, she could hear her uncle's voice and Gavin's answering one.

She stepped in the doorway and their conversation ground to a halt. "Sorry, not interrupting, am I?" Her breath caught as Gavin stepped into view. Damn, she gave Alexi's earlier description credit. He was definitely a walking wet dream.

In a black tux with an oriental collar instead of bow tie,

the man was a threat to any woman's hormones. His dark hair was held back at his neck by a leather band, and the embroidered edge of the collar was the same vibrant emerald green as his eyes. Her gaze slid over his broad shoulders covered in black, across his solid chest clothed in pristine white, drifted to his tapered waist, and down his long, black-clad legs.

She realized she was shaking her head slowly and stopped. "Wow, Gavin," her voice was a bit husky, and she coughed to clear her throat. "You clean up well."

"Thanks. Not so bad yourself." His voice sounded deeper than normal and she could've sworn it carried an edge of heat.

Dear gods, she had to get herself under control! Where in the hell were these stupid hormones coming from? Didn't they know it was futile? No way was he making any moves in her direction, not after their little "discussion".

Turning to her uncle, she caught his glimpse of amusement. *Great, just great.* She took a deep breath, which turned out to be the wrong move, as the laces in the corset's back loosened, allowing the blade to slip. She pressed a hand to her chest in an effort to keep both her weapon and her top in place, cursing as heat filled her face.

Doing her best to ignore her embarrassment, she asked Mulcahy, "Is Rachel around?"

"No, she went home a few minutes ago. Why?"

Her face flamed brighter. "I need someone to help me lace up the back. I couldn't reach it."

The amusement in Mulcahy's eyes spread to his curving lips, but it was Gavin who spoke. "Drop the coat, Raine. I'll do it."

Lovely. Now she was giving everyone a good laugh. Another reason to hate wearing things like this.

Sighing, she moved closer and gave him her back. Only

then did she shrug her coat down her arms, to reveal the loosely laced top.

As he tied it off the laces, his knuckles brushed her bare skin and sent a shiver through her. Before he finished she swore she felt his fingertip trace the line of her spine. Either that, or her over active hormones were playing tricks again. Regardless, there was no stopping the eruption of goose bumps.

"There, all tied up," his voice reverberated against the bare skin of her neck, igniting wicked images in her fevered mind.

Murmuring her thanks, she put some space between them and pulled the coat back on, hoping he hadn't noticed her reaction.

"Here," Mulcahy handed the heavily embossed invitation to Gavin. "It's your ticket into the party. Keep in mind, you two are representatives for Taliesin Security tonight. Talbot hinted he was making some big announcement. Let him talk, get information on his projects, see if he lets anything slip." He reached into one of his desk drawers and drew out a slimmer envelope, which he also handed to Gavin. "This is Taliesin's donation."

Raine looked at Mulcahy. "We're giving Talbot money?"

Mulcahy got up and grabbed his coat hanging near the door. He motioned for the two of them to leave, and then followed them out, pulling his office door closed behind him. "Yes, McCord. It's a fundraiser. We're a prominent company, and regardless of what we think about Talbot and his foundation, we are going to play the game. If we didn't contribute, not only would Talbot wonder why we won't support his philanthropic endeavors, so would the rest of the mundane world. We don't want to clue him in to the fact we know what he's up to."

The group boarded the elevator and waved to the night

security in the lobby. With his hand on the door, Mulcahy eyed them both. "I told Talbot I had a conference call I couldn't reschedule, but would send my top two employees in my place. There will be press, so keep it calm in front of the cameras and don't start a fight."

She smiled. "We won't embarrass you, Mulcahy. We'll play our parts. We'll ask questions and listen, that's it."

Her boss studied her. "I hope so. Be careful." Then he was out the door and slipping inside the waiting dark sedan. She watched him settle in and give directions to the driver. Gavin moved up behind her, and she met his gaze in the reflection of the glass door.

His arm appeared around her, and pushed the door open. "Ready?"

She held his unreadable gaze and stepped outside into the chill night. "As I'll ever be."

WITHOUT SAYING A WORD, Gavin opened the passenger door to his car. Raine muttered a subdued thank you and slipped inside. He shut the door with a little more force than necessary as she occupied herself with arranging her skirt.

All right, maybe he was still angry with her. Not a big surprise. For the last few days, she made sure to be anywhere he wasn't. The few times she found herself alone with him, she discovered any possible reason to escape. For a woman who normally faced things head on, running scared did not sit well. Yet she couldn't figure her way across the very wide chasm between them.

His door opened and he climbed behind the wheel. His quick assessing glance faltered briefly on her nervous hands.

After he started the engine, she looked down and felt heat spike her cheeks. Thanks to the skirt's side slit, her twitchy hands managed to move the leather in such a way as to frame the white skin from mid-thigh to just below her knee. *Great, just flash the man!* She tugged the skirt over, hiding her pale flesh.

The silence lay heavy in the car, the tension so thick she battled the urge to scream. This shouldn't be so hard, he was just a man. Yet, here she was, stomach in knots, racking her brain for something to say. She'd rather face a rabid shifter than start this necessary conversation. Finding the courage to open her mouth took more effort than was pretty. "Do I owe you an apology, Gavin?"

He didn't even look at her. "I don't know, do you?"

His answer set her teeth on edge. Okay, so maybe this was his idea of punishment. Part of her yelled to shut up and let the conversation drop, but for the first time in a while, she ignored it. "I'm not sure."

Her answer earned a considering glance. She didn't know what he saw, but for a brief moment he seemed almost amused. Then his attention returned the road. "Look, Raine, are you really sorry you didn't tell me, or are you just sorry that you did?"

She opened her mouth to respond and then stopped. She wasn't sorry she had told him. She was actually glad. It had been a relief to tell someone, especially him. She studied him, this time to really see him.

Yeah, he was damn attractive, but she had worked with other good-looking men and hadn't felt the need to share something so personal, so painful. This man was different. His opinion mattered, because when she was with him, she wanted to be more than what she was. In him, she saw a glimpse of what she once hoped to be, before life threw her detours. She wasn't ready to put a halo on him, but the fact he knew exactly who he was and where he stood, drew her like a magnet. He made her feel safe, and that scared the crap out of her.

She cleared her suddenly dry throat. "I'm not sorry I told you." She dropped her gaze to her lap where her hands were clenched. "I actually wanted to tell you. I could never figure out when."

He gave an inelegant snort. "Any time after the initial meeting with Mulcahy would've been nice."

"Right." Her sarcasm was so thick she could have smacked him with it. "Because telling the hunter his prey is sitting right next to him is always a healthy choice."

His mouth thinned in anger at her flippant reply.

She sighed. "I messed up. I screwed up whatever partnership we had, and for that, I'm really sorry." Even to her own ears, her voice sounded wistful. "Strangely enough, I like working with you. I don't know how to fix this, but for once, I actually want to."

"I don't know if it can be fixed," his serious tone made her eyes burn. "If we were partners, you shouldn't have left me in the dark on this. It makes me wonder what other secrets you're hiding."

Her laugh was strained. "I could sit here and tell you, 'I'm not hiding anything', but you wouldn't believe me. I get it." She paused, took a breath, and gave him a bit more. "The thing is, Gavin, these 'secrets' I have? Some of them are secrets even to me. Can you understand that?"

He stopped at a light. Before she could react, he reached out and grabbed her chin between his fingers. Forcing her to meet his penetrating gaze, he leaned forward until his breath fanned over her parted lips. "Maybe I can, but if I'm going to get through this with you, you need to start facing things. Can *you* do that?"

Her heart stopped. Staring into his eyes, she realized he knew exactly what he was asking of her. The real question was, did she have the courage to take the journey, with him? The blaring of a car horn broke the moment. He muttered a curse under his breath and drove through the intersection.

The silence wasn't so heavy now, but expectation still rode the air. She stiffened her spine and kept her voice low, "I can't make any guarantees, but I can try."

His fierce smile was her only answer.

CHAPTER NINETEEN

As Gavin pulled up to the valet in front of the beautifully lit Governor Hotel in the heart of downtown Portland, Raine took in the ornate exterior. Built in the early nineteen hundreds, the landmark hotel exuded a quiet elegance now lost in some of the more modern buildings. It was a perfect setting for Talbot's fundraiser.

Gavin opened her door and offered her a hand out. She grasped his warm palm, and let him assist her out of the car. After handing his keys to the valet, he wordlessly offered his arm.

Gently placing her hand above his wrist, she savored the warmth rising from his skin, despite his clothing. His glamour lent his face a cold, glowing arrogance. She set her face to mirror his aloofness. Their arrival made those around them stop what they were doing and watch them cross the entryway. Raine wasn't surprised by the reaction. Alexi told her once that the glamour was a stark reminder of the old tales of the Shining Ones, those emotionless creatures who once preyed on the poor defenseless mortals.

Inside the lobby, ornate ceilings soared high above their

heads. While Gavin led her toward the elevators, Raine couldn't help but admire the exquisite Italian Renaissance craftsmanship.

They approached the Heritage Ballroom and the din of voices and soft music, accompanied the tings and clinks of crystal, that wafted through the double doors. The entryway framed a picture of Portland's elite. Dressed in a dazzling rainbow of colors and adorned with priceless gems, the impressive crowd glided underneath thirty-foot ceilings held aloft by detailed columns and raised panels.

On either side of the door stood two burly men in tuxes, guarding the wealthy from the peons. They straightened as Gavin and Raine approached. She didn't miss the combination of fear and awe that flashed over their faces before they managed to mask it. Inwardly, she laughed. It was amazing how jumpy mortals got when one of the Fey got a little shine on.

With supreme arrogance and barely a glance, Gavin handed their invitation to the man on his left. Within the Kyn community, the Fey were notoriously good at playing the aristocrat. Gavin did it better than most.

The guard read over the invitation, then checked it against the clipboard resting on the stand next to him. He cleared his throat, his voice almost painfully deep, "Thank you, sir. Enjoy your evening."

Without taking his attention from the room in front of them, Gavin nodded and pulled her forward.

A small, nervous looking young man appeared to their right and offered to take their coats. Raine went to remove her long coat, and her fingers brushed Gavin's as he held it steady so she could pull free. The small electric tingle when they touched pulled her gaze to his. There was a small flame hidden deep in the green shadows, an indication the momentary connection was not one sided.

"Thank you," her voice was husky.

He raised her hand as she pulled it free from the last sleeve, and brushed his lips lightly across her knuckles. "You're welcome."

She fought to keep her mask in place. *Shit! It wasn't fair.* He rattled her cage with ease. Pushing her heightened awareness of the disturbingly, sexy man next to her behind a thick mental door, she locked it down. She wasn't here to jump his bones. She was here to do a job. Despite their tentative peace, the sting of his comments on the way to Mayson's was too fresh. Tonight, they had to find out what Talbot knew.

Speak of the devil.

She caught sight of Jonah Talbot's tall figure weaving through the crowd as he made his way across the room to them. Sensing her slight stiffening stance, Gavin turned to see who caused it. They watched the blond man headed their way. Gavin leaned his head in close and asked in an undertone, "Is that Talbot?"

She turned to look up at him, which put her mouth within inches of his. "Yes."

His eyes narrowed slightly and gaze sharpened. "When did you meet him?"

Her mind blanked for a second and the realization hit when she recalled what she hadn't told Gavin days ago. "That meeting I interrupted with Mulcahy a few days back? It was with him."

Gavin searched her face for a few moments, then straightened and faced the approaching man. As the crowd ebbed and flowed around Talbot, she noticed the striking redhead attached to his arm. Raine and Gavin stood still, waiting for Talbot to reach them.

His blue eyes shone with excitement as he held out his hand to Gavin. "I'm so glad Mr. Mulcahy was able to find someone to come in his place."

Gavin shook the proffered hand. "He sends his apologies. I'm Gavin Durand, and this is Raine McCord."

Talbot's smile grew. "Ah yes, Ms. McCord, I believe we've met earlier."

She gave him her hand with a cool smile. "We have, yes, Mr. Talbot. You have a lovely gathering here." Pulling her hand back as soon as was polite, she placed it over her other one that was still resting on Gavin's arm. What she wanted to do was scrub it off, but she refrained.

The redhead gave Raine an assessing look. Her pale green eyes tried for unimpressed but failed miserably. When she turned to Gavin's dramatic figure, those same pale eyes gained an avaricious light. She must have tugged on Talbot's arm, because he looked at her, his smile cooling at whatever he read in her face.

His look was a little less friendly, and Raine got the impression he was not very happy with his companion. "My apologies, may I introduce Dr. Eden Lawson? She's the head of our research staff."

Gavin took her proffered hand, pressed a brief touch of lips, and then dropped it gently. "A pleasure."

"Jonah mentioned you two were with Taliesin Security." Icily polite, Eden flicked a glance at Raine, but it was if she was unable to tear her gaze away from Gavin. "We're so glad to have your support tonight."

"Mr. Mulcahy asked if we would review your pending projects to see if there was one which rose above the rest," Raine said, hoping to break Eden's fascinated stare. "Taliesin is always happy to lend our support to worthy causes." *And bring down those not so worthy.* Not able to say the last part out loud, it made her feel better just to think it.

"I'd be more than happy to run over those projects with you both a little later tonight," Talbot's smooth voice cut in.

"For now, Eden and I must welcome some more guests. Until later?"

"Until later," Gavin responded.

The two Kyn watched the human couple move on to the next set of guests. Gavin looked down at Raine. "Shall we?" He motioned toward the bar located on the other side of the milling crowd.

She nodded, and let him lead her out onto the floor.

As they moved through the scattered groups whispers blew like a faint wind. The two of them drew stares as they glided across the floor. An itch started up between her shoulder blades. Gavin must have noticed her reaction because he covered her hand, the one still lying on his arm, and gave it a small squeeze.

She never liked formal gatherings, and this was proving to be no exception. The small, viciously polite conversations, the edged barbs, and the insincere observations, was like fighting with invisible, edged blades made out of words and hidden implications. She found comfort in the fact, that unlike a Kyn gathering, this one should remain fairly bloodless.

An older couple intercepted them a few feet from the bar. The man stood a couple of inches shorter than Gavin, but his straight-backed posture and dress uniform made it clear he was military. His face held the polite mask, which seemed to be the norm for such get-togethers. Brown hair, silvered at the temples, was in the short cut favored by most of those in the armed forces. Sharp hazel eyes made a quick assessment of her and Gavin.

On his arm was a fine boned, gracefully poised woman whose ash blonde hair and smoky blue eyes created a picture of feminine contrast. An actual smile accompanied the delicate hand held out to Gavin, her voice smooth and warm.

"Hello, I'm Erica Cawley and this is my husband, General Mathew Cawley."

Gavin bent over her proffered hand. "Gavin Durand, and this is Raine McCord."

As Erica pulled her hand back, a slight blush tinted her cheeks a pale rose.

Raine inclined her head in acknowledgement and smothered the sigh begging to escape as another female became flustered with Gavin's attention. She needed to remember to tell him to tone it down next time he got his shine on. It was like he turned into the pied piper of women—and that was not a good thing.

The general's mellow baritone cut through his wife's slight pause. "Mr. Durand, Ms. McCord, a pleasure to meet you." He tilted his head slightly, and as he studied her, his gaze sharpened. "My apologies, Ms. McCord. Have we met before?"

"Not that I'm aware of, general." Mentally donning her armor, she entered the game. Cawley could very well know exactly who she and Gavin were and what they truly represented.

His intense regard strengthened her suspicions. "Perhaps I've had dealings with your company?"

"It's possible," Gavin interjected smoothly. "Taliesin Security works closely with various military personnel."

She caught the flash of comprehension in the general's face. Oh yeah, the man knew exactly who he was dealing with.

"Taliesin Security, the security specialists?"

"Yes sir," Raine kept her voice friendly and pleasant.

Cawley shifted his stance slightly, and subtly placed his wife behind him as his voice noticeably cooled. "I've heard of your company."

"Good things, I hope," Gavin responded.

Cawley shrugged. "Depends on who's listening. Taliesin has quite the reputation." He threw out the bait, and Raine gritted her teeth.

They had no choice but to stick this out. Reminding herself of the role she played, she forced her voice to remain calm and unconcerned, "Reputations are sometimes blown out of proportion. Professional jealousy runs rampant in every industry."

His expression gave nothing away. "Very true. Rumors say Taliesin employs some very rare and unusual talent."

Her smile never faltered, and she laughed lightly. "Rare and unusual talent? I suppose our employees could be seen as rare. We try our best to lure the top minds to our company. I would say a combination of excellent training and highly honed skills can set our employees apart, but," she shared a look with Gavin, before turning back to Cawley, "I'm not sure what you mean by unusual."

Something unpleasant drifted through the older male's gaze. "I've heard a couple of stories surrounding a small elite group employed by your company, their names known to only a few. It's my understanding they exist to take on cases others refuse."

Her heart skipped a beat, and she was grateful the Cawley's were human and couldn't hear it. Her mind worked furiously. How had he heard of the Wraiths?

Gavin's laugh almost startled Raine. "I'm not sure who you've been talking to, but I wouldn't put too much credence in their tales." If she hadn't known him so well, she would have been fooled by his light grin and easily swallowed his denial. "Our company specializes in security jobs. We protect everything from bodies to objects. We turn away business on a daily basis. Obviously someone is desperately digging for any mud to fling in our direction."

The general turned away, and snagged a drink from a

passing waiter before responding. "Perhaps you're right." He raised his gaze to Gavin's as he took a sip. "Rumors generally come from those who wished they were true."

Gavin's smile remained unruffled. "Unfortunately, in this instance, they would be sadly disappointed."

The men reminded Raine of two large dogs at a standoff.

"So General, Mrs. Cawley," she stepped into the slight silence. "What brings you out to the Talbot Foundation fundraiser?"

Erica's eyes lit up. "The foundation has made tremendous headway into developing possible cures for various illnesses. Something I follow closely with my own charity work."

"Really?" Gavin asked. "Which work is that?"

Erica seemed to falter under his attention, but she pulled herself together, apparently intent on sharing her own passion. "I work with various health care organizations in trying to find solutions to the variety of birth defects and illnesses endangering our children. It's an important cause, and one Mr. Talbot has helped out many times in the past. Without supporters like him, these causes would be lost and the children abandoned."

Raine realized Erica Cawley was a modern day crusader, one of those rare people who actually believed in her charity work. Her conviction showed in the burning intensity of her blue eyes and the fervor of the faithful, that echoed in her voice.

A small flicker of resentment flared to life inside Raine. Why was it the truly devoted people tended to be conned more easily? If, when, she silently corrected herself, Talbot was brought down, this fair haired woman would be one of those left behind to pick up the pieces. *At least she'll still be human and in one piece, though.* The quick slice from the cutting thought stilled Raine's breath for a second. Ideals, unlike a person's sense of self, could be rebuilt. Those who fell under Talbot's experiments were truly the lost ones.

"A worthy cause," Gavin's voice brought Raine back to the conversation. "The children are blessed to have such a protector as yourself on their side."

"Thank you." The pale pink returned to Erica's face.

Her husband touched her arm and turned to Gavin and Raine. "Our apologies, but unfortunately I'm required to mingle with a few others. If you'll excuse us?" The Cawleys took their leave and moved away. Raine and Gavin watched them weave their way through the ballroom.

Gavin wrapped his arm around her waist and bent his head toward her. "Shall we dance?" At her nod, he took her out on the dance floor.

Dancing with Gavin was easy, her body followed his lead naturally. Swaying in his arms, she tilted her head back and kept her voice soft so the surrounding couples wouldn't hear their conversation. "Where do you think the general heard that little tidbit?"

His jaw tightened fractionally as he moved his head closer to hers. To the other partygoers it would look intimate, when in reality he was shielding their conversation. When he answered, his voice sent shivers down her spine, "I don't know, but I don't like it."

Neither did she. The Wraiths weren't known to the mortal world. Even within the Kyn, the groups was not a commonly held belief. Mulcahy made certain no one really knew how strong they were. A necessity as they were one of Taliesin's most closely guarded Kyn secrets. The fact that a human military chief heard tales worried her. Especially since the rumor was more fact than fiction.

She turned into Gavin, nestling close as his familiar woodsy scent filled her senses. There was only one way

Cawley could have heard the stories. "We have a traitor in the Wraiths," the words came out on a mere breath of sound.

His arms tightened around her in acknowledgement.

They both knew when Mulcahy found out, things would get dangerous, real quick. If the traitor was a Wraith and working with Talbot, the threat to the Kyn community had increased dramatically. The only good news was it dropped their suspect pool to ten, instead of the whole Kyn community.

Gavin slowed and then stopped, drawing her out of her thoughts with a light touch to her chin, as he gently tilted it up. The drone of music and voices seemed to drop into silence as she felt herself falling into those shards of jade. His thumb rasped across her lower lip, once, twice until deep inside a coil of tension drew tight.

She closed her eyes in an attempt to rein in her reaction. It took a few seconds before she felt strong enough to open them.

His face was neutral, but his eyes burned.

Someone accidentally jostled her, and sound snapped back with a pop, jerking her out of his spell. She stepped away slightly, regathered her composure, and hid her spinning emotions behind a blank mask.

The edge of a sardonic smile curled his lips. Silently, he offered her his arm and led her off the dance floor.

He confused her. She had no idea what the rules were to this game he was playing. Although they seemed to have reached a tentative peace on the ride here, it was hard not to remember his reactions to her dark confession. A part of her yearned to trust these overtures, but another, more hardened part wondered if he wasn't setting her up for a humiliating fall.

Granted, her confusing emotions could make her read

things into his small actions, but why her? There were tons of women, human and Kyn, who would trip over themselves to get into his bed. Raine didn't want to ruin their working partnership, and there was no doubt sex would do just that. As long as they could work together, she didn't want to push her luck.

She hated games and so help her, if he was playing one, she didn't want a turn. It didn't help that she had her own internal argument going on. Her heart wanted to see where it would lead, but logic warned there was nowhere to go.

Oblivious to her inner turmoil, he guided her around the room. She forced her personal concerns to the background, and concentrated on the people around her. Before long, the music drew to a close and the crowd turned to the head of the ballroom where Jonah Talbot stood with a microphone in hand. His commanding presence seemed to encompass the room. As his voice filled the room, he proved that charisma was just a human form of glamour.

Gavin and Raine listened as he thanked everyone for coming out to support the Talbot Foundation. He went through the normal rounds of acknowledgements and then moved on to the sales pitch. "You all know Talbot Foundation has many arms, but there is one in particular I would like to discuss with you tonight." His face was alight with excitement as he continued, "Our research arm has been working tirelessly to help find a way to eradicate various birth defects and common diseases. Recently, we may have stumbled upon a breakthrough."

The hush filling the ballroom was deafening.

"We may have found a unique DNA strand, which so far has proven immune to most infectious diseases. We are working on duplicating this strand to create necessary antibodies to help in the fight against various illnesses."

Quiet exclamations and muted conversations ebbed

through the room like ocean waves. Raine tightened her hand on Gavin's arm as dread began to rise.

Talbot waved his arm to get everyone's attention, not a hard feat since he already had everyone's focus. The rumble of whispers died down as he continued. "Most of you don't know this, but the Talbot Foundation has been working on this particular solution for many years. Our previous attempts to pinpoint this unique DNA sequence generally ended in failure. However, as Dr. Eden Lawson, our head of research, will explain, we may be closer than ever before."

Eden took the microphone and addressed the audience. "Thank you, Mr. Talbot. Ladies and gentlemen, thank you for support tonight. I want to take a moment to publicly thank Mr. Talbot for his generous support of our research team. It's his support which has made my job such a source of joy." She turned and smiled at Talbot who stood off to the side. He smiled back.

Her smile faded and her face took on a more serious expression when she turned back to the gathering. "My team spent years trying to track down the elusive elements found in those lucky few who seem to hold a natural immunity to some of our more serious diseases. I won't bore you with the scientific details, but will simply say the discovery of this particular DNA strand may hold the key to unlocking those elements. We are on the edge of breaking the genetic code to find the answer to the ultimate antidote."

Quiet filled the ballroom as Eden continued, her smile wide, eyes bright. "For years there have been rare patients throughout the world who held a natural immunity to a variety of diseases, such as the common cold or flu, cancer, and the multitude of other debilitating illnesses. When it comes to their innate immunity, we tried to find the key that sets them apart. With the discovery of this DNA strand, we feel we are on the right path to deciphering these key genetic differences. We here at Talbot Foundation are hopeful our research will be beneficial to the entire global community."

Eden's pale green eyes paused on Raine and Gavin, held for a moment, and then moved on. "We have been able to use volunteers to aid in the gathering of information and materials. We want to thank those patients for their sacrifices. We have a long road ahead of us, but we're truly excited that this crucial first step has been made. Your donations tonight will help us in continuing our research toward improving the lives of future generations."

Loud applause filled the room at the end of her speech.

Raine's mind whirled at this new development. She didn't hear the rest of Talbot's speech, but watched Eden move off to the side, and shake hands with various individuals. The redhead worked her way toward the Cawleys. She managed to pull the general away from his wife and the two began a conversation. The general's posture was board-stiff, which made Raine wonder if he and the good doctor had an uneasy relationship.

Raine watched the conversation without appearing to stare. Cawley did not look happy with whatever Eden was saying. They seemed to have a brief argument before the general said something and Eden nodded. A few more exchanges and then they parted ways.

Gavin had been silent, watching as well. Did he have the same questions she did? What exactly did a head of research have that could be so important to a military leader? Eden's speech triggered several of Raine's internal alarms. Those so-called "patients" had to be Kyn. From the beginning, those humans in the know had marveled at how immune the Kyn races were to human illnesses.

Where on earth did Eden find her "volunteers"? The Kyn community generally steered clear of such things. Could she be behind the drug company trying to gather Kyn for its drug trials? Worry nipped on the heels of that thought. What exactly had Eden's team discovered in the unique DNA strand? Raine wasn't buying the altruistic line being spouted at tonight's gathering.

If she heeded her own line of paranoia, she could easily see how research done on the Kyn would benefit a military organization. If humans could recreate the powers the Kyn inherently held, they could strengthen and fine-tune them to what they wanted. The natural immunity the Kyn held to blood born and infectious diseases, was countered by their low birth rate, their intolerance to iron and, for some, to silver.

Add in Cawley's probe on Taliesin housing a bunch of Kyn warriors, and her sick feeling grew stronger. What if the human military wanted their own special secret weapon? What if, as had happened fifteen years ago, the humans were once again trying to play creator, except this time they may have succeeded? What if they were already able to change a human to hold some of the best traits of a Kyn, without the weaknesses?

Her face paled as she acknowledged how dangerous such a being could be, and how high the price would be for its creation.

She leaned into Gavin, and tried not to let the terrifying images playing in her mind reflect on her face. She wrestled back the nightmares seething deep within her, images she carried since she was fifteen.

Gavin looked down, his eyes blazing out of an unemotional mask, revealing he made his own unhappy conclusions. She wanted to leave immediately and report to Mulcahy. However, looking past Gavin's shoulder she saw Jonah Talbot heading toward them.

Her fingers dug into Gavin's arm and she forced her

mouth into a welcoming smile. Under her breath she warned Gavin, "Talbot's heading our way."

A deep breath shuddered through Gavin's tall frame. When she glanced back at him, his face had dropped back into character. He took her cold hand in his, rubbed his thumb slightly over the top of her hand reassuringly, and turned to face Talbot.

Talbot's smile was wide and excited. Raine couldn't figure out how he was able to hide his inner monster so well. "Thank you for staying, and I'm sorry I took so long to track you back down."

"You're a busy man, Mr. Talbot," Gavin answered. "Such gatherings require a great deal of time and effort."

Talbot chuckled softly. "That they do, a necessary evil."

Raine kept her voice light and airy, a difficult feat when she wanted to take her blade and plunge it deep into the man's heart. "That was a quite an announcement you and Dr. Lawson made. Congratulations on your discoveries. You must be so proud."

Talbot's mouth twisted into a wry grimace. "Not so much proud as relieved. I considered closing down the research branch a few years ago, before I brought Eden on board. She's brilliant and turned the department around dramatically."

"Shutting it down?" Raine prompted. This was an interesting twist.

Talbot nodded and snagged a drink from another of those passing waiters. "Genetic research is costly and has more failures than successes. Before I brought Eden on, I lost my head of research, Dr. Manheim. I started to believe the department was a loss. When I hired Eden, I told her she had two years to find something or it would be finished." He raised his glass slightly in a mock toast. "She came through, so I'm honoring my end of the bargain."

"I'm impressed," Gavin said.

Talbot raised a quizzical eyebrow. "With?"

Gavin's smile held a hint of the predator beneath his clothes. "Your research team. They must be very persuasive to have been able to find such willing patients to take part in your research."

Talbot's face cooled a notch. "I'm aware of the stories surrounding my father and his work. I am not the man my father was, Mr. Durand." His gaze was steady, seemingly sincere, but Raine wasn't sure she bought it. "However," he added, "Dr. Lawson assured me all volunteers were just that —volunteers."

Not expecting Jonah to make such revealing statement, Raine's mask slipped for a second.

What kind of game was he playing? Searching his face closely, she couldn't detect any signs of the madness his father displayed. A sickening thought wormed its way into her mind. What if Jonah had nothing to do with what was going on?

Her world tilted.

"Mr. Talbot," she said, struggling to keep her voice level, "we did not mean to offend you, but you must recognize our concerns."

He dropped his head for a second and when he looked back up, she caught a glimpse of deep sorrow. "I know the rumors surrounding my father and his work, Ms. McCord. All I can say is as far as I am aware, that mentality no longer exists at the Talbot Foundation. I know under my father's leadership the foundation took turns I would never support. I've spent most of my life trying to make up for my father's mistakes."

She wasn't sure she believed him, but if she read him correctly, he meant every word he said. She wanted away from this gathering, away from Talbot and his foundation. She needed to think and she wanted to talk to Gavin.

Gavin and Talbot continued chatting for a couple of minutes. Then Talbot shook Gavin's hand and said good night to Raine.

His gaze turned considering as he placed a kiss on her hand. "It's been a pleasure meeting you, Ms. McCord. Please send my heartfelt thanks to Mr. Mulcahy for his generous donations."

She nodded absently and wished him a good night. Gavin gently led her out of the ballroom. She said nothing as they waited for the valet to bring his car around. When they headed off into the night, she softly voiced the one question spiraling in her head. "What have they done?"

CHAPTER TWENTY

Raine was still asking herself the same question the next morning when she scanned the parking lot as she strode to Taliesin's front door. With her hair pulled back in a ponytail, dressed in faded jeans, boots, and a soft green sweater, she no longer looked like the magically untouchable Fey who attended last night's function.

She crossed the lobby and hit the elevator. On the ride up, she found herself unconsciously stroking the silver lynx charm. She found she liked wearing Cheveyo's gift for some reason. Besides, right now, she could use all the comfort she could find.

Talbot's frank statement regarding his father's activities created small cracks in her deep seated belief of Talbot and his foundation. The whole 'admit to knowing the evils of his father'—and then making it oh-so-clear he didn't tolerate such behavior—could be a clever way to deflect suspicion.

She got off the elevator and headed to her office, her mind churning. She closed the door, crossed to the tall window, and stared blindly at the city and wilderness intertwining into a typical Portland landscape.

If Talbot wasn't just an evil prick who could lie better than anyone she had ever met—which was saying something —and was truly an innocent dupe in whatever scheme was going on, then who was pulling the strings in this game? She crossed her arms and leaned against the windowsill, her breath fogging the glass.

The more disturbing question that kept her tossing and turning the night before still remained. What if Jonah Talbot was exactly as he appeared? So wrapped up in her own anger and need for revenge, she never tried to look in any other direction. If she had, would she have found someone else?

Okay, she needed to start back at the beginning, remove Jonah Talbot from the equation, and try this again. She turned toward her desk when a knock jerked her out of her thoughts. "Come in."

The door opened and Gavin, dressed in his typical jeans and T-shirt, stepped inside, his gaze scanning the small office. There wasn't much to it. Empty of personal pictures or touches, the warm wood tones and potted plants filling the corners and niches gave it a cozy vibe.

She snuck a quick look at the clock sitting on her desk. "Wasn't our meeting in another fifteen?"

"It is." He studied her carefully. "But I wanted to talk with you before we head into Mulcahy's office."

She waved him to one of the chairs in front of her desk. "I'm listening."

He didn't move, but asked, "Long night?"

She grimaced. Figured he'd notice the dusky circles under her eyes. "Couldn't sleep."

"Yeah, I get that," he muttered.

Guess she wasn't the only one tossing and turning last night. She took her chair and pulled one leg up under her.

He settled into the chair in front of the desk. "We need to

figure out what's going on here because we're missing something."

She sighed. "I was just thinking the same thing."

Running his hand impatiently through his hair, he managed to dislodge the leather tie holding it back. "Want to talk through it with me?" He leaned down to pick it up.

She nodded, captivated as he refastened the tie in his hair. It was so silly, but no matter what he did, it fascinated her. She dropped her gaze quickly, not wanting to be caught staring.

Hair secured, he leaned back. "Okay, so we start at the beginning. Jonah Talbot comes to Taliesin to look into the deaths of his employees. He's waited a while to do this, so we have two possible conclusions. Either he failed in his attempt to breach Taliesin's security and wants a way to watch how we work, up close and personal."

"Or," she broke in. "If he's on the up and up, he really is concerned about his life. Maybe the last death was one too many for his peace of mind and he wants answers."

Gavin continued, "Either way, he turns down protection from Taliesin. Why?"

She absently played with a pencil. "Say he's involved, protection from Taliesin would put us too close to his personal life. He could be worried about slipping up some-where. If he's not involved, he may not want our protection. Especially given what he knows his father did to the Kyn. It's not smart to ask the fox to guard the henhouse, especially if it involves a fox with an ax to grind."

Gavin nodded. "I can see that. So our next piece is the company behind the drug research, Polleo. We can trace it back to the Talbot Foundation. That same company approached a wizard and a witch, and shortly thereafter the wizard disappears and the witch goes into hiding."

"Don't forget, we got jumped outside Zarana's." She tapped the pencil's eraser against the desk. "Which means our questions set off alarms somewhere."

His smile was grim. "Right, then there's our trip to Polleo, which ended with nothing more than a bunch of cryptic notes and possible traces of our wizard, but nothing definitive."

There was one thing about their B&E adventure that still bothered her. "Don't you think it was a tad easy getting into that lab?" When he frowned, she added, "If the lab was involved, wouldn't it be heavily guarded?"

The frown smoothed out as he considered her point. "Very possible. Could be our tracing the finances set off some flags and they cleared out what they could."

Yeah, maybe. "Or it could've been a ruse to keep us chasing our tails," she muttered.

"Either way, the lab is a dead end." He shifted slightly. "Which takes us to Bane Mayson's call, saying he has information to share."

She used her foot to rotate her chair from side to side, as she turned the pieces over. "And a handful of hours later he's dead. That tells me someone's watching us, or they were watching Bane."

"Right." Gavin ran a hand around the back of his neck and rubbed. "Whoever it is, they're coordinated and fast."

She aimed a quizzical look his way.

"We hit Portland, what? Three, maybe four hours later to find our missing wizard sliced and diced at Zarana's. No one sees anything, no one hears anything."

Okay, granted, that was worrisome. "Alexi said she felt something against her wards, something she didn't recognize. It's why she went out. She wanted to see who, or what, managed to breach them."

"I can see that." He rubbed a hand over his chin. "We end

up at the party last night where Talbot's head of research drops her bomb that they think they've found a unique, highly immune, DNA strand." A thread of heat wound through his voice and his face darkened. "I'm damn sure that DNA is Kyn, which raises another set of questions and concerns despite Dr. Lawson's assurance her guinea pigs were volunteers."

Raine's lip curled in disdain, while contempt bled into her voice. "I don't quite believe that. No Kyn would voluntarily put themselves in a scientist's hands. Where the hell is she getting her samples?"

Gavin shrugged.

Raine sighed. "In case all of that wasn't enough, we've got the general fishing for information on a secret Kyn army."

"Someone's talking out of school," Gavin growled.

"No shit," she shot back. "And the cherry on top," the hardest to swallow as far as she was concerned, "we have Talbot's fervent denial of not being a chip off the old block."

Gavin's eyes narrowed. "Do you believe him?"

She stilled her chair, shrugged, and sent the pencil rolling along her desk. "I'm trying to figure out if he's the world's greatest liar or a naïve dupe. If he's lying, then he's even more dangerous than his father."

She pinched the bridge of her nose. "But if Talbot's telling the truth, is he truly ignorant of what's happening in his company? Because someone at the foundation is involved."

She dropped her hand, took a breath, and listened to her own voice say, "If it's not Talbot, my next bet is Dr. Lawson and the general."

She must have flinched because Gavin gave a wry grin. "Bet that hurt to say."

"You have no idea," she groused. "What do we tell Mulcahy?"

His grin faded and exhaustion etched lines around his

mouth. "That the human military is working with the Talbot Foundation and may be creating their own Kyn/human hybrid army. Just in case that's not enough of a challenge, there's a leak somewhere in Taliesin, and the next Kyn they trap will likely be a Wraith."

CHAPTER TWENTY-ONE

Raine and Gavin met with Mulcahy to share their thoughts and conclusions. Mulcahy didn't react until they came to the part where they voiced their theory the leak was a Wraith.

His eyes went scarily cold, as did his voice. "How sure are you it's a Wraith?"

"We're not," Gavin stated. "But since we're the only group of Kyn who know the Wraiths aren't an urban myth, evidence suggests a Kyn in the know would have to spill for Wraiths to ping on the humans' radar."

Mulcahy nodded and gestured for them to continue. When they finally finished, he was quiet for a few minutes, thinking things through. Raine could almost see him running various scenarios and drawing conclusions, dismissing those that didn't fit.

Finally, he broke the silence. "We need more information on this Dr. Eden Lawson and what she's found. I'll see if Rachel can get a hold of Talbot and the good doctor. I need to take them up on their offer of a tour of their offices. Durand, I need you to dig up as much background as you can on Dr. Lawson." He turned his attention to her and kept issuing commands. "McCord, if I can get this tour, you're coming with me. In the meantime, I want you to see how much information you can gather on the Cawleys."

Orders delivered, he waved them out of his office. Raine closed the door behind her as he asked Rachel to contact Talbot and arrange a meeting, today if possible. She headed down to research to start unearthing what she could on the general and his wife.

Interestingly enough, there was quite a bit. Cawley had a distinguished record of service to his country. He came from a military family and carried on the family tradition of service, rising quickly to his command post.

He married Erica Waverly, the daughter of a southern businessman who made his first million at the tender age of twenty. The Cawley's had two children, both high school age and currently residing at private boarding schools. The practice of sending children away to school always puzzled Raine. If you had children, why wouldn't you want them around?

The general's history read like a perfect example of a military man on the fast track. His current post was blacked out. Trying to get into sealed military records was more than she could handle, so she turned it over to one of the research techs. Hopefully something would pop, but she wasn't holding her breath. Cawley's current project was sealed under so many locks it would take a computer Houdini to release it.

She made a point of asking the tech to get through without raising any flags. The general's records were squeaky clean—almost extraordinarily so—and it set off her internal alarms like a klaxon. Something was buried deep, but she wasn't sure anyone at Taliesin would be able to uncover it.

Around one, she got the call from Rachel to meet Mulcahy downstairs for their appointment with Talbot. She headed toward the elevators, and sighed when she caught sight of her jeans-clad reflection in the glass doors. She was definitely underdressed for the meeting, but there wasn't much she could do about it.

A few minutes later, she sank into the dark leather passenger seat of Mulcahy's sleek black BMW sedan. He and Gavin seem to share a love of a fine automobile.

Unobtrusively, she studied her uncle. He drove with the same deliberate control that marked every aspect of his character. His hair was unruffled and his Armani suit impeccable. Watching him, she realized not once in their relationship had she ever seen him off balance or unsettled. There had been anger, coldness, hints of a wickedly dry humor, and his normal business-like mien, but she couldn't remember any softer emotions. For the first time she wonders at what happened to make him such a controlled being?

"Do I have something on my face, McCord?" his voice broke through the silence simmering in the plush interior.

She shook her head slightly, mortified to have been caught staring. "Are we meeting just Talbot for this little tour?"

"Actually, no. It seems Dr. Lawson was excited at the prospect of visiting supporters and would enjoy showing us her lab and research."

She frowned. "Excited?"

He shrugged.

"That makes zero sense if she's been doing what we think she has."

She met Mulcahy's gaze briefly before he focused on the road again. For a moment, she thought she'd seen a flicker of gentle amusement. It made her wonder what he saw when he looked at her.

When she was younger, she would comfort herself with stories of how he loved her. She convinced herself his cold demeanor was a shield, covering his guilt and shame at being unable to save his beloved sister and her only child.

The illusion faded when she ran across a picture of her mother and realized how alike they looked. Similar enough that Raine decided it wasn't any gentle emotion tightening Mulcahy's face when he really looked at her, but resentment. Resentment she was alive, not her mother.

His voice brought her back to the present. "It makes perfect sense. It's the concept of hiding in plain sight. Dr. Lawson has probably decided it will negate any questions we have on her work if she appears to be open to letting us see what she's accomplished."

She raised an eyebrow at the dry tone in his voice. "So she's showing off?"

"That would be my guess."

She watched the passing scenery as they headed into downtown Portland. Trees gave partial glimpses into buildings hidden behind thick foliage. The overcast skies lent the developing downtown skyline a blurry edge. "Is Talbot a player in her game, do you think?" Her deceptive casualness belied the importance of his answer.

Out of the corner of her eye, she caught the reflexive tightening of his fingers on the steering wheel before he relaxed them once more. "I don't have enough information to give you an answer." His response was as bland as his tone. When the BMW pulled into a parking spot outside the Talbot Foundation's main office, he slid her a sharp look. "Why is it you want him to be guilty?"

She met his penetrating gaze with an unemotional one and challenged, "Why is it you want him to be innocent?"

"I never said he was, Raine." There was an edge of something she couldn't identify in his voice. "However, I don't judge the children for their parents' actions." With that, he opened his door and got out.

Liar! Her mental voice hissed. The barb wedged deep as she watched him stop at the doors to look back at her. She kept her expression blank, hiding the impact of his verbal hit. She wasn't up to playing on her uncle's level, but one day he would stab too deep, and when the bleeding stopped, there would be nothing left between them.

She straightened her shoulders, got out, and walked up behind the man she knew would never love her, never trust her, and forever blame her for his beloved sister's death.

CHAPTER TWENTY-TWO

The Talbot Foundation was almost as impressive as Taliesin's offices. To Raine's mind the sleek lines, modern edges, glass walls, and gleaming steel were more intimidating than welcoming. She followed Mulcahy across the marbled tiles to the front desk where he gave their names and, like the magic they lived with, they were ushered into a private elevator. When the doors opened, plush carpet stretched along the hallway of the top floor and lead to a set of imposing wooden doors.

As they approached, one of those doors opened and Talbot appeared, dressed in modern businessman attire, complete with dark pinstripe slacks, deep blue shirt, and a tie that brought the shirt and slacks together. Raine bet there was a jacket somewhere in his office. He wore a welcoming smile and an air of excitement. In her role as Mulcahy's official bodyguard and unofficial extra set of eyes and ears, she stayed a couple of steps behind.

"Mr. Mulcahy," Talbot's greeting was cheerful. "I'm so glad you found the time to visit." He aimed his charm her way and offered his hand. "Ms. McCord, a pleasure."

She took it and gave him a nod.

Jonah turned back to Mulcahy. "Won't you come in?" He motioned them both inside. "I have coffee, or tea if you'd like, before we tour the offices."

She followed Mulcahy in, but stayed near the door. Her boss took a seat in front of the black walnut desk, behind which a set of floor-to-ceiling bookcases dominated the wall space. A nice, flat-screen TV, complete with sound system, hung on the wall beside the door. Papers were strewn across the desk, while a sleek desktop computer sat on one end. Like Mulcahy's office, the occupant could enjoy the breathtaking scenery afforded by massive windows on the far side of the room. The only difference was the view—Mulcahy's was courtesy of Mother Nature, and Talbot's was the manmade beauty of downtown Portland.

The two men exchanged pleasantries and general conversational gambits about mutual acquaintances while she listened with a half an ear. She scanned the titles of the books lining the shelves behind Talbot, and noted a variety of subjects. Not only were there a great many historical texts involved, but a few Kyn texts were tucked discreetly in-between. Photos of Talbot alongside a number of local movers and shakers were scattered throughout the office. The typical one with the mayor, the governor and, if she wasn't mistaken, he even had one with the current president. Interestingly she didn't see one with his late father.

There was a soft knock at the door, and Raine turned as it swung open.

Dr. Eden Lawson strolled in, her expression cooling dramatically when she caught sight of Raine. Today the good doctor sported a black skirt ending just above the knees and three-inch heels to showcase her legs. The ivory colored shirt was severe, but on her looked feminine. Her red hair was in a complicated French twist Raine would never master.

After a quick dismissive appraisal of Raine's worn jeans, scuffed boots, and oversized sweater, Eden turned her charisma on Mulcahy. "Mr. Mulcahy, a pleasure to meet you, finally," her sultry voice wrapped around the room as she offered him her hand. "Jonah has told me so much about you."

"Nothing too unpleasant, I hope," Mulcahy answered, bringing Eden's hand up for a brief brush of lips across her knuckles. A faint rose tinted the good doctor's cheeks. Raine stifled a grin as Mulcahy played the charm game with innate ease.

Eden gave a tinkling laugh. "Not at all, I assure you."

"Well then," Jonah cut in, regaining Mulcahy's attention. "What would you like to see first? We have a few projects in progress which might interest you."

"Why don't we start in the lovely doctor's lab?" Mulcahy suggested, turning to Eden again. "I'd be honored to see your work on DNA. It sounds fascinating, not to mention ground-breaking."

Appearing slightly flustered at Mulcahy's intense regard, Eden tucked a non-existent strand of hair behind her ear. "I guess we'll start in the labs, then." She glanced at Jonah and demurred prettily, "If that's all right with you, Jonah?"

Watching the show, Raine thought she caught a glimpse of irritation in Talbot's guileless eyes. It was so swift she wasn't sure. Instead, she gave herself a mental shake. More likely, she was projecting her own irritation at the shining Eden and Mulcahy seemed intent on doing to each other.

Talbot came from behind his desk and headed toward the door. "Sounds like a plan to me. Shall we?" He held it open as Eden walked out, followed by Mulcahy. Talbot gestured to Raine. "After you."

She kept her expression casual and her tone light, "Actually I prefer to stay in the background while I'm working, if you don't mind."

He raised an eyebrow, his tone teasing, "You consider this visit work?"

She managed a polite close-lipped smile. "I'm not here for the visit. I'm here for Mulcahy." She followed him into the carpeted hallway and waited while he closed the office door.

He moved to walk beside her as they headed toward Eden and Mulcahy who waited by the elevator. "For Mulcahy?" He sounded puzzled. "Like a bodyguard?"

"Exactly that," she answered.

"Why would he need a bodyguard here?" There was a hint of offense in his question.

Mulcahy caught the tail end of the conversation, and answered it smoothly, "An unfortunate drawback of my position. I rarely go anywhere without an assistant."

"Assistant?" cut in Eden as the doors gave a soft ping and began to open.

Mulcahy waved her in before holding the doors for Talbot. Only then did he step in ahead of Raine. "McCord is one of a handful of my employees with the ability to combine her considerable talent in security details and extensive skills as an executive assistant into one efficient position."

"So I shouldn't be offended you feel a bodyguard is a necessity when visiting me?" Talbot's tone carried a wry twist.

Mulcahy's smile was his most civilized. "Not at all. For us it's simply standard procedure. Besides, I always have need of an assistant."

Eden shivered delicately. "It seems such a harsh way to live."

"Not harsh, Dr. Lawson," Mulcahy was casually dismissive. "It's simply the way things are."

The elevator doors opened into a bustling lab, which would be the envy of any research center. Raine followed behind the group, noting the various station littered with esoteric equipment she couldn't even begin to understand. Muted conversations flowed from one area to another. She tuned out the historical tour as she followed behind the small group.

The lab was laid out in a circle. Closed doors with retinal and fingerprint security guarded various entry points. These doors seemed to lead into another level. There were surveillance cameras placed thorough out. Computer stations were locked down, unless they were in use. Walking between stations, as Talbot and Eden expounded on their lab's achievements, Raine watched a tech place his thumb on a fingerplate sunk into the desk before the computer screen lit up, requesting a login and password. Whiteboards were covered in a jumble of letters and numbers, which were totally incomprehensible to her.

"What do you think, Ms. McCord?" Talbot pulled her back into the conversation.

"I think your security here is impressive," she kept her tone polite. "I do have one question for you."

He smiled briefly. "Ask."

She motioned out to the lab floor layout. "Why a circle?"

His smile widened. "Actually, it worked security-wise to design the labs this way. Each progressive floor requires a higher level of security clearance. There are five levels, each a bit smaller in square footage, but more defined in their objectives."

"Each project requires a different amount of research and experimentation," chimed in Eden. "Unfortunately, we can only show you this floor, as some of our other projects are under a higher level of security. Our religious artifacts must be kept in temperature-and-humidity-controlled rooms to protect their integrity." She led them into a white walled conference room.

"That makes complete sense," Mulcahy agreed. "We wouldn't want to endanger any of the progress your labs have achieved."

Eden gave a light laugh. "We aren't worried you'd endanger our progress. We like to keep things to ourselves until we're certain of our findings."

Talbot, Mulcahy, and Eden took seats around the black table. Raine picked a spot behind Mulcahy and resumed a familiar post against a wall. Her position gave her line of sight to the only door. A laptop sat next to Eden's chair on the far end of the table and a white screen blanketed the opposite wall.

"Speaking of findings," Talbot said. "Why don't we show you how we found the DNA strand, and how we hope it will benefit society?" The lights dimmed. He and Eden moved into their presentation with a confidence that spoke of a well-rehearsed routine directed toward interested backers.

The information Eden shared was not much more than what she had relayed at the party. It didn't take long before Raine realized Eden was quite aware of the existence of the Kyn. Two years ago, Eden, as the assistant to the previous head of research, was given access to quite a few delicate secrets. It took her two more long years and many frustrating tests before she managed to get the genetic strands separated. She made it clear the reason this particular discovery took so long was due to the fact it was hard to find volunteers with Kyn blood.

"How did you find Kyn willing to donate, Dr. Lawson?" Raine broke in, her quiet voice slicing through the room.

"To be honest, Ms. McCord," Eden said, her voice stiff. "Our volunteers were difficult to come by as they tend not to want to make their presence known."

Raine held Eden's icy gaze. "That's an evasive answer, doctor."

Anger sparked, but was quickly banked. "Some of our employees were able to persuade friends to come in for blood work. However, due to confidentiality, we are unable to reveal those donors."

Eden moved onto the next slide and opened her mouth to discuss the next point, but Raine cut her off. "Excuse me, but I have another question."

Eden's mouth snapped shut and her lips tightened in annoyance. "I'll try to answer as best I can."

Civility, coated in frigid tones indicated Raine was indeed pissing off the good doctor. Too damn bad. "It is my under-standing—and past experience—that scientific tests do not generate consistent, definitive results with organic Kyn samples."

Eden's shoulders tightened and her gaze hardened as it gained a speculative gleam. "I was unaware you have a scien-tific research background, Ms. McCord."

"I don't."

"Then your understanding is based on what?"

Raine kept her tone even. "Working a variety of murder scenes with the FBI, local law enforcement, and their crime technicians."

Talbot cleared his throat. "It's a fact that most labs are unable to get consistent data or clean results off of Kyn traces. The magic inherent to being Kyn interferes with the scientific laws."

"How did your labs manage to get clean results?" Mulc-ahy, clearly following the thread of Raine's question, joined in.

Talbot appeared undaunted and self-assured. "We have superior equipment. In combination with Dr. Lawson and her team, we've been able to cull those results which vary, and isolate the variables so we could formulate a solid conclusion based upon what was remained."

Mulcahy tilted his head, his gaze sharp. "How close are you really to isolating and replicating this DNA strand?"

"Our test results are coming in at ninety percent accuracy at this point," Eden announced confidently.

Mulcahy's lips took on a sardonic curve. "I'll ask again, how close are you really to achieving your claims of curing humankind?"

Eden smiled, emanating supreme confidence in her work and skills. "Closer than anyone else has ever come."

A light knock on the conference room door interrupted the meeting. Talbot turned up the lights and opened the door, while Eden shut off the presentation.

A polished young man stood in the doorway, his voice low, but not so low for Raine to miss what he said. "I'm sorry to interrupt, Mr. Talbot, but General Cawley is here to meet with Dr. Lawson."

Talbot's stance stiffened slightly as he thanked the messenger, closed the door, and turned to Eden. "Dr. Lawson, your appointment is here," he said, his tone cool.

The doctor shot Jonah a look before turning smoothly to say goodbye to Mulcahy. There was some tension there over General Cawley, which made Raine curious. Why wouldn't Jonah approve of the general?

Mulcahy rose to take Eden's hand. Talbot watched with a closed expression as she left the room. He gave himself a slight shake. "My apologies, shall we continue on with the tour?"

Mulcahy glanced at his watch. "Perhaps next time, Mr. Talbot," he said, his voice apologetic. "I also have a meeting I must attend. Perhaps we can make another appointment?"

Raine followed the two men out of the lab. Eden and General Cawley were on the other side of the reception area, waiting for an elevator. While Talbot and Mulcahy exchanged goodbyes, Raine watched Eden use a sharp hand gesture during an obviously heated argument with the general.

What the hell was going on with those two? The general was plainly not happy with Eden, nor she with him. Maybe between Gavin's research into Eden's background and the Taliesin research team's on the general, the key between the two would be revealed.

Just then the general looked in their direction and met Raine's stare. The palatable fury in his gaze sent a shiver down her spine. That man was seriously pissed.

"Until later, Ms. McCord?" Talbot's voice broke the unexpected staring contest.

She turned and met those blue eyes, eyes from this close up, she realized, came from his father. She fought back another shiver and shook his hand briefly, keeping her tone cool. "Perhaps, Mr. Talbot."

She couldn't afford to forget where this charming man came from. It was too dangerous. Turning, she followed Mulcahy out of the Talbot Foundation building and its myriad of secrets.

CHAPTER TWENTY-THREE

The waning sun heralded the coming evening. Cool air, with a hint of a bite, flowed into the SUV as Raine drove home. When she and Mulcahy returned from Taliesin, Gavin's report was waiting. Eden Lawson's history was interesting to say the least.

Her mother died from ovarian cancer when she was young, and her father worked for one of Aaron Talbot's labs. When Eden was sixteen, her father had a fatal stroke, leaving her everything. Money enough for her to go off to medical school, where she earned top honors in biogenetic chemistry. Upon graduation, determined to solve various genetic defects, she went to work overseas, jumping around third world countries with a research team. When she returned a few years later, she approached the Talbot lab for a job. Once hired, she worked her way steadily up the ladder.

Last year, with the tragic death of the previous head of research, Dr. Evan Manheim, she was promoted from assistant director to director. Manheim was one of the three deaths that did not belong to Raine. It made her wonder what his cause of death was, and if Eden had anything to do with it. Raine made a note to remember to ask Gavin if Manheim was part of the two-for-one car accident or the suicide. Of course her dislike of Eden Lawson could be coloring her assumptions.

Eden was single and appeared at a number of functions with Jonah Talbot. Remembering Talbot's behavior the night of the party, and again today at the lab, Raine figured the couple situation was more about convenience than actual chemistry. Not to mention Talbot and Eden seemed married to their jobs, another good indicator dating wasn't a huge priority.

As for the Cawleys, the research team hit dead end after dead end. One team member told her he could keep digging and break through the security levels, except there was a very high chance his movements would send up a flag and bring their actions unwanted attention.

She turned onto the road leading home, and drove through the few acres that created the isolation she craved. Even more appealing was the natural forest that made up the majority of her backyard. A small touch to her wards confirmed no company had dropped by. Grateful for the respite, she parked the SUV in her garage and walked to her house.

After relocking her front door, she took off her boots, and padded over her wooden floors in sock-covered feet. She dropped her keys in the purple glass bowl sitting on the small entry table, and headed into her bedroom.

Restless and antsy, she decided to go for a run. She stripped out of her jeans and sweater, and pulled on a pair of black running pants and matching shirt. She laced up her Nikes, and decided not to take any blades with her. Sweat under the blade sheaths made them itchy—besides she was in her own territory. Should anyone decide to come visit, her wards would give her plenty of warning.

After warming up on the back porch, she headed into the woods. As she concentrated on her breathing and the soft sound of her feet hitting the ground, her restlessness slowly started to calm. Testing her body, she moved faster, doing her best to stay silent and not disturb the natural rhythms of the night.

Moonlight traced silvered patterns through the leaves, and shadows fell fast and thick like an inky cloak. Her night vision kicked in, bathing her surroundings in a surreal glow. The air was cool, crisp, and its fingers caressed her face as she lifted it to the rising moon.

Moving through the thick woods like smoke, she lost herself in the magic and freedom of the night. She didn't have to watch her every move or word. Here, in this place, she was free to just be the Kyn she was—magic held in human form.

Suddenly the night sounds fell silent. A tremor ran through her wards and she stopped as if hitting an invisible wall. She dropped her psychic barriers and sent that magical part of her out to locate the intruder. She tilted her head slightly. *There—to the west, back near the bridge over the creek.*

She waited, barely breathing, and then a second tremor hit, a little more south, quickly followed by another. Three intruders had penetrated her wards. It wouldn't matter if they were human or Kyn, either way they were trespassing.

She turned around and started back to her house, trying to determine how many were headed toward her. She used the deep shadows as camouflage and made her way silently. This was her land and she was intimately acquainted with every inch of it.

Her dark hair and clothing helped her disappear into the night-shrouded forest. Shadow Walking wasn't an option because she could miss too many details on the prey she tracked. Right now, she was reconsidering her decision on her blades.

As she closed in on the edge of the woods, she paused, then crouched down to watch.

A few minutes passed before she saw a dark-clad figure stealthily creep around the edge of her house and up the steps to her back door. When his fingers touched the knob, a silent explosion threw him backward. No noise, no light, just his crumpled form indicating he tripped a ward.

She smirked, her night vision coloring the scene in shades of red and orange. The asshole should've known better than to break into the house of a Fey. Too stupid to recognize when a door was warded, they had to be human.

He groaned softly, rolled to his knees, and shook his head. Another figure appeared, darting toward the kneeling man. The two males—one standing at least six two, the other still kneeling—spoke in low voices that carried on the night air. With her enhanced sense of hearing, she had no problems eavesdropping.

"You okay?" the tall one asked.

"Yeah," the first one hissed. "Damn door was a trap."

Quick on the uptake, aren't you, buddy? She waited to see if the third one would come out to play.

The taller of the two helped the other to his feet. He was shorter, maybe five ten or so, but solid. The two men headed toward the woods. Their hand gestures hinted at military training.

Considering the mistakes made so far, their training had to be minimal. Something to consider. Still no sign of the third one, but she could lead these two on a merry chase.

Silent and quick, she slipped through the trees to a middle point between the two intruders. Their progress was slower, and their efforts to move quietly, futile. As they drew near to her position, she snapped a fallen twig with her foot.

The noise echoed like a gunshot in the night. The men's foot-steps stopped short.

She sprinted across their path—giving them a glimpse of her dark shadow—then raced into the woods.

The chase was on.

Eventually she'd have to circle around behind them, but for now she would stay far enough ahead to keep them hooked. Locating the tree she needed to put her plan into action, she leaped onto a huge bough stretched across her path. Grabbing ahold, she pulled herself into the branches and scrambled out of sight. Although, the last was probably unnecessary as few hunters ever looked up.

She stretched along a higher branch whose ample leaves provided cover, and waited until her two pursuers stopped underneath her position. They communicated with economic hand signals, and then spread out in a search pattern. When they moved away, she slipped out of the tree, careful not to give her position away, and dropped lightly to the ground.

The hunters' invasion on top of her rising frustration over the situation with Talbot, and—on some deeper level—the confusion and hurt from Gavin and her uncle, all came together, loosening the chains that kept her in line.

Throwing caution on the metaphorical trash heap, she summoned her twisted magic. It answered with a roar of dark glee that reverberated in her mind. Refusing to listen to the small voice warning her there was no going back, she cracked open that locked door—just enough to pull on the magic she needed.

It was time to utilize some old skills.

She focused on her right hand, and her nails slowly lengthened into sharp, deadly claws, the fingers slightly longer and thinner than normal. The transformation stopped when all five nails were as lethal as knife blades.

Gliding to her left, she followed the shorter one. The hunters were now the hunted. Stalking him with cold efficiency, she waited for the right spot to take him down.

He paused near a large tree, apparently unsure which way to go.

Moving up behind him, she tapped him on the left shoulder. As he turned his head toward her, eyes wide with surprise, she whipped her right hand, claws extended, in a quick, deadly stroke across his neck, ripping out his throat. Scarlet ribbons exploded from his carotid artery and jugular vein.

He raised his hands in a futile attempt to stop the bleeding while she sent up a silent prayer his partners were too far away to hear the faint gurgling emanating from his shredded windpipe.

She caught the man when he collapsed, dragged him behind a huge old tree, and covered him with leaves and debris. The coppery smell of blood combined with the adrenaline from the hunt sent her heart rate racing, even as it fed the vicious monster under her skin. She wiped her clawed hand on the fallen leaves as the thin level of civility that allowed her to function in the world crumbled to ash, leaving behind the predator.

The thrill of the chase rose, and she pulled her lips back from her sharpened teeth in a nearly silent snarl. Her reality narrowed to the hunt for the second man and the eventual kill. The third showed no signs of joining the party. Yet.

She struggled with her animalistic nature, and forced it to obey her will. Her animal moved instinctually, not intelligently, and she couldn't afford to make any mistakes tonight.

Heading in the direction of the taller man, she noted the faint signs of his passing. A broken leaf there, an impression of a heel here, the tingling sense—of something close by—that niggled at her gut.

A slight noise to her right pulled her up short. Acting on impulse, she threw herself flat on the ground.

The unmistakable sound of metal driving into wood assaulted her ears. Glancing over her shoulder she saw a black handled knife, still vibrating, impaled in the bark of a tree where her throat had been.

Her prey had gotten behind her. Bastard.

Rolling to her left, she surged to her feet, just in time to block a savage kick aimed at her head. Grabbing his leg just below the knee, she twisted hard, throwing her attacker to the ground.

He executed a twisting somersault and regained his feet, another knife clutched in his hand. His face was covered in camouflage paint, making the whites of his eyes and teeth the only features she could discern in the darkness.

The man growled low in his throat as they slowly circled each other.

Raine kept her right hand down along her side, hoping he hadn't seen her unique set of knives.

Without warning, he moved in, knife slashing, as he executed a series of punches and kicks designed to keep her off balance.

She dodged each thrust. Then made her first mistake. She jerked out of the way of his knife and ended up in the path of his incoming kick. The impact numbed her right arm.

The man's laugh was low and evil.

The animal inside snapped its leash and snarled. Her vision turned red with rage, and she succumbed to the searing heat.

Her attacker slashed out with another punch-kick combination, but she blocked the incoming strike. Ignoring the pain in her right arm, she grabbed her assailant by the wrist, dug her claws in, and snapped the bone with one quick twist.

His sharp cry of pain was quickly followed by a soft thud as he dropped the knife.

Lost in her animal's hunger and rage, she didn't stop. She seized his throat and dug her nails in. His pulse thundered against her fingertips. She flexed, carving her claws in deeper and squeezing his larynx like a pair of vice-grips. She shook him once, hard, then threw him against a tree.

His head rebounded with a solid *thunk* and he slid to the ground.

She secured the man's dropped knife and stalked toward him.

Propped against the tree he watched her close the distance, his eyes the only thing moving in his grease-painted face. Muddy brown and filled with panic they darted from side to side as she advanced. Unable to get his broken body to respond, he struggled to breathe through his partially crushed throat. He had one arm behind him, the other scrabbling for purchase on the leaf-strewn ground.

She knelt before him and his eyes widened. A flash of insight hit her as she read his fear. With her blood spattered face, feral snarl, misshapen clawed hands, and glowing silver eyes she was the nightmare of the Kyn, a demon from deepest night. A living, breathing monster from human horror stories come to life.

She could work with that. Her voice was rough, almost a growl. "Where's the other one?"

The man stilled, staring at her in wide-eyed terror. Caught up in her magic and bloodlust, she almost didn't catch the quick, jerky movement when he brought up a small gun from behind him and aimed.

She knocked the weapon away, but not fast enough.

The bullet missed her stomach, but the sharp, hard punch in her side evidenced a hit. The fierce burn told her it was iron. Furious with both him and herself, she drove the knife she retrieved, up and under his breastbone and shredded his heart.

Threat eliminated she stood and hissed at the pain. She fought to reverse her magic, as she pressed her now normal looking, right hand to her side. When she lifted it, blood coated her fingers. Strange how her blood seemed more black than red. She lowered her hand and took a deep breath before checking for a corresponding wound on her back.

Please let it be a through-and-through. If the iron bullet was still inside, it would poison her.

Relief hit when she touched the gaping exit wound. She stripped off her shirt and ripped it into strips to wrap around the wound. She took a precious minute to tie the strips one handed so she wouldn't leave a blood trail and moved into the shadows,

Unwilling to miss the other man who was still hunting, she choose not to Shadow Walk. Either he would come to investigate the gunshot or run. Gripping the unfamiliar knife, she crept back home.

Five long minutes later, she hit the edge of the forest. The wound in her side burned like a brand, but she didn't have time to deal with it. She worked her way behind the garage, and headed to the creek to see if the vehicle the three-man team arrived in was still there.

The night sounds had yet to return to normal, which made her hesitate. The third man had to be nearby. As she started to creep forward, the hair on the back of her neck rose in alarm. The slight warning gave her just enough time to raise a circle of protection. The incoming spell hit her circle, then flared over it.

No human could do that. Which meant the third attacker had to be Kyn.

She curled her left hand around the silver lynx at her throat, and drew on her magic, readying herself. Peering around the edge of the garage, she ducked back as a streak of fire scorched the side of the building. If she couldn't see, she couldn't aim.

The sound of car door opening had her darting out from behind the dubious protection of the wooden structure. The dim outline of a small, dark truck gave her a target. Rushing her shot, she sent an energy spell in its direction.

She missed and hit the ground behind the fleeing vehicle. The explosion rocked the truck, but the sound of the vehicle being slammed into gear, told her she wasn't going to catch him. She charged toward the creek, hoping for a second chance, but the flash of taillights was the only thing she caught.

Frustrated, she turned back and slowly trudged toward her house. The rage and adrenaline faded, leaving only dull pain and exhaustion behind. Tremors racked her body, but she had to hold it together. She needed to call Mulcahy and take care of the two bodies out back. Only then could she patch up her wound, which was now a constant, biting ache.

Remembering the locked front door, she cursed, then staggered unsteadily to the back and stumbled up the porch stairs.

Was that her phone ringing? Who the hell was calling her now?

Undoing her protection ward, she stepped into her house and headed into the kitchen to answer it. She clenched her fist to keep her blood-covered hand from shaking. Grime coated her hand.

Was that flesh under her nails?

"McCord," she said in a voice that sounded nothing like her. She slumped against the kitchen table and tried to concentrate.

"Raine, are you okay?"

She didn't recognize the male voice on the other end. "Who is this?"

"Cheveyo. Are you all right?"

"Well—" Hearing the raspy tone of her voice, she cleared her throat. "I am now. Why do you ask?"

"Did you have any visitors tonight?"

"Yes."

Cheveyo was silent for a moment. "Are they still there?"

A short, harsh bark of laughter erupted, then it ended in a groan. "In a manner of speaking."

"How many?" His voice was strained.

"One got away. The other two are going to be around for a while." Why was he calling her? What was the point of his questions? She collapsed into a chair, the burning pain of the bullet wound turning her legs to Jell-O. Damn it, iron or not, it was just a bullet. It shouldn't hurt this bad.

So caught up in analyzing the pain, she missed his next question. "I'm sorry. Say that again."

"Raine, what happened?"

She could've sworn she'd heard Gavin's name in Cheveyo's terse comments. She put her head down on the table, closed her eyes, and pressed the phone to her ear. "One of them shot me," she mumbled. "I'll be fine. I just need to rest for a second before I take care of the bodies."

"I'm coming over." His voice grew fainter.

"'Kay." As waves of pain and darkness rolled her under, she lost her grip on the phone and slipped into nothing.

CHAPTER TWENTY-FOUR

Searing flames consumed her bones and muscles. Her skin popped in the intense heat as the fire devoured the darkness. She jolted awake with a shriek.

Panic spiked as hands held her down. She struck out blindly, determined to escape. Something growled and panted—like an animal caught in a trap—and she realized, distantly, it was her. A voice close by called her name, telling her to calm down, that she was okay.

She raked her nails down the arms attached to the hands on her shoulders. Above her someone cursed, while someone else gave a low laugh.

"Damn it, Raine!" The harsh words broke through her terror bringing recognition—Cheveyo.

A hard shudder wracked her body. Jerking her hands back, she fisted them as she fought to regulate her breathing. She forced her eyes open and stared into Cheveyo's deep black ones.

"Let me go!" The words tore at her sore throat, leaving her voice rough.

"Gladly." Anger shaded his face in grim shadows. "Just as

soon as you calm down. You'll pull open your wound." He leaned over her, his hair falling forward. "Now, will you please lay still?"

Giving him a slow nod, she watched him back slowly away and let her go. His caution, as if dealing with a wild animal, was almost amusing. He pushed his hair out of his face and half turned away.

A slight movement behind Cheveyo drew her attention to a man stepping out of the shadows. Standing roughly six feet tall, there wasn't much to set him apart from the crowd—brown hair, equally dark eyes—but the electric tingle skipping over her nerves as he closed in, certainly did. He was a Lycos, and based on her reaction, a very powerful shifter.

That aura of power triggered an unexpected response from some unacknowledged part of her. A snarl surged up from her chest and erupted from behind her clenched teeth before she could stop it. She scrambled into a sitting position and ignored the pain streaking through her side.

The man stopped in mid-movement, watching her with calm brown eyes.

Cheveyo stepped between them. "Raine, are you okay?"

She could almost hear the pop as she and the stranger broke eye contact. She glanced around and realized she was in her own bed. She drew in a breath and went to rub her face only to catch sight of the smeared blood on her hand, topped with fresh smears that matched the ones on Cheveyo's arms. The night's events came back with a rush.

"I don't know." Actually, she did. She was far from okay. Not that Cheveyo or the stranger behind him would understand.

Tonight she freed a part of her nature typically chained deep, an aspect closer to a wild animal than either man could ever suspect. She frantically began reinforcing her mental walls, hoping to rein it in, but it fought back, refusing to retreat. She sucked in deep breaths as she patched her identity back together, not daring to let Cheveyo know just how close she was to losing it. What if she couldn't cage this aspect of herself—the part that thrilled to the hunt, to the kill? Her walls trembled under the onslaught of doubt, so she shoved it aside. A few breaths later, she could at least fake normal.

The shifter stepped forward, and jerked her out of her thoughts. "My apologies, Ms. McCord, for the pain my bringing you back to consciousness caused. We wouldn't have done so if it wasn't important."

His pleasant baritone only put her more on edge and there was a knowing light in those dark eyes, as if he could see right through her flimsy façade. "Sorry, it's been a long night, Mr..." she trailed off, unsure what threat he brought.

He gave a short, elegant bow. "Vidis, Warrick Vidis."

She froze. Warrick Vidis was the head of the shifters—definitely not the social type. Acknowledged as the most powerful shifter in the Kyn community, he wasn't one to interfere in the business of other Kyn. He served next to Cheveyo, Mulcahy, and Natasha only because the other shifters wanted a representative who could hold his own when it came to the machinations of the supernatural community.

According to Chet, one of the closest friends she had in the shifting community, Vidis was a power to be reckoned with. He was generally fair and even-handed in his dealings —until you crossed him. At which time you best have your grave dug, because what little he left would need a resting place.

What the hell was he doing here in her house with Cheveyo? Deciding to ask, she said, "Mr. Vidis, I don't mean to be rude, but why are you here?"

His smile changed his face from average to charming. "I

was with Cheveyo when he called you. I have some ability in healing, and we thought I might be of some use to you."

"You dropped the phone," Cheveyo told her. "I tried yelling, but when you didn't answer, we headed over." His sharp scrutiny scoured her face as he perched precariously on the edge of her bed. "You were passed out on the table."

"I remember talking to you on the phone," she said softly. "I needed to rest for a second before heading back out to—" she hesitated, slicing a look at Vidis. "Take care of things."

Vidis's smile flared briefly, his tone gently mocking. "No need to be delicate. I can handle it, I assure you."

She bet he could, but sharing such things with a virtual stranger was disconcerting. Especially when both men chose to hover over her. She glanced around. "Please have a seat, Mr. Vidis. There should be a chair somewhere nearby."

He rocked forward, but checked the movement before it completed. "If it's all right with you, I'd like to finish healing the wound on your side."

She stifled the urge to glance at Cheveyo, uncertain what about the shifter made her so nervous. Mortified at her uncontrolled responses, she could only nod. Cheveyo moved aside and Vidis took his place.

She turned on to her left side and exposed the bullet wound, thankful she still wore her running pants and sports bra. Having these two intimidating, powerful men in her house left her uncomfortable. As Vidis sat down beside her and his warm energy pulsed outside her own aura, noticeable but not unpleasant.

Recalling the intense fire that woke her, she sucked in a breath and stiffened. "What exactly are you going to do?"

With his hands half raised, Vidis stilled. "I'm going to heal it from the inside out." He moved his palms over the wound. "You should feel warmth, no pain."

She gripped his wrist gently, stopping him. "It hurt last

time." He might make her nervous but letting a stranger work magic on her was even more unsettling. Scrutinizing his face, she took in the serenity and deep-seated calmness reflected in his expression and slightly almond-shaped eyes. "When you woke me up, it felt as if I was burning from the inside out."

His lips quirked. "We needed you awake, and the only way to make that happen was to provoke you."

She released his wrist, rested her arm along her upper ribcage, and watched Vidis warily. Cheveyo remained a silent shadow, watching them both.

Vidis placed his right hand over the wound in her front and his left over the one in her back. His eyes went slightly out of focus. Heat seeped into her side and the soreness slowly ebbed away.

She fought her instinctive urge to move out from under his touch. It took concentrated effort to hold still while someone worked magic on her.

A few moments later, he raised his hands, briefly closed his eyes, and stood up. "It should be fine."

She rolled over, pulled her legs around, and prepared to get out of bed. At the absence of pain, relief spiraled through her. Cheveyo shifted toward her, as if to help. She waved him off as Vidis went to the far window and clasped his hands behind his back. Once on her feet, she stretched gently, feeling her muscles respond. Cheveyo gave her a look and she shook her head.

Still shaky, she walked over to the unsettling man by the window. "Thank you, Mr. Vidis." Quiet respect filled her voice. He gave a short nod, and she turned to Cheveyo. "I have to go take care of the two men out back."

"Already taken care of," Cheveyo's voice was neutral, giving nothing away, his face stoic.

She didn't ask for more. No need. He knew the score. The

bodies were probably already buried deep in the woods. Just how long had she been out? "What time is it?"

"One in the morning," came his answer.

"I was out for three hours?"

He nodded.

Well, that would explain why she was still shaky. "I need to take a shower."

What she needed was to get the blood out from under her nails and off her skin. She didn't need the visual reminders of the consuming dark joy when she dug her claws into that man's throat. She'd thrown him so she wouldn't rip his throat out, and then took a bullet for the small kindness. Go figure.

Vidis turned from the window, his face in shadows. "Of course, but hurry if you please. We need to discuss things." He left the room.

Cheveyo stepped close. She tilted her head back, but refused to retreat, no matter how much he loomed over her. His mesmerizing eyes were an inky black, but his expression remained undecipherable. He lifted his left hand and gently traced the bruises marring her skin below the intricate knots and the battle ravens on her right arm. Then, without a word, he turned and followed Vidis.

The minute she was alone her shoulders slumped. Lord and Lady, she was tired. Not so much from her wounds or the fighting, more from her internal struggles. Cold and paralyzing fear curled around her as she considered just how much damage that wild, uncontrollable part could cause. Tonight had been close, too damn close. Freeing it to hunt had nearly ripped the length of her tightly held leash from her hands. If she ever lost her grip for good, it would be a disaster, creating danger to herself and everyone around her.

She stripped off her pants and bra to hit the shower. Stepping under the warm water, she lifted her face to the spray, letting the heat seep into her. Bloodlust still simmered, fueling the urge to rend and tear those who hunted her. Long ago, after her time in the lab, she'd been forced to admit such urges—so intense they were almost primal—were forever a part of her, until it seemed as if a wild animal shared her soul.

Learning to cage it had taken time. Reining it back once it was set loose took even longer. In her darkest moments, she considered letting it free once and for all, but something always held her back.

Once she washed the stains of the night off her skin and got dressed, she braided her wet hair back. She set her two wrist sheaths in place, then strapped her longer blade into its spine sheath. Against her dark T-shirt and hair, the black hilt was indistinguishable. Steadier with her mental walls and physical weapons in place, she padded barefoot down the hall to the kitchen.

The low rumble of male voices drifted toward her but fell silent when she appeared in the doorway.

She got a cup of tea and ignored the weight of their silent regard. Keeping her face blank, she took a sip and sat down with them at the table. "I'm assuming, Mr. Vidis, that you being with Cheveyo when he called me was not a happy coincidence?"

"Not quite, Ms. McCord."

"Call me Raine, or McCord, the Ms. sounds too stuffy."

Vidis nodded. "All right then, Raine—"

"Three Wraiths were attacked tonight." Cheveyo did a piss poor job of hiding his impotent fury and frustration. If he was even trying.

A tight feeling clutched her stomach. "Who?"

Cheveyo held her gaze. "You, Chet, and Gavin."

Terror snatched at her bones, sinking talons deep. "Are they okay?"

Cheveyo's jaw clenched. "Chet was killed."

A silent scream started somewhere deep inside as dread surged. It took everything she had to keep her voice steady as she asked the next question, "And Gavin?"

A flash of pity proceeded Cheveyo's gentle, "He's missing."

The world spun. The tabletop disappeared as white and gray spots danced over her vision. The internal scream turned into a wail. "Is—he still—alive?" The words stumbled over the block of ice in her chest.

"We're not sure."

Gavin was alive. She would accept nothing less. She reached for her tea and wrapped her cold fingers around its pitiful warmth. Her imagination strayed down twisted paths, the images scraping deep gouges across her mind and heart. Closing her eyes, she clung to the inner core of anger and determination, which brought her back from hell more than once.

It hurt to shove her terror for Gavin away, to bury it deep, but she didn't have the luxury of falling apart. Gavin needed her, needed her to do her job. If she got lost in her sickening, internal maelstrom, she would be useless to him.

Refocusing, she cleared her throat. "How was Chet killed?" It took a great deal to kill a Wraith. Sharp grief at loosing Chet joined her emotional upheaval.

"From what we could tell," Vidis answered. "There was more than one attacker. Based on his wounds, one of them had to be a fairly powerful spell caster. The other had claws." For a moment, Vidis's inner predator peeked out, green and gold flames burned deep in his brown eyes. "They came in behind Chet and took his head." He looked down at his clenched fist and forcibly relaxed it.

A shiver skated down her spine at Vidis's full-blown rage. His emotions triggered hers, and she was unsettled to discover she was fighting the urge to snarl in an answering fury. Her voice came out harsh. "Neither one would walk blindly into a trap. They are…were…smarter than that. The only way Chet could have been ambushed was…"

"If he was with someone he trusted," Cheveyo finished.

Dread coalesced in her stomach. Before she could reply, the jarring of her wards warned her of incoming company. She stood so fast the chair fell to the floor. She was half way down the hall to the front door before Cheveyo caught up with her.

"Raine!" He grabbed her arm and pulled her to a halt. "You can't just charge out there."

She blinked at him. "It's my land, my territory. I can do what I damn well please." She jerked out of his grip. When he went for her again, she slipped to the side, and gave him a slight shove which sent him stumbling back into Vidis, who'd come up behind. If she'd been thinking rationally, she would've been shocked by her actions.

As she slipped into the night, she caught the soft purr of a well-tuned engine, but not the same vehicle used by her attackers earlier. She charged down the porch stairs toward one of the taller trees guarding her front yard, sensing both Vidis and Cheveyo coming up behind her. She held up a hand, signaling them to halt.

Headlights cut through the inky night and illuminated the yard. As the sedan came to a stop, recognition hit. The door opened, and a shadowy figure emerged. Slowly he turned and scanned the shadows. "Raine, why are you outside?"

Mulcahy's unexpected presence tipped her tension level up a notch. Her uncle never came out to her place, and for him to be here now? Yeah, that wasn't good. "I needed some air."

He paused at her obvious sarcasm before nudging the car door shut. The dull *thud* followed him as he moved across the yard only to pull up short. "Vidis. Cheveyo."

She caught the wary coolness in her uncle's greeting and wondered at it.

He stopped at the foot of the porch steps, one hand brushing absently over his dark suit. "Shall we go in? I believe we have some planning to do."

She waved her arm toward her home. "After you."

Mulcahy made quick work of the stairs and headed in. Vidis fell in behind him. Cheveyo waited for Raine to join him. Watching her uncle and Vidis head deeper into the house, she appreciated Cheveyo's solid presence beside her.

She sighed deeply. It was going to be a long night.

CHAPTER TWENTY-FIVE

Raine's kitchen had never been quite so full. At the table, Mulcahy and Vidis sat opposite her and Cheveyo. Vidis was quietly listening to Mulcahy share Raine and Gavin's investigation, going so far as to lay out their various conjectures. When he finished, the silence flowed back like a thick blanket.

Raine broke it. "Chet was betrayed by a Wraith." She wasn't intending her statement as an accusation, but feared she failed miserably.

"Not a Wraith, McCord," Mulcahy corrected. "But an employee of Taliesin? Highly probable. However, my prime suspect is dead."

"Are you sure?" Maybe exhaustion and tension exasperated her need to provoke her uncle. Either that or, her inner beast wasn't as tightly leashed as she thought.

Unruffled Mulcahy calmly answered, "Since you killed him, yes."

His admission sent her reeling. A surge of anger, so deep it was almost hate, washed through her. One of the Wraiths' cardinal rules was anonymity, especially when it came to elimination jobs, their names only known to Mulcahy. His blunt statement in front of these two high-ranking members of the Kyn community blew that anonymity to hell.

It was one more cut to her growing collection of wounds, inflicted by a man who considered her nothing more than a tool. His obvious disregard of her rank and responsibilities in front of the other two men was a wicked blow to her already lacerated emotions.

If he wanted to trade hits in front of Cheveyo and Vidis, so be it. Tonight she had no problem with it. "And which job would that be, sir?" she asked with a vicious politeness.

Seeming to realize how she interpreted his words and actions, Mulcahy raised his hands and rubbed them over his face, a frustrated gesture she never before seen him use. "My apologies. That was out of line."

She stayed silent, unable to believe him.

He grimaced. "It was Quinn."

"Quinn wasn't a Wraith." The tone of Vidis's voice wobbled on the thin line between accusation and statement.

A flash of discomfort crossed Mulcahy's face and an awful thought hit Raine. Before she could reconsider voicing it, she blurted, "It wasn't about him taking out those college students, was it, Mulcahy?"

His face stayed blank, except for a small flinching around his eyes, that indicated she scored a direct hit.

"Why did you have me kill him?" Her voice went soft and cold. "What else did he do?"

For the first time ever, her uncle's legendary control faltered. "He was behind those deaths, of that there is no doubt. He was the last person they were seen with. However, he obtained information on a number of the Wraiths."

"What kind of information?" She refused to back off.

He held her furious gaze. "Information such as their names, where they lived, and their weaknesses. He used that information to persuade me to allow him to join the Wraiths."

Truth rang through Mulcahy's explanation and eased some of her tension. Quinn had always been a bit cocky—sure he could win in any situation. He was not above a little blackmail to get what he wanted. "He threatened to make it public knowledge?"

"Not just that, he threatened to expose us." Something flashed across his face, and had her realizing he was no longer talking about the Wraiths now, but their relationship, the one he refused to acknowledge.

That he was so close to disclosing their blood ties in front of Cheveyo and Vidis left her shocked.

Not missing her expression, he braced his arms on the table and leaned in. "Warrick won't tell and Cheveyo already knows."

Such a simple sentence to shatter years of secrecy. A thread of hysterical laughter threatened to choke her. She waited years for him to admit to being family and now that he was, she wished he would shut the hell up.

Underneath the laughter was a rising tide of hurt. That Mulcahy shared her past with Cheveyo was one thing. However, him now acknowledging their blood ties in front of Vidis made her question why. In all their years together, he made it painstakingly clear their relationship must remain a secret. Her uncle never made a move unless there was something in it for him.

Dark paranoia lifted its ugly head. There was something else behind her uncle's strange behavior. Since it couldn't be worry over her, it had to be something near and dear to his heart. He lived for his position at Taliesin. If he wanted to strengthen that position, he would need to remove perceived obstacles. Her mind took a sickening turn. Could he be behind tonight's attacks? Could this deadly night be about power? Unable to shake the disturbing thoughts, she held his gaze and asked, "Who did you bring with you?"

Cheveyo and Vidis froze, an eerie stillness filling the room. Their reactions revealed she wasn't the only one harboring such suspicions. It was almost funny to discover she wasn't the only one who had issues trusting her uncle. If Mulcahy wanted to get rid of possible competition and tie up loose ends, now would be the time. No way could she defend herself or Cheveyo and Vidis against Mulcahy and whatever team he brought in as back up. Considering tonight's mess, opportunity didn't need to knock. It could waltz right in.

Mulcahy's head jerked back, his eyes widened. "Is that what you think of me, Raine?" His harsh question snapped the tension like a rubber band.

At her continued silence, he shook his head, pushed away from the table, and paced.

"I had you kill Quinn because he was blackmailing his way into the Wraiths. It would've only been the beginning. With that one action, he proved himself untrustworthy. No matter what decision I made, he would always go to the highest bidder." He stopped behind his chair, gripping the back. "He signed his own death warrant. I had to make sure he wouldn't be a threat to Taliesin ever again."

She wanted to believe him, and any other night, probably would have. Right now, her world was so on edge she had a hard time believing anyone. Too many hits with too much damage to her emotions left her questioning not only herself, but everyone around her.

"How do you tie a dead man in with Chet's death then?" Vidis's voice slid in between Mulcahy and Raine.

Mulcahy sat back down and regained some of his formidable control. "There were rumors Quinn had a lover."

"Do we know who the lover is?" Vidis rose from the table and took his cup to the kitchen sink.

Mulcahy shook his head. "No, that's part of the problem. The information about his lover came from Chet. Chet's death leads me to assume this lover has access to the same information Quinn held. I believe whoever it is, is sharing it with whoever is taking out our people."

"I don't understand." She was either slow, or there was something Mulcahy was leaving out. "Why would Chet know about Quinn's lover? Quinn worked on a personal security detail that Chet headed."

"He wasn't supervising Quinn, he was following him. The security detail served as a cover so Chet could keep an eye on Quinn's routine."

"And?" she prompted.

"He found Quinn was leaking information, but he never found out to whom."

She took in his rigid posture. There was something more to this story. "Who was Quinn supposed to be covering?"

Self-directed rage burned deep in Mulcahy's eyes. "Erica Cawley."

It started to click into focus. Laying it out verbally so Vidis and Cheveyo could follow along, she said, "So Quinn wanted to be a Wraith, and was pissed when you told him no. He decided to get inside information on the Wraiths, and use it as a bargaining tool." She shook her head. "That was stupid. Blackmail wouldn't work with you."

"No one said he was smart," Cheveyo noted.

Her lips twitched. "You put him on a cushiony security detail with Erica Cawley so Chet could watch his movements. However, Chet wasn't able to find Quinn's contact, so you decided to neutralize Quinn before too much damage could be caused."

"Then I got the call from Talbot to look into those deaths," Mulcahy added. "Which put you and Gavin onto

Polleo and raised enough warnings to make someone go after you unprepared."

Gavin's name brought a flare of pain. "They didn't know we were Kyn at that time," she mused. At Cheveyo's steady look, she explained, "Tonight they used iron bullets. That night they used regular lead bullets. Either it was a rush job, or they didn't know who we were."

Mulcahy nodded in agreement. "We found nothing strong at Polleo. Just a tease about Rimmick, then Mayson's murder, which was quickly followed by Rimmick's body."

"They were cleaning up behind themselves." Frustration leaked through as she traced the edge of her teacup. "They're staying one step ahead of us. What about Dr. Lawson's little announcement? Was the run-in between Gavin and me and the Cawleys planned?"

"Maybe. I don't know." Mulcahy rubbed his chin. "If the military is looking to make the ultimate army, then setting you and Durand onto Lawson's research would be enough bait to set up a Wraith, based on the information Quinn or his lover gave them."

Vidis leaned against the counter between the kitchen and the dining room.

Raine agreed with Mulcahy's conclusion. She and Gavin had been set up, which meant Lawson, Cawley, and possibly Talbot had information on both of them. A thought struck and she narrowed her eyes. "Mulcahy, how much information did Quinn have on me?"

He shrugged. "He knew you were my niece and a Wraith."

"Nothing about my past?" she prodded.

He shook his head. "No."

She felt a grim smile stretch her lips. "Then we're one up on them."

"How do you figure?" Cheveyo asked.

She turned to him letting her anger and determination fill her gaze. "I'm much more than they anticipated."

"We need a plan, and you going off half-cocked is not going to work," Mulcahy's tone was sharp with reprimand.

She bared her teeth with a growl. "We don't have time to fuck around, sir." Heavy sarcasm coated the last word. "We know who has Gavin. Both you and I know what he's going through right now." She refused to let anyone stand between her and Gavin, including her boss.

Her uncle's gaze was shuttered. "Perhaps."

"There is no perhaps. Whether you want to admit it or not, we have to get him out."

"That's going to be a little hard to do since we have no idea where he is," he snapped back. "Get yourself under control."

It was one challenge too much. A red curtain of rage hazed her vision, but before she could respond, Vidis slipped behind her and put a hand on her shoulder. "We can track Gavin."

Turning, she took in the Lycan leader's lethal expression and understood his unspoken suggestion. Vidis didn't care about anything but killing those who had murdered his shifter. "Who are you thinking of?"

"Xander." Vidis's smile was more a snarl of white teeth.

Her wild side surged in answer to his baring of teeth. A fierce hunger awoke and ran under the excitement of an eminent hunt. She needed to move. Instead, she held still and forced herself to hold Vidis's gaze. The scrape of a chair snapped their silent communication.

She blinked to find Mulcahy watching her, lines marring his brow as he witnessed the strange byplay between her and Vidis. A small sense of relief welled at her uncle's concern. At least she wasn't losing her mind. She slid a glance to

Cheveyo, only to find him watching all three of them, his thoughts hidden.

"You want to send out a hunting party, Warrick?" Mulcahy's voice was back to his impersonal best.

Vidis nodded. "I do. You and I both know Xander is the best tracker, next to me."

"If you're the best, why don't you come?" Cheveyo asked.

Vidis barked out a laugh. "Because I am the least politically adept head of house at Taliesin. We want our hunting party to bring back someone or something alive for questioning. Plus, we don't want to leave anything behind that would bring the humans to our door with questions. When our prey is found, I cannot guarantee either outcome."

Raine's respect for Vidis rose. It was rare to hear any Kyn admit to a failing, much less a head of house. Perhaps the stories about Vidis walking a thinner line between animal and man weren't exaggerated. Typically those with Lycos blood faced the wonderful challenge of dealing with a dual nature, man and animal. Some managed to keep the man aspect first and foremost. Strong emotions, such as anger, pain, or the thrill of the hunt, tended to bring the animalistic nature to the fore. Vidis's frank admission showed a leader who knew his own strengths and weaknesses—a rare but admirable trait.

Mulcahy nodded. "Xander, Cheveyo, and Raine, then. I'll ask Natasha for her suggestion and have her send them to Taliesin." He rose from the table and turned to Vidis. "You'll contact Xander then?" At Vidis's nod, he gestured to Raine. "Get yourself armed and meet me at the office. I want you to find out who is behind this and bring them to me. Alive." The last was direct order. He turned and walked away, pulling his cell phone from his suit pocket. The front door snicked quietly closed behind him.

She stared at her hands on the table as the wilder side of

her soul calmed and settled. She should be tired, and maybe she was, but too many emotions coalesced inside, leaving her unable to consider sleep.

Tonight she claimed someone. Maybe not out loud, but she wouldn't lie to herself. Gavin was hers. The possessiveness shocked her into momentary stillness. Wonder sparked at how far she let him in. Instead of pushing the feelings aside, she held them close, needing the small warmth. Maybe there was still hope that she wasn't completely lost yet.

To get Gavin back, she needed the ruthlessness of the dark, twisted part of her. Out of the two men still with her, Vidis would have the least qualms about who and what she was. What Cheveyo would think, she refused to worry about. He already witnessed her earlier handy work tonight. Besides, this was no time for a personal crisis of conscience.

Time to embrace her full nature. Vicious humans made her into a weapon, and she was ready and willing to turn it back on them. No one would ever again hurt someone who belonged to her. Promise made, she released her grip on the chain holding her civility together. Her mental cage collapsed, setting her free.

Gavin was out there and she needed to find him before she lost him for good. She had no idea how much he could take before he broke, but she held tight to the belief that he was stronger than most. She refused to accept anything else.

Cheveyo touched her hand. "Ready?"

Both men were on their feet, watching her with unspoken demands. A fine edge of trembling energy, a sense of something barely contained, emanated from them, calling to her. They were hunters, warriors, and it was time to do what they did best.

She felt a feral smile twist her lips. "Oh, yeah. Let's go hunting."

CHAPTER TWENTY-SIX

R aine followed Cheveyo's black Jeep to Taliesin. She could have gone with the two men, but she wanted her own car. The areas under the mat in the back held more hidden weapons, which were a bit less conspicuous than if they loaded them into Cheveyo's Jeep. No sense in taking a chance on butting heads with local law enforcement should they happen to be pulled over. A high probability as she broke most of the speed limits heading back into Portland.

She pulled in next to Cheveyo in Taliesin's parking lot and noted a sleek black Ducati bike parked near the doors. She crossed the lot, met the other two men at the door, and rode the elevator up, all without saying a word. Flanked by Cheveyo and Vidis, she stepped out of the elevator and strode toward Mulcahy's office.

The door was open, framing the small, curvy figure of the only other female Wraith who epitomized the concept of unique. An intricate tattoo ran from temple to chin on the right side of her delicate face, adding to mystique of her hazel eyes shot through with gold. Spiky blonde hair tipped in metallic purple matched the sleeveless shell in the same color. The shirt stopped above a silver and diamond stud that pierced a small belly button riding above smooth, shiny, vivid green pants that appeared painted on, only to disappear into heavy steel-toed bike boots decorated with silver chains and buckles.

Xander's ability to create an unforgettable fashion statement others could never dream of pulling off amazed Raine. "Damn, Xander, I will never understand how you get colors like that to work."

"You know how it is, Raine. Some have it and some don't." The husky voice did not match Xander's small frame. She moved back to let Cheveyo and Vidis through, and waited for Raine to clear the door before closing it.

Mulcahy placed his phone back in the cradle, his face set in unreadable lines and his tone ruthlessly hard. "I'm having the GPS in Gavin's car traced. Ryder will call and let us know where it signals from. You, Cheveyo, and Xander can go meet him at the car. Warrick and I need to be at Chet's to deal with The Division."

In a subtle claim of the Lycos leader, Xander perched on the arm of Vidis's chair. Her face and voice were all business when she addressed Mulcahy. "I found traces of humans and an unknown at Chet's house."

Too keyed up to settle, Raine paced the back length of the room. "Anything else?"

Xander turned and eyed her coolly. "A warding spell had been cast, but it wouldn't have triggered until he stepped across his threshold. From the signs I could follow, the spell was set by someone with Kyn blood and little training. It was more as if they relied on brute strength. The humans and the unknown were waiting for him when he came through the door. The humans attacked and the unknown came in from behind."

Raine's agitated movements ground to a halt, and she

gave the female shifter a sharp look. "How's that possible? If he came through the door, then the one behind him couldn't just pop out of thin air." She jerked as it hit her. "They Shadow Walked?"

Xander nodded slowly.

Raine cursed in a low, vicious tone, her rage straining the fragile control she fought to maintain. Her cell rang and jerked her back from the edge. She took a deep breath, snatched it out of her pocket, and checked the display. The number came up blocked.

Unsure of the caller, but not willing to miss the call on the slim chance it was Gavin, she excused herself and went outside the office to answer it. "McCord."

Static filled the line, then cleared. "You're going to have to move fast if you want to save your boyfriend, Raine."

"Who are you?"

"Let's just say you and I are kin of sorts," the voice was a vibrating growl.

Her heart rate kicked up and the static increased even as she struggled for calm. "Strange, I don't remember attending a family reunion recently."

The static eased. "Perhaps because you have no family left."

Her blood froze. "What do you want?" she demanded, her tone cold, merciless.

"Ah, ah, ah," the voice chided. "No need to get so upset, *cher*. I just wanted to let you know, if you want lover boy to make it out sane, you best starting moving on Dr. Lawson's little lab."

Her pulse spiked. "What lab?"

There was a huge elaborate sigh. "I'm so disappointed at how slow y'all move. Hasn't your boss found lover boy's car yet?" The gruff voice didn't wait for answer. "Check the glove compartment. I'm sure you'll find what you're looking for."

Her mind raced furiously. "How do I know this isn't just another trap?"

"You don't," the growl rumbled. "But since you and I know exactly what's happening to your man, I have a feeling it won't matter. That Chet character, he was getting way too close, but this one, they're keeping alive. For now. He shows promise."

A guttural scream cut through the airwaves, and her breath stopped.

"You recognized that, uh? Ah well, that's going to hurt. Good hunting, Raine." The line went dead.

Trembling in a fury-coated panic, she let out a short snarl of frustration, then hissed as the sharp, jagged edges of her now broken phone pierced her palm. She spun around and stormed back into Mulcahy's office on a wave of anger. Her abrupt entrance brought Vidis to his feet, while Xander stayed protectively in front of him.

"Gavin's at Lawson's lab." The tight leash on Raine's volatile emotions was stretched to a breaking point. "That phone call was Chet's attacker, and he's playing both ends against each other."

"Explain." Mulcahy's order cut through her rage, and brought her focus back enough to continue. She rocked up on the balls of her feet, body poised, and fists clenched at her side as she strove to contain the turmoil within. "He claimed Chet was too much of a threat. For now, they're keeping Gavin alive."

"Then we have a little bit of time to plan this out," Mulcahy stated.

Flames of panic spiked. "No we don't, sir. We need to move now. Our little font of information indicated I have personal experience with what's happening to Gavin. Every minute we waste, is one more piece of his sanity lost."

Her confrontational approach did not go over well with

Mulcahy, a man who did not tolerate his decisions being questioned. "What are you talking about?"

It was stupid, dangerous even, to push, yet she couldn't stop. The combination of fear, guilt, and heart-wrenching panic at what she knew Gavin was suffering was too much. For Gavin's sake, it was time to rip those damn blinders off her uncle's eyes and make him admit the truth as to what was happening to his Wraith in that thrice-cursed lab.

She let the beast prowling inside her surface. Freed from its chains, the violent energy rose and created a physical wave in its wake. Cheveyo shot to his feet, but the storm of magic and emotion gathered around her, tightening the air in the room with suppressed violence. On her other side, Vidis and Xander moved into defensive positions.

With an inhuman snarl, Raine threw a shield around her and her uncle to keep both the shifters and the witch away. She just needed a few minutes. She reached deep into her soul and grasped the twisted ropes of magical energy, before weaving them together. Her teeth sharpened, her nails stretched into claws, and the bones in her face shifted and reformed. She lifted arms now covered in black fur and threw back her head, letting loose an eerie scream of frustrated rage.

Intellect warred with instinct and she stopped the transformation half way through. Painful though it was, she wanted her uncle to witness the half-woman, half-monstrous leopard the humans managed to create. For Gavin, she would reveal her darkest self to those in the room as proof of the monster twisted humans could create.

Mulcahy's eyes widened and he took an involuntary step back, his back hitting the edge of her hastily erected shielding. A small dark part of her enjoyed the quickly suppressed flicker of fear in his deep brown eyes.

Fear is good, whispered the beast.

"We are not waiting, Uncle." Her voice emerged, lower than normal and carrying the edge of a growl, though still understandable despite her partial muzzle. "Gavin is not going to be sacrificed because you don't want to face the fact the humans can create the very monsters you fear. Look at me. This is what you want me to embrace." She placed her sharp-tipped claws on his desk and leaned forward until she was almost crouched on top of it. "I am not Kyn. I am a monster!"

Mulcahy's face was pale but he stepped in and cupped her twisted face with his hands. Shock and his unexpected touch held her still. "You are still my niece and still Kyn. Even more, you are a Wraith." A heartbeat passed, then another, before let her go and stepped back. "We cannot afford to rush into the lab unprepared or we will lose more than just Gavin."

She searched for a glimpse of disgust in her uncle's face. "The killer called me kin. He knows I have no family."

Mulcahy's brow furrowed in confusion. "I am your family. Taliesin is your family." He shook his head. "If you rush in, Raine, we will lose not only Gavin, but all those who will be with you. Then not only will they have Gavin, but they will have the weapon they created and lost years ago. Is that what you want?"

"I don't want Gavin to be twisted into me!" Anguish echoed under her rage. She raised claw-tipped hands to cover her face and began caging the beast. As her magic receded, she lowered her hands, and watched the magic shimmer over her arms. When it dissipated, her claws had been replaced by very human hands that now rested on the mahogany desk. She raised her head and met her uncle's steady gaze.

Unsurprisingly, practical ruthlessness stared back, like a

general assessing a powerful solider. "Do you think Chet's attacker holds the same powers you do?"

"I don't know," her voice was empty. "He could be more or less, depending on what they did to him."

"It would be better if we had a clearer picture of what we may be up against," Mulcahy's tone was brisk.

She gave a harsh bark of laughter and pushed back from the desk. "We have no idea what we're up against." She waved her palm and dropped the shield as she turned her back on her uncle. "As soon as we hear from Ryder we need to get to that car."

"McCord," Mulcahy's voice was sharp as glass.

Raine turned to face him.

"Don't ever threaten me again. You are not the most dangerous person in this room and rage doesn't mean power."

"I know, Mulcahy," she answered. "But I don't have to be the most powerful, just the most deadly."

CHAPTER TWENTY-SEVEN

The sleek convertible blended in with the pre-dawn shadows that lay over the heavily forested road outside of Oregon City. However, the shiny red muscle car that sat in front of it, did anything but blend. Raine pulled up behind the two parked cars as a young man in chinos and a collared, baby blue shirt made his way to her. Cheveyo got out of her SUV's passenger side and rounded the hood.

The smiling young man strode over. "Hi, I'm Jamie Ryder. Natasha sent me." The artistically messy, sun-streaked brown hair moved with every step. The look must have cost a pretty penny to achieve.

Raine nodded in greeting. "I'm McCord, and this is Cheveyo." When Ryder got closer she noted he was a bit taller than her, and there was the slight ring of red around the brown iris. Without those eyes, he could be any college boy on any campus. Between that tell-a-tale ring and the unnerving sense of other swirling around him, it was clear that Frat Brat possessed a fair amount of demon blood in his veins.

While he and Cheveyo exchanged words, she tried to

figure out why Natasha felt sending this boy on a hunting party was a smart idea. Regardless of his bloodlines, he seemed soft around the edges. Since Natasha wasn't a fool, there had to be something Raine was missing. Hopefully it wasn't something that would come back to nail her.

She walked to Gavin's car and noted there were no signs of it being forced off the road. The rumble of Xander's bike caught her attention. The other woman came to a stop, pulled off her helmet, and made her way over. At her arrival, Ryder stopped in mid-sentence, and as Xander went to Raine, his face took on a stunned expression. At any other time his reaction would make Raine smile because Xander's petite appearance fooled most males into underestimating her. Not a healthy thing for any man to do.

"Xander," Raine called. "Do your thing and let me know what you find. I'm checking the glove compartment."

"You think there's a map?"

The ever-present fury she fought to contain, sparked at Ryder's derisive tone and she shot him a venomous look. Without answering, she pulled open the sport car's passenger-side door and slid in. Her control was shot to hell and there would be no getting it back until Gavin was safe and whoever took him was in small bloody pieces.

Trapped by the car's interior, Gavin's woodsy scent surrounded her, causing her lungs to catch and her stomach to clench. She kept her focus on her search, first noting that the keys were still in the ignition. Ignoring the tremor in her fingers, she popped the glove compartment open. The map her anonymous caller mentioned lay inside.

She pulled it out, left the car, and moved to her SUV's hood, so she could spread the map out. She located their position just outside of Oregon City, then found an inked blue circle that framed a blank spot nestled between a small river and South Hayden Road before it turned onto the

Woodburn-Estacada Highway. The location was a bit farther out and surrounded by two Federal Reserve parks and the sprawling Philip Foster Farm, but she'd bet good money it was Eden Lawson's hidden lab.

"Got it," she snapped.

Cheveyo and Ryder came up beside her and studied the map, while Xander continued to prowl around Gavin's car. Raine could sense the bursts of power as the other woman tracked down any lingering magical traces.

Cheveyo placed a warm, restraining hand on Raine's arm, a subtle warning to keep it together. "Dawn's around the corner, and there is no way we can safely bypass security and get him out until we have more information."

She knew her eyes were unfriendly. "I'm highly aware we have to wait until nightfall, Cheveyo. I won't put this op at risk by striking out blindly."

He measured her look against her words, and then nodded—seemingly satisfied she meant what she said—and dropped his hand.

She re-folded the map and moved around him to Xander. She didn't get far.

Ryder stepped in front of her, bringing her up short. Young and arrogant, he swept her with an appraising look. "Damn, Natasha is never wrong."

She didn't have the patience to deal with cocky little demon frat boys and cursed herself for asking, "About what?"

He gave a low, evil laugh. "You, of course." Then he deliberately invaded her personal space.

She froze, her muscles coiled and prepared to strike.

Ryder kept moving his mouth, unaware of how close to danger he stood. "You like to live dangerously."

She gave him a sardonic look. "I hate to be bored."

He pushed, testing her, like some naughty child. "She

didn't mention you're another prime example of why you don't have to be male to have stone cold balls."

Fortunately, she wasn't anyone's mother. She met his smirk, only then noting the signs of his latent handsomeness. However, his ability to grow into that promise was currently up for debate. Only a breath separated them and with a subtle flick of her wrist, she had her blade a hair's breadth away from his groin area. "If you don't want to lose yours, you'll step back, little boy."

For a second his eyes flamed red, then he looked down to find her blade perilously close to his prized package. He stepped back, but not before he flashed a taunting grin and raised his hands to indicate he was unarmed. The tension between them stepped back just as Xander called her over.

Raine shook her head as she headed to the tracker. Demons were such a pain in the ass, always pushing until someone bled. Frat boy from Hell better have some serious skills or when this was over, she and the demon queen were going to go a few rounds.

Xander knelt on the far side of the car and without looking up, addressed Raine. "There was a female here. It looks like a meet, but I can't be sure because Ryder's car tracked over any earlier tire markings. These—" She pointed to the faint indents and smudges in the damp ground, barely discernible even with Raine's superior vision. "Are what gets left behind if you wear those designer heels."

"Figures," Raine muttered. "Dr. Lawson seems to have a penchant for heels."

"Yeah." Xander shot Raine a look. "Most women do."

"Not me. I'm not into pain."

Xander snorted, then straightened, and moved deeper into the surrounding forest. "Come here."

Raine followed her in to the shadows.

After a few feet, Xander stopped, and turned back to the

now almost invisible road. "Notice how you can't see anything?"

Raine nodded.

"Not only that, but Ryder and Cheveyo can't see us." Xander's hazel eyes were steady. "There were five of them hiding in the forest, probably shielded."

"So," Raine kept her tone flat. "Some sort of spell was used to make sure Gavin couldn't detect them?"

Xander nodded and crossed her arms over her chest. "I think that's the best guess, but maybe Cheveyo can test it."

"He pulls up, scans, gets nothing." Raine gazed unseeing toward the direction of the road as she pieced together what Gavin walked into. "The woman was already waiting for him. Has to be someone he knows or recognizes."

Xander nodded. "If he headed out this way to check out Lawson, he wouldn't just stop and pull off."

Raine considered it. "Maybe, or maybe she had a flat, you know, the whole damsel in distress thing. She'd have to be driving something big, a van or an SUV or—"

"SUV would be my top choice," Xander cut in. "They're everywhere and wouldn't set off alarm bells like a van."

"Yeah, a van screams serial killer or kidnapper," Raine agreed as Xander flashed a quick grin. "They're chatting and what? The five hidden men jump him?" She shook her head and started toward the parked cars. "It doesn't make sense, because there would be at least one body or blood."

"Maybe," Xander agreed as she kept pace. "But what if the woman had some way to incapacitate Gavin?"

"Like what?" Raine stopped and shot the other woman a scornful look. "Some Kyn tranquilizer?"

The blonde halted and shrugged her shoulders. "I'm just saying, we have no idea what these people have access to." Her gaze was sharp, watchful. "If they can mutate a Kyn into whatever it is you are, why can't they have some drug to disable Kyn?"

Raine buried her instinctive flinch at Xander's comment. "Point. Okay, say they drug him and take him away." They began moving out of the trees. "Would there be signs near his car?"

They headed back toward the cars and the two waiting men. Xander stepped up to the front of the sports car, and pointed at the ground, her smile was almost smug. "You mean like these?"

"Drag marks." Raine was disgusted at missing them on her first pass around the car. She needed to be sharper than this. She called Cheveyo over and asked him to check out the area Xander discovered to see if he could trace any spell.

While he worked, she leaned her jeans-clad hip against the convertible and faced Xander. "What happened at Chet's?" Raine hadn't wanted to ask, but she needed to know. He'd been a rare friend and even though her worries about Gavin shadowed most of her thoughts, she hadn't forgotten Chet.

The smaller woman's face went blank, but her eyes darkened with grief and anger. "Spelled trap," she answered. "He walked into his house and tripped it. Based on what was left behind, it didn't produce the desired effects of limiting his abilities. He fought those lying in wait before he was killed."

Obviously eavesdropping, Ryder walked up to them. "If the spell was tripped only when he walked in, it means it was set before he got home."

Xander nodded shortly. "There were faint traces of an unknown Kyn who was able to bypass Chet's wards. They probably set it and let the others in."

"They knew his movements, his habits, then," Raine said quietly. "Which points to Quinn's mysterious lover."

"Fucking coward." Xander's face was hard. "They Shadow

Walked into his home, and then slashed his throat so deep it pretty much decapitated him."

"There are very few Wraiths who can Shadow Walk," Ryder pointed out, throwing Raine off balance. "They need to have some Fey blood to accomplish it."

"You're a Wraith?" she blurted.

"What?" He flashed her one of his annoyingly smug smiles. "You thought I was here because I'm Natasha's flavor of the month?" He laughed.

Red tinged Raine's cheeks, and her voice was gruff, disconcerted at being so off the mark, "My apologies, Ryder."

His smile got a bit larger, but his eyes remained flat. "Bet that hurt, uh?"

Raine ignored him. "I thought Shadow Walking was an ability known only to Wraiths?"

"Not always," Cheveyo cut in, catching the last part of their conversation. "It's not a widely mastered skill, but there are those outside of the Wraiths powerful enough to do so."

"Look," Xander said. "It doesn't matter who trained the killer to Shadow Walk, only that he can."

"Okay, so he comes in behind Chet, and slashes his throat." Visions of the man she killed earlier stopped Raine. Had her strike been so deep he was nearly decapitated? She didn't think so, and she didn't want to ask Cheveyo in front of the other two. She shot him a look to find him watching her. Again the weird sense he could read her mind flashed through her. She cleared her throat and didn't break eye contact with Cheveyo. "Xander was the weapon a blade?"

"No, it was too ragged. I'd say it was claws." Xander's answer snapped Raine's head around. "We aren't sure if it's shifter or demon. The smell is off."

"What do you mean?" Raine's voice was sharp and her pulse raced as the image of a ragged, torn throat whipped through her mind.

"I mean it didn't smell right. There were familiar elements of shifter and demon, but like nothing I've ever encountered before." Her attention didn't waver. "The closest I've come to anything like it, is you."

The blood drain from Raine's face. "What do you mean, me?" She wasn't sure she wanted to hear this.

Xander's voice didn't change. "You smell a bit like Fey, a bit like Magi, a bit like shifter, all intertwined with something feral. You're not as clear cut scent wise as say, Gavin or Ryder here."

Ryder's face lost its boyish charm and turned harsh as he studied Raine. "How sure are you that McCord didn't kill Chet, Xander?"

"The scent has a different twist and it's male," she said, her tone scathing. "Which is why she's still breathing, demonling."

"Besides," Cheveyo pointed out. "She can't be in two places at once."

Raine blocked out their conversation and underlying threats, as she struggled to put it all together. "It was the Kyn out at my place who had to set the spelled trap for Chet." Her words stopped the conversation cold. "Which means they split their strengths. This Kyn has to be Quinn's lover."

"I agree," Cheveyo said. "It's the only explanation on how they were able to penetrate Chet's home and get out to your place."

She began to pace. "So this mysterious Kyn heads out to my house with two men, on the possible chance I would be an easier target. While my anonymous caller is sent out with his own group for Chet, more manpower, so they think he's the bigger threat. In the meantime, Lawson lures Gavin out to the middle of nowhere and her little band of merry men takes him down."

"They keep underestimating us," Xander pointed out.

Raine nodded. "And Quinn's lover isn't as experienced as we are."

"How do you figure that?" Ryder asked.

Cheveyo was the one to answer. "The spell meant to trap Chet failed and their only option was to kill him. The spell used here to shield the hiding men was basic but strong. You don't have to be skilled to shield, but you do to disable a Wraith."

"So Quinn's lover isn't a Wraith?" Xander asked.

"I don't think so," Raine said. "There were too many mistakes. Basic mistakes no self-respecting Wraith would make."

"It doesn't bring us any closer to figuring out who Quinn's lover is," Ryder stated. "If anything it makes our suspect pool a hell of a lot bigger."

"Doesn't matter." She pocketed Gavin's map. "We go after the one we know for sure, Dr. Lawson. We break her, we get the other two." She felt their stares and looked up. "What?"

"You are one cold bitch, McCord," Ryder broke the silence. With a wicked grin he added, "It turns me on."

Raine snorted. "You're a sick puppy, Ryder."

His soft *woof, woof* followed her back to her SUV.

CHAPTER TWENTY-EIGHT

W hile dawn painted the sky with soft pinks, deep blues, and a range of purples, Cheveyo, in Gavin's convertible, led the mini caravan back to Taliesin. Raine rode alone in her SUV as music pounded through the speakers and into her body. The volume deafening in a futile attempt to block out her thoughts. Nightmare images of her past were now superimposed with Gavin's face, and by the time she pulled into the parking lot her head was throbbing.

Exhaustion left her ragged, and after dutifully reporting to Mulcahy, who sported a rare five o'clock shadow—his own indication of a sleepless night—she headed to her office. Now armed with the possible location, the research team was pulling information on the lab. After working through the layers of a tricky paper trail buried among Eden's inheritance, they were able to link the lab to the good doctor. Now they were trying to track down the security plans because there was no way to utilize Shadow Walking, not if Gavin was badly injured. Therefore, Mulcahy assigned a team to keep an eye on the lab and note security details before Raine's team infiltrated tonight.

Behind the drawn blinds and closed door of her office, Raine waited for the research team's call. Her concentration was shot, but she managed to make one call on the slim chance of finding out information on Quinn's lover. Unfortunately, Alexi never answered. Since it was still early, it wasn't unexpected.

Raine curled up in her chair and stared sightlessly out the window. Her mind ran in useless circles, and her emotions were in turmoil. Fear-laced worry and anger pushed against each other like never-ending waves. Drained, she closed her eyes and let oblivion take her under.

It didn't take long for the dreams to start.

She was crouched naked in a cage and in front of her, Gavin was strapped to a metal table. Blood dripped steadily from the edges, and his screams echoed in her head. White lab coats moved around, taking samples, writing notes, and making observations. The *click click* of high heels on the hard floor brought her gaze around. Another white lab coat adorned the redhead with a hard smile twisting her face.

Eden moved passed Raine's cage without a glance and stopped next to Gavin. "You'll make such a good solider, Mr. Durand." Her voice, cool and even, seemed to echo and fade. "Don't worry, it won't hurt for long."

Mocking laughter filled the sterile room, ebbing and flowing like the ocean, louder, then softer, then louder.

Struggling harder against the bars, Raine snarled, "Leave him alone, bitch!"

The woman ignored her completely, and leaned over to stab a needle into Gavin. His scream echoed off the walls, making Raine cover her ears while she muttered, "No, no, no, no," uselessly.

A shadow fell over her cage and when she pried opened her eyes she found Gavin's jade green ones caught in a twisted mask of wolf and man. "This is your fault, Raine."

She reached trembling fingers through the bars to touch him, but he wrenched away.

His voice came from a snarling muzzle in an accusing growl. "Why didn't you stop them? You should have killed them all."

"I'm sorry." It came out in a whisper. "I'm so sorry."

The cage disappeared, leaving her naked and kneeling in a dark hallway. She got to her feet and ran, desperate to find the door to Gavin and get them both out. Snarls, groans, and whispers followed her fleeing form. They grew louder, pounding at her until she screamed with despair, even as she covered her ears in a futile attempt block the noise beating at her mind. They crashed against her barriers, tore at her sense of self, and stripped her of all control.

Like a thrown light switch, the noise flicked off into a sudden, deafening silence. All that remained was the harsh sounds of her breath, as it rattled through her hollow chest. She dropped her shaking hands from her ears and opened her eyes.

She stood at the end of the hallway in front of a full-length mirror. The reflected image wavered, and she leaned closer only to find Gavin's half-wolf, half-man face staring back. She centered on his green eyes, and tried to bring his image into focus, but green bled to silver until she faced a feral woman. Her tangled dark hair and blood-stained hands tipped with pointed nails, matched her mouth stretched to reveal sharp, tearing, red-rimmed teeth. She crouched on the floor, her hand disappearing into the thick black fur of a large leopard.

The instant Raine met the leopard's silvered gaze the world went still, holding its breath. She went to touch the woman, and stared in horrified fascination as the woman's hand reached out to meet her touch. Just before their palms met, Raine let out a sharp gasp, which snapped her awake, her heart racing.

She rubbed her trembling hands across her wet face and waited for her phone to ring.

CHAPTER TWENTY-NINE

The rain from earlier had stopped, although the cold bite in the air left no one in doubt that winter was coming. Raine took the clouds obscuring the moon as a good omen.

She deftly dropped the now-dead security guard behind the tree, confident Ryder and Xander had the other two taken care of. Cheveyo held the concealing spell, also known as the Abdo spell, steady. At her signal, he followed her to the side door.

Suspending all movement, she waited, listening to the night. The side door was still propped opened by a rock. They got lucky when the newly deceased guard indulged in his unhealthy nicotine habit. Otherwise, they would need the dead man's eye and finger to get through the door. Since Raine refused to wait any longer, they were going in half blind.

The research team managed to uncover dated security permits, but they weren't able to find anything more current. They confirmed fingerprint and retinal identification were required for entry, and bypassing the interior electronic surveillance needed an access code.

Raine and her team discussed the possibility that the security had been upgrade at some point in the last few years. However, Mulcahy pointed out that the interior security may not have been upgraded, especially if Dr. Lawson was working on Kyn subjects. The magic inherent to the Kyn tended to interfere with electronics, making it unwise to invest money in a high-end security system, which would bring unwanted attention to a forgotten lab.

Raine wasn't so sure, and when she recognized the finger/retinal scan on the outside doors, her doubt crystalized. The security measures bore an uncanny resemblance to those used at Talbot's labs.

Day watch confirmed a small staff of about five individuals, plus three security guards. When Raine's team arrived, the outside guards grew to five and two of the staff members left.

As far as Raine was concern, four to eight was not bad odds. She sent Xander and Ryder to remove the two guards on the far side. Then she watched as Cheveyo proved not all witches held tight to the three-fold law. He shot off a spell that took out the guard coming around the corner, while Raine snapped the other guard's neck. That left the cigarette smoking guard who so nicely left the door open.

Signaling Cheveyo to call the other hunters back, she kept her attention trained on the surrounding darkness. The witch sent a small pulse of magic toward the talisman Xander wore. A sort of magic communicator, the talismans enabled the two groups to signal each other without noise, and kept the shielding spell in place.

Raine was impressed with Cheveyo's skill. It took tremendous ability to hold the Abdo spell in place on two separate groups while working with the talismans. Being head witch brought some definite advantages.

The shadows deepened and reformed into Xander and Ryder as they moved around the corner. Raising a brow, Raine caught Xander's short nod, confirming the guards were down and out.

Motioning for the others to follow and spread out, she headed toward the thin beam of white light coming from the propped door. With efficient hand signals, she directed each member to their assigned positions. Cheveyo would cover any video cameras with a perception spell known as the Conspicio spell. It made anyone watching the cameras believe nothing was happening in the hallways—kind of a magical looping of the security feed. The down side to the spell—when the magic hit the wires, it would most likely short the cameras out, eliminating the element of surprise.

Raine was willing to take the chance.

She reached up and silently pulled out the fighting knife from her back sheath. The black-coated weapon was an intimidating total length of thirteen inches. The eight-inch, double-edged, carbon-steel blade held a blood groove. She tightened her right hand around the solid hilt. Releasing one of her wrist blades to her left hand, she flicked a glance over the three figures beside her. Everyone was armed with various blades, except for Cheveyo.

The small group moved up behind the door. Xander grabbed the door handle and waited. Positioned on the opposite side with Ryder, Raine gave Xander a nod. She yanked it open, giving Cheveyo a clean shot at the cameras. Working quickly, his hands swept through the spell grace- fully, his fingers appearing to flick off some small insect. The rush of his magic, brushed by Raine's aura as she slipped into the point position, poised for a confrontation.

A high-pitched whine came from the two cameras aimed

at the door and a small whisper of smoke puffed from one of the casings. The other still worked, if its green steadily blinking light was to be believed. Raine headed swiftly down the narrow hallway to the closed beige door, and stayed low and in front of Cheveyo.

To the left of the door was a small computer pad. She stepped to the side to peer through the heavily reinforced slat window as Ryder came up behind her. Nothing moved in the brightly lit outer hallway. She lifted her chin to Ryder, and he placed his hand on the metal handle. Standing as close as she was, Raine watched the red ring in his eyes bleed over the brown as his power focused on the now twisted metal handle.

She finally figured out why Natasha sent him. It seemed his Fundo demon father left him with an affinity for metal. Which meant none of the locks in this place could stand against them, as Ryder was able to soften or strengthen any metal with a touch. It also gave Raine a hunter with no weakness to silver or iron. Cheveyo was a strong asset, but Ryder wouldn't hesitate to kill quickly, something they might need before the night ended.

A soft thud caused her to shoot Ryder a sharp look. He held the handle in his left hand as he pushed the door open with his right. Before the alarm on the door could sound, Cheveyo sent another small burst of magic into the pad, disabling it.

The antiseptic smell hit her first, causing old memories to rise. She fought the fear, scrabbled for control, and motioned the others through. Following Xander, Raine kept her hand on the door until it closed.

Now it was Xander's turn. She stepped forward, raised her head, and closing her eyes, all the while drawing in deep breaths. She turned until she faced the left hallway, cocked her head, and opened her eyes, indicating she caught Gavin's scent.

Raine covered their backs as they traversed the sterile white hallway. The edges of old fear and panic beat at her, but she forced it back by concentrating on getting to Gavin. The murmur of voices brought the small group up short just outside the double doors leading to the main lab.

The floor plans indicated a simple lay out. The main floor held a large space, most likely the lab, a couple of smaller rooms, and the reception and security areas. The basement was an unknown, but Raine bet that would be where they would find Gavin. The problem was, to get there, they had to go through the doors in front of them, and then cross through the main lab.

She pushed her braid aside and re-sheathed the short sword in a practiced move. She let everything quiet inside her until there was nothing but anticipatory silence. Then she moved to the front of the group. At her nod, Ryder sent his magic barreling into the metal doors. They blew off their hinges and half way across the lab, leaving a wide path of destruction in their wake.

The two men on the right side of the room, jumped to their feet, and set their backs to the far wall. The doors shot through the lab with Raine striding in their wake. She caught the older, dark-haired one by the throat, and had his feet dangling off the floor before the younger, blond haired man could react.

Xander was right behind her, and the scream bubbling up in the blond's throat was abruptly cut off as a wickedly sharp blade was laid none too gently against his neck. Xander bared her sharp teeth and the man's legs collapsed under his weight, terror leaving a smelly stain at his crotch.

Savage joy danced through Raine as horror widened the

washed out eyes of the now-gasping man she held. His hands scrabbled at her left wrist and would've drawn blood if her sleeves were shorter or looser. She placed the point of her wrist blade just under his right eye, pressing the tip in until a drop of blood appeared. The frantic hands at her wrists abruptly stilled.

"Where is he?" Menace rode her voice. She loosened her grip enough so he could suck in a breath and find his voice.

"Who?" his question emerged thin, shaky.

"Don't fuck with me." She pressed the knife deeper, letting his blood bead on the blade and forcing a terrified whimper from him. "All I have to do is push this in, straight to your brain. Answer the damn question."

"Down—downstairs," he stuttered, sweat popping out on his brow.

Raine threw him to Cheveyo, who stood beside her. "Bind him. He's going to take us downstairs."

Cheveyo yanked the man to his feet, securing his arms behind his back, and with a soft word froze his vocal cords.

The computer monitor the two men had been huddled around snagged Raine's attention. Glass slides lay near the powerful microscope sitting beside the computer. She looked closer, identifying blood on two of the slides. Rage swept through her. The paper-thin substance on the third piece of glass was skin. Snatching it up, she stalked toward the younger man Xander still held.

"Who took this?" She leaned into his waxen face.

He clamped his mouth shut, his body shaking so hard, it forced Xander to pulled the blade back before he slit his own throat. His muddy colored eyes frantically flicked from the man Cheveyo held to the two huntresses accosting him.

"He won't answer you," Xander drawled to Raine. "You're scaring him to death."

Raine felt a fierce smile bloom. "Yeah, well, I guess we'll light a fire under him to help find his voice." With a small movement, she brought a flare of white flame to her left palm. The blond's eyes widened and latched onto the eerily silent tongues of white flames flickering over her left hand.

Leaning in, she brought her burning hand up as if to caress the side of his face. He jerked back, frantically trying to get away from the flame. Her voice was low, soft, deadly. "Who took the skin?"

His frantic movements became jerky and wild causing Xander to lose her grip. The man pulled back sharply, stumbled, and scrambled with hands and feet in a desperate bid for the door. Sobs and gasps accompanied his frantic dash. He managed to get halfway across the lab before Raine's flying blade impaled itself to the hilt at the base of his skull. His body jerked upright, as if yanked by strings, and then did a half-turn, revealing the dimming light in his eyes as he crumpled to the floor.

She felt no sympathy as she pulled the small knife out of his neck. Wiping the bloodied blade on the white lab coat, she lifted her ice-cold gaze to the remaining man shaking in Cheveyo's grasp, his face a horrified mask.

Her voice sounded remote, even to her. "I guess he took the sample."

"Nice aim," Ryder commented as he casually walked around the dead lab tech.

Raine stalked back to Cheveyo and his prisoner and re-sheathed her throwing blade. The scientist stumbled back against the tall witch as she approached. "Xander, Ryder, clear the rest of this level." She motioned to Cheveyo. "Let's move."

Cheveyo dragged the man with him as they headed toward the elevator that would take them down to the lab. At the card-reader on the button panel, she reached out and yanked the cringing man's ID card off his neck, leaving angry red marks behind.

She flicked a glance at his picture. "Ethan Carver. Nice to meet you, Ethan." She swiped the card through the reader, and watched the lights go from red to green. The door slid silently open and she gestured, "After you."

Cheveyo shoved him to the back of the car while Raine slipped inside and hit the button sending the elevator to the basement.

She directed Cheveyo to move Ethan to the front of the elevator until he was centered in front of the doors. Standing to the side, she kept her blades sheathed. She needed her hands free as she mentally gathered her magic together in anticipation. Tension held her body poised for action.

The elevator gave a soft ding as it came to a smooth stop. The doors slid open. The first thing she saw was the empty examining table standing in the center of the room, enclosed in reinforced glass. A distant voice in her head wondered why evil labs prominently displayed that cold metal slab. Ranged around the edges of it were various machines.

Behind the glass cage, there were three locked doors with small windows carved into each entry. Chances were they were one-way glass, so the lab coats could observe whoever was inside. All three windows were dark, giving no clue as to which one held Gavin. On the left side of the basement a door opened, and out stepped Eden Lawson.

Catching sight of Ethan bound and held immobile by Cheveyo, the elegantly coiffed redhead drew up short. When Raine moved out of the elevator and into the room, Eden's gaze shifted from startled to wary.

"Well, Ms. McCord. To what do I owe the honor of this visit?" Still framed in the office doorway, Eden was cool and composed.

Raine kept a tight rein on her emotions. "It seems you took someone who doesn't belong to you."

When Raine stepped forward, Eden pulled a small

device from the pocket of her lab coat and shook her head. "You might want to stand still." A small smile played around her lips. "Do you know what this is?" She didn't wait for an answer. "This will send an electric current into the collar attached to my guest—a strong enough current, even a Kyn might have some problems recovering. Not to mention what it will do to his cells when the current hits a few of our injections now running through his body."

Raine stopped, her gut churning. "Following in your father's footsteps?" She needed to keep the doctor talking as it would give her or Cheveyo an opening.

Ethan began struggling in Cheveyo's grip and drew Eden's attention. She frowned at Raine. "Do I dare ask what happen to Toby?"

"He ran into a knife." There was no inflection in Raine's voice, and Eden's gaze hardened. Raine moved from behind Cheveyo and kept her hands visible and relaxed.

"Is that so?" Some of the anger held in the scientist's eyes leaked through and her grip on the small device tightened. Raine's breath hitched as Eden said, "You do realize how hard it is to find good help these days? He was such a bright young man, quite filled with potential."

Raine shrugged and despite her internal upheaval, managed to keep her tone conversational. "Want to trade? You can have Ethan back. I'll take Gavin." She shifted until her left side was partially behind the petrified Ethan.

A twisted smile lit Eden's face. "No, that's all right. I think I'll get more out of Gavin than you will out of Ethan."

"In that case." Keeping her eyes on Eden, Raine dropped her left wrist blade into her palm and with deadly speed, slammed the lethal weapon into the base of the helpless man's skull, giving it a sharp twist. When she pulled it back, Cheveyo let go, and the lifeless body fell to the floor.

Eden's face paled, but her voice was steady. "That was unnecessary."

Raine shook her head. "I disagree." She brought her other hand up and reached for the twisted magic running through her. "But then, I think I have something better to bargain with." Her nails lengthened and her arm began to shift.

Eden let out a small, excited gasp. "There were rumors some of the tests were successful, but I haven't been able to find any proof."

Raine dropped her arm, let it return to normal, and managed to move a step closer. "Oh, they were very success-ful, at least for me." She lowered her voice. "I can't say the results were the same for others."

Derision swept across Eden's elegant face. "Bane Mayson was a failure from the beginning. I read the initial reports and lab findings. They should have never used him."

Raine's mind sped through options as Eden talked. If Cheveyo threw a spell, there was a chance Eden could depress the button before his spell hit. It wasn't a risk she was willing to take. That meant she needed to lure the scien-tist closer, and to do that she needed to utilize the curiosity that started this, while the good doctor was in a talkative mood.

Obviously, Cheveyo's thoughts ran along the same lines because he drew Eden's gaze away from Raine. "What did your father miss, Dr. Lawson? What did you find?"

Raine didn't hesitate, but used Cheveyo's distraction to move a few more inches forward.

Eden flicked her gaze between her and Cheveyo, and then edged out of the doorway. "No more moving forward, Ms. McCord." Warning given, she answered Cheveyo's question. "The strength of the test subject's inherent magic. Mayson was a human psychic, but his magic was too weak. It twisted the results so they were unusable. The stronger the magic, the more defined the results become."

"You're going to blame Mayson for his own torture?" Raine's voice was sharp as old anger and resentments simmered.

Eden moved slowly down the hall. In an attempt to split the scientist's attention, Cheveyo shifted toward the other side. His move served another purpose as it created more room between him and Raine.

"It wasn't torture," Eden's voice was practical. "It's science. Don't you understand the benefits these discoveries will create?" Fervent belief lit her face. "Do you understand how many diseases we can eradicate once we isolate this DNA strand? Not only will we save countless human lives, but we will be able to de-mystify what sets Kyn and humans apart."

The slight brush of Cheveyo's magic rushed over Raine's skin and she caught his casual hand gesture to move forward. Together, they slid another step closer. When Eden's expression remained unchanged, Raine realized Cheveyo was once again utilizing the Conspicio spell, hiding their changing positions. The illusion would work in small increments, and maybe give enough time for Xander and Ryder to join their little party.

"So if a few Kyn died in the process, it's all worth it in the long run?" She kept Eden talking.

Eden's light laugh sounded so normal, it gave Raine the creeps. The echoes of the laugh faded. "You're a dying breed. The rewards such a discovery will generate for the human world heavily outweigh the lives of a few Kyn."

"I'm surprised Talbot agreed to your research, considering his father's reputation." Raine felt another soft brush from Cheveyo and slid another few inches forward.

"Aaron Talbot was a man of vision." Irritation filled

Eden's face. "His son, on the other hand, is hampered by his misplaced sense of compassion."

"Jonah doesn't know about this?" Raine asked, inwardly reeling from the shock of Eden's revelation.

"Of course not." Eden absently waved the hand holding the electronic device, and Raine tensed. "He would have never let me get this far. This is my discovery, and it will set me far apart from the Talbot Foundation. I'm going to change the history of humanity."

"What about what General Cawley wants?" Cheveyo asked, his voice smooth.

"The perfect solider?" The words were mocking and disdainful. "I needed funding, and the government is a wonderful source of income. Cawley believes my research is going to give him some kind of superhuman soldier."

"But?" Cheveyo prompted.

"The magic skews the results so radically, it's a lost cause." Her smile was angelic. "However, I won't be sharing that with him. He's doing this behind his agency's back. Did you know that? In the meantime, I can continue my research." Eden drew level with the first barred door and stopped, her shoulders straightening.

Raine sucked in a breath realizing Gavin was behind that door. "How about you give Cawley me? Won't it bring in more funding if you can prove to him such a solider exists?"

"You want to take Mr. Durand's place, Ms. McCord?" Eden asked, dryly. "How self-sacrificing."

Undaunted, Raine kept pushing. "I'll let Cheveyo chain my hands and feet. I'll put all my weapons on the floor." She dropped the bloodied blade from her left hand. "You can get Gavin out of that room and pass him off to Cheveyo so he can take him out of here. They'll leave. No retaliation." She watched Eden give the suggestion serious consideration. "I'm a much better weapon than Gavin will ever be," she tempted. "Jonah's father made sure of it."

Eden tilted her head to the side in a birdlike motion. "How long did they have you?"

Raine fought hard to keep her tone empty. "Three months."

Eden's fingers moved over the keypad by the door. It unlocked with a quiet snick. There was no movement from inside the dark cell. The simmering rage Raine held tight to all night joined the rising fear for Gavin, and formed a leaden ball in her stomach.

Eden didn't even glance inside the unlit cell. "You'd make an excellent study, Ms. McCord, but I'm afraid you're too much of an unknown to take such a risk."

Her gaze was still locked on Raine when Ryder's grinning face appeared out of the shadows behind her. Quick as a snake, he wrapped her left wrist in a crushing grip that caused her fingers to loosen on the device. Raine sprang forward and caught the little black remote before it hit the ground.

Eden shrieked and raked Ryder's face with her long nails, scoring three long gashes before he could stop her. He cursed and yanked her arms behind her back, and forced her to face forward. Without sparing her a glance, Raine dashed into the cell with Cheveyo right behind her. She summoned a small ball of light to chase back the darkness.

Gavin huddled in the corner, naked. Fresh cuts, seeping burns, and trickles of blood, threw macabre abstracts over his shaking arms, which were wrapped around his drawn-up legs. His sweat-drenched, tangled hair curtained his face.

Seeing him like this broke something inside of her. Furious tears burned against the back of her eyes. She ignored them and motioned for Cheveyo to back out.

Memories of her own time in captivity made it easy to

imagine what nightmares stalked Gavin's mind and twisted his reality. She edged closer carefully, doing her best not to set him off and kept her voice at a bare whisper. "Gavin, can you hear me? It's Raine."

Eden's angry shrieks echoed through the room, and Gavin's bruised shoulders tensed. Raine attention didn't waver from him, but she directed her next order to Ryder. "Get that bitch out of here. I'll deal with her in a minute."

The shrieks faded as Ryder pulled Eden down the hall. Raine sensed Cheveyo poised in the doorway, but she didn't look away from the one who mattered most. "Gavin?" She dared to crouch a few feet away from his huddled form. "Gavin, look at me, please."

His shaking stopped abruptly. He raised his head, his eyes blind to everything except what crawled through his mind.

Seeing the deep lines of pain and fear etched into his strong face a wave of cold, bitter fury surged over Raine. She struggled to hide her raging emotions, and kept her voice to a soft murmur. "Gavin, do you recognize me?"

His jade green eyes focused on her for a brief second, then narrowed at something over her shoulder. Instinctively she glanced to her left. It was a mistake.

He leapt, knocked her backwards, locked his hands around her neck, and squeezed. The noises coming from his mouth weren't even words, more the sounds of an animal in unbearable pain.

Cheveyo moved in, but Raine signaled for him to stop. She managed to get both of her arms in-between Gavin's and broke his hold. When lost his grip, she twisted her hands, shackled his wrists, then using his own weight as leverage, she threw him off.

It took all her strength to restrain him until Cheveyo could use a spell to put him under. As Gavin's struggles ceased, she loosened her grip and cupped his large hands in hers before gently laying them down next to him. With the barest touch, she shifted the long dark hair out of his face and tenderly traced his cheek. "I'm so sorry, Gavin."

"Raine?" Cheveyo put a hand on her shoulder. "I need to get him out of here."

She took a shaky breath. "I'll send Ryder to help you. Take him back and get a healer." She got stiffly to her feet. "Have Mulcahy use whichever healer he used with me."

"Are you bringing Lawson back to Taliesin?" Cheveyo asked.

She faced the one-way mirror. Red marks from Gavin's fingers ringed her neck. Distracted by her merciless reflection and incandescent silver eyes, she didn't answer, just turned and left the cell.

Her lethally intent emotions blew before her like an ill wind as she headed down the hall toward the still struggling Eden and the bored-looking Ryder. "Go help Cheveyo get Gavin out of here."

Ryder nodded and let go of Eden's wrists. Before the scientist could react, Raine snatched a handful of Eden's unraveling hair and yanked hard enough to earn a short scream of pain. Then using her grip in Eden's hair, Raine dragged the struggling woman down the hallway and toward the glass enclosed exam room. Eden's French-manicured fingernails ripped and broke as she clawed at Raine's hand. One high heel was left in the wake of their passage and her nylon-clad foot scrambled frantically against the smooth floor.

None of it fazed Raine. She tightened her grip and lugged the cursing, sobbing bitch down the hall.

When Eden grabbed the examination room doorframe in an obvious try to halt their forward progress, Raine wrenched her free with one sharp, hard jerk. Eden screamed

—a high-pitched screech of pain—as more fingernails rico-cheted off the floor.

Dragging Eden around to the floor in front of her, Raine jerked her hand free of Eden's hair, and delivered a vicious slap. Eden's shocked silence filled the room, and she froze momentarily—just long enough for Raine to body-slam her onto the frigid metal table. The force of Eden's back hitting the icy steel knocked the breath—and the fight—out of her, allowing Raine the time to shackle one wrist and ankle before Eden began struggling in earnest.

The restraints, a combination of iron and silver, stung Raine's hands, but she welcomed the small pain. It spurred her on and kept her focused. With the scientist locked down, Raine snagged Eden's chin, and forced her to meet the glacial steel of Raine's gaze. Her grip tightened until her nails sliced small cuts along Eden's jaw. When she spoke, ice coated her voice. "Give me a reason. Just one."

The metallic stink of fear radiated from Eden, the scent pleasing the wilder side of Raine. The whimpers escaping from Eden's bloodless lips added a savage spark of glee to Raine's soul as she made quick work of the remaining two leg restraints.

Leaving Eden strapped to the table, Raine studied the room. She spotted a number of syringes, loaded with some clear liquid, lying in the cooling unit and smiled. Eden's terrified gazed followed Raine's every move, as she wrenched open the cooler and grabbed one of the syringes. She turned back to Eden with a savage smile and Eden's breath hitched.

Raine dragged a small, backless chair over to Eden's left side. "Now what could this little syringe hold that scares you so much?" Her voice was a purr of malice.

Eden's eyes never left the syringe.

Raine kept her voice calm and made sure to hold the small instrument in clear view. "Where shall we start?

Hmm?" She tapped the syringe lightly against her palm. "I know, let's start with how you managed to get Quinn to turn over other Kyn to you."

"I don't know what you're talking about," Eden declared, her voice shaky, but determined.

Raine made a *tsking* sound. "Wrong answer." She jabbed the syringe into the vein threading the inside of Eden's elbow. Eden gave a short scream and began to pant. Raine wiggled the syringe. "Would you like to try again?"

"Quinn approached me with an offer."

That could be true since Quinn was an opportunistic bastard. "What kind of offer?"

"He heard about the discreet inquiries we made about Kyn volunteers, and he informed me no Kyn would come forth willingly." Eden seemed to calm a bit when Raine held the needle still and listened. "He said he could get me a couple of volunteers," she continued. "Kyn who wouldn't be missed."

"How?"

Eden sucked in a shallow breath. "He indicated he had a source who could identify which of the Kyn hung on the fringes of society—where no one would raise an alarm about their sudden disappearance."

"Who was the source?"

Eden licked her lips while her eyes flickered once. Raine applied pressure to the syringe, and depressed the plunger a fraction. "Okay, okay, stop!" Eden's voice broke. "His girlfriend! She owns a bar, Zarana's. Her name is Alexi Savriti!"

Shock blasted Raine's world off kilter. Everything inside her went still. Then like a black tidal wave, the pain and rage of betrayal swamped her. Alexi was the last name she suspected to emerge from Eden's lips.

Barely aware, her hands tightened on the syringe and she pushed the plunger a bit farther. She fought a silent, desperate battle for control like a diver reaching for the surface. If she lost, the woman strapped to the table wouldn't be answering any more questions, and the surrounding lab would be no more than a pile of rubble. Raine ruthlessly clamped down on her venomous emotions. Her first breath was shallow and shaky, but the second one was stronger, steadier.

Frantic sobs broke through her chaotic thoughts and snapped her attention back to Eden, who was mesmerized by the needle in her arm. Raine lifted her finger off the plunger. The level of the concoction in the syringe had dropped slightly. Raine gave a mental shrug and got back on task. "Once Quinn was dead, did his girlfriend take over?"

"Wh—what?" Eden sobbed.

Raine coldly repeated her question.

Eden's sobs died down, broken by the occasional hiccup. "Yes, she helped him with bringing in the wizard."

Seething inside, Raine concentrated on getting answers. "When Rimmick didn't perform to your standards, you killed him."

Eden shook her head, her face pale and clammy. "I didn't kill him, he was already dead. Alexi offered to get rid of the body for me."

"You killed him with your fucking experiments, Dr. Frankenstein," Raine snarled. Eden whimpered. "At least Rimmick found release in death, unlike Mayson. Which reminds me, how did you get to him so quickly?"

Eden's eyes remained fearful but blank. "I don't know what you're talking about."

Raine put her finger back on the plunger, and Eden's voice rose half an octave. "I swear I've never met Mayson. I just saw the reports my father had on him."

"I have one more question for you, doctor," Raine

sneered. "Who's the freak who took out the other Kyn when you attacked Gavin and me? Where did he come from?"

"Tarek." Disgust lightly undercoated Eden's trembling voice. "He's not sane, but he's useful."

"Created another monster you couldn't control, huh?" Raine shook her head. "See that's the trouble with you, with your father, even with Talbot. What all the twisted, greedy scientists never considered." She leaned closer and plunged the syringe half way down, her voice a sibilant hiss as Eden's scream echoed through the room. "You made us, and now we'll destroy you."

As the echoes of Eden's shrill scream faded, a slight movement brought Raine spinning around.

Xander stood in the doorway, her face an empty mask. "Anything left for Vidis to work with."

Raine straightened and shot a disgusted look at Eden, who was now unconscious. "Yeah, but it will be fun to see what her little poison does to her." She dropped the half-empty syringe on the floor and crushed it underfoot. She went to the cooling unit, pulled out three syringes containing the clear liquid, and then located a small container. Filling it with the syringes, she stuffed the padded pouch in her pocket.

"Grab her," she said to Xander. "And let's get out of here."

Xander let out a hiss as she released Eden from the restraints. She took a moment to bind Eden's hands and feet, and then heaved the limp form over her shoulder. Raine followed her out of the room. When Xander went left, Raine went right, heading to Eden's office. Behind her, Xander paused and called her name. Raine didn't turn back, but said, "Head for the elevator."

Raine didn't wait to see if Xander followed orders. Instead, she called forth her magic and sent it into Eden's office. The flickering flames began to consume the contents of the room, dancing over the desk and climbing the walls. Satisfied, Raine turned away and headed back to the elevators. She let her magic drip from her hands as the white flames left a path of destruction in her wake.

At the examination room, she gathered her magic, checked to make sure Xander was in the elevator, and sent a ball of energy spinning into the room. Then, she leapt over Ethan's crumpled form and darted to the elevator where Xander waited. Safely inside the metal container, Raine watched the room ignite then flash into an inferno before the doors slid shut on the hurtling flames. As they exited the elevator on the top floor, a muted explosion shook underfoot.

Raine smiled.

She maneuvered through the twisted wreckage of the lab, stepped lightly around the blond's wide-eyed corpse, with its surrounding puddle of blood, and held the doors open for Xander. Once outside the final door, she took a deep breath of the biting night air.

Xander readjusted her hold on Eden's unconscious body.

"Take her back to the car," Raine ordered. "I'll do clean up. Let them know we're on our way back."

Xander nodded and melted into the darkness. Raine waited a few moments until the shifter was clear, then heaved the bodies of the dead guards into the building. Satisfied all the evidence was inside, she sent a burst of magic into every computer, every camera she could find, and fried the drives, guaranteeing no information could be salvaged.

Back at the double doors, she tapped into the roiling rage to fuel her magic. A ball of flame blazed to life between her outstretched hands. The flames were white, ghostly, and silent. With a soft word, she sent it rushing into the building. Every available surface that could burn, would. The rest would melt beyond recognition.

She whirled around, raced for the tree line, and reached the edge just as the explosion rocked the air. Stripped of her civilized veneer and socially imposed restraints, the true Wraith was revealed. Her sense of satisfaction was cold, feral, and the gleam in her silver eyes would strike fear into the stoutest of hearts.

As the unearthly flames ate the remains of the lab, she strode into the night, merged with the shadows of the surrounding forest, and disappeared.

CHAPTER THIRTY

I t was just past one in the morning when Raine pulled her
SUV to a stop in a natural clearing, miles from civiliza-
tion. Other than Xander's terse directions, the drive was
made in silence. Eden remained an unconscious lump in the
back seat even when the SUV bumped over the barely there
paths threading through the forest.

Dual urges battled inside Raine. Her aching heart needed
to see Gavin, while a darker part wanted to drive back to
Portland and confront Alexi. But she had to follow her chief's
orders. Mulcahy's instructions were clear, the two Wraiths
were to bring Eden before a tribunal of shifters, including
Warrick Vidis, to answer for Chet's death.

Cheveyo and Ryder were on their way to the small home
of Cassandra Miwa, the old witch healer who helped bring
Raine back after her captivity. Cheveyo told Raine he would
call and let her know what was happening. He cautioned her
not to expect an update for a few hours, as Cassandra would
need time to get through the drugs before she could reach
Gavin.

Raine sent a fervent prayer to the Lord and Lady for Gavin's recovery.

She cut off the headlights and got out of the car. By the time Xander shut the passenger door, Raine had dragged Eden out of the back seat. She threw the limp body over her shoulder like a sack of wheat and followed Xander down a winding deer trail. Within minutes, they stepped into another clearing. This one was surrounded by a ring of small, lichen-encrusted boulders hidden among the foliage. There was an unnaturally silent, blue fire glowing in the center of the circle. The azure flames cast shifting shadows over the four figures on the opposite side.

Mulcahy's rangy form was easily discernible, as was Vidis's slight figure. There was also a great shaggy wolf sitting quietly next to what looked like a very lumpy boulder. The boulder rose and straightened. Raine braced as the figure unfolded to a height of about six-foot-eight. Gold eyes gleamed in the firelight.

Mulcahy motioned Xander and Raine closer, as they did so, he gave a soft command. Magic rushed over her skin as the circle closed with a snap. Realizing her boss had trapped them inside the judgment circle, she almost snarled in frustration. She wouldn't be able to leave until the tribunal was complete, which meant going after Alexi would have to be put on hold.

Sensing her impatience, Mulcahy shot her a sharp look. "Put the doctor down, McCord."

Raine shrugged her shoulder and Eden landed with a resounding thump on the hard ground. It brought a small wince from Xander and a soft groan from Eden.

Mulcahy moved to Eden. "*Expedio.*" His command was soft, but the binding holding Eden's hands and feet dropped to the ground. "*Conscius.*"

Raine's reluctant admiration for her uncle rose as Eden's

eyes fluttered open. The scientist sat up and glanced around, shakily rubbing her head. It seemed to take a moment for her surroundings to register. Then her eyes widened, her breath hitched, and she scrambled backwards from the silent quartet facing her across the wicked blue flames.

Panicked noises escaped her white lips, until her wildly spinning eyes caught on Mulcahy crouched by the fire. Apparently, the sight of someone she recognized reassured her. The mewling noises shut off as if she'd flicked a switch, and her scrambling movements ceased.

Her gaze locked onto Mulcahy as if he was the only sane thing in the universe. "Mr. Mulcahy, thank God! You have to get me out of here." She reached out her hands in supplication. "Your employee is insane."

Raine snorted. The foolish human actually thought Ryan Mulcahy was her savior. Either that, or she figured he was stupid enough to fall for her helpless female routine.

Mulcahy's smile was icy, his brown eyes dark, as he completely ignored her imploring hands. "We need you to answer a few questions for us, Dr. Lawson. I'm sure your cooperation will help in determining your sentence."

Eden's mouth dropped open. She lowered her hands and pushed herself shakily to her feet.

Mulcahy straightened and stepped back. Turning, he addressed the waiting judges. "Honored tribunal, *breithimh*, Dr. Eden Lawson is being brought before you to answer for the death of Chet Hilliard." His voice was oddly formal. "She is our *deontas bais*, our payment, in the event of death, to you, to our fallen brother, and his family. Do as you will." Finished, he stepped back to the edge of the circle, and left Eden to face the three Lycos standing in judgment.

Eden's eyes darted from place to place as if something kept winking in and out of sight. She began to sway a bit on her feet and sweat beaded across her forehead. Her hands clenched and unclenched. Whatever was in that syringe was definitely having an impact on her and Raine wasn't the only who noticed her strange behavior.

"Raine," Vidis's baritone rode smoothly on the night air. "Is the woman going to be able to answer our questions?"

Raine kept her tone bland. "I'm sure she'll be able to—for a while."

"She doesn't look sane enough to have planned Chet's death," the golden-eyed giant muttered. His voice gave the impression of tumbling rocks.

The large wolf next to him stalked around the fire and advanced on Eden. The scientist gave a shrill scream of terror and stumbled backward. Xander sprang forward, with disconcerting speed, and prevented Eden's retreat. The wolf sniffed a few times, then a low growl passed its lips. As it turned away, a light mist enveloped its form. When the haze dissipated, the wolf was gone and in its place stood a tall, naked, dark haired woman.

She stormed back to the giant's side. "She doesn't smell right." Her voice was a growl. Her eyes were almost black as she shot a considering glance at Raine.

Feeling her own hackles rise, Raine fought to leash her temper. Without a doubt, the woman was an alpha. Her carriage was too straight, too arrogant and noble, to be anything but a leader.

Seeing a wolf shift into a nude female was apparently too much for Eden. She screwed her eyes tightly shut and muttered, "This isn't real. None of this is real."

Everyone ignored her.

Raine faced the three judges. "In the interest of getting some straight answers, I used a form of encouragement."

"Such as?" Vidis asked.

"I let her try out some of her own medicine." She caught the flash of satisfaction in Vidis's gaze.

"Do you know what this medicine does?" the giant asked.

Raine shook her head. "I don't, but I can give a few guesses." She noticed the alpha woman arch a brow. "I think the drug is designed to remove the inner barrier a Kyn holds between the mundane world and the magic world," she continued. "It causes a Kyn to be bombarded with magics not their own. It can also amplify the Kyn's natural magic to a very uncomfortable level."

"Have you had the substance analyzed already?" the woman asked.

"No." Raine's shoulders tightened but her voice remain detached. "However, from personal experience, I can say it is one very twisted ride."

The woman cocked her head, and studied Raine. "And for humans? What does it do?"

Raine shrugged. "I'm not sure, since humans have very little to no magic. I'm guessing it creates extremely vivid hallucinations." She stared at the still cowering scientist. "We could ask her."

"Not right now." The sharp predatory smile crossing the raven-haired woman's face sent shivers down Raine's back. "We have other, more important questions to ask."

The giant motioned to Xander to hold Eden. Xander used her grip on Eden's arm to yank her upright. "Pay attention."

Eden shuddered.

Raine listened as the three Lycos judges interrogated Eden. They got the same story she gave Raine in the lab, only with a few more details. Quinn had funneled information on the Kyn to Eden by utilizing a subtle illusion spell, which allowed him to listen into private conversations at Taliesin. When he ran across bits and pieces about the existence of the Wraiths, he decided to share with Eden, going to far as to expound on the benefits of such information falling into General Cawley's hands. Using the promise of the ultimate solider, she was able to gain more funding for her research from Cawley.

Being assigned to Erica Cawley's security detail was a perfect cover for Quinn. It allowed him to act as a go between for Cawley and Eden. However, Quinn mentioned he would have to be careful with his communications because Chet was his supervisor on the assignment.

After Quinn's death, Alexi was out for blood, convinced he was killed by a Wraith. When she found Chet sniffing around who Quinn was involved with, she convinced Eden the nosy shifter was becoming too much of a threat. Alexi began pushing Eden to take Chet out, but initially Eden refused. She believed, rightly so, that taking out a Kyn like Chet was too dangerous.

The final nudge came from Talbot's gathering that Raine and Gavin attended. Cawley managed to corner Eden and demand visible results from her research. Not wanting the general to clue in on the fact she was far from developing the perfect solider, Eden went back to Alexi for help. Alexi glee-fully provided three names, Raine McCord, Gavin Durand, and Chet Hilliard.

Together, Alexi and Eden planned the simultaneous attacks, knowing they would have one chance to hit the top level of Taliesin. Once the three were removed, the Kyn community would close ranks and infiltration would be harder than ever. Eden felt even if two of the three hits were unsuccessful, the results she gained from just one would be enough to set her research over the edge.

Raine's stomach roiled and her fists clenched as the story spewed from Eden's mouth. The doctor's voice remained clinical as she described the attack plan. Alexi brought in Tarek to spell a talisman to shield the five men sent to ambush Gavin. Eden brought along a palm size injector to knock Gavin out long enough to be overpowered.

When Alexi found out Tarek could Shadow Walk, she kept him on standby. A good thing, since the spelled trap Alexi set at Chet's home failed to work as intended. With Eden's agreement, Alexi ordered Tarek to kill Chet before he could wipe out his attackers.

Raine took a twisted kind of pleasure in hearing how Alexi threw a tantrum after Raine wiped out the attack team. Alexi's consistent underestimation of Raine's capabilities would come in handy.

Once Eden ran dry, silence descended into the glen. Even after laying bare all of the twisted plans, her inability to see the three Kyn as anything more than minor lab experiments was glaringly obvious. She stood there in front of Xander, trying to pull her tattered pride together, unaware her actions had signed her death warrant.

Eden ran her hand through her tangled hair, but stopped when Vidis's voice made her jump. "We are the judges of Motoki Pack, and our punishment is final. This mortal must pay with the same coin she cost Chet Hilliard."

Eden raised a trembling chin. "You are not the police and—"

"Actually," Raine interrupted, happy to burst psycho-bitch's bubble, "they are your judges, jury, and executioners."

Eden swiveled, her panicked gaze landing on Raine. "You can't eradicate my research, even with my death."

Raine bared her teeth. "Already done. Your little chamber of horrors is nothing but a pile of rubble." Anticipating Eden's next thought, Raine shook her head. "Do you know what magic does to electronics, Dr. Lawson? There isn't one recoverable byte."

The scientist began to shake in earnest. "You can't just kill me. They'll be questions. People will know, and they'll come after you." She turned to the tribunal, pleading, "You can't do this! I didn't kill anyone! It was all Alexi!"

Eden's composure crumbled, her mind buckling under the pressure of the earlier injection and her current state of terror. Mulcahy took a step forward and with a quiet command, froze her in place. Eden's eyes were the only things moving on her bound form.

Mulcahy turned to the three judges. "Do you require us any longer?"

Vidis shook his head. "No, we'll take it from here." A savage smile broke over his face as he read Mulcahy's anxious expression. "We'll make sure there are no questions on her death. It will look like an accident, we swear it."

Mulcahy's shoulders relaxed at the reassurance, and with a quick motion, he dropped the protective circle. With a twist of his wrist, the blue-flamed fire disappeared. Xander moved up behind Eden and caught the woman's arms behind her in a tight grip. Mulcahy released the spell holding her captive.

Eden opened her mouth to scream, but the sound was quickly cut off as someone else's spell rendered her mute.

Through the fitful moonlight, Raine caught the hazy transformation of the black-haired woman back into a wolf as she moved toward the doctor. Vidis and the golden-eyed giant joined the lady wolf and surrounded Eden. A little regretful at not taking part in the bloodletting, but anxious to move on to Alexi, Raine followed Mulcahy out of the circle and back into the night.

CHAPTER THIRTY-ONE

"When are you going after her?" Mulcahy's question cut through the SUV as they drove along the main highway.

Raine kept her eyes on the road. "As soon as I drop you off and check on Gavin."

She didn't turn to meet Mulcahy's gaze. Instead, she braced for his objections, because she had no doubt he would share some. Her knuckles whitened on the steering wheel. The pounding waves of betrayal and anger needed an outlet. Shedding Alexi's blood would be the perfect solution.

"I know how personal this is," Mulcahy said softly. "But you need to have a plan in place."

Hearing the unspoken permission in his words, a malicious glee burst into life with unholy light. "I've got a plan, Uncle. I plan on hunting the devious bitch down and spilling her blood as painfully as possible."

Mulcahy simply sighed and changed the subject. "Do you know where Miwa's is?" When she shook her head no, he continued, "It's closer than the office. Let's head over and see how far she's gotten. I'll get a ride from Cheveyo when he heads back in."

Raine shot him a quick look.

"You'll be able to go hunting quicker this way," he added drily.

Sneaking a quick glance at the man next to her, she caught the edge of a cold smile. Turning her attention back to the road stretching into the pre-dawn darkness, she echoed it.

She followed his sparse directions west, and the hour and a half ride gave her plenty of time for her worries and fears to create a sickening roil to her stomach. Knowing firsthand what could emerge from Lawson's little experiments left her wondering. Would the healer be able to bring Gavin back? If she did, would he be the same?

Never ending fears spun through her mind, and battered her brain until her head was pounding. It was a relief when they reached a small town with dimly lit streets. During the day, the rustic buildings and clean sidewalks would give tourists a sense of stepping back in time. Right now, the lightless storefronts, deserted streets, and dark homes gave the impression of a ghost town.

They pulled in behind Cheveyo's black Jeep parked outside a small cottage-type home that sat on the outskirts of town. A pristine white with silver trim, the house fairly glowed in the darkness. The lawn was a neat square and potted plants graced the steps leading to the front porch.

Raine followed Mulcahy up the wooden steps. A weary looking Cheveyo answered his knock. Seeing his obvious signs of exhaustion sent a tremor fissuring through her composure. Not once could she remember Cheveyo looking so tired and drained.

He led them into a small, neat room, which smelled like a rain-washed forest. She took in the well-used, but durable furniture, and the flickering fire in the stone fireplace, candles, and flowers. Through a doorway on her right, dried herbs hung from the ceiling in the kitchen. All of it added to the feminine vibe. There was peace here, and it quieted some of the night's ugly vibrations.

In the cozy living room, Cheveyo took a seat and braced his arms on his knees as Raine and Mulcahy found a spot on the plaid couch. "Cassandra's made some headway," his voice was soft, as if someone slept and he didn't want to wake them. "She's been able to erect a partial barrier for Gavin. When he's stronger he's going to have put his own in place."

"Is he—" Raine swallowed over the unexpected lump in her throat. How did she finish the sentence? No way in hell would Gavin ever be okay.

Cheveyo's expression softened. "He's more aware of what's happening. We don't know yet what all was unlocked —and probably won't for a few more days."

Mulcahy's voice was equally quiet. "Do you think he'll make it through?"

Cheveyo ran a hand through his hair, and it was obviously not the first time as his hair wasn't its normal styled self. "If he's as strong as I think he is, yes. The real question will be, does he want to be okay?"

Raine frowned. "What do you mean?"

He sighed. "You both understand that whatever drug Lawson used on him dropped his natural barrier to outside magic?" They nodded. "Well, it also increased his natural ability and, we may come to find out, added new ones."

The blood drained out of her face. "You've got to be wrong. They didn't have him long enough to do that."

Cheveyo shook his head. "I'm not wrong. It seems Lawson improved upon whatever was used when they had you." Reading her expression he added, "It's not like what happened to you, Raine. It's different."

That snapped her gaze to his. "Different?"

Cheveyo rubbed a hand over his face, as he tried to explain. "With you they added, twisted, and then increased, whatever existed into something more…unexpected. With Gavin, it's as if his abilities were given a steroid injection. All of his talents—they'll be stronger and harder to control. He'll have to relearn to master his magic."

An ached settled like a rock in her chest. "He can do that. He's strong enough." Something on Cheveyo's face had her pulse thudding heavily. "What else?"

"When they erased his natural barrier, his defenses tried to protect him. Instead of holding it at bay, they broke and reformed in to something different."

Dread curled in her stomach. "How different?" Cheveyo stayed silent, his gaze unreadable. Frustration made her voice sharp. "How different, Cheveyo?"

"We don't know," he finally answered. "We may not know for a while."

Silence flowed back into the room. The peace Raine felt earlier was washed away under the tidal wave of panic and undercut with fear. What this would mean for Gavin's future? Unable to sit still, she pushed to her feet and began to pace the small room as Mulcahy and Cheveyo talked quietly behind her.

The damn scientists never once took into account that their lab rats had souls. Their twisted experiments left horrific scars that never disappeared. Violence, like lethal flames, flowed around her as she tried to wear a trench in the floor. Her fists clenched and unclenched. Her emotional upheaval left her blind to her surroundings.

The snap and crackle of the fire brought her to a halt. Staring into the flickering flames, her disjointed thoughts clamored for attention. The irrational thought that this wouldn't have happened if she hadn't introduced Gavin to Alexi lodged itself in her head.

Yeah, it was a stupid, but if she could do it over, she would've never taken him into Zarana's. Her nightmares were right. She was partially at fault in this. She wouldn't blame Gavin if he held her responsible. Her worries and fears coiled deep. Would Gavin be able to handle the challenges facing him? Would he be strong enough to rebuild his sense of self?

Knowing the man he was, his strength and determination, she had faith he would. Granted, it would take time. And while he did, she couldn't do anything to help except present Alexi's head on a platter. Of course, taking Alexi out as slowly and painfully as possible might not be enough to make amends. Gavin could still walk away. From her.

Sharp, numbing pain cut through the mental excuses and laid bare how much the man lying in the other room meant to her. Damned if Alexi hadn't found Raine's Achilles' heel.

She rubbed the heel of her hand against the hollow ache in her chest. This was why she couldn't let anyone get close. Either she screwed them up, or they screwed her over. Something she lost sight of when she first called Alexi friend. And again, when Gavin became her partner. The current situation would leave a lasting scar and serve as a brutal reminder of that philosophy.

It's a good thing I won't be able to forget. Every time I see him, I'll remember.

Cheveyo's voice broke through her dark thoughts. "Do you want to see him, Raine?"

One last time, before he pushes me away. Aloud she said, "Yeah."

Cheveyo led her toward the back of the house and stopped in the doorframe of a candle-lit room, before stepping aside so she could enter.

Tiptoeing to the old, cast iron bed, she stood over the one man she wished she could protect.

Gavin's sherry-colored hair framed his still face. Long lashes feathered out, and the spark of life that normally lit his angular face, was buried deep. His bare shoulders and arms rested above the faded quilt, while the new cuts and wounds served as reminders of his ordeal.

The vibrant colors of his protection markings along his right shoulder and arm stood out like a painting on a pale gold canvas. *Could she wake this warrior with a kiss?* Shaking her head at such a sappy thought, she delicately traced his tattoos with a gentle fingertip.

She'd give herself this last moment with him, then leave. When he was back on his feet, he wouldn't want her around. She'd be a stark reminder of what he suffered and what he might become. As she traced the intricate markings, she silently admitted she wasn't sure she could handle the weight of blame and anger he'd level when all was said and done.

Shame at her cowardice left her hand trembling. She wasn't sure she could ever forgive herself for getting him into this whole mess.

Bending over, she placed a gentle kiss against those unresponsive lips. Still bent, she cupped his face in her hands, her voice a bare whisper, "I'll make her pay. She's already dead. She's just not smart enough to lie down."

Unexpected tears pressed hot and heavy and one escaped, falling down her cheek. She brushed his hair back, enjoying the silky texture and the way it curled around her fingers. Slowly she dropped to her knees and nestled her head in the space between his head and shoulder. Her broken whisper was full of pain. "I'm so sorry, Gavin."

Nearby someone shifted slightly, and Raine jerked to her feet, her gaze drawn to the woman sitting in the corner in the shadows. Raine tucked her raw emotions away, and fell back into the warrior who stood protectively over another.

The older woman rocked steadily in the chair across the bed. Strands of white hair the color of moonlight was worn in a loose braid. The piercing blue eyes belied the impression of age. They were sharp, intelligent, and discerning. Even her face, with its lack of lines and clear complexion broken by a smattering of freckles, added to the ageless image. "Hello, Raine. Remember me?"

Her voice echoed in Raine's memory, the one calm thing during those hideous months when she first came back to Taliesin. Some of her tension ease with recognition. "Cassandra. You were the one who helped me come back."

Cassandra's smile was gentle. "A good way to put it, 'come back.'" She studied the still figure in the bed. "He'll make it, you know."

Raine looked back at Gavin. "Yeah." She cleared her throat. "Yeah, he will. He doesn't know how to do anything else."

The other woman stood and moved around the bed. "I'm sorry. I should have warned you I was here earlier."

Heat flooded Raine's cheeks.

Cassandra gave a soft chuckle. "You're a lovely young woman, Raine."

Raine's mouth opened in shock at the comment. Lovely was not a word most people associated with her.

Cassandra came up to Raine's side and the older woman's head barely reached Raine's shoulder. In her memories, the healer was taller. Cassandra had been the guardian between a frightened young girl and the madness swirling inside her mind.

The healer straightened the quilt and her voice flowed around Raine. "You know, he'll need help when he wakes up."

Raine shook her head and took a step back. "Not from me. He won't want to see me."

Cassandra's hand stilled as she cocked her head to study Raine standing so stiffly beside her. "You didn't do this to him. You didn't put the needle in his arm."

"I introduced him to the one who betrayed him." Raine met those intense blue eyes and made the damning admission aloud. "I made the mistake of trusting someone I shouldn't have, and now he's paying the price."

Cassandra made a soft humming sound in the back of her throat as Raine turned away, and her soft words chased Raine from the room. "So are you."

CHAPTER THIRTY-TWO

As anxious as Raine was to head straight to Zarana's and confront Alexi, she didn't. Tipping Alexi off now would gain Raine nothing. She needed time to set her plan into motion. Dawn was chasing the shadows of the night when she bumped over the unpaved road to her home. Testing her wards, she found them stable with no new breaches.

As she moved through her kitchen, it felt as if eons passed since she left, not just a couple of days. She left Friday night with Cheveyo, Warrick, and Mulcahy, and now it was early Sunday morning. With Gavin in Cassandra's capable hands, she could take this time to think and plan.

She cleaned up the remnants of Friday's late night tea party, and restored her kitchen to its normal order. Lining her knives along the oak tabletop, she pulled her cleaning supplies out of a cupboard, sat at the table, and began taking care of her blades. As her mind went over various options, her hands moved by rote until the blades emerged clean and sharp.

She needed to get Alexi somewhere quiet, somewhere

they wouldn't be interrupted. Maybe an early meet at Zarana's? It wasn't out of character for Raine to request, especially if she was hunting for information. The thought of moving the meet to the evening crossed her mind, but she didn't want to give Alexi any time to rabbit. Nor did she want to have unexplainable casualties which would result in dealing with The Division.

Which reminded her, she should probably call Vidis or Xander to see how much time she had before Lawson's body turned up. Since it was Sunday, chances were good the body wouldn't appear until Monday.

The ringing of her cracked cell phone interrupted her thoughts. When the number came up "blocked" her pulse quickened, but her voice remained steady, "McCord."

"Morning, sunshine," greeted her caller.

"What do you want, Tarek?"

Laughter rumbled through the phone. "I see you got the good doctor to talk. Are you going hunting, Raine?'

"For you?" she snorted. "Not worth my time."

"Now, now, chickadee, insults will get you nowhere," he chided. "I thought I'd give you a little bit of help with your plans."

"Now why would you do a thing like that?"

"Can't it just be out of the kindness of my heart?"

Some of her festering rage warmed her voice and static crackled through the line. "The same kindness that had you Shadow Walking behind Chet before you slit his throat?"

The *tsking* sound on the phone had her clenching her teeth in an effort to stifle a snarl.

"Now that was business, little girl. I had to fulfill my contract. Bills to pay, you know."

She got up and walked over to the bay window in her dining room, and stared unseeingly at the quiet forest in her backyard. "So you go to the highest bidder? Even if they're the same sick fucks that made you?"

A rumble of dark laughter echoed in her ear. "Don't you get it? Money is power, and I like power."

She narrowed her eyes as a final puzzle piece fell into place. "You weren't paid to take out those three men of Talbot's."

A second of silence stretched into two. "No, that was personal." His voice cooled. "You know about personal, don't you? I watched you take out some of my targets, but you stopped short. Now, why would you do that, hmmm?"

Tarek wanted to talk to someone, to explain, to brag, to vent, whatever, and she was happy to let him, so long as he gave her more clues. "I decided I didn't want to be the monster they created. Gave them too much control. No one controls me."

"Then you understand," he said. "Why I took those three out."

She swallowed despite her dry throat. "Yeah, I do." And Lord and Lady help her, she really did. She rubbed a hand across her forehead, as if wiping away the haunting faces.

"Now that they're gone, I decided to put my skills to use," Tarek continued. "I figured since they went out of their way to create me, why not make a few dollars?"

"Lawson was doing the same thing," Raine said. "I don't get why you'd help her do that to someone else."

"At first I didn't realize I was working for the good doctor." There was a smile in his slightly rueful tone. "It was Alexi, not Lawson, who approached me about a few tools."

"Like the shielding talisman?" Raine guessed.

"Boy, the woman just can't shut her mouth, can she?" he muttered.

Fierce satisfaction seeped into her voice. "Oh, that's not a worry now, Tarek. I do hope she paid you already."

"Ah well," he sounded philosophical. "She wasn't the one paying, but still, it's a good thing I demanded the majority of my payment up front."

Determined to keep the talkative dick on track, she pushed, "When did you realize you were working for the good doctor?"

There was a noticeable pause. "Does it help if I say it was right before my first call to you?"

Despite a faint note of truth, Raine wasn't buying it. "How do I know you're not lying?" She paused, but didn't expect an answer. When he stayed silent, she continued, "Let's say you aren't, so I don't know if it helps. I'm not sure there's enough money for me to kill Kyn who haven't done anything to me."

She could hear him shift as if settling deeper into a chair. "Now see, little girl, we'll just have to agree to disagree on that point. You kill for Mulcahy, and he pays your bills. How is that different from me? Just because I'm not some cherished Wraith who works for the blessed Taliesin Security, how does it make us different?"

She spoke to the underlying resentment that threaded through his words. "I kill those who harm others, or threaten the Kyn community. You kill for money. That's a big difference."

"You keep telling yourself that and maybe someday you'll believe it." His voice was droll. "Moving on, I've decided I don't quite like being lied to, so I'm going to give you a leg up to help even the score."

Her fingers tightened on the phone. "Lied to about what?"

"You do know your best friend hates the Kyn, right?" He paused. "Oh right, you don't. So let me clue you in. I don't mind doing a job as long as those paying me are on the up and up about why. She lied through her pearly whites and now Taliesin Security is out for my blood."

Raine let that stand because he was right. On both counts.

"I'm going to help you get your own back," he said. "In turn, you're going to give me the time to go under for a while."

Seriously? He expected her to stand between him and Taliesin? He had to be crazy. "How exactly do you think I can do that?"

"You call your boss and have a chat. Get me a head start of a week. After that, it's on me if I'm found."

She didn't bother hiding her derision. "And I get what in return?"

"You get a secluded meeting with your best bud, a little girl-bonding time." Strangely, his voice gentled. "No one should be betrayed by a best friend. Even I have a level of honor to stand by, and that falls below it." She opened her mouth to take a shot about his so-called honor, but he cut her off before the words escaped. "You best call the boss man and start dancing, Raine. I'll call back in fifteen."

The sharp click of disconnection echoed in her ear. She held the phone and considered his offer. This could easily be a trap, but her need for revenge—and some gut level instinct —told her Tarek was on the level. Growling in frustration, she dialed Mulcahy.

After an infuriating ten-minute call where Mulcahy pointed out all the possible faults with this deal, plus reiterating his anger at being forced to play nice to the one who killed his Wraith, she pinned her boss down to a four day head start for Tarek. Mulcahy, determined to send in back up, wanted details on her meeting place. Not that she agreed to it. Who needed the hassle of ditching or incapacitating them? This was a solo mission.

The clock struck fifteen minutes exactly when her phone rang again. She picked it up.

Tarek's low rumble filled her ear. "Do we deal?"

"Depends on you," she answered. "You get four days, not seven."

He gave a surprised laugh. "Damn, little girl, you did better than I thought. You ever need a job, come see me. I could use someone like you."

"Not in this lifetime," she snapped. "When and where?"

"Impatient chickadee, aren't you?" he teased. "Why is that, do you suppose? Is it because lover boy is down and out for the count?"

With a ruthless grip she strangled her emotions. "He'll be fine, and this isn't about him."

"Who's the liar now?"

Her only answer was a snarl.

Chuckling, Tarek continued, "I'm to meet the little demon Gypsy at about three today, at a little hunting shack that used to be mine."

"Used to be?" Raine asked.

He sighed. "Well, I'm not going to have much use for it where I'm going, so consider it a small bonus gift to the one who walks away." He gave her directions. "If I were you, I'd get there a bit early to scope out the place. Just because she's there to give me the final payment, doesn't mean she won't try to take me out."

Raine's voice was cold. "I'm not a novice."

His low chuckle filtered through. "Never said you were. By the way, don't waste your time searching the place for clues to me, there won't be any."

"How do I know you won't be there to help Alexi take me out? She was pretty pissed she missed me last time."

"You don't," he answered. "However, I'd be a stupid man if I didn't take advantage of my four day head start as soon as I could, now wouldn't I? *Au revoir, cher.*" The phone went dead.

She studied the blades on her table as her mind found a quiet center. She glanced at the clock. She had some time—

an hour at best. She flipped open her cell and dialed one more number. After it was answered, she asked a few questions, waited for the response, and then hung up. Deliberately, she removed the sim card from her phone and set both pieces on her counter.

Time to finish this.

CHAPTER THIRTY-THREE

It was just past eleven in the morning when Raine found the ramshackle hunting shack. "Shack" was being generous. Gaping holes spotted the weathered wood, and a simple, gray tarp played the part of the door. Green vines twisted in and out of the boards and added the appearance of stringy, green hair.

After leaving her SUV behind in the garage of an unoccupied cabin, she walked the few miles back into the nearest town. A battered backpack held her well-padded weapons. Just off the main road, at the bait-and-tackle shop, she found what she was looking for.

She hitched a ride in an ancient truck with older man in stained overalls who smelled strongly of fish. She had him drop her off at the entrance to some unnamed, unpaved road. The old man thought she was a young college student intent on backpacking some of the trails. He made noises about young women not being safe out on their own. Reassuring him she would be joining up with her group that was already at the campsite, she left him somewhat mollified and he let her go with barely a rumble.

She backtracked, and hiked the next five miles in, studying the terrain. It didn't take lone to realize Tarek was true to his word. It really was in the middle of nowhere, and that brought a terrible sense of pleasure.

She circled around the ramshackle shelter and scouted through the surrounding foliage. She took her time and searched for any sign that Alexi had made it there before her. Satisfied she was the only one around, Raine headed in. She walked the perimeter of the structure and sent out testing probes for any nasty traps lying in wait. When it came up clean, she pulled aside the tarp. Winged insects rushed out and she waited for them to dissipate before stepping inside.

She let the tarp fall close behind her and called forth a small flame of light. Tarek had left her nothing but the four somewhat sturdy walls. Weak sunlight and soft breezes filtered through the cracks and caused dust moats to float like fairy-dust on the drafts.

She shrugged her pack off and placed it in the corner. Then she removed her flannel shirt and stripped down to her black T-shirt and jeans. After stuffing the flannel in the back-pack, she slipped off her hiking boots. She could move quieter and quicker in bare feet, while barely leaving a trail.

Back outside, she ignored the chill of the mountain air and moved stealthily through the forest. She set up a subtle spell that was enough to send an alert when someone headed her way. Then it was time to determine which way Alexi would most likely come from. Raine's choices were limited to the overgrown path from the road to the east and the faint hikers' trail to the west.

Behind the shack was dense forest growth, which eventually backed into federal land. In front, the forest ran a couple of miles before dropping off sharply at the edge of a very steep cliff that met a rambling river below.

Once she spelled the east and west sections, she moved back to the shelter and pulled out various blades. The silver lynx Cheveyo gave her spilled out of her T-shirt. She placed her hand over it and felt the warmth of it. It would come in handy later.

Facing Alexi would be difficult, especially since she could set a ward to cut a Kyn off from accessing their magic. Raine couldn't depend on her ability with natural magic. Instead, she'd have to rely on her skills as a Wraith—skills honed with deadly precision. The well of twisted power residing inside her would be an added bonus.

Her plan centered on running Alexi down. Raine wanted the chase, needed to hear Alexi's heart beat furiously as she ran, to smell the cold sweat of fear as she became nothing more than prey. It wasn't just a just a need, she craved it.

She set the knives neatly on a towel, sat back, and ran a finger absently down one of the blades. She stood and went out to sit in the sunlight with her back against the weathered boards of the shack. She closed her eyes and opened her senses.

The wind curled around her, its chill nipping at her skin. The rustling of the leaves, like whispered conversations, flowed and changed with the breeze. Wildlife flittered in between branches, burrowed under roots and rocks, and wound through overgrown paths. Her tension slowly retreated, washed away by the cool air and the sounds of nature.

Then she did something she never tried. She dropped her barriers and reached for the magic she never fully embraced. She pushed open the mental door and hovered at the threshold knowing this would change her fundamentally. If she survived Alexi, she might not survive her magic. No matter what happened—even if she left here alive—she would be different. Maybe not at first, but eventually it would show.

The outcome scared her, but she was willing to pay the price. Never again would someone else pay for her mistakes. In this quiet moment, she admitted this wasn't entirely for Gavin, but for her, for her sense of betrayal, and her pain and anger. As selfish as it seemed, she wanted restitution, no matter how much it cost her. Even having Alexi's blood on her hands didn't give her pause.

Raine took the last step through the doorway and tumbled willingly into the abyss.

RAINE LOST her sense of time as she delved into the swirling magic. Power flowed around and through her. At first, she tried to separate each wave, but gave up as the waves came faster and faster. The first few washed over her and left her untouched. Then they grew in size and strength, slamming into her, and barreling into her mind in a sickening dance.

Some of the magic she could easily grasp, but the stronger waves were overwhelming, almost frightening. Dimly, she realized perhaps she should've listened to Cheveyo and done this with him. Her physical body wasn't meant to hold such power, and she was pretty sure that same engulfing power could destroy her mind.

After the first few painful struggles each time something clicked into place, she stopped fighting. Like a gigantic jigsaw puzzle, the years old missing pieces slid into place, some smoothly, while others needed a metaphoric pounding. When the puzzle was complete, she stood before a tall mirror, much like the one in her dream. The surface wasn't clear, but swirled with colors and distorted images. Just when she thought she could make something out, it would shift and change. She watched the patterns form and reform, trying to understand.

The mirror disappeared and left her in a well of darkness.

I'm Raine McCord. I'm a Wraith. I can survive this.

Her silent mantra served as an anchor in the storm. She bit back screams as more and more magic hit. Then suddenly the barrage stopped. For a moment, everything stilled. The sound of her breath rasping in her chest was overly loud.

The mirror in front of her swirled with memories triggered by the wild trip. She saw herself at fifteen, huddled in a corner, and a brief glimpse of Cassandra kneeling in front of her, hand extended. It all came back to her—the struggle to get through the noise of the magic dwelling inside her to find something that didn't shift, something stable.

Her breathing hitched, then sped up as the spinning mass in the mirror expanded and reached for her. Her first instinct was to step back, to run and close the door. Instead, feeling battered in spirit but determined to see this through to the end, she made her feet move forward.

She reached out and watched as her fingertips touched the nebulous image. Surprisingly, it wasn't cold, but warm. Her eyes widened and she forgot to breathe when her image emerged on the mirror's dark surface. It wavered and reformed to the feral woman of her dreams. Her hands and teeth were still rimmed in blood, but the large black leopard with matching silver eyes lay calmly beside her. Raine dropped her hand and froze while the woman and leopard watched her warily. Meeting the woman's silvered gaze, a hush fell over the world.

She stepped closer. The woman moved with catlike grace to match her movements. Gathering her mental strength like a ragged cloak, her gaze never wavering, Raine reached out again and felt the silent white explosion when her hand met the woman's. Blinking to clear her eyes, she realized she was now naked, and under her palm was soft fur. Looking down she met the silver gaze of the leopard beside her. There was a final shift in her magic then it locked into place.

The leopard's triumphant scream blended with hers before everything went dark.

CHAPTER THIRTY-FOUR

Raine woke with a start, as the cool breeze tickled her face and the weathered boards pricked against her back. She shifted her wrist to look at her watch and was surprise to note only an hour had passed. Such a short amount of time to alter her whole world. Under her skin, the predatory cat prowled, as anxious as she to hunt. *Patience*, she whispered to herself and the cat. They still had a couple more hours to go. Instead of feeling beaten, her body was relaxed and ready for action.

Uncertain of what happened or how much of an impact her decision would have on her magical abilities, she remained calm, accepting the fact she and the leopard could easily interchange control. Cats were notorious hunters—quiet, lethal, and quick. Attributes she would need when facing Alexi.

The magic part of the package...well, she'd handled it as it came. Who knew if she would be able to call on any magic, or how reliable it would be once it manifested. Better to stick with what she knew than try for something new.

No doubt Alexi would show early, so Raine went into the

shack to prepare. She tied her hair in a knot and slipped two throwing blades into the mass. Most people thought they were hairpins, and they could be, but they made even better darts.

Next came the stiletto blades, which rode low on her hips. She kept her lynx charm tucked under her T-shirt. The she stuffed her flannel back into the now almost empty backpack, took it into the forest, and tucked it into a hollowed out log on the south side. There was no tell-a-tale marks leading to it, but she made a point to remember where it was, as she might want to retrieve it when… if she made it out alive.

Back at the shack, she erased all signs of her presence before heading toward a large tree overhanging the barely discernible path on the east side. If Alexi came up the west path, Raine could catch her by surprise. If the Gypsy came up the east path, then all the better. Raine picked her spot in the heavily shaded branches, then hunkered down to watch and wait.

The slight vibrations of the various wards she placed around the perimeter of the shack vibrated softly against her psychic skin. Even if Alexi got lucky and took her out, Raine had a couple of nasty surprises waiting for her former best friend. Some would injure, some would simply slow Alexi down, but Raine's favorite was the intricate blood tracer spell.

Her earlier question and answer session before leaving her house had produced the recipe for this particular spell. The tracer spell would be an invisible thread leading her uncle to Alexi's doorstep regardless of where she tried to hide. Raine trusted Mulcahy to take Alexi out—not because of the death of his niece, but because Alexi was the one behind the attacks on his Wraiths.

The spell required blood magic, something most of the

Kyn shied away from as it deeply involved the caster. Raine never professed to be the shy type. The spell used a part of her, an essence of what made her who she was, and it wasn't replaceable. But if Alexi was the one who left here alive, that part would no longer be required.

She let the surrounding silence filter through and a calm settled in her bones. Regardless of today's outcome, she was ready. For today, she accepted the fact she would never fully fit into the Kyn world. She might walk this path alone for many years. That was okay, though. Sometime during her mental trip, Raine took the first step in facing her fears and started embracing what she was and what she would become.

If she made it out of here alive, she was fairly certain she would be taking Cheveyo up on that training—if it remained on the table. Not to say she would go quietly into that good night. Oh, hell no, that wasn't who she was.

Her mind calmed and her wards vibrated with a steady hum. Every now and then, she reached out and touched the part of her crouched and waiting, tail twitching. Keeping her rage locked down, she hoarded it for later.

Maybe an hour passed before the first trip of her wards slice across her awareness. Someone was approaching from the west road. Moving only her eyes, Raine waited to see who would step into the clearing.

A faint jolt of pain surprised her as Alexi's short, dark cap of curls moved into view.

Raine's last spark of naïve hope sputtered and died, quickly followed by disgust at Alexi's inability to be subtle on her approach. Either she was stupid or arrogant in thinking she could stroll in bold as brass. No self-respecting hunter waltzed into a meet without scoping the place out first. Maybe all those deaths were just luck on Alexi's part, not skill. Either way it was more proof of

Alexi's egotistical belief in her own skills, and it would be her downfall.

Alexi moved cautiously out into the clearing and neared the shack. She scanned the area, going so far as to send out pulses of magic to search for spells. They found nothing.

The magic powering Raine's wards beat seamlessly with the energy found in the natural world making them magically invisible. Score one for her Fey blood versus demon blood. Her eyes stayed focused, and a spark of anticipation fired as Alexi took the last step clear of the forest.

Alexi moved toward the tarp doorway and shoved it aside, peering in. Pulling her head back, she scanned the forest. Her face was cold and unamused. "All right, enough games. I have your payment. Come get it. I need to get back to open the bar."

Raine's lips curled into a feral smile. She pulled her shields tight and dropped lightly into crouch at the head of the hiking trail. "Fancy meeting you here, Alexi." Ice dripped from her voice as she strolled into the clearing.

Alexi's face whitened in shock. "Raine? What are you doing here?"

Raine stopped and cocked her hip. "You know, I was just wondering the same thing about you."

A sheepish expression bled across Alexi's features. "I got a call saying if I met a source at this location I could get some information to help you find out who killed that wizard."

"Really? Funny, so did I." Raine raised an eyebrow and gave her former friend points for her acting ability. It was truly amazing how good an actress she was. "However, my source has a name. Tarek. Recognize it?"

Undiluted fury transformed Alexi's face. "That traitorous bastard! I should have killed him earlier."

"Yeah, you probably should have." For the first time Raine witnessed the warped being that lived under her friend's mask. Tucking away the sickening pain—at being so obtuse as not to see this—she focused on the deadly force swirling inside her. "Should have done it before he killed Chet though." She shook her head. "Really, Alexi, did you think you could try to take the three of us out and no one would be the wiser?"

Alexi snarled. Without warning a ball of flame arrowed straight toward Raine.

With a negligent flick of her wrist, Raine blocked it and stepped to the side as the flame petered out and fell like orange rain to the damp ground. She *tsked*. "Temper, temper. You're going to have to do better than that."

Alexi visibly pulled herself together. Her dark eyes, rimmed with red, turned shrewd. She circled to Raine's right and put the ramshackle building to her back.

Raine waited, her stare focused, like a cat with a small mouse. There was a rush of magic as the demon halfling threw a quick warding up to block Raine's magical attacks, even as she tossed out a testing flicker of a spell in return.

The warmth of Cheveyo's charm burned against Raine's chest as her shields strengthened. They wouldn't hold long, just long enough to get the chase started. Hopefully.

Frustration bloomed in Alexi's red-rimmed eyes. "Bitch!" Her lips curled back in a twisted grimace. "They won't hold long."

Raine glided a couple of steps to her left and slowly herded Alexi along the shack wall and toward the forest sitting behind it. "Maybe, maybe not." She kept her hands down and loose. "Before we start this, can I ask you something?"

Alexi moved a couple more steps to her left, her attention never leaving Raine. In her hands, fire bloomed like flickering blades. "Are you going to go with the standard, 'Why?' You should be more original."

Raine said nothing, just waited and watched, her body coiled.

"Did you know the only thing of worth my father gave me was this?" Alexi moved her hands and brought the two tongues of fire together, then she weaved the flames into what resembled a staff. "The wonderful ability to twist and mold fire into any shape I choose. I used it to kill him." She briefly fingered the four thin scars on the side of her face. "He did leave this behind." She cocked her head to the side, her curls bouncing innocently. "Does that shock you?"

"At this point, not really," Raine drawled.

Alexi's smile held a hint of madness. "Oh, that's right. You're one of the brave and noble pieces of shit known as Wraiths. All that bullshit about protecting the Kyn community from humans and humans from crazed Kyn. You're just a bunch of hired killers, drawing a paycheck in blood."

"Don't hold back," Raine said dryly. "Tell me what you really think."

"Don't mock me!" Alexi's face contorted before she took a deep breath. "You're supposed to protect the Kyn and mortals alike, right? So why did I find Quinn in his own blood? Who stood for him? Who stood for my mother after one of your thrice-cursed demons raped her? Who stood for me when she killed herself when I came into my power?" This last was wailed—the echoes of a tortured child threading through the madness.

"So, what?" Raine quashed the pity whispering through her. "You're not the only one with a troubled past. Is that how you justified your actions?" She shook her head and let her contempt show. "Quinn sold out other Kyn for experimentation. Why should anyone stand for him?"

Alexi took a few more steps.

Raine held steady and waited for the woman to drop her guard long enough for Raine to make her move.

Alexi began to twirl the flaming staff in her hands, her mad gaze locked on Raine. "I loved him." Alexi's voice was calm, almost normal, her tone soft. "Quinn was it for me."

Without warning, Alexi shifted her grip and struck out with the burning staff. Flames ripped through the air between them. When they hit Raine's shields, the magic shimmered briefly, but held.

Alexi's smile was confident. "A couple more hits, and you'll be a smoldering pile of ash."

Raine shifted closer. She needed Alexi out of control, so she let derision fill her voice. "You know it's a pretty fucked up relationship if date night includes the murder and evisceration of a wizard. Perhaps the two of you should've looked into counseling."

Alexi snarled and hurled another wave of flames.

Raine dropped, covered her head with her arms, and rolled. The blasting heat shimmered above her. Her hand came away with one of the throwing knives and, as she came up to her knees, she threw it. At the sound of Alexi's short scream, Raine's smile flashed, savage and cold. The throwing dart sliced into Alexi's right shoulder. With a quick mental push, Raine released the attached magic activating the embedded blood tracer spell.

Cursing and unaware, Alexi let her flaming staff falter. Her right arm hung uselessly at her side. Without warning, she turned the staff into a snake-like whip in her left hand and sent it lashing out.

Shocked at Alexi's speed, Raine barely managed to roll away from the flames. Unfortunately, they breached her weakening shields and seared her left side. She hissed as the pain streaked from shoulder to hip.

Alexi's eyes narrowed and an evil smile played along her lips and twisted the scars on her face. "Bet that stung." She watched Raine stumble to her feet, then reached up and gripped the small throwing knife. With a grunt, she yanked it free from her shoulder.

Raine straightened slowly, kept her breathing even, and her voice rock steady. "I can't figure out why you had someone kill Mayson, or how you got to him so fast."

"Quinn's spells were still active, and he placed one on that freak after a meeting." There was a sort of perverse pride in Alexi's answer. "I just continued to monitor them."

"You killed him?" That was an alarming bit of news. If Alexi was able to pull off such an intense spell, she was much more dangerous than Raine anticipated. Not that being a crazy, psychopathic demon was any better, but Raine would have rather attributed Mayson's death to Tarek.

"What?" Alexi laughed, correctly reading the shock on Raine's face. "Did you think I let you know the full extent of what I can do?"

Raine shrugged and ignored the whiplash of pain down her left side. "Obviously not, since you're a sick murdering bitch."

Alexi faced her, blood trailing down her right side in a red stain while malicious humor flashed in her eyes. "Oh come on, Raine. Your hands aren't any cleaner than mine."

"Depends on your definition of clean."

Alexi snorted. "I took out those who took mine. Chet killed Quinn, I killed him. Tit for tat."

"Wrong, Alexi." Raine shook her head and slowly let her recently embraced darkness shine through. "He didn't kill Quinn. That pleasure was all mine."

Alexi froze, and for a single moment, sanity broke through the haze of madness, then rage took over. She took a flying leap at Raine.

Raine braced and let Alexi slam her to the ground. Alexi's fingers curled into claws and she raked them down the right side of Raine's neck, drawing blood. Using Alexi's own momentum against her, Raine got her feet and hands between their bodies. With a quick shove, she threw the smaller woman off. The adrenaline rush blocked out all pain as she flexed her hands and legs and lunged back to her feet. She put her back to the shack and faced Alexi, who now knelt on the ground at the foot of a tree.

The woman pushed herself to her feet, her eyes bleeding to red. "Speaking of men, how's your walking wet dream?" Her voice was a sibilant hiss. "I heard he hooked up with a redhead." A trickled of blood marked the corner of her mouth, and she used an arm to brush it away.

Raine banked her fury at Alexi's verbal strike. Too bad it hit so close to the mark. "I guess you didn't hear," she said, her voice scathing. "He's fine. The redhead? Well…" She shrugged. "She's had better days."

Alexi snarled and shot forward, leading with her fist.

Raine didn't go for her blades. No, she needed the sensation of flesh meeting flesh. Blocking Alexi's clumsy attack, she struck out with a short arm jab into Alexi's ribs, sending the woman to her knees again. Raine stepped back and circled while Alexi struggled for breath. "Oh, Alexi." She watched the dark haired woman regain her feet. "You know how you forgot to mention a few things?"

Alexi raised her eyes as Raine removed the two stilettos and tossed them into the forest. They were quickly followed by the other throwing dart.

Raine's deepening voice and glowing silver eyes held Alexi immobile. "Well, so did I."

One moment Raine stood there, in the next a large black leopard with the same glowing eyes crouched in her spot.

Shocked, Alexi took a step back then turned and did exactly what Raine hoped she'd do. She ran.

Letting loose an eerily feminine scream of triumph, the big cat dashed after its prey.

CHAPTER THIRTY-FIVE

Deep inside the cat, Raine marveled at the power held in the leopard's body. The padding footsteps were nearly silent on the spongy ground. She used her whiskers to catalog the scents of the forest and reveled in the bouquet of odors that assailed her.

Over there was a rabbit—quivering, hoping not to be seen —the faint smell of deer, the crispness of the air cutting through the trees, the earthy smell of fertile soil buried under the fallen leaves. The leopard's head came up sharply, there— just there—the sharp smell of other, something that didn't belong in the natural world. The leopard's lip curled with a silent baring of teeth.

The woman inside recognized the stench of demon, even if the animal didn't.

Raine tried not to dwell on the alien sense of invasion as her mind and the leopard's shared the same body. Ceding to the animal's intellect, she submerged her sense of self and trusted the leopard to stalk and hunt their prey.

There was no more conflict over hunting Alexi down and shedding her blood, no guilt for Raine's part in Gavin's condition. Just the anticipation of a good hunt, fresh meat, and warm blood.

The leopard stopped, bunched its muscles, and sprang up to the overhanging branches. It moved along a barely discernible pathway overhead as it tracked its prey. It didn't take long before the cat was crouched like a menacing shadow above Alexi's head.

The demonic gypsy rested against a tree, her eyes darting around frantically for a glimpse of the big cat.

The sharp scent of blood and fear made its way to the leopard's nose. The mouthwatering aroma made the whiskers twitched once, but at the inner woman's urging, it held still.

Alexi cursed softly as she slid down the trunk of the tree —just as the leopard landed like smoke in front of her. Unable to stifle her short scream, Alexi scrambled to her feet and took off.

Deep inside the leopard, Raine grinned. Woman and cat bounded after the fleeing prey. The scent of blood and the tantalizing smell of fear-soaked sweat drifted back to them.

When Alexi tripped over a log and struggled back to her feet, the cat crouched and waited, wanting to play with this mouse. Raine got lost in the fun of the hunt, the joy of chasing down that which was weaker. Time after time, the cat pulled up short as Alexi stumbled blindly through the forest.

Strung out with exhaustion, Alexi tripped once again and fell. When she didn't rise, the cat took a couple of cautious steps closer.

"Bitch, you think this is a game?" Alexi's harsh breathing made her words difficult to understand.

Both the cat and the woman were taken by surprise when Alexi—moving with unnatural quickness—threw a whipping tongue of flame at them, while muttering indecipherably under her breath.

Raine fought the cat for dominance. When the flame whipped along their chest, they screamed. Pain made the cat angry. It wanted to jump on its tormentor. Hissing, it began circling Alexi. Raine finally cut through the animal's instinctive need to mindlessly attack and shred. Such a move could kill them both.

Alexi's chanting grew stronger, but Raine didn't recognize the language rolling from her mouth. She did, however, recognize the energy building up as some serious magic.

Raine pushed the cat to jump and slash out, and caught Alexi across the chest with the leopard's razor sharp claws. The woman stumbled back, her words cutting off abruptly as bloody furrows bloomed bright red.

While Alexi fought for footing, Raine shifted back to human form. Years of training blocked out the screaming pain of a fast shift of bones and skin that merged with the wounds and burns down her left side and across her chest.

She stood naked, except for Cheveyo's charm, as blood dripped from her hand. There was one moment to wonder distantly what happened to her clothes before Alexi let out a blood-curling scream and launched herself at Raine.

Alexi managed to catch Raine mid-body with a shoulder, and sent them both rocketing to the ground. Raine's bare back painfully met a tree trunk. White light exploded behind her eyes as air rushed out of her lungs in a whoosh. She fought for oxygen, as red rage broke free. She blocked Alexi's swinging right hand and countered with a vicious left that snapped Alexi's head back and sent her stumbling backward.

Alexi's red eyes were lost in a haze of hate as she rushed Raine again. When they crashed together, Raine could hear Alexi still mumbling through the spell. Some internal sense warned Raine she couldn't afford for the demon to finish. Desperate, she slammed her right arm into Alexi's diaphragm. Alexi's eyes widened as she gasped for air and stumbled back.

Raine got her feet underneath her and stalked menacingly toward the woman sprawled on the ground. "Come on, you traitorous bitch," she growled. "Get up."

Alexi lumbered to her feet again, a calculating gleam in her eye. "Come get me, kitty cat."

Raine took a running leap and got both legs up to slam into Alexi's face. Alexi moved with that unnerving quickness, and Raine's feet hit her left shoulder instead. Alexi used the spinning motion to reach out and wrap her hands around Raine's right thigh. Unexpected heat seared through Raine's skin and bone, ripping a scream from her throat, and momentarily drowning out Alexi's crazed laughter.

Lying on the ground for a timeless moment, Raine waited for the sickness rolling in her belly to calm. Then, gritting her teeth, she forced herself to her feet once more. Her right leg wouldn't support her so she shifted her weight to her left. Streaked with blood and covered in dirt, she could feel the anger burning inside her, the depth of which equaled the madness in Alexi.

Alexi struggled for air but her eyes were sharp and preda-tory. "Did you like that one?"

Raine kept her left arm behind her as if wounded, hoping to lure Alexi closer. Raine's strength was waning and Cheveyo's charm was close to empty. She kept her gaze on the other woman and allowed her left arm to shift. "It was definitely interesting."

Alexi moved toward her. "I have something even more interesting."

Raine held her body still and ignored the tremors running through her injured leg. She couldn't afford any weakness, and from the amount of magic amassing around

Alexi this was it. Raine watched Alexi's body and at the moment Alexi's legs tensed to spring, Raine braced.

Alexi hit her hard riding her down to the ground. Raine whipped her left arm up and used her claws to rip a bloody trail from shoulder to belly. At the same time, Alexi's spell slammed into Raine and both women screamed.

Raine fought the burning pressure that tried to burrow its way into her soul. With blind instinct, she used her arm and slashed across Alexi's throat. Blood fell in a warm rain across Raine's face, but she barely noticed as she fought against the deadly spell Alexi had unleashed.

The pain became unbearable, worse even than what she went through when she was younger. Her vision whitened, the edges going black. She couldn't feel her body, just an all-encompassing fire that burned her from the inside out. She fought to breathe and mindlessly slashed out at the weight on top of her.

Lost in the agony, survival instincts kicked in. Her internal barriers shoved up, struggling under the weight of the spell and its killing magic. Lost in her internal battle, Raine felt the moment her barriers started to crumble, and her awareness began to fade. She centered her concentration and strength of will on shoring up her barriers, but she was so tired.

Her defenses buckled.

Raine found comfort in knowing she managed to keep her promise to Gavin and take Alexi out. It was her last coherent thought. Distantly she heard someone calling her name, but found she didn't care as the blackness swallowed her whole.

CHAPTER THIRTY-SIX

R aine was cold. Unfortunately, a wave of pain quickly chased the chill away. A soft groan escaped.

"She's coming around." There was a male voice, but she was having trouble figuring out who it belonged to.

She struggled to open her eyelids, but they were weighted down. It took her a bit, but she finally managed to pry them open. Dappled sunlight washed across her face, and she focused on the burnished leaves above her, trying to remember what she was doing here.

Someone ran their hands over her body. Her naked body. *Okay, that had to stop.* She tried to move her arms to push the hands away, but they wouldn't respond. Panic spurted and her breathing hitched as she struggled to make her body move.

A deep voice rolled overhead. "Stop, Raine. Just lie still. You're safe."

Her gaze flickered down to find Cheveyo kneeling next to her. He studied her face for a moment and then turned back to finish running his hands over her body. When his fingers whispered over the burn on her thigh she hissed at the biting pain.

"Stop." The croak was barely there, but he must have heard it.

His hands stopped and he looked at her.

She licked her dry lips and tasted something metallic and brassy. "Need to sit up." She struggled and Cheveyo moved behind her to help her upright. Her vision swam, then steadied. She was still naked and it bothered her. "Clothes?"

Cheveyo shifted behind her and skewed her balance. She placed her right arm on the ground to steady herself, but as weak as it was, she wasn't sure it would hold long. A soft warmth draped across her shoulders. Looking down she saw Cheveyo's flannel shirt.

She tried to figure out how to button it up without falling over, but his hands came around and quickly did up the buttons. Good thing he was a tall man, because the tail end of the shirt would brush mid-thigh when she stood. If she could stand.

She leaned back against him, on some level realizing he had a T-shirt on under the flannel. Taking a deep breath, she looked around.

Xander sat tailor fashion a few feet away, while Ryder leaned against a tree in front of her. Both of them watched her closely with identical blank masks.

Raine kept her mind empty and just breathed. A coppery smell hit her nose and drew her gaze to her right. The sight of what remained of a body brought everything back in a flash.

Cheveyo's grip tightened as Raine's body jerked, stiffened, and then stilled. She studied the bloodied remains huddled on the ground. Alexi's face was slack and her red-tinged eyes were staring emptily up through the canopy of leaves. She looked as if she'd been mauled by a large cat—which, essentially, she had.

Raine's first swipe had carved deep grooves along the side of Alexi's torso, which now showed small glimpses of white ribs. Her second slash opened Alexi from throat to belly. Seeing the bulge of exposed entrails, Raine felt nothing. Distantly, she wondered if this image would haunt her. There were more wounds, but they ran together, until all that remained was a decimated mass of torn flesh and ripped viscera, barely discernible as humanoid.

She raised her gaze to the two Wraiths warily eyeing her. "How did you find me?"

Cheveyo's voice rumbled behind her. "The charm I gave you."

She gave a weak laugh. "You used it to track me."

"It's good we did, McCord," Xander said. "A few more minutes and the spell would have finished you."

Raine coughed and then winced at the pain in her ribs. "I just had to last longer than she did."

"No," Cheveyo's denial was sharp. "Her spell tied the two of you together. If she died, so would you."

She tried to twist around to see him, but hissed as her injuries pulled and shot sharp needles of pain through her body. "I'm here, she's not. She must have not done the spell right then."

Something close to a growl emerged from Cheveyo. Surprised by the unexpected sound, Raine's eyes widened.

"You idiot." His hands clamped down on her shoulders as if to shake her. "The only reason we were able to break the spell was because we got here before she died."

"Okay." She kept her voice steady and her eyes level as she took in the frustration in his face. "Then I owe you my thanks."

"Actually," Ryder's voice brought her attention to him. "You owe him a lot more than that."

"What do you mean?" Her stomach lurched at the darkly humorous look in the pretty boy's eyes.

Ryder smiled as he answered, "Cheveyo broke the spell by tying your life force to his."

She jerked forward and despite the jolts of resulting pain, faced Cheveyo. "You did what?"

He stiffened and folded his arms across his chest. "It was the only way to snap you out of the spell. I used the link the charm forged between my magic and yours to drag you back."

"You had no right!" Her hands clenched. "Explain what happens now, Cheveyo. Can you undo it?"

"No, it's permanent." Both his voice and his eyes were unreadable.

She gritted her teeth and fought down the bubbling panic. "What does that mean?"

"It means you both can tap into each other's magic to some degree." Glee filtered through Ryder's voice and made him sound like a boy who had a titillating secret.

It took Raine a second to process Ryder's answer. She stared at Cheveyo. "To what degree?"

He shot Ryder a disgusted look. "It's fairly limited. We'd have to be close together for it to work, and I have no intention of utilizing this bond."

"But it's still there," she whispered.

It was another chain that linked her to someone else. A powerful someone who could use her. She dragged in a shuddering breath. She couldn't deal with this right now. Later—she'd deal with it later. "We need to get rid of Alexi's body, and I'm sure Mulcahy would like a report."

"What he'd like is your ass in a sling," Ryder commented.

Raine stared at him.

"You disobeyed your chief and didn't tell him where the meeting was." Undaunted, he shrugged, obviously enjoying the tension filled atmosphere. "He's not happy."

"Good," she muttered as she struggled to push herself to her feet. "At least I'm not alone in that."

Cheveyo moved to help steady her and ignored her slight stiffening.

"Ryder and I will take care of the body." Xander got to her feet. "You need some medical attention."

Raine shuffled over to stand by what remained of the woman she once considered a friend. She felt nothing but relief that she was standing and Alexi was dead. Without a word, she let Cheveyo lead her away.

It was slow going as her body made its numerous aches and pains known. She was hunched over, like an old woman, because something in the center of her body still hurt. Not a deep hurt, more like a sore, seriously-pulled-some-muscles hurt. It meant Alexi managed to hurt her worse than she first believed.

Cheveyo was a tall, silent shadow beside her. When she stumbled, he reached out to brace her, and when she was steadier, he pulled back.

The sun was heading toward the west and giving way to late afternoon when she and Cheveyo reached the clearing with the shack. She caught a dull glimmer out of the corner of her eye and took a few steps before carefully reaching down to retrieve one of her knives. A slow scan netted the other one a short space away. She made her way over and picked up the second blade. Having the two blades in her hands made her feel steadier, more in control.

Cheveyo said nothing, not even when she faced him with a blade in each hand. She searched his face, the high cheeks bones, the impenetrable obsidian gaze set deep under slashing black brows, the slightly crooked nose, full lips, and angled chin. His expression was difficult to read. She took in the faded jeans, the deep blue T-shirt, and the worn hiking boots. Distantly she admitted that he looked good enough to earn second, even third glances, but right now she felt nothing. She was exhausted, physically and emotionally.

Perhaps it was better to be emotionally drained, since she could pretty much assume if she felt better, Cheveyo wouldn't be standing so nonchalantly in front of her while she was armed. Her voice was as empty as her heart. "Why?"

Cheveyo's expression didn't alter and his voice eerily echoed hers. "I could not stand by and watch your spirit bleed away."

"And because you decided I should live, what do I owe you?"

A flash of something too fast to understand washed over his face. "I've said it before, Raine, you have trust issues. You owe me nothing."

She snorted, and then winced as her ribs protested. "Everything has a price, Cheveyo. You're too old not to understand that."

"Is this where I'm supposed to say something about you being too cynical?"

A spark of dry humor rose. "It's the way of my people. We're rarely disappointed that way." She turned away as her brief humor faded. "What did you do to us?"

Out of the corner of her eye, she caught the flash of confusion, frustration, and pained male ego that was there and then gone. "It's an old magic, the sharing of life forces." His voice took on a lecturing tone. "When one person is gravely injured in spirit, another person can help them survive by sharing a small piece of their personal power. However, the person sharing must be strong enough to create and forge the link and the one receiving must be willing to take it."

That brought her head around. "Are you saying I willingly took part in this? I remember a lot of pain, and passing out, but I'm pretty certain I would remember you asking."

"No, but you were willing to live at any cost."

She shook her head. There were times when being Kyn was more trouble than it was worth. This was turning out to be one of those times. What, she mused briefly, would it be like to just be human? To face such problems as how to find the money to replace the transmission in a beater car, or what job to do for the rest of your life.

Nope, instead she faced mad scientists, psychotic demons, covert military generals, a pissed off boss who'd make the psychotic demon seem like a walk in the park, and a witch who now held a piece of her soul. Not to mention the man she cared for was still in a coma and would probably wake up hating her for what she dragged him into.

To hear Cheveyo say she wanted to live at any cost was disconcerting. She was bone tired, not just in body, but in spirit.

Before turning fifteen, she and her mother lived a quiet life. Once, she thought, staring sightlessly out in to the woods, life had been quite simple. Her mother loved her. That she never doubted. It didn't matter if she hadn't shared who Raine's father was, she'd done nothing but protect Raine. Together they found joy in the simple things, a well-planted garden, treasures rediscovered in antique shops, and lessons to help Raine's emerging natural magic.

Her mother's face was a hazy memory, but the long dark hair that smelled of jasmine, the gray-blue eyes always sparkling with laughter, and the graceful hands that showed Raine the basics in warding spells—those stayed clear.

She held those details close while at the lab. Her personal talisman against the onslaught of pain and the dehumanizing —what an ironic term—experiments. When she realized her mother was dead—and how she died—Raine hadn't even been able to grieve. Escape had become the all-consuming goal. Through the insanity of relearning how to block out the screaming chaos of the magic around her, to burying deep those magical traits which seem to frighten those who knew her, she held the kernel of her mother's love close. Protecting the small flame of love, could, in her darkest hours, bring a tiny whisper of comfort.

She lost sight of that spark. Something she could admit now.

At some point when she was hunting down those who twisted her, she hid the spark so deep it almost sputtered out. Yet, when Cheveyo reached out to bring her back from the death she could have sworn she would've cheerily welcomed, it burst forth, strong enough to have her accepting Cheveyo's offer.

His voice wove through her thoughts. "Raine?" She shifted her gaze back to see puzzlement etched on his face. "Where did you just go?"

"I'm just surprised," her voice felt rusty. "To find out maybe you're right."

"About what?"

"Maybe I did want to live. Shit," she muttered.

He blinked slowly. "You are a very confusing woman."

She started toward him. "Yeah, I get that a lot." When she reached his side, she handed him the two blades. "Don't drop them." Then she headed to the log behind the shack to get her backpack. She had used clothes to pack her weapons, but now she wanted her jeans. Being naked sucked.

She dragged the pack out of its hiding spot, went into the shack, and changed. Once back outside, she handed Cheveyo his flannel shirt. He took it without a word. She started to shrug into her pack, but Cheveyo's hand shot out and took it from her.

She didn't argue. Exhaustion pulled at her, but the trek to the road remained. "How far is your Jeep?"

"It's back near the park entrance." Cheveyo gestured toward the road she knew was five miles out. "It's the closest we could get by car."

She sighed and started out, Cheveyo trailing behind her. They walked in a weird sort of comfortable silence for a while before she needed a distraction from her body's whimpers. "What did Ryder mean about you and I tapping in to each other's magic?"

Her sudden question didn't seem to startle Cheveyo. "When you combine life forces, you are combining magics and creating a sort of door between the two people."

"Dumb it down for me, Cheveyo."

He sighed. "If we were in close proximity and in need, we could open the door to create a secondary source of power. Take your last situation. If we were bound, you could've countered the demon halfing's hold by opening the door and drawing on my knowledge of defensive spells."

She concentrated on putting one foot in front of the other as she shifted the information around. "So I could have just gotten a peek at your mind, found what I needed, and pulled it out?"

"No, more like I would feel what you were going through and reacted as if it was happening to me."

She stumbled to a halt. "Wait a second. If I'm attacked, you're going to feel it and visa versa? I don't need any more enemies. I can barely handle the ones I have now."

Her statement brought a small quirk to those full lips. "You don't have to worry. The only way the mental door will open is if you open it and I answer."

Frowning, she studied his calm face. "If you knock and I don't answer, what happens?"

He shrugged. "I'll deal like I would've before."

"And if you die?"

"You have a decided lack of confidence in my skills."

She pushed. "I'm not kidding around. What if I don't answer, or can't answer, and you're killed?"

The witch's gaze shuttered. "You will feel it, but you will survive it."

"How deeply will I feel it?"

"I don't know," frustration laced his voice. "It's not like I go around tying myself to every person in trouble."

Whoa, pushed a button there. "Okay, but that brings two questions to mind. One, how can you not know? Don't you know this stuff? And two, why did you tie yourself to me?"

He raked a hand through his hair. "As I said before, the magic used for such a spell is old and the tales accompanying it have faded into the past. I was taught the spell by someone older and wiser than me. Since I haven't seen what happens if one side of the equation falls, I can't tell you what to expect."

"Then how do you know I'll feel it?"

"Logic. If I die, you will lose a small piece of yourself, and visa versa."

She took a moment to digest that little tidbit. The hope that the little piece she could lose would be one of the worst flitted through her mind and then drifted away. A twisted piece of humor to stave off hysterics at being linked to a man she barely knew. She shot him a look. "You didn't answer my second question."

He raised an eyebrow. "I'm not going to." When she opened her mouth, he raised a hand. "I can't, actually. I reacted and it's done."

She heard the finality in his tone, turned, and began making her way back to the cars.

Time passed, and she concentrated on breathing through the ache of her screaming muscles as she pushed herself relentlessly, blocking out her surroundings. Cheveyo brought her back to her senses with a gentle hand on her elbow when she stumbled onto the relatively clear path that lead to the parking lot. She raised her weary eyes and if she was a lesser woman, would have cried in relief when she made out Cheveyo's Jeep.

Cheveyo's voice was a low murmur, "Just a little bit more."

Unable to speak, she jerked her head in a nod. She didn't realize how much she was leaning on him until they reached the Jeep and he stood her against the vehicle. Her legs were watery and she feared passing out. The witch helped her into the passenger seat, then snapped a belt across her lap.

She leaned her head back and closed her eyes. The other door opened and the vehicle shifted under Cheveyo's weight as he settled in. Before he could turn the ignition, she rolled her head, and pulled her lids up just enough to look at him. "My SUV is parked at a cabin."

Cheveyo picked up a cell phone and hit a series of numbers. "I need you to pick up Raine's SUV." She heard Ryder on the other end. Cheveyo got the directions from her and passed them on. "Just take it back to Taliesin. Thanks." He snapped the phone closed.

She lost the fight to keep her eyes open. "He doesn't have my keys," she mumbled.

Cheveyo pulled out of the parking lot and headed back toward Portland. "He doesn't need them."

"College boy ruins my ignition, he's paying for it."

Cheveyo didn't answer.

The hum of the tires lulled her into a light sleep. She had no idea how much time passed before she was roused from her semi-conscious state. Couldn't have been long, judging by the slight change in the sun.

"How upset is Mulcahy?" her voice was rusty.

Cheveyo didn't even startle. "Fairly pissed."

She sighed. "Why aren't you with Gavin and Cassandra?"

"When you didn't call back in, Mulcahy knew you were heading out alone. He contacted me. Considering I was the best bet at tracking you, it was a logical call."

She stared out the window at the passing scenery. She would need every bit of strength to cope with her uncle. He wouldn't take lightly to her disobeying his orders. Especially since she had been bucking his authority on a consistent basis lately. Which meant this would be a big argument. She didn't want to deal with it. She would rather go home and hide for a while. And that was a weakness she couldn't afford. Time to pay the piper. She sighed.

"You scared him." Cheveyo's voice brought her head back around.

"Mulcahy doesn't scare."

He shot her a look. "I don't know why you can't see it, but where you're concerned, he can scare."

She couldn't stop the snort. "I'm just a very valuable weapon to him."

He shook his head. "I think you're selling him short."

"No, I'm not." She turned away, happy she was so exhausted her emotions barely made a dint. "Every time he sees me, it reminds him of my mother's death. He blames me. Not that I hold it against him." The last was said under her breath.

Unfortunately, Cheveyo's hearing was as good as hers. "I sincerely doubt that. You were a kid when it all went down."

"It doesn't matter." She pulled at the seatbelt until it was no longer digging into the burn on her chest. "I don't want to talk about it."

She shifted on her seat as the burn on her right thigh throbbed under her jeans. "I'm going to need to clean up before I see him." She spread her fingers out and took in the reddish brown tint to her nails. Despite using water and a T-shirt to wash the worst off her face and hands, she still needed a shower.

"You'll get maybe fifteen before he'll expect you in his office."

She nodded and closed her eyes for the remainder of the trip.

CHAPTER THIRTY-SEVEN

When they reached Taliesin, Raine headed straight toward the gym and a shower, while Cheveyo made his way up to Mulcahy's office. Some of her tension dissolved with his departure. Not knowing what to think or feel about the tie that now existed between them, she felt no urge to try and figure it out. She stripped, left her clothes in a pile, and walked naked into the shower.

She stood under the warm spray while the reds and browns streamed down her body and swirled into the drain. She closed her eyes, blanked her mind, and raised her face to the falling water. For a few precious moments, she reveled in the warm, relaxing pressure of the shower. When the water hit her thigh, it stung, but eventually even that changed to a dull ache. The burns that shackled her leg looked like some weird hand-shaped tattoo. As she studied them, she realized she was now the proud owner of another scar.

The observation tore a harsh laugh from her throat. Without warning, her legs gave out and she slid down the wall. She wrapped her arms, marred by a variety of cuts and scratches, around her trembling legs, and drew them toward her chest. Unable to bring them too close—due to the slashing burn along her chest and the stiffening of her left side from the burn working its way from her shoulder to her hip—she rested her forehead on her knees. Her long hair untangled, providing a spotty barrier against the stinging sensation of water on the deeper furrows Alexi had left along the right side of her neck.

Battered inside and out, all the emotions Raine blocked out for the last few days came crashing through her compromised barriers. Why was it every time she reached out and opened herself up to others, she turned it to shit?

She made a mistake, one that cost her dearly. Not seeing Alexi for what she was had left Raine burying one friend, losing the illusion of another, and fearing for the sanity of a third who very well might leave her. Plus, she was now tied to a powerful man—one who rivaled Mulcahy—and worried about her sanity at tapping into powers long denied.

The fear of losing her hard won independence and self-sufficiency made her blood run cold. Not to mention how watching Gavin walk away would shatter her. There, huddled in a shower stall in the gym at Taliesin, she made herself a promise. She would rebuild her emotional barriers, master her skills, and depend only upon herself. She wouldn't open the door between her and Cheveyo, and she would avoid Gavin. He wouldn't want her around anyway.

Leaning her head back against the wall, she couldn't tell the difference between the water from the shower or the tears trailing down her face.

CHAPTER THIRTY-EIGHT

Twenty minutes later, Raine stepped out of the elevator and moved with something close to her usual grace. Exhaustion still dogged her steps, but her emotions remained blessedly numb. Not a bad thing as Mulcahy would dress her down, as was his right. She had ignored his orders to fulfill her need for vengeance. Therefore, she would take whatever he dished out.

His door was open.

She stepped through and stopped before his desk. He stood with a cup of tea in one hand, and watched the dying evening light out his window. They stood that way for a moment before he turned and moved to the desk and set the cup down. He motioned for her take a chair. She hesitated a second, but then chose to follow his unspoken order as her left leg still had a tendency to quiver.

"Are you all right?" His voice was even.

She nodded. "I'll survive."

He sat in his chair and studied her for an unnerving minute. Could he see the exhaustion behind her mask? His gaze traced the red gouges on her neck as they disappeared into the collar of her long-sleeved shirt. No doubt Cheveyo had given him a full report on what happened.

"Cheveyo explained what he did to save you." By neither voice nor expression did he reveal what he felt about the witch's actions. "Are you going to be okay with that tie?"

"I have no choice but to be okay with his decision. However, I have no desire to draw on that bond. Ever."

"Ever is a long time, niece." There was a hint of humor in his voice that knocked her off balance.

She spoke without thinking. "Why aren't you reaming me a new one?"

A glint of something, which might be sadness, washed through his gaze before it returned to its indecipherable best. Maybe her exhaustion had her imagining things. "I think I can figure out why you went out by yourself. I can even understand it." He picked up his tea and took a sip before continuing, "Revenge is an emotion I understand all too well."

She shook her head. "It wasn't revenge." At his raised eyebrow, she corrected herself, "All right, not just revenge." She struggled with how much to share with her uncle, since this was who she was talking to, instead of her boss. "I made a mistake that others paid dearly for. It was my responsibility to correct that mistake. I didn't want to endanger anyone more than necessary."

"If she had killed you…"

Her smile was cold. "It wouldn't have mattered. I linked a blood-tracking spell with one of blades. It would've led you straight to her. Either by my hand or yours, she was dead."

He sighed and tapped his fingers on his desk. "Did you ever consider yours wasn't the only mistake made with this situation? That you weren't the only one involved in this whole debacle."

She remained silent.

He leaned back in his chair. "I made mistakes." His words were serious and remorse was a light undertone. "Decisions I can now look back on and say weren't the best ones. That is the beauty of hindsight, niece. If you live your whole life looking backward, you will never move forward. Do you understand?"

This was so unlike any conversation she ever shared with her uncle, it rattled her. "I do, but I also understand learning from your mistakes."

His sharp scrutiny almost made her squirm. "I could ask what you've learned, but it's not my business." There was no answer she could give, so she stayed silent while he continued. "Do I need to worry about you going rogue?"

She understood this was now her boss asking the question. "No, sir."

Mulcahy nodded. "All right." He pulled some papers over and began scanning them. "Tomorrow, news of Dr. Lawson's death is going to hit the air waves. I also need to close out Talbot's case." He paused and shot her a very pointed look. "Does he need to worry about any more deaths hitting his company?"

She heard the underlying question and the knowledge behind it. It barely made a ripple in her numbed state. Was she going to go after anyone else at Talbot's for what was done to Gavin and Chet? No, but she wasn't going to give Talbot carte blanche, either. "It's a big company, sir. Death is very indiscriminate, but I don't think he has a need to worry at this time."

He smiled a bit at the twisted, enigmatic reply. "You still think he had something to do with this?"

She shrugged, uncertain how to explain the deep-rooted suspicion that could well be her own personal paranoia. "It worries me that Dr. Lawson worked so closely with Talbot, and he still, supposedly, had no idea what was happening. Lawson was clever, but I would've sworn Jonah Talbot was smarter than that."

"Perhaps," Mulcahy answered as he made a note on the papers in front of him. "We'll keep an eye on him, but at this time we have nothing concrete to tie him to Lawson."

"What about the general?"

His pen stopped and there was nothing comforting in his small smile. "The general has lost his researcher and her research. He will soon discover all her promises were lies. For now, we have to watch him." He leaned back in his chair. "Removing him would bring too much attention to the company, not to mention the Kyn community. The human military has always, and will always, try to infiltrate the Wraiths, one warrior community to another. It's a matter of staying a few steps ahead of the humans."

"And if he hooks up with someone else?" Arrogance was really an issue for the Kyn. Somehow, she didn't think just because you outlived your human counterparts, you were that much more infallible.

Mulcahy's smile went so sharp it could've drawn blood. "Then, questions or not, he'll be taken care of." The smile faded. "Which brings me to my next question. What about Tarek?"

She took a deep breath and let it out. "He's gone for now. We could try to track him down, but he seemed awfully anxious not to go up against Taliesin."

"Will he stay away, or are we going to have to go after him?"

"I think he'll stay away." She rubbed at the ache in her thigh. "Giving me the meeting place with Alexi was his way of making amends."

Mulcahy nodded briefly. "For now, he's off the radar. However, if he comes back up, it's your responsibility." Raine expected as much. "That's it for now, McCord. Go home and get some rest." He pulled another document over and started reading it.

She stood, then paused. When he raised his head, she asked, "How is Gavin, sir?"

"I wondered how long it would take you to ask." When she remained silent, he nodded, apparently approving of her restraint. "He regained consciousness a few hours ago. Cassandra said he's doing better than expected."

She fought to keep her voice neutral and won. "Will he be coming back?"

"When Cassandra approves it, yes. Gavin expressed a strong desire to be back at work." His brown eyes were shrewd. "Anything else?"

Did he ask for me? She shook her head. "No, I'm glad to hear he's doing okay. Have a good evening." She turned and left the office.

Downstairs she found her SUV parked near the doors. There were no signs of Cheveyo, Ryder, or Xander, for which she was grateful. She got in and heaved a sigh of relief when her key slid in smoothly and the engine turned over. The deafening sound of industrial rock brought a weak smile to her face. Pounding, angry music and Ryder were hard to picture. She figured him to be more of a pop music person. It so fit with his looks.

She headed home, bone tired and soul weary. The fact Gavin hadn't asked to see her broke her heart a little, but it wasn't unexpected. If their positions were reversed, she wasn't sure she'd want him around.

For now she just wanted sleep. Tomorrow, she would clear her desk and put in for an overdue vacation. She wanted to get away for a bit. She needed time to shore up her defenses. Maybe she'd call Cheveyo to take him up on his offer of training. It couldn't hurt. It was better to master your weapons instead of letting them master you.

At the end of the day, when all the blood was washed away and the bodies disposed of, she was what she was—a Kyn and, Lord and Lady help her, a Wraith.

CHAPTER THIRTY-NINE

THREE DAYS LATER

High above downtown Portland, Jonah Talbot watched the hustle as Wednesday commuters rushed to and fro. On Monday, he received a call that Dr. Lawson died in an electrical fire in her house over the weekend. Unfortunately, when flames hit the gas heater in the garage it touched off an explosion. The house was nothing but rubble and ash. Eden Lawson was identified by dental records. The officer who called him explained there were no signs of arson or foul play. A tragic accident.

Perhaps, but he wasn't altogether certain it was an accident. First thing this morning, his very efficient secretary brought him the final report from Taliesin's investigation into the deaths of his employees. According to Mulcahy's report there was no decisive evidence linking the deaths. Some could be murders, but each death carried different, distinctive traits. The final supposition was some of the deaths were purely accidental, while a couple might be the result of personal vendettas against the victims. Mulcahy added a personal note, stating that Taliesin found no eminent threat to Jonah Talbot at this time.

At this time was a curious way to word things, but Jonah admired Mulcahy's ability to be subtle. The ringing of his desk phone interrupted his train of thought. "Talbot."

"The lab was destroyed along with any and all research." General Cawley's voice came over the wire. "It looks as if a damn bomb went off over here."

"Pity. I hate to lose that much research. However, don't you have some of the earlier notes and results?"

"Some, but it's going to take time to rebuild what we lost here."

"I'm a patient man, General."

There was a disgruntled sigh. "I'm not, and my superiors are getting itchy. We need to give them some proof of advancement to keep them calm."

Talbot let the frustration of dealing with politics color his voice, "They may call me directly if they need reassurance. I would remind them that moving too quickly on this will set off alarms within the Kyn community. If they wish to avoid whatever happened to Dr. Lawson and her research, they will remain calm. Every experiment encounters setbacks."

The general paused. "I'll soothe whatever ruffled feathers I can at this point. However, are there any other names you want me to add to the list of who we're watching?"

The flash of silvered eyes ran through Jonah's mind. "Yes, Raine McCord and Gavin Durand." He hung up the phone softly, then turned and watched the flow beneath the glass window, a slow cruel smile playing across his face.

END OF BOOK ONE

Turn the page for an exclusive Kyn short story - Submerged in Shadows

SUBMERGED IN SHADOWS

A KYN SHORT STORY

Forced on an unwanted vacation, Raine soon discovers that boredom is the least of her worries when danger washes ashore, bringing unexpected complications.

"Y̶ou call this a vacation?"

"Until a few moments ago, yes."

The man didn't bother to respond, but picked up the extra blanket from the second chair and sat down. The night was closing in, the light fading under the gathering storm clouds on the horizon. It brought along a chill with more teeth than bite, but what else could you expect in November? At least it wasn't raining. Yet.

"Why here?"

Taking another sip of tea, Raine McCord savored the delicate combination of chamomile and spice in hopes it would wash away the bitterness his presence wrought. He waited, his silence creating more pressure than being battered with questions. Ryan Mulcahy, CEO of Taliesin Security and head of the Northwest Kyn, knew how to work the non-verbal interrogation. She focused on the waves lapping the edges of rocky sand. "It's quiet."

And here, on Shaw Island nestled among the San Juan Islands in Washington, quiet was an understatement. No street lights glared, no busy streets rumbled, no bustle of shops distracted. Endless starry skies stretched above, while water whispered over sand and stone below. Between them, there was silence.

With under three hundred residents, she didn't worry about nosy neighbors or unexpected guests during her impromptu vacation. Well, except for the man currently sitting next to her, comfortable in his tailored slacks and pressed shirt sans tie. He didn't fit here. Hell, she didn't fit here, but she needed this after…Her mind shied away from the memories and the guilt.

"Not the vacation spot I expected," he said.

Her lips twitched. She couldn't help it, but to hide it she brought the mug to her lips and murmured, "Did you think I'd go to Hawaii or something?"

"Or something." Quiet humor drifted in his voice.

"Yeah, sorry Uncle, that's not really my style." The moody waters surrounding the island matched her thoughts. Besides she was much more comfortable in the shadows. Hawaii would have required a bikini, something she didn't own. "Surprised you made it out here."

"Caught the last ferry in from Anacortes."

The tension she fought so hard to lose came back in a heartbeat. For her maternal uncle to make an effort to come out did not bode well. Her hands tightened on her mug, and her jaw locked. It was difficult, but she managed to keep her voice level. "You can't stay here."

"Can't leave until the morning ferry, and you choose the one spot without a hotel or B and B."

Damn him. He was a master game player, one she had no

hope of ever outmaneuvering. Why did she even try? She glared at him, but the effort was lost as he continued to stare out over the inky stain spreading across the waters. "Why are you here?" Each word escaped with a snap.

His head turned slowly until he faced her. The light spilling from the small cabin behind her and the last gasps of dusk brushed over his face, carving illusions of emotions she knew damn well he'd never show. "He's coming back."

Her heart stalled, then picked up a panicked pace. *He* was Gavin Durand, the man she led straight into a nightmare because she trusted the wrong person. A nightmare he was still fighting.

"You need to be there when he arrives."

Guilt rushed in and wrapped choking hands around her throat. Under it, shame coursed. She turned back to the water and brought her shaking mug to her lips. The incoming storm clouds crept closer. Winds nipped over the water and curled around her, leaving the tea's warmth useless against the chill in her veins. When the cruel grip of memories eased, she choked out, "I've done enough to him. He won't want me there."

"I want you there." There was no give in her uncle's voice.

"Is that an order from my Captain?" Because if it was, she could dance around his command, but not outright ignore it. She used up all her markers with her last stunt, and she wasn't in a hurry to lose her position as one of the elite Wraiths. Her uncle ran the twelve member, highly secret, highly specialized team of Kyn who kept the nightmares from tearing through humans and Kyn alike. They were already down one man. If Gavin didn't make it back completely, they'd be down two. Take her out of the equation and things would get dicey quick. The Kyn might not be as plentiful as the humans, but there were enough monsters out there to keep the Wraiths hopping.

"No, but I didn't take you for a coward."

There was no controlling her flinch as his words left a mark.

Mulcahy blew out a breath, and ran a hand over his jaw. "You can't avoid him forever." Then he muttered, "Correction, maybe you can, but it won't do you or him any good."

Bitter remorse rose, and her lips curled. "Says who?"

"The voice of experience," he offered, wry amusement taking the edge off his answer. It unsettled her when he pulled shit like that, sounding as if he cared. Before she could respond, he kept going. "Things are going to get worse before they get better, and I'm not willing to lose anyone else because of it." This time, all amusement had faded, leaving simple truth.

"How much worse?" Because if anyone could see the future, she wouldn't put it past her uncle, one of the oldest, most secretive Kyn she'd ever met. She learned the hard way if he said something was barreling toward you, you had two choices—gear up or get gone. Personally she was all about the gearing up, not much sent her running. Except maybe facing Gavin.

The wind died. A deeper quiet flowed in to fill the void. Even the sound of water licking along the sand disappeared.

Into the silence, his voice emerged with a prophetic cadence. "Our world won't stay in the shadows much longer. Humans have short memories. They've forgotten about our kind, and why we're behind their fairy tales. Instead, they see only the results of our natures, and they fear what we are and the power we wield." Thunder rumbled over the water, darkness taking over completely as the impending storm clouds pushed closer. The tide surged in with a hiss.

"Some want it," she added, not that he needed the reminder.

He nodded. "We've managed to keep our presence from

the general population, but it won't last. When we're finally exposed, we can't afford to have divisions within our ranks. A cracked shield will shatter under the weight of fear and mistrust. The Wraiths can't afford internal division, which means you need to suck it up and work with Durand. Sooner rather than later."

Logically she understood where he was coming from, but she wasn't ready. Not yet. No way could she mend that tear without first facing the rips bleeding inside her. "Why don't we let him make the decision on when that moment should be? He deserves that much."

Instead of agreeing, he studied her, as if seeing beneath skin and bone. "And in the meantime?"

Damn him for pressuring her, but she knew it was coming, knew she needed to do it. So she would give him this, instead of her promise to be there when Gavin returned. "In the meantime, I'll work with Cheveyo." Between the two men, Cheveyo, the intimidating witch and head of the Northwest Magi house, was the lesser of two evils.

He dipped his chin in acknowledgement and together they watched the storm crawl in.

RAINE LEANED against one of the porch's posts as she stared into the storm-drenched darkness. Drizzle fell, easing from its earlier deluge, and the waves weren't ravaging the cove's edge so much as snapping at it. In the small two-room cabin behind her, Mulcahy slept. Or, at least, occupied a bed behind a closed door.

Sleep didn't bother to visit her.

She stared out into the night, feet bare against the cold wood, jeans damp from the blowing precipitation, hands fisted inside the lined slicker keeping the weather's edge away. She'd come here for peace, but his arrival had screwed that six ways to Sunday. So much for a vacation. Hell, she only wanted a break, but since he brought all the shit she was trying to leave behind along with his damn overnight bag, she was screwed on that front, too. She sighed.

Something moved out by the edge of the cove. A darker shadow against the night. Every sense on alert, she didn't move, didn't react, simply watched. Against the dark backdrop of the water and cloud-covered night sky, it was hard to determine who or what stumbled along the sand. The muttering of the waves almost drowned out a soft cry. She raced off the deck and crossed the distance before it faded. Sharp rocks and scattered driftwood bit at her bare feet, but didn't slow her down.

As she closed in, the shape sharpened into a child. A very scared child crawling on her hands and knees at the edge of the water. Raine slowed, then stopped a few away, sinking into a crouch. Children weren't her forte, but terror held this little girl in tight, merciless claws. It screamed from the big eyes peeking from behind tangled hair, and the tiny body shaking so hard, Raine worried she might shatter any second.

Instead of reaching out, Raine sank her hands into the sand in front of her and kept her voice soft. "Hey, there."

The little one whimpered and ducked her head, curling her spine.

Seeing that sliced Raine deep, and she fought to keep her anger at whoever created such a reaction out of her voice. "Shhhhh, I'm not going to hurt you." She continued to croon reassurances, calculating her best approach. Water crept up the sand, and washed over the girl's wrists and knees. "It's too cold for us to be here. Can you come inside with me?"

Instead of an answer, another shiver wracked the small body.

Shrugging out of her slicker, Raine inched closer, crooning nonsense, not wanting the child to bolt. Finally, she was close enough to lay her hoodie over the girl. On a vicious gust of wind a harsh, guttural cry whipped through the night, and Raine barely had time to brace as the little girl threw herself into Raine's arms. The lined slicker acted as a blanket. Her face burrowed against Raine's chest, muffling her raspy whimpers. Another brutal gust hit, and the fading rain took on new strength. Raine's T-shirt didn't stand a chance.

Gathering the girl close, Raine rose and dashed back to the cabin. She burst through the door, kicking it closed behind her. Away from the reemerging storm, the sounds falling from the child's mouth broke through the quiet, tearing through Raine's normal stoic demeanor. They mixed with haunting memories of another girl and another time, and left both the woman and her armful shaking, lost in their separate nightmares.

"Raine?" Her uncle's baritone curled around her. Warmth settled on her shoulders, dissipating the chill of the past and anchoring her in the present.

Mulcahy turned her.

She blinked, bringing him into focus.

A small frown furrowed his brow as he took in what she held. "Who's this?"

Raine shook her head and reached for words. Finding none, she coughed and finally managed, "Not sure, but she was stumbling down the shore."

Wind battered at the door, rattling the knob before knocking along the windows. Mulcahy looked out the dark pane of glass.

Raine caught an uneasy shadow crossing his face. "What?"

When he turned back the shadow was gone, probably just a trick of light. "I'll grab a blanket from the bed. Take the child to the bathroom. No telling how long she was out there and we need to get her warm."

Dipping her chin in acknowledgement, Raine followed him down the short hall. They split halfway down, her to the bathroom, him to his room. The girl's trembling had slowed, but not stopped, so Raine sat on the edge of the porcelain tub and shifted the girl to one arm. With an arm free, she ran water in the tub, keeping the temp warm, but not too hot.

As the tub filled, Raine slipped from the tub's edge to the floor. Better to be on solid ground when she unwrapped the little one. She finally managed to get the jacket off, uncovering shifting shades of brown and darker strands of...was that seaweed? Gently snagging a strand, she held it up. Yep, seaweed. Completely puzzled, she muttered, "Where did you get this?"

Another raspy whimper vibrated against her chest, and the tiny hands twisted in Raine's wet T-shirt. The child's quiet desperation tunneled devastating cracks under Raine's emotional walls. "Hush little one, you're okay. I've got you." Her words were soft, her hands gentle as she began to untangle the child. A difficult maneuver as she kept trying to crawl into Raine's lap. "Okay, kiddo, we have to get these wet things off you."

Utilizing a rare patience, Raine divested the girl of the oversized slicker. As she held one small hand, she noticed a fine webbing between the delicate fingers.

A sound at the door, brought her head up as her arms gathered the girl protectively close. Her uncle stood in the doorway, blanket in hand. "Is she hurt?"

At the sound of his voice, the little body pressing against her shivered hard. Raine shook her head. "Not from what I can tell, but she's scared out of her mind."

He handed over the blanket. "Here, I'll watch the door while you get her warm. Someone might be looking for her."

Unable to quell her unsettling sense of unease, Raine murmured, "Don't let them in."

Instead of honoring that with a response, he simply arched an eyebrow.

"Right." She set the blanket on the floor out of the way. The soft click of the bathroom door closing echoed through the bathroom as she grasped the girl's shoulders and pushed back gently until there was room between them. She made *shh*ing noises until the girl's harsh breathing slowed, and the time between shudders lessened. When she was sure the child wouldn't face plant against her chest, she adjusted her hold, one hand support the girl's back, the other carefully moving the long, wet strands of hair back until she could see her face.

Deep pools of darkness stared back and Raine sucked in a sharp breath. What the hell? It wasn't the swallowing black of fear, but as if the girl's entire eye, including the sclera, were dipped into fathomless ink. "Selkie." The word slipped out on a whisper.

Thick lashes drifted down, lifted, and thin fingers dug into Raine's arms. "He took our skins." Sorrow and fear added depth to the childish whimper. "Mama said to run. I ran."

Locked deep where memories couldn't hurt, the guilt under the last two words struck an old chord. Raine squeezed one small hand. "You did the right thing." Needing a moment to recalculate her next step, she reached back and turned off the water. The tub was half-full.

Selkies shared much with their seal counterparts, such as an affinity for salt water versus fresh, which meant the bath may not be the best move. Better to let the child decide, than accidentally do more harm. "Bath or blanket, kiddo?"

With an unexpected lean, the little girl nabbed the blanket. Raine's quick reflexes saved her from smashing face first on to the floor. It took a few moments to get her wrapped in the blanket, but once she was covered, she sat in Raine's lap, still and watchful. As hard as it was to hold the little girl's stare, Raine managed. Time for introductions. "My name is Raine, and the man who was just here, is my uncle."

The girl dropped her chin, small white teeth nibbling her lower lip. Raine didn't press, simply waited as the girl worked through the wisdom of sharing. It wasn't long before her spine straightened with determination, and her head lifted, a bit of bravado adding a flush to her pale cheeks. "Maris."

Raine's lips twitched. Someone had a liking for Latin, since that was a direct translation of 'sea'. "Maris, it's nice to meet you." Now came the hard part, finding out who the hell was after her. "Can you tell me what happened?"

With impeccable timing, another hard gust battered against the small window above the tub, and what little color Maris's face held, seeped away. Her alien gaze snapped to the window even as she inched closer to Raine. "He'll come for me."

Cradling the back of Maris's head, Raine tucked her close, the soft blanket brushing her jaw while Maris's jagged breathing sent warm puffs over her skin. "He'll have to go through my uncle and me, sweetie."

"He's meaner than a sea snake. Even daddy says so."

From the quaver in her voice, sea snakes were her epitome of fearsome. "Right then, so we'll just have to be extra careful."

Shifting the girl's weight, Raine tightened her hold and got to her feet, not that she had to hold on too tight. With her arms and legs locked around Raine, Maris could give an octopus a run for its money. "We're going to go into the front room so you can tell your story. Then we'll figure out what we're going to do next, okay?" Because if anyone knew how to deal with a traumatized Selkie child, her uncle would.

Maris nodded without lifting her head. Raine walked down the short hall to the front room to find Mulcahy, arms crossed over his chest, shoulder braced on the frame of the front window, frowning into the blind surface. Taking in his position and the raging storm outside, Raine chided, "Really think that's a good place to stand, Mulcahy?"

He turned away from the glass and watched as she settled on the couch with Maris. "I'd rather know who's coming up my steps than wait for them to barge in."

He pushed off the wall and walked over, his attention focused on the little girl huddled in Raine's lap. He slowed, then crouch in front of them until his face was level with Maris's. The hard lines of his face eased, and a spark of wonder crept in. He held out his hand. "Hello, love."

Stunned by the rarely heard gentleness in Mulcahy's voice, Raine could only blink and wonder who had replaced the ruthless son of a bitch she knew and tolerated with this man.

In her lap, Maris untangled a hand from the blankets and took his larger one. "Hi."

Raine was mesmerized as Mulcahy carefully brushed his thumb along the back of Maris's hand. "What are you doing so far from home?"

For the first time in years, the musical lilt of Ireland whispered through his voice, bringing an unexpected ache to Raine's chest. She remember that voice, so long ago, trying to ease her tears. Funny how she'd forgotten that. Memories of her mother's laugh and her uncle's teasing banter crowded close. Biting the inside of her cheek hard, she shoved it back. Not the time or the place to deal with such things.

"This is Maris," her voice came out choked. "Maris, my uncle, Mulcahy."

"Ryan," he corrected never looking away from the little girl. "Easier for younger tongues." He let go of her hand and settled on the floor in front of them, his back resting against the coffee table, one arm resting on a bent knee. "What's a young lady like you, doing out so late, young Maris?"

Maris's head turned back to look at Raine, the movement causing the blanket to fall around her shoulders. Those solid black eyes should be difficult to read, but Raine caught the little girl's question. Offering a small smile, she dipped her chin in encouragement.

Maris turned back to Mulcahy, and blew out an audible breath. "Mom and me came to visit the sisters and play with the llamas. We weren't going to stay long, just a little while, because daddy's coming home today and mom needed some vegetables from the market for dinner. We were getting ready to head back, but he was there." Her tiny shoulders hunched and her voice got soft. "He had our skins. He wouldn't give them back, and he…" Her voice trailed off as a shudder wracked her body.

Raine's stomach dropped, as image after horrific image raced through her mind. While Selkies could walk on land for short periods of time, they needed their skins to survive. If some man held them hostage, there's no telling what Maris's mother was enduring for her daughter's safety.

She wrapped her arms around Maris's waist, tugging her back so she'd feel safe. She rested her cheek against the damp strands of Maris's hair, the tang of salt water biting her nose. She didn't want to ask, but they needed to know. "He, what, sweetie?"

A harsh sob escaped the little girl and Mulcahy's hand curled into a tight fist, even as Raine held her closer.

"He hit mom, over and over until she couldn't get up." Maris lifted her face, tears streaming over rounded cheeks. "She was hurt bad, and I couldn't help. She told me to run, so

I did. I shouldn't have left her, but I was so scared. Daddy'll be mad I left her."

Mulcahy leaned forward and captured Maris's face in his hands, holding her still. "Hush, baby girl. Your daddy won't be mad, he'll be proud you did what your mom said to do."

"But I shouldn't have left her!" The little girl's wail echoed through the small cabin. Outside, the storm paused as if taking a breath and then charged back in, stronger than before. The lights flickered under the onslaught, adding to the eerie sense of being hunted.

Mulcahy ignored it all, focused solely on the terror-stricken child in Raine's lap. "You did exactly what you should've done. Had you stayed, he would have hurt you. Something neither your mom nor your dad would want."

Raine made a noise at her uncle's lack of finesse. His gaze flickered to hers, and his sharp headshake cut off her protest before it escaped. His attention dropped back to Maris. "Do you know where your mom is now?"

Maris nodded, the drying strands of hair curling around her face. "In the tower."

"Tower?" Mulcahy met Raine's gaze above Maris's head.

"By the pond," Maris added. She titled her head back to look at Raine. "Back at the next cove." She twisted in Raine's lap and her arm emerged from her blanket to point to the west.

Shaw Island housed a small nunnery and very few residents, but on her way to the cabin, Raine had marked the closest homestead about a mile or so out. There were small buildings cluttered around a pond, but a tower could've been tucked away in there. It wasn't the next cove over, but two. Still with the way the island was laid out, a little girl could get confused, especially in this weather. Considering the strange situation, best if she called on her neighbors now instead of later. No telling how bad of shape Maris's mom was in, and Raine didn't want to be the one to break the little girl's heart.

"Well then, Raine will have to run over there and check it out." Mulcahy met Raine's gaze over Maris's head.

Yep, time to do some neighborhood drop-ins.

THE FIRST COVE to the west came up empty, so Raine didn't waste time making her way to where she noted the buildings from earlier. Sure enough, while most of the buildings remained dark, one small home was nestled under the shadow of an attached stone tower, a dull glow behind the covered windows.

Under the cover of the storm, she managed to get up close to the weathered boards of the structure. Protected from the rain by the hood of her black slicker, she hunched next to the rickety planks of the porch, ignoring the chill. Instead, her focus was on the leakage of light seeping around the metal slats of the cheap blinds covering the window. Filtering out the wailing wind, the chittering rain, and the hissing waves, she strained to lock on to some sign of life. Minutes dragged by with no shadows playing peek-a-boo with the light and no rasp of movement emerging from within.

Instead of creeping closer, she made her way around the back of the small structure until she could see the tower rising like a dark finger against the sky. There were slits high up, near the roof, but it was too dark to tell how big those openings were. Better to use the door. Maybe. Her other option? Climb up and hope for the best. Tilting her head back she considered the rain-slicked stones. Yeah, not really a smart move. Door it was then.

Dividing her attention between the tower and the

cottage, she located the heavy wooden door with the shiny, new lock. Picking the little sucker would take time, and she hadn't exactly brought her tools with her. Instead, she only had her blades, because who needed an arsenal when you went on vacation? If Gavin was here, he could've made quick work of the pesky piece. She was limited to kicking the door in or something equally noisy. Since she was on her own and had no idea who or what she was facing, best to be cautious.

Prowling around the base of the tower, she considered. A new lock meant there was something worth hiding in the tower, and chances were that's where she'd find Maris's mom. Ignoring the storm's lash she began to cull through various ways to get through the thick door.

She could use her knife and break the lock. Probably better than trying to scale the slick stone surface. However doing that would warn whoever was inside to her presence, which might not be smart. With no idea of who or what she was facing, it would be better to go in quietly or with the edge of surprise on her side. Considering the weather, knocking on the door with an offer of Girl Scout cookies wouldn't cut it.

Coming around the tower's far side, a wink of a light in the distance froze her in place. Dropping into a crouch, she pressed her spine against the wet stone and merged into the surrounding shadows. The light disappeared, then reappeared, and it took a moment for her to identify the sporadic pattern as someone walking with a half-hidden flashlight. Drawing on the animal that shared her skin, she tapped into her leopard's senses crafted by a mad scientist's desires.

The night snapped into crystalized focus, banding into reds, greens, and yellows, while every hair on her skin stood at attention in predatory warning of an approaching threat. A sudden lull in the storm's fury gave her the opportunity to hone in on the soft sound of sand squelching underfoot.

Through her unique night vision a form appeared, but it was strange. Instead of the expected red and yellows indicating body heat, it was a combination of blue-tinged yellow and greens.

She blinked once, slowly, but nothing changed. Right then, so definitely not human.

Whoever or whatever it was, continued to make its way to the tower, but based on the pattern of the muted flashlight, they were looking for something. Say, like a little girl? She could feel her lips curl back over her teeth and managed to shut down the soft snarl rumbling in her chest. The storm kicked back into noisy gear as the figure moved forward, and she began to form a nebulous plan.

Her fingers flexed, and she felt the burn as her retractable claws slide forth. Using the freeze frame movements inherent to her cat, she crept around the tower's base, back toward the door, never taking her attention from the approaching figure. Because of how the cottage was situated against the attached tower, the shadows were heavier on the far side of the door. Using their cover, she coiled the muscles in her thighs and pushed off, going straight up to land lightly on the cottage's roof. The wood creaked under her weight, and she winced. Hopefully, between the storm and the distance, the noise of her landing wouldn't be detected. Several careful movements later, she was on her stomach, knife in hand, eyes trained on the figure.

It wasn't long before she could make out the thick chest and heavily muscled arms plastered by wet cotton and paired with lean legs covered in denim and bare feet. The incongruous sight trigger the memory of another pair of small, bare feet. Besides a frightened child running from monsters, who the hell else would be out in bare feet?

A dark tangle of wet hair obscured the face, but no doubt it was male. One who wasn't happy considering how he stomped up to the door. In fact, he slammed the heavy wooden door back with a resounding *thwack* as if pushing back a piece of paper. Some kind of light existed inside, because for a moment, as he did a side-to-side check, it revealed a very inhuman face and glinted strangely off the bare skin of his arms.

Considering the Fey were one of four races making up the Kyn, unnatural beauty wasn't a shock. But combine sculpted masculinity with a double row of sharp, pointed teeth bared in a silent snarl and shock was a definite reaction. As he stepped more fully inside the door, that weak interior light bounced off his skin, adding an iridescent sheen.

Shark teeth and scaled skin.

What the hell was a Triton doing this far inland? The much fiercer and violent cousin to the Selkies weren't much for playing on land. And why the hell was he hunting Selkies? Her knowledge of Tritons and Selkies was a little shaky, but she could've sworn the pompous nature of the Tritons kept them from pestering those they considered beneath their notice.

Eons ago, Tritons served as servants to the gods and goddesses of the sea, which is what probably started their egotistical belief that they were the top predators of the sea. Considering that mouthful of razors, maybe there were other reasons for it. Still, it didn't explain why this one was here and terrorizing a mother and child.

His broad back began to move further inside reminding her she didn't have time to ponder such things. She had one shot to find out what happened when you pit a cat against a fish. Just one.

Muscles coiled, grip solid on the hilt of her knife, claws extended on the other hand, she leapt with single-minded focus. Her impact knocked him forward a few stumbling steps, before he twisted in attempt to smash her into one of the walls.

Her blade sank deep, high in his back, missing her intended target, his spine. Dammit. With no other choice, she raked out with her clawed hand scoring a bloody, diagonal furrow from shoulder to hip. His deep roar shuddered over her ears, but he arched away from the attack, giving her the necessary room to drop to the floor and under his beefy arm swinging her way.

Needing more room to escape being caught between him and the wall, she kicked out. Even before her foot hit, she knew it wouldn't be enough to disable, the angle was all wrong. Still it was enough to send him off balance and gain her a few more precious feet of freedom so she scramble into the middle of the room, retracting her claws. She slipped her two boot knives free so when she gained her feet, she was armed. With her feet set she faced the pissed off Triton.

"What the fuck?" His question rolled over her carrying the depth of fury found in rough surf.

"I think that's my question." She met his gaze, barely controlling her flinch. Color swirled around the rounded slit of his pupil. They changed so fast she couldn't tell what the colors were, only that they made her stomach churn as if she was falling into a fathomless pit.

She forced her gaze away, keeping her attention focused on the minute movements of his body. They circled each other, weighing strengths and weaknesses. The injuries he sustained didn't seem to impede his movements, which caused a small niggle of worry. She brushed it aside. She didn't have time for that shit.

The soft light came from two lanterns hooked high on the walls. The room was bare except for steps curling up into the deeper dark above. The Triton edged toward the steps, and she matched his movements in a strange, lethal dance. The storm picked up strength, and wind and rain pelted her shoulder closest to the doorway. Rain sprayed across the stone floor.

He continued to watch her, never blinking, barely moving. The terse standoff was interrupted by a soft groan of pain drifting from above. It sank into Raine, reminding her why she was there. Her simmering anger flashed white-hot then morphed into a solid core of determination. Maris's mother was alive, and somehow Raine would make sure she stayed that way.

The Triton's lips stretched into a nightmarish smile, revealing the double rows of thin, curved saw blades doubling as teeth. "Maris." The little girl's name ended in a hiss. "Troublesome git."

Raine didn't bother rising to the bait. Let him think what he wanted, she just needed an opening.

He managed another inch closer to the stairs, his movement smooth and deadly. "You shouldn't get involved in situations you don't understand, girl. The females are mine."

"Yeah, that doesn't work for me." She mimicked his stillness. He had to move soon, but she didn't have clue one on how Tritons fought.

Then he gave her one.

There was no twitch of muscle, no tell-a-tale movement or warning. One second he was across from her, the next, his scary ass mouth was going for her stomach and ribs.

Instinct and luck were on her side. She spun, slashing out even as her foot slid through a small puddle of water, knocking her balance off. Her unexpected move meant she escaped his reaching hands, even as her blade carved a deep gash along one of his arms.

Unfortunately, it gave him the perfect opening. His head snapped around and those sharp ass teeth clamped on her arm.

For a moment, she wondered if he missed, then fire sparked along her nerve endings as those curved teeth ground against skin and bone. A burst of caustic iron-rich scent hit air while agonizing fire tore through her arm. Her hand spasmed and the dull *thunk* of her knife hitting the floor was lost under her sharp scream.

Calculation disappeared under basic survival. Adding any movement with the sawing bite wasn't smart, but the need for escape trumped rational thought. She dragged her injured arm close, bringing the Triton with her.

Her scream of pain morphed into the feline scream of a leopard as she brought her other hand up, still clutching her last knife, and stabbed it deep into one of those merciless eyes. She twisted the blade, unmindful of the pulpy mess she created. All that mattered was getting her arm free, and the brutal move worked.

The Triton opened his mouth to roar in agony, freeing her mangled arm from his bite. One hand went to cover his eye, the other arm swung out blindly. She managed to stumble back and took the punch on the shoulder of her injured arm instead of her face. Pain lanced her shoulder, only to be replaced by a blessed numbness. There wasn't much time to enjoy the respite, because he was coming back.

The fight had switched their positions, putting her closer to the stairs and the Triton between her and the door. Outside, lightning struck somewhere close, the flash illuminating the room in bright white. It edged the Triton in black as he began to glide toward her. With her arm out of commission, there was no more time to screw around. This had to end or she wouldn't be able to keep her promise to Maris.

As he lunged, she harnessed the magic living inside her and directed it to her blade until it was lined with blue-white flames. Committed to his forward movement, the Triton had no option but to follow through. Raine braced her feet, dropped into a crouch and leapt straight up as he barreled into the wall where she had been standing. As she dropped down, her flexible spine twisted, letting her turn in mid-air and land on his back, sinking her blade to the hilt against the base of his skull.

His knees hit the floor, his hands scrambling to reach the blade imbedded in his skull. She let go and stumbled to her feet as the silent flames spread, following her will, licking over his shoulders and up his skull, devouring him with lethal hunger. His screams rose, competing with the wailing winds of the storm now curling around the room. They choked off as he toppled face down to the ground. Rain and ice-edge wind whipped Raine's hair around her face, but she didn't look away from the burning form at her feet.

RAINE RETRIEVED HER BLADES, tucked them back into place, and dragged her abused body up the stairs. It was time to get Maris's mom. Each step hurt, but once she tucked her injured arm against her chest, the pain became bearable.

How many damn stairs did this place have? The steps seemed unending, what kept her going were the occasional moans drifting down. Finally, she made it to the top. There was no light, and the slits in high in the stones didn't help since storm clouds blocked whatever moonlight existed.

"*Tachair.*" At her soft command for light, a small globe of white popped into existence above her shoulder.

A whimper sounded.

Raine sent the light up, illuminating the room.

Curled back against the far wall on a pile of ragged blankets lay a tangle of limbs and dark hair. Sucking in a bracing breath, Raine cleared her throat and tried for a gentle reassuring tone. "Maris sent me to help."

The pile jerked, then the mass of tangled hair lifted, revealing solid black eyes ringed in purpling bruises. "Maris is safe?" The words were rough, as if her vocal cords weren't working correctly.

"She's safe." Raine stepped closer and slowly sank to a crouch in front of the battered woman. "My uncle is guarding her."

"Keep her safe from Kaimana." The woman struggled to rise, and Raine moved forward trying to help as much as she could with one arm.

Through a combination of stubborn determination and a handful of curses, Raine managed to get the injured woman to sit upright against the wall. "If Kaimana is the Triton downstairs, he's dead, so no worries there."

The woman's body gave a jerk at her words. "Truly?"

Raine nodded taking in the damage Kaimana wrought on the female before her. Both eyes were bruised, with heavier discoloration along one delicate cheekbone. Her lips were split, and through the tangle of hair and shredded material, her pale skin was decorated in shades of blue, green, and purple darkening to a painful maroon. One thin arm was wrapped around her ribs, which were either broken or cracked. "What's your name?"

Those dark eyes watched her, a wary tightness drawing tiny, white lines around them. "Eirene."

"Eirene, my name's Raine. We need to get you out of here. I promised Maris I'd bring you back."

Her head dipped in acknowledgement, but she didn't look away. "He's dead?"

Eirene's fear scraped over Raine, leaving her raw. "My word to you."

The battered woman caught back a sob of relief. "Finally."

Raine's stomach clenched. Why did that word make dread curl in her stomach? "Finally?"

Eirene ran a shaky hand through her tangled hair, trying to drag it out of her face. "Do you know what Lyr's Seat is?"

Wracking her brain, Raine recalled a dusty piece of Kyn history. "The Undersea throne, right?"

Leaning against the stone wall, Eirene nodded. "In an attempt to alleviate strained relationships between the Tritons and the Selkies, the last ruler appointed court representatives to ensure an equal voice between the courts. Aidan, the current ruler, gives heavy credence to his Selkie advisor, to the displeasure of others."

Pieces began to click. "Let me guess. You're the advisor?"

Eirene's smile was shaky, but there. "No, that dubious honor belongs to my husband."

"And Kaimana decided to use you and your daughter as leverage against your husband?"

Eirene's smile faded, fear and feminine loathing twisted her face into a grimace. "That may have been the initial plan, but I think it was an excuse for what he really wanted."

"You."

She gave a short jerky nod. "And, perhaps, Maris."

The agony in her whispered comment, made Raine wish she'd taken a bit longer in killing the monster downstairs. No mother, or child, should ever have to come that close to such a blood-chilling nightmare. But dead was dead, and it was time to get Eirene out of here, before anything else happened tonight.

"We've got quite a trek ahead of us. Can you make it?" Because between their injuries it would be a hell of a haul. Another nod, and Eirene used the wall behind her to brace as she struggled to her feet. Even with her dress ragged and torn, her body battered and bruised there was no mistaking the delicate beauty of the woman. Raine's stomach tied itself in Gordian knots. She didn't want to voice her next question, but it needed to be asked. "Eirene, did Kaimana rape you?"

That delicate chin lifted, and her split lips curved up revealing sharpened teeth, much sharper than Maris's. "He tried, but some things males won't risk losing." She snapped her teeth together in two vicious bites.

Seeing that savage response made Raine smile. "Good, but you can't go out in that, you'll freeze to death." She shrugged out of her slicker. Even with the ripped sleeve, it would be better than what Eirene was currently wearing.

As Eirene took it, she said, "I need our skins."

"Do you know where they are?"

She shook her head and pushed off the wall to shuffle over to Raine. "No."

Raine stifled a sigh and wrapped her working arm around Eirene's waist, careful of her ribs as they made slow progress down the stairs. "Okay, well since neither of knows where he stashed him, I have an idea." Because uncovering secrets were her uncle's thing.

As concisely as possible, she explained to Eirene how they would go get Maris and her uncle, and he could help them locate their missing skins. She took Eirene's lack of argument as consent and concentrated on getting down the last few steps with falling.

They stepped onto the bottom floor and Eirene's hiss brought Raine up short. Eirene stared at the burnt remains of the Triton sprawled by the wall. "By Stygian Darkness, you did that?"

Refusing to let the other woman stand and stare, Raine just grunted and inexorably led her out into the now calming storm. The wind had died down and the rain had tapered off into a light mist. It took twice as long to make it back to the cabin, but as she lifted a heavy foot for the first step to the porch, the door swung open.

"Mama!" A tiny blur hurtled forward and slammed into Eirene.

A soft groan escaped as she held her daughter close. "Baby, Maris, my baby."

Listening to the woman reassure her tiny daughter and hold her close, their two dark heads together, brought a choking pressure to Raine's chest. Her knuckles whitened on the railing and she looked away only to find her uncle standing in the doorway, the light from inside spilling around him, leaving his expression shadowed.

Locking her aching memories away, she choked out, "Eirene, we need to go inside."

She followed the mother and daughter up the stairs and stopped as Mulcahy let them through. As she came even with him, he set his hand on her shoulder. "How bad?"

"Bite to my arm, dislocated shoulder, otherwise I'm fine." She turned to meet his eyes. "It was a Triton, so the bite's pretty bad. Unfortunately, Eirene has no idea where he hid their skins."

"And you want me to find them?"

She went to shrug, only to stop with a small hiss as her damaged shoulder protested. "It's what you do."

Humor lit deep in his amber gaze. "Very true," he murmured. "Let's get you patched up and find their skins."

Two hours later, Raine and Mulcahy followed Eirene and Maris away from the tower. Like Raine expected, Mulcahy made short work of finding the skins. The tracking spell he used wasn't one she was familiar with, but it was old.

Kaimana had stashed the skins in the tiny attic of the cottage. The two Selkies took their skins and Mulcahy hauled the dead Triton down to the nearby beach, while Raine followed behind.

Standing at the water's edge, Eirene and Maris waded out into the now calm surf. A song started, haunting and illusive.

It drifted above the ocean, sinking beneath the incoming waves. The last notes died away as the clouds drifted from the moon, and a cresting wave rushed in to break gently against the shore, a figure stalked towards the two females.

Raine held her position next to her uncle.

The figure became a man who gathered Eirene and Maris to him, holding them tight. Maris clambered up his chest to curl her thin arms around his neck. He caught her close with one arm, and wrapped his other gently around Eirene. Together the trio waded to shore, the sea lapping at their feet.

They stopped and the male spoke. "I'm Afon."

"Ryan Mulcahy." Her uncle dipped his head as his arms were full of roasted Triton.

Afon's attention turned to Raine.

"Raine McCord," she offered, noting the raw markings on the male's chest. It looked as if he tangled with Jaws.

He stared at what Mulcahy held. "You saved my family when I could not." When he looked up, Raine had no problem seeing the guilt and fury warring in his face.

She motioned to his raw torso with her bandaged arm. "Looks like you did your best."

"It was not enough to stop Kaimana from taking what wasn't his." He brushed Maris's hair with his chin. "A debt is owed."

The offering left no response but the nod she gave.

Another wave crested and two more figures stepped out of the surf, moving closer. A harsh bark broke the night, and Afon turned his head to respond. When he turned back, he addressed Mulcahy. "We'll take his body."

Mulcahy handed over the Triton to the larger of the two males walking up the beach. Everyone remained silent as the body exchanged hands and was taken back to the sea.

Pale streamers lined the horizon where sea met sky,

announcing the sun's approach. Maris whispered something in her father's ear. He looked from Raine to his daughter, a small smile curving his lips. He unwrapped his arm around Eirene, then slowly sank into a crouch to set Maris's feet in the surf. He searched the sand and grabbed something, holding it tight in his fist. A series of lyrical notes fell quietly into the still pre-dawn, and a soft luminance covered his fist, then faded away. He opened his hand and Maris grabbed whatever it was nestled there. She turned and walked back to Raine.

Dropping down to the girl's eye-level, Raine studied Maris's young face. The little girl held out her closed fist. "For you."

Extending her palm, Raine caught the object. A stunning iridescent stone of swirling blues and greens lay in her hand. She curled her fingers around it and brought it to her heart. "It's as beautiful as you, baby girl."

Maris giggled, dashed forward and gave Raine a quick hug. "Someday, I'll be a warrior like you." The girlish whisper tickled Raine's ear.

Closing her eyes, she tightened her hold on Maris. "You already are, kiddo."

She let her arms dropped, but stayed on her heels as the little girl rejoined her family. The three slipped further into the sea, until Eirene offered one last wave before disappearing.

A light touch against her hair startled Raine. She tilted her head back to find her uncle standing next to her. Unable to bear the depth of emotion shadowing his face, she turned back to the sea. "Maybe next vacation, I'll choose Hawaii."

His quiet laugh echoed over the sea as dawn chased the rolling waves.

THANK you for reading SHADOW'S EDGE. Stick with Raine in **SHADOW'S SOUL** as she takes on a simple assignment for Cheveyo that turns into a vendetta fueled nightmare that threatens to destroy the fragile threads between her and Gavin.

Slip into Raine and Gavin's next adventure, now available.

Do you want to share your exciting discovery of a new read? Then leave a review!

Don't miss out on exclusives & new release information by subscribing to Jami's newsletter at:
https://www.subscribepage.com/Jami-Subscription-Books

Or you're welcome to swing by and visit Jami's website at:
http://jamigray.com

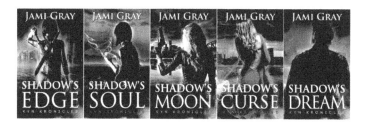

SHADOW'S CURSE

When the queen of chaos locks horns with death's justice, Natasha and Darius set a dangerous game in motion, leading two predators into a lethal dance of secrets.

SHADOW'S DREAM

Tala can't forget the past. Cheveyo can't change it. As the dreams they shared linger, can they escape the encroaching nightmare before it's too late?

Stay tuned for the final installment arriving late 2021

ABOUT THE AUTHOR

"...a fantastic paranormal action novel is quite possibly the best book I've read this year. I could not put it down, and had to exercise serious self-control to keep from staying up all night to finish it."
—The Romance Reviews

Jami Gray is the coffee addicted, music junkie, Queen Nerd of her personal Geek Squad, Alpha Mom of the Fur Minxes, who writes to soothe the voices crammed in her head. You don't want to miss out on her multiple series that combines magical intrigue and fearless romance into one wild ride -- Arcane Transporter, Kyn Kronicles, PSY-IV Teams, or Fate's Vultures.

[a] amazon.com/author/jamigray

[f] facebook.com/jamigray.author

[BB] bookbub.com/authors/jami-gray

[g] goodreads.com/JamiGray

[twitter] twitter.com/JamiGrayAuthor

[instagram] instagram.com/jamigrayauthor

Made in the USA
Las Vegas, NV
16 January 2022

41436663R00226